STEEL WILL

The Life of
Tad Sendzimir

Vanda Sendzimir

HIPPOCRENE BOOKS
New York

For information, address:
HIPPOCRENE BOOKS, INC.
171 Madison Avenue
New York, NY 10016

Library of Congress Cataloging in Publication Data
Sendzimir, Vanda.
    Steel will: the life of Tad Sendzimir / Vanda Sendzimir.
        p.   cm.
    Includes index.
    ISBN 0-7818-0169-9
    1. Sendzimir, Tadeusz. 2. Inventors—Unites States—Biography.
I. Title.
T212.S46   1993
672'.092—dc20   93-32962
                                                       CIP

Printed in the United States of America.

for Berthe

Contents

Diagrams

ACKNOWLEDGMENTS

This book would not have been possible without the extensive cooperation of members of my family, especially my mother Berthe and my half-brother Michael. Thanks also to my brothers Stanley and Jan Peter.

My understanding of the steel industry and of my father's place in it began at zero. Whatever progress was made could not have been possible without the patient help of the following: Don Armstrong, Charles Baker, Andrew Beck, Tad Bijasiewicz, Ted Bostroem, Bill Chess, Ken Coburn, Ruth Dinan, Howard Doolittle, Kurt Dunbar, John Eckert, Jim Fox, Ed Frank, Jacek Gajda, Nicholas J. Grant, Stanislaw Grazynski, Bob Hart, Jerry Jablonski, Roman Jerczynski, Franciszek Kaim, Adam Kotula, Sam Lebowitz, Roland Lessage, Fritz Lohmann, Claude Martin, Dick Martin, Tad Mlynarczyk, Kaz Oganowski, Louis Perdu, Marvin Pierson, Jan Postula, Zig Protassewicz, Eugeniusz Puslowka, Paul Reeder, Andrew Romer, Masaharu Sakatani, Tim Sakovich, Roy Seeling, Thaddeus Sendzimir, Ralph Shunk, Bill Sidaway, Emil Skulski, Charlie Smith, Joseph E. Smith, Jan Swiecicki, Tetsuji Taniguchi, Jan Tomczycki, Bill Trettel, John Turley, Fujio Umetani, Wieslaw Wozniak, and Roman Wusatowski.

For their personal recollections of my father, I'd like to thank: Nicholas and Luba Alferieff, Marya Lilien Czarnecka, Evelyn Day, Rodney DeLeon, Tadeusz Gromada, Feliks Gross, Gina McWeeney, Teresa Piombo, Vera Lundberg, and Betty Walters. For their help in Poland and with the numerous Polish translations, I'd like to thank Jacek Dobrowolski, Jadwiga Gajewska, Inka Meystowicz, Krystyna Tolloczko, Jerzy Sedzimir, my aunts Teresa Nechay and Aniela Kecka, and all the members of the Nechay family here in the United States: Jacek, Rysia, Marc and Bettina.

Many friends and acquaintances helped with advice and with their comments on this manuscript in its many permutations. It is all the better for it. Thanks to: Scott Badler, Laura Benne, Archie Brodsky, Hiyaguha Cohen, Steve Edelheit, Marcy Fischer, Stephen Fox, Jim Goldberg, Steve J. Heims, Melle Katze, Iver Kern, Alice Crane Kovler, Janis Lewin, Lynn Liccardo, David Ludlow, Alicja Mann, Musa Mayer, Andrew Phillips, Lynne Potts, Susan Quinn, Michael Robinson, Pamela Rockwell, Judith Rosenberg, Wickie Stamps, and Ross Terrill.

PREFACE

At nine o'clock in the morning on August 25, 1987 smoke was rising from three of the ten giant smokestacks of the Huta Lenina steel plant. Outside the main gate, on a traffic island between two fortress-like administration buildings, a thickset woman hoed a circle of stunted red geraniums. The morning sun was barely able to penetrate the heavy, smoke-drowsy atmosphere over Krakow.

I sat on a small bench at the edge of the traffic island with Jacek, my friend and translator. We spoke quietly, to calm our nervous excitement, as we watched the last of the graveyard shift queuing at the bus stop and buying cigarettes at a small kiosk. We were early.

Somewhere beyond those high gates, somewhere past the soot-smudged trees and cathedral-sized slag heaps of Poland's largest steel plant, two of my father's inventions were muttering and chuckling rhythmically in the hands of the day shift. We had come to see these machines, and to talk to the people who bought them and the people who run them. My father is Tad Sendzimir; the Sendzimir name, and connections at the Mining and Metallurgical Academy in Krakow, had gotten us in. I'm writing his biography, I had explained, the biography of one of Poland's, and the steel industry's, most famous inventors.

Tad Sendzimir transformed steel making in the early 1930s with a dramatically improved way to galvanize steel and a new type of mill that could roll steel strip down to half the thickness of a human hair. His inventions wrote and spread a new gospel for galvanized and thin sheet metals; he made it possible, for instance, for radar to be mounted on airplanes in World War II, and material from his mills formed the outer shell of the Apollo spacecraft. Today over ninety percent of stainless steel in the world is rolled on his mills.

He has received every top international award in steel, including what for engineers is their Nobel Prize: the Brinell Gold Medal.

At 9:30, Jacek and I presented ourselves and were led up to the office of the technical director. He and his assistant sat with us at a broad conference table and answered my questions. Huta Lenina owns a small rolling mill and a galvanizing line—their prototypes were born in 1933 on Polish soil, less than 50 miles away. This plant had purchased them in the late 1950s, after touchy negotiations with the Cold War-inclined U.S. government, which didn't believe that micro-thin steel for electrical transformers was all this Warsaw Pact country wanted to produce with the Sendzimir mill. When I asked the two men how this particular mill worked, they loosened and warmed up, and began to scribble diagrams on sheets of paper and talk faster than Jacek (a poet, not an engineer) could ably follow. But their enthusiasm didn't need translation. That a Pole had invented these machines was icing on the cake: the concepts were elegant, in and of themselves.

A driver came to take us to the site. We were issued hardhats, and driven a mile or so down a road lined with poplars to a long, four-story-high factory building. We descended on foot into a dimly lit, underground corridor, and surfaced many minutes later in the center of a cavernous hall. The air was thick with dust, visible in the few slanting, diaphanous pillars of sunlight. Above our heads, cranes glided silently by clutching rolls of steel strip as big as passenger vans. We were surrounded by five-foot-high stacks of galvanized sheet, like decks of cards awaiting delivery to a giant's blackjack table. A medley of chugging and booming echoed from a mill at the far end of this cavern, and mingled with more muted thunder from other parts of the building, the din never so loud as to drown conversation. The foreman, a large man wearing blue coveralls and a warm smile, greeted us and immediately apologized that the rolling mill was down for a sixteen-hour break. But the galvanizing line was running, he said, and that was far more spectacular.

We walked on the black floor, spongy from decades of dust and grease, in the direction of the chugging and booming. On our left, a long line of purling rollers passed an endless, four-foot-wide strip of steel swiftly forward to its baptism in zinc. In a few yards, we came to the zinc bath, a small tub of silvery, molten metal. Shooting out and up from the tub came the strip of steel, a wide shimmering ribbon of silver, dazzling and gleaming like a wet razor, racing straight up and up, four stories into the air. Near the top, the zinc was "dry" and had crystallized into the familiar icy patterns, the spangle, we see on watering cans and drain pipes.

I was mesmerized.

The foreman then brought us over to see their Sendzimir rolling mill. The compact, squarish mill sat quietly in a far corner. The foreman opened the cast-iron door on the side to let us peek in at the black, dormant rolls of its internal organs, resting from their regular work of squeezing hard steel strip to the thickness of tissue paper.

As Jacek and I were riding on the bus back to Krakow, I began to wonder: why was I only seeing these fascinating machines now, in my mid-thirties? These processes were twenty years older than I. Why had I not been brought, on my father's shoulders, to gaze at a sight any child would find entrancing?

In fact, I was not raised in a steel mill. My father's office walls were cluttered with photos of him in tuxedos, receiving medals from the King of Sweden and presidents of scientific societies, but all I knew was that he packed up his briefcase in the morning and came home in the evening for supper. Unlike my friends' fathers, after supper Tad went to his office in a corner of our large house in Waterbury, Connecticut, and I would go there later in pajamas to kiss him goodnight. I often would go with my mother on the long car trip to Idlewild Airport to drop him off, and weeks later return to lean excitedly against the glass of the balcony high above the U.S. Customs counters, trying to spot him among the scores of weary men in gray suits and felt hats coming back from Europe and Japan.

I remember, on his return from these trips, the love I saw in his twinkling eyes and warm smile under the scratchy moustache. But I also remember my slight disappointment (which grew, as I grew) that the relative calm and freedom of our days out from under his domineering presence were ending. (I wonder now how much I even missed him. He was smoothly replaced by his surrogates on television, Walt Disney and Walter Cronkite, two father figures who resembled him closely.)

I had an idea that he was famous, but I was often confused, as a small child, when asked, "What does your daddy do?" Sometimes I'd boast, "He's an inventor," and that would do. But sometimes I'd fill in the blank next to "Father's Occupation" with "executive," or "businessman." I'd spell out the word hesitantly; I knew that wasn't the whole story, but those titles were more, to my eyes, true-to-life. That's what *I* saw him do.

My early experience of real inventing was confined to his automatic pancake maker, a contraption of heated steel drums his handyman had been set to putter with in the garage. Nothing to draw awards, or even inquiries—but a four-year-old knows pancakes. She does not know steel, even if she might slide down it all afternoon at the playground. On rare occasions—examining drain pipes in a hardware store, or picking up a stainless steel knife in a restaurant—he'd remark to me, or to my brothers, Stanley and Jan, "This was rolled on your daddy's mill." We'd sit and watch, in those restaurants, as he scribbled circles and coils on paper placemats, lost in thought, using the fat, multi-colored ballpoint pens my mother would find for him. When the waitress came with the food, my father would look up, startled and sheepish, and request a new placemat as he folded up and pocketed his sketches. That's as close as we got to Tad Sendzimir's world-renowned genius.

I was astonished to learn, when I was older, that his first jobs had been as an auto mechanic. I never saw him fix a broken lawnmower, or a leaky faucet. Recalcitrant cars were taken straight to the dealer's garage. Tad's intimate feel for machinery was entirely cerebral; he claims (with utter self-delusion, I later learned) to have constructed his inventions down to the smallest coupling entirely in his imagination before explaining them to his draftsmen—as if he were Mozart, with his head full of completely orchestrated, yet-to-be-written, symphonies. After the anomalous and short-lived pancake maker, our garage had no disemboweled machines around with which my brothers and I could spend a Saturday afternoon watching our father tinker. We never learned to love, as he had as a boy, the smell and feel of grease and warm metal.

I did not resent this then, though I know Stanley and Jan did: our father wasn't around for baseball, or any other childhood pursuits, either. As my brothers and I, with our mother, collected shells on the beach in front of our Florida home, Tad was off alone in the distance, scurrying beside the water's edge like a skinny, upright crab. He was hard at work, in solitude, calculating and reasoning machinery out in his head.

I do not remember resenting his distance. I do remember resenting how eccentric and odd he was. Like most children, I wanted desperately to be like everyone else. It was futile. My father was past the age of a grandfather. His accent was thickly Slavic, and at home my friends could hear him on the telephone, sprinting in Polish. He, we, ate strange things: yogurt and carrot juice and wheat germ. Family outings were a source of despair: he'd drive the wrong way down one-way streets; he'd order liver in restaurants and make a commotion if it arrived "overdone"; he'd never book ahead in motels, so we were often turned away into the night. Only my mother showed up at school functions. As I grew older, I was glad of this: my father was an embarrassment to me.

With adolescence, my distance from him grew, both physically and emotionally. I loved and hated him, admired and resented him. When I began reading about feminism, my anger took political shape. Big deal that he's a genius! How about being a decent father, a considerate husband? At my most bitter, in conversations I'd explain that, "My father's *real* children are his inventions. My brothers and I are just his biological children."

But time and physical distance eventually did their work. He began to mellow, going into his eighth decade; he became less tyrannical, more joking and relaxed, more willing to listen and to compromise. The scribblings on placemats now were more likely to be puns than patent drawings ("Oliver North's greatest asset is his LIE-ability," was a favorite in 1988.).And I began to look on Tad's eccentricities more with fondness than annoyance. I was proud, in a backhanded way, that this wealthy man's favorite clothing store was J.C. Penney. And we all would smile, on the afternoon of Christmas Eve, when he would disappear to K Mart. He had suddenly remembered the date. My mother had already done the Christmas gift buying for the family, and she'd stacked the boxes in elegant red and green paper under the tree. But Tad would emerge just before supper bearing a handful of his own small packages wrapped in white paper napkins, our names printed on the top of each in thick black marking pen.

In 1983, the Mining and Metallurgical Academy in Krakow hosted a celebration commemorating the fiftieth anniversary of the Sendzimir galvanizing process and the first rolling mill. The whole family went to Poland for the occasion.

In Krakow, we were invited to a family gathering at the apartment of my father's cousin Olek, a retired doctor who lived with his wife in a high-ceilinged, three-room apartment. When we arrived, the rooms were crowded with people, the tables heavy with cream cakes and glass teacups. Octogenarians, eyes damp, came to embrace my father, and each of us in turn. Cheeks were kissed. Hands were kissed. As I watched the animated scene, I realized that for the first time in my life, I was in a room full of Sendzimirs. I was in a town where the name Sendzimir was not strange and foreign, but perfectly ordinary, and in fact revered.

The next day, as we drove by cab down the central Krakow boulevard to the ceremony, we saw from a block away the white banner stretched above the Mining Academy's stained granite portal: "JUBILEUSZOWE SYMPOZJUM TADEUSZA SENDZIMIRA," "Jubilee Symposium for Tadeusz Sendzimir." Inside the assembly hall, we sat among several hundred in the audience, watching the collection of twenty or so white-haired men take their places on velvet seats on a dais, our father in the front row. One by one, each rose and made a short speech in Polish, frequently gesturing and glancing back to Tad, who sat quietly, smiling—pleased, slightly embarrassed at the effusiveness of praise, honored.

This scene of respect and awe was replayed several times in the next couple of years. The family came together again in 1985 for my brother Stanley's wedding, in Linz, Austria. The giant Austrian steel concern, Voest-Alpine, invited us to tour their Linz plant, and asked Tad to give a brief talk about his current work. Tad lectured in German to a roomful of engineers. Both the younger engineers and the older managers were quite plainly enthusiastic; they asked him to consider a joint research and development project with Voest-Alpine.

A couple of months later, the same look of enthusiasm spread across the faces of three hundred Chinese engineering students in a hot, sunny lecture hall in Lanzhou, China. Tad had been invited to return to China in August 1985, to cement a joint venture project he had begun negotiating on his first trip in 1984 (he had just turned ninety). I asked to tag along. We spent ten days in Lanzhou, on the high, arid plateau that cradles the just-maturing, well-named Yellow River. Tad spent most of the time with Berthe on couches in a small sitting room at Lanzhou Steel, drawings and contracts spread out among the cups of jasmine tea, working painfully through the details with a group of engineers and interpreters in white short-sleeved shirts, gray pants and sandals.

After Lanzhou, we spent three days in Shanghai. Tad had lived there from 1918 to 1929, managing a nail factory. Our hosts from the Shanghai Number Five Steel Plant had dug through old city records and maps to locate Tad's factory. We were driven through neighborhoods of tightly knit two- and three-story wooden houses. At last the car stopped in a cul-de-sac next to a low brick building. Inside, the rickety machines and bales of rusty wire made the place look like an unprofitable and abandoned New England mill, even though the plant was still in business, sixty years after its founding.

I would return to the States, after these trips, and notice our bond growing. We were beginning again to have shared experiences. And in his frailty, my father was beginning to rely on me to help him and my mother in these travels: to get the visas, to negotiate with guides, to carry bags. I felt a respect and gratitude from him I had not felt before.

But this old tiger, Tad Sendzimir, was not just changing his stripes. It was I who was also seeing, in those few years, other sides of the beast. My perception of my father was opening, click by click, like the aperture of a rusty, wide-angle lens: his roots in nineteenth-century Polish history, visible in the cracked stucco and cobblestones of 1980s Krakow; his scientific contributions to the steel industry, heard in the voices of professional colleagues, in half a dozen languages; his, my, living, doting family in Poland, stuffing us with cakes and canapes. I was finally seeing my father as more than the petty tyrant, the harebrained, eccentric inventor. I had entered his element, and stopped, finally, to take a look around.

In 1985 a growing frustration and dissatisfaction with my job came to a head. I had been feeling for a number of years that my talents lay elsewhere, in writing. On a Christmas visit home, a couple of months after I quit my job, my father suggested, "Well, how about writing my biography?" I knew he'd had an interesting life, and it would make a good story. But I also knew it would be a ticklish task. I was not an engineer. I was not a historian. And I was not altogether clear on how I felt about the protagonist. My life was then in upheaval, and I would have liked to say, "Let me get my feet on the ground. I'll take this up in ten years." But you don't say that to someone who's ninety-two. It had to be done now. This was either a unique and exciting opportunity, or quicksand.

My interest in the subject was already in ferment. The yeast had been sprinkled back in Krakow in 1983, in Linz, in Lanzhou, in Shanghai in 1985. I took up the task with an eye to the man, the fascinating individual. But I still was taking up the subject of my very own father. The challenge encompassed a search—revealing, painful, nourishing—through my past and my relationship with him. As a journalist, and as a feminist, I had to discover and show not only the great man, but the great man's faults, the burdens on his loved ones, the failures. And I said to him, straight out, "You're no saint, you know." And he said, "Oh, I'm well aware of that. The book would be pretty boring if I was. Write what you like."

I spent weeks interviewing him over the stacks of paper and blueprints and Polish journals on his desk in Florida. I found his memory sharp for stories from his childhood, and crystalline for the details of machinery, but blurred and superficial as to personal relationships. The task was fascinating, and frustrating. Was I still too hostile, I wondered? Would a more patient, sympathetic, and above all *removed* person be better able to elicit honest and heartfelt responses? But perhaps an outsider would go home satisfied with Tad's glib and often contradictory answers. Perhaps our tension was necessary, at least for this version of the story. It was frustrating also because not much indeed seemed to be heartfelt. His tone was frequently flat, his responses about personal matters—his relations with his parents, his disastrous first marriage—were often monosyllabic, and above all unexamined.

Our denouement came in 1987. Tad brought the family to the Soviet Union, to visit for the first time the town of his birth, Lwow. This city in the western Ukraine had been Polish for six centuries, until 1939, when a large chunk of eastern Poland was taken over by the Soviets. My father had lived there from his birth in 1894 until 1915. I had great hopes for our trip: to see his homeland with him, and to record his reactions to the old and the new of this city, once idyllic for a middle-class Polish boy.

But Tad's reactions remained deadpan. We walked the streets, unchanged since his boyhood. We visited the Polytechnic, where he had studied. We stood outside the ornate provincial administration building, where his father had worked. I would pump him, poised, pen in hand, about his reactions and impressions, and he would be noncommittal. "Oh, it all looks the same. I'm glad I got to see it."

It was only when we found his family home that some feeling at last slipped out. The street names had been changed, but Tad eventually recognized the four-story stucco apartment building. A young Russian woman welcomed us in, and led us to a corner sitting room. There painted above the doorways were the simple landscapes my grandmother had done seventy-five years ago. In one, a girl in peasant dress stands in a wheat field; in the other a dark lake shines in the moonlight. The room had been Tad's bedroom. For a brief second, his eyes grew wet as he pointed up to these paintings, describing how his mother had worked on them.

We left the house and returned to our hotel for lunch. "Well," I asked him, "what did the lady say? How did it look to you?" "Oh," he said, "I don't remember. Nothing much." And nothing more. I had gotten more emotion out of his descriptions of zinc plating.

Reviewing my notes glumly in my hotel room later that afternoon, the light finally dawned: this male, this engineer, this person most at home in the world of mathematical equations and the laws of thermodynamics, was *never* going to be able to articulate his feelings. But I had just seen him in his former bedroom looking at his mother's paintings, and I had seen him reciting Polish poetry of 150 years ago, and I had seen him passing around the traditional flat Polish wafer on Christmas Eve before the first star appears and wishing each of us happiness in the coming year—each time with a halt in his voice and a glisten in his eye.

His emotions do leak out, only I hadn't been watching. I wanted them served up on a silver platter. When he wouldn't, it was easy for me to put the blame on him, to pronounce him cold and unfeeling, and so continue our old pattern of miscommunication.

My task did not then become easier, but my understanding of his character, and of our relationship, and of this book, was deeply changed. I began to accept him as he was: a man, a man of some greatness and some weakness, who just happens to be my father. And I began to accept our relationship, and accept the difficult dynamic between two hard-headed individuals who can argue but can still love each other.

The book finally was taking shape in my mind. And as much as I had gone through with my father, in the battles and their resolutions, it remained clear to me that this is *his* book. His life can and does amply fill these pages, on its own. I am the daughter, but here I am just the scribe. This is the end of my story, the beginning of his—told, nevertheless, by a scribe with particular eyes, voice and heart.

CHAPTER ONE

LWOW

1894 - 1914

In August 1914, a month past his twentieth birthday, a semester shy of graduating from the Polytechnic, Tad Sendzimir's formal education came to an abrupt halt. The Czar's armies were approaching Lwow, his hometown. The inaugural skirmishes of World War One were bringing his idyllic boyhood crashing to a close. Born the scion of a Polish noble family that likes to trace its name back eight centuries; raised in one of the few cities where Polish art, science and culture flourished; trained in engineering in one of Poland's most prestigious polytechnics—he, Tadeusz Sendzimir, was bound, *he* knew, for greatness. First a doctorate in Vienna. Then maybe an apprenticeship in America.

But now his parents were packing up suitcases to flee west with the children into the safety of Austria. And he was staying behind, to avoid conscription into the Austrian army. He was staying behind, in this soon-to-be-empty house, in this soon-to-be-occupied city, looking at a now very uncertain future. History was throwing him a curve, as it had before and would again.

*   *   *

The first curve of history Tad faced, along with all Poles, was that at the time of his birth in 1894, his native country could not be found on a contemporary map. Local demographers would have

21

counted the Sendzimir family in Lwow as loyal citizens of the Austro-Hungarian Empire, in the province of Galicia. Galicia was the generous chunk carved out by Austria in 1772 from the underbelly of a proud but mismanaged Poland. Poland's complete dismemberment among Austria, Prussia and Russia was finished by 1795. One hundred years later, when Tad arrived, not even Poland's name remained on the map.

The Sendzimir family handled this situation as all their countrymen did. The map that could not be found on printed paper still lived—in shades of blood red, forest green, straw yellow and Vistula river blue—in the hearts of 20 million Poles. It lived on the vellum sheafs of poetry dispatched by homesick, angry, venerated exiles in Paris; it lived in the strains of Chopin's polonaises played by blue-eyed young girls in the parlors of the fallen gentry; it lived in the whispered arguments of university students—resistance versus conciliation, idealism versus realism, the heat of rebellion versus the cold sweat of community work; and it lived in the stories of kings, queens, heroes and martyrs told around supper tables, but deleted from the official history books given to schoolchildren.

Because of the Partitions (as Poland's dismemberment was called), recreating the map of Poland's history became a national pastime. It fulfilled a need for self-awareness that comes passively to other countries, countries that enjoy a standing government, sovereign borders, and a freely-spoken language. Nineteenth-century Poles, with little of these, had to work at it.

So Tad grew up with grand and noble stories, of Poland's heyday in the sixteenth and seventeenth centuries, of the days when King Wladyslaw IV's dominion extended east of Kiev, and of his own prestigious ancestors. Early in his life, he joined the long list of gifted Poles who were forced to go abroad for safety, sustenance, fulfillment or recognition—Kosciuszko, Mickiewicz, Curie, Conrad, Chopin, among many others; these stories helped him then to sustain his own map of national honor. Through his life, the ideals of the nobility (to which he added his own twentieth-century spin) guided him. Late in life, he insisted that his ancestors' accomplishments were more important than his own, that he but continued a saga.

The stories of these ancestors gained depth and color with each retelling, and a retelling would commence on any excuse—in rambling letters, in rambling supper conversation. "I am the descendant of a noble family in the service of the Polish Republic since the twelfth century, and probably before," he'd repeat, tapping his fingers rhythmically on the desk. "You recall the family insignia? That embroidered cloth—I believe it's red and gold—on the wall above the couch." He'd draw a small sketch of it on a scrap of paper, next to a rolling mill design. Leaning back, gazing into the distance, he'd proceed to the story of the famous magnate who supposedly arranged the royal marriage that united Poland and Lithuania in 1386. "That move proved to be a stroke of genius. The dynasty ruled Poland for two centuries and it was the most glorious chapter of our history." Now his eyes were shining. Next came Tad's forebear Michael Sendziwoy, an influential alchemist and philosopher in several European courts, who is reported to have transmuted metal into gold in 1604. Tad would wind up the story in the last century: "Most recently, my great-grandfather Stanislaw, an officer under Napoleon, distinguished himself by initiating the defense of Plock against the Austrians. He received the Golden Cross, *Virtuti Militari*, from Prince Poniatowski, and was later a judge of the Supreme Court."

Tad would halt the tale just then, at the death of the illustrious Stanislaw in 1831, from stomach cancer. His pause is significant, for Stanislaw is truly the last Sendzimir representing the proud and anarchical Polish nobility, the *szlachta* which had ruled (many say misruled) for six hundred years. The *szlachta's* legal status was annulled in 1795 by the partitioning powers. But those powers could not with the same stroke erase the *szlachta's* social status, nor its deep moral beliefs: the primacy of the individual, the superiority of their class (especially over the Jews), and their duty to the nation. These tenets were handed down like the family silver to the *szlachta's* nineteenth-century successors, the newly-forming intelligentsia, and passed untarnished to the sons of the sons and so to Tad. His re-telling of the ancestors' stories served primarily as annotation of an attitude about his place in the world—a Pole no matter on what shores he stood—and of his pridefulness and canonic belief in the strong-willed individual.

Tad always claimed to be "a product of the nineteenth century," and his character comes into focus as he continues his story, tracing the family and their social strata through that age.

By 1864, two failed insurrections against the partitioning powers had led to deportations and massive confiscations of land and title—obliterating, root and branch, the *szlachta*. Most disappeared into the ranks of the intelligentsia—artists, teachers, doctors. Some became bureaucrats, even merchants and entrepreneurs. Some had success, especially in the Austrian-held area of Galicia, where a more liberal imperial policy allowed for an independent Polish administration and major Polish universities, theater and culture. But some in the new intelligentsia failed, and Tad's family stories now become homilies.

His two grandfathers acted out the best and the worst of what became of the Polish nobility in the nineteenth century. One grandfather, Karol Jasklowski, is revered, and still presides over the clan from his large, formal portrait in the apartment of Tad's cousin in Krakow. The other grandfather, Julian Sendzimir, presides only in family gossip.

Julian was the ne'er-do-well of Stanislaw's thirteen children. He gave up the family domain, joined a theater troupe (his love for the stage far outstripping his own talent), and married a seventeen-year-old dancer. They moved to Warsaw and settled, on slender means, into the life of dilettantes. Five children came in quick succession and then, on a summer's day, the young mother suffered a heart attack and drowned while swimming in the Vistula river. Julian moved his brood to Krakow—to the freer atmosphere of Galicia, where Polish could be spoken in the schools—and spent the rest of his life drinking in cafes around the beautiful *rynek*, the market square, leaving the eldest son, Kazimir (Tad's father), to care for his younger brothers and sister. Tad inherited Kazimir's shame and contempt for this wastrel. Julian's ghost would haunt, in Tad's worried imagination, the stage career of Tad's own son, Stanley.

The story of Tad's maternal grandfather, on the other hand, was one of virtue, patriotism and success. Karol Jasklowski came from a noble Lithuanian family. He fought in the 1863 uprising against Russia. During a retreat, the story goes, Karol hid in a barn under a pile of hay, and whispered Hail Marys while a detachment of Cossacks pierced each stack with their long pikes, missing his arm by inches. He escaped to Switzerland, then came to Galicia, and became the plenipotentiary for the estate of Prince Czartoryski (one of Poland's richest and most influential magnates) and president of the Czartoryski bank. Tad was a small child when Karol died of heart trouble—he remembered him sitting in a black armchair gasping for breath—but this grandfather lived on in family lore as almost a cult figure, as the celebrated patriarch to be replaced a half century later only by Tad himself.

In that half century, patriarchy of the Sendzimir family was shared by two of Julian's sons, Kazimir and Czeslaw, who came to Lwow and fell in love with two of Karol's daughters, Vanda and Malgorzata. Both men shunned the profligacy of their father but never quite made it to the eminence of their father-in-law. Both entered, with their generation, the "gainfully employed" professional class: Kazimir a hard-working but unambitious bureaucrat, Czeslaw a socialist-sympathizing country doctor.

Thus they fill out the map of Poland's nineteenth century *szlachta* cum intelligentsia that was sketched as much into Tad's consciousness as into his genealogy. In three generations every option this class turned to, except exile, was played out: nobleman and war hero, artist and dilettante, insurrectionist turned banker, and finally two professionals, a civil servant and a doctor, one loyal to the imperial regime, the other still hoping for something better.

Tad's father Kazimir joined that segment of Poland's intelligentsia which, in the final decades of the nineteenth century, rejected romanticism and insurrection in favor of peaceful work and conciliation with the foreign powers. He studied agriculture in Vienna, worked briefly in Prussian Poland until Bismarck expelled all non-Prussian Poles in 1885, and landed a job in Lwow as manager of the Empire's salt monopoly. Tad was forever conscious of, and vain about, his noble lineage. But his father's station as a bureaucrat was held as a mark of distinction for the Sendzimir family, not a descent from higher status. That is due to the peculiarities of Galicia at the time.

*　　*　　*

Galicia is spoken of as the Polish Piedmont, an intellectual center for a stateless nation. The Czar and Bismarck bore down on recalcitrant Poles in the territories held by Russia and Prussia. But Austria, juggling seventeen different nationalities in her weakening empire, let the Galician Poles be Poles. In the last decades of the nineteenth century, Krakow and Lwow became hothouses for a culture and language then in deep freeze in Warsaw and Posnan.

Lwow, known as Lemberg during Austrian rule, gained the nickname "Little Vienna" more for its political atmosphere than for its ornate buildings, fancy shops and high quality universities. Galicians were called the "pillars of the Habsburg Empire," and none was so upright as the intelligentsia in Lwow.

Lwow also became a magnet for the disaffected and disenfranchised in Russian and Prussian Poland. They came as students and professors in Lwow's fine Polish university and Polytechnic; as exiles, like Karol Jasklowski, after the failed 1863 uprising against Russia; and as professionals, like Kazimir, seeking posts in the burgeoning state bureaucracy, where they prospered in the fading light of fin-de-siecle Central Europe.

They took their white-gloved children to the new Parisian-style Opera House. They rode in carriages after Sunday Mass to eat cream-filled cakes in the pastry shops, or strolled to the top of Wysoky Zamek, the city's central promontory, to enjoy the view of the Gothic and Baroque cathedral spires that sprout from Lwow's green hills. University students crowded into smoky cafes. Laced and bustled ladies boarded the new electric streetcar line to meet their friends for tea in the *rynek*, the central square surrounded by the narrow, ornamented facades of sixteenth century noblemen's houses.

But Lwow's location on the eastern edge of Galicia lent it a taste quite different from its rival city, Krakow, to the west. Lwow lies roughly equidistant between Krakow and Kiev. Its founders were

Ruthenians (known now as Ukrainians), who built it as a fortress against the Tartars in the thirteenth century. The city soon fell to the Poles, who over the next six centuries layered on their occidental, European culture. The Poles' diligence was hampered, however, by the currents from the Ukrainian sea in which this Polish island floated, and by Lwow's status as a regional trading center: through it came flocks of merchants—Jews, Armenians, Greeks, Hungarians, Germans and Italians—many of whom liked the place and stayed. Lwow never became a sugary slice of Polish pastry, but something more akin to a sweet and sour Slavic borscht. Christians knelt in their Roman, Ukrainian Catholic and Armenian cathedrals. Jews prayed in their synagogues. Gaily-colored signboards hung in front of the Jewish stores; gypsy wagons, festooned with bright copper pans, clattered over the cobblestones; and Ukrainian peasant women walked into town with baskets of eggs and kefir to sell door to door.

Nevertheless, by contemporary account Lwow in the 1890s was a thoroughly Polish city. Over 80% of its 150,000 people were Polish, and it was a town where a Polish boy could grow up believing he, and Emperor Franz Joseph, owned the world. The backwardness of the Ukrainian villages in the surrounding countryside of eastern Galicia, called by some the poorest province in Europe, concerned all too few of those who passed their time in Lwow's shops, cafes and theaters.

* * *

One who did see Galicia's villages, every one large enough to support at least a small store, was Tad's father. Salt was sold in paper-covered cones, weighing one kilogram, called a "foot" of salt. Grocers bought them wholesale from the Galician state monopoly, and Kazimir's duties included traveling the length and breadth of the province to inspect the stocks and accounts of each store.

Perhaps his calm stability attracted Vanda, the banker's daughter. This suitor lacked the colorful background of Karol Jasklowski, her father. But Kazimir's jovial nature, his love of concerts and opera, and his seat in the bureaucracy made him a commendable prospect. Deep in Tad's file of family photographs rests one on thick cardboard, edges made soft from years of handling: a portrait taken in Lwow at the time of his parents' wedding, in the month of August 1893. Vanda sits on the edge of a bannister while Kazimir stands behind on the stair two steps above, their figures close, nestled but not visibly touching, like intertwining branches of a tree.

Vanda did not settle into motherhood as smoothly as she settles into this picture (but—perched on a hard bannister, under layers of linen in the August heat, facing domesticity—perhaps that's why her smile is so circumspect). The artistic training she received in high school tugged at her spirit and ambitions. In her early years of marriage, she paid less attention to her children and more to painting landscapes, arranging the garden, and decorating the house. Tad was cared for by his aunt Malgorzata, who lived with them and worked as a school teacher before she married Kazimir's brother. He remembers Aunt Malgorzata taking him to see the locomotives, and talking to him as an individual, a person with a young mind of his own, while his mother treated the children like children.

Kazimir did not seem to mind, or perhaps he did not notice, Vanda's initial disinterest in the family—Tadeusz, Aniela (the angel) two years younger, Zbigniew (the trouble-maker) four years after that, and Terenia (the baby)—but Vanda herself later regretted her attitude, and spent more time with the younger children. It was only the baby, Terenia, who was to see and appreciate firsthand her mother's strengths. Later in life Vanda channeled her energies into work with the church, into caring for her ailing husband through the 1920s, and in her last days into bringing color and warmth to the labor camp in Kazakstan—organizing a Christmas pageant in her barrack, for instance, with religious figures pasted together from newspaper and straw—where she, Terenia and Terenia's two small children spent the Second World War. She would die there in 1944.

The marriage of Vanda and Kazimir was a good one. They were openly affectionate and protective of each other, and with time their personalities balanced. Vanda's acquisitive tendencies were held in check by Kazimir's frugality; Kazimir's deep devotion to his children compensated for Vanda's artistic and church activities outside the home. While Vanda fed them chocolates, Kazimir, who held rigorous ideas about health, packed the children off for daily walks in Lwow's large parks. The parlor was often full and the cake trays seldom empty. Together Kazimir and Vanda established a loving and stable middle-class atmosphere for a young boy to grow in: strict, but allowing a great deal of freedom for a strong character to develop, unchallenged by overweening personalities. The home was Tad's private Galicia, and his parents let Tad be Tad.

He was born on July 15, 1894. (During that same year Tad's most famous Polish predecessor in sciences, Marie Sklodovska, met Pierre Curie, while she was studying the magnetic properties of various steels.) The year 1894 was the 100th anniversary of the insurrection against Prussia and Russia, led by Tadeusz Kosciuszko, so Tad became one of Kosciuszko's many namesakes christened in Poland that year.

His closest sister Aniela, two years his junior, remembered Tad as a small boy, in their first house on Domsa Street: "Most of the time we spent on the balcony; we played ball and we brought the dolls there. There were two toilets at the end of the balcony, and when Tadeusz went there he usually sang. He sang a lot of songs, even Christmas carols, and Mother scolded him for singing Christmas carols in the toilet, which she believed was not appropriate. He would take to the toilet booklets on machines and construction and their prices, and he would read them there." When Tad was not reviewing small machinery catalogs he could often be found in the basement of the Galician parliament building where his father worked. The small boy passed many hours with their downstairs neighbor, Mr. Kaczmarski, who ran the repair shop for the machines packing salt into the paper covered cones. He took to that workshop, with its ample supply of tools, the doll he "borrowed" from Aniela— to saw the head open to find out how the eyes were able to open and close. A few years later he nailed and screwed together pieces of wood to construct a clock mechanism.

He was willful, single-minded, and even, on personal matters, selfish. "I usually played alone," he remembered, "I didn't like company." He grew bored with family conversations. He got his way. He was deeply attached to his Aunt Malgorzata, who once let him see an illustrated physics book she was studying. He begged for it, and she promised it to him after she married. When his mother came to the children one morning with the sad news that their favorite aunt would be moving out and marrying their uncle Czeslaw, Tad shot like an arrow to her room: "Aunt Madzia, please give me that book on physics!" His most vivid memory of his grandmother Octavia, Vanda's mother, is that when she died she left him what became his most prized possession: her simple, large wooden desk with a shelf of lockable drawers on top. This became his fortress. He piled books high up along the sides, and set chemical experiments hissing and steaming on top. A dutiful boy, he would, when asked, clean up his end of the room, but the makeshift desktop laboratory was guarded jealously: "This is off limits!" His mother, proud of her bright and determined son, acquiesced. He built his own camera when he was thirteen, and for developing the glass plates he commandeered the bathroom as his darkroom, for hours at a time. "I knew I must have been quite a nuisance," he said. In one chemical experiment he accidentally set the sofa on fire.

"I had inventions as far back as I remember," Tad boasted. "I was in my eighth grade at gymnasium when I applied for my first patent, through a Vienna patent attorney, for a special holder for a draftsmen's pen for Chinese black ink, that prevented it from drying out. I got the patent, but no buyers!"

Yet he also sang operatic arias in the bathroom, recited long verses from Polish poets he revered, and bought small presents for his brother and sisters with his weekly allowance at the Jewish dry goods shop around the corner. The budding scientist had a heart.

The only member of the household Tad was unable to charm was his brother Zbigniew, born six years behind him. A dark-eyed, handsome boy, by all accounts Zbigniew was relentlessly peevish. His bile flowed mostly toward his elder brother—noticeably the gifted and favored one. "He was always trying to find some way to annoy me," Tad recalled. "I remember the family out on a walk, and the sun was shining behind and throwing shadows. Zbigniew saw me walking ahead of him and cried 'Oh Father, Tadzik is walking on my shadow!'" Zbigniew never outgrew his jealousy toward Tad.

Apart from Zbigniew's belligerence, life in the Sendzimir house at 12 Saint Teresa Street was calm, cheerful and dignified. In 1906, Kazimir built in Lwow a three-story apartment house across from the tall gates of a private girls' school, a ten-minute walk down the hill through the park to his office. The house was divided on the first floor by a tall passageway which allowed carriages to pass through to the garden. Its small iron balconies and rococo flourishes in the beige stucco made the building slightly more elegant than its neighbors—accurately reflecting, in Tad's opinion, the slightly grander stature of its occupants.

The atmosphere Vanda created in their first floor apartment was of the heavy, ornamented stability of turn-of-the-century Galicia: the bear-skin rug on the sofa, the large standing mirror in the corner, the brown-edged potted palm, the small altar for the Virgin Mary, and Tad's precious desk in the corner. Above each door Vanda painted into the triptych frame moulding a landscape from the eastern Carpathian foothills where the family spent their summers. (None depict, unfortunately, the dam that Tad organized his playmates to construct on a mountain stream. Some mountaineers came up from below to find out why the stream had stopped flowing, and promptly destroyed the structure. The eleven-year-old civil engineer was mortified: "This was so beautiful, so well constructed. Now it's all ruined!") The center of family life on Saint Teresa Street was the half-acre, private garden where Vanda's decorative talents and Kazimir's agricultural training joined hands. In the summer the family ate its meals in the shade of cherry, apple and plum trees on a wrought-iron table. For Tad, the sweet taste of gray pears decades later could bring him back to Lwow.

Tad's solitary, driven nature did not completely cut him off from family life: the walks in the park, the occasional public lectures, the frequent opera and theater trips. But in the summer, when the family visited the resort town of Zakopane, high in the Tatra Mountains, Tad would go off on his own: "Sometimes in Zakopane you had low-lying clouds and fog that would stay for a week. You'd never see the sunshine. I took a cape, I knew the road very well, and I went clear through and up and finally got into the sun, and then I had all the day in sunshine." He spurned his father's strict ideas about health until he was fifteen, when he read on his own a book by a Swedish hygienist that converted him to a lifelong fanaticism for long walks and fresh vegetables.

He continued to visit Kaczmarski's repair shop. When he matured and developed some dexterity, Kaczmarski set him to work. One afternoon when Tad came in, Kaczmarski handed him a solid block of iron, several inches thick, and asked him to make it into a perfect cube. Tad already knew how to use a file, and figured this would be quick work. He fit the chunk of metal into a vise, found a file and a ruler, and began. The block became smaller. And smaller. And smaller. Weeks later, he had at last a cube, and an appreciation for precision. "I learned shop knowledge the hard way," he said. "Then only he gave me the lathe and the other machines, the stamping machines, the drills. He liked me very much. I went there and stood long hours and watched him working." And the sharp, cold smell of iron filings and lubricating oil seeped into his veins.

A couple of years after Tad entered gymnasium (roughly equivalent to high school combined with junior college, running from age 10 to 18), a new theater of operations opened up to him. Stanislaw Tolloczko, a heavy-set, goateed uncle on his mother's side of the family, was a professor of Inorganic Chemistry at Lwow's University of Jan Kazimierz. Uncle Tolloczko took a liking for, and saw the potential in, his thin, energetic young relative. He invited Tad to spend time in his laboratory at the University. Almost every afternoon, from age thirteen until he was finishing his Masters Degree at the Polytechnic, Tad made the twenty-minute run over to the University to work with his uncle. The lab was over a hundred feet long, divided into three rooms filled with strangely twisted pipes, funnels, vases, distilling flasks, glass tubing, bulbous bottles and metal receptacles. Copper sinks and tanks of gas lined the side walls. Jets of blue flame sprouted from thin pipes on the work tables. Each bottle and tube had to be fashioned from scratch—nothing came ready-made—and Tad was first taught by his uncle how to carefully heat the glass to a uniform temperature, and in one smooth motion bend or blow it to the desired shape. Other students required the attention of their amiable professor, so Tolloczko let Tad putter away on his own, giving counsel and encouragement only as needed.

Tad had been conducting his own experiments at home for years. Even his book-knowledge of science sometimes surpassed that of his professors. "I did quite a lot of extra-curricular work," he boasted, "because I knew the weak side of the teacher, and sometimes I wanted to make it that the teacher didn't know and I did." Despite such self-aggrandizing behavior, Tad was popular with the gymnasium faculty, who nicknamed him "The Senator" for his serious and aloof demeanor. He did not get into fights, and he excelled even in subjects he had no liking for: that is, anything taught by rote. In addition to the Gymnasium's extensive science curriculum, by age eighteen Tad had taken eight years of Latin and six of Greek, as well as French, German and Polish language and literature. On his own, he studied English. (He was amazed when his children, in private schools in the United States, had a much less rigorous program.)

He shared the self-righteous, individualist traits of many young men who went on to shake up the world—Newton, Edison, Bohr, Einstein—but he was not a recluse; he had a circle of close friends (one, Joseph Beck, later became Foreign Minister in the Polish government between the wars) who came to his home and danced with Aniela and her girlfriends when the parlor doors were opened and the cake trays set out. At graduation, Tad made from heavy paper and his own snapshots small albums with pictures of his classmates and professors, and gave one to each member of the class.

While Tad felt the most rapport with his science teachers, he was just as excited by philosophy, poetry, Greek and Latin. At ninety-five he could still quote aphorisms in Greek and bring dispatches from the Peloponnesian War into supper conversation. As a teenager, he spent many hours browsing for volumes on Polish history and literature in the dusty shops of Lwow's antique book dealers, the "Antykwariat," crowded along one street in a nearby neighborhood. He would walk to the other side of town and back in the late evenings to attend a discussion group held by a local philosophy professor. He wasn't searching for the meaning of life; his love of philosophy was a love of logic, a love for the mental exercise, and its purpose was to serve his science. "Philosophy *is* science." he once explained. "To me it's even more, because to me philosophy showed that even in sciences I had to be very strict in logic, and not admit anything unless the proof is sufficient. Philosophy is very good for learning to say, 'This is proof,' or, 'No, that is not enough.'"

But his love of Polish poetry cannot be justified in the pursuit of science, and needn't be. It was like his love for hiking in the Tatra Mountains around Zakopane: a source of inspiration and national pride, as much for Tad as for the generation of the 1830 Uprising, the generation of rebels and romantics. This hard-headed student was soft for the bold, patriotic epics of Adam Mickiewicz, the Polish Byron, for the mystic lyricism of Juliusz Slowacki and the dark, complicated verses of Cyprian Norwid, passages from which he could still recite, without faltering, in his nineties.

These pursuits ebbed when Tad entered the Lwow Polytechnic in 1912, and had to leave liberal arts outside the gate. The massive Italianate main building of the Polytechnic, founded in 1871, was a five-minute walk from home. This quick rush to school in the morning, and occasional bike trips in the country, were all he saw of the open air. Tad chose the study of mechanical engineering over chemistry, became somewhat of a bookworm, and rose to the top two or three in his class.

Tad's choice of mechanical engineering, instead of the chemistry study he had spent so many adolescent hours on, reflects the childhood love of machines that he never outgrew. But it also reflects his ardent individualism. His chemistry mentor, Uncle Tolloczko, was a source of inspiration, not of direction. Nor did Tad go to his father for advice. Kazimir was proud of Tad's achievements, but Kaz's philosophy exposed a diffidence and lack of ambition that to the son was thin, sour gruel: "In life," Kazimir said, "you can go so far and no further." Tad lived and breathed otherwise.

He was truer to the advice of—and the fantasies about—his more distant ancestors: the nobility's ideals of pride, superiority and (only much later) patriotic duty. He consistently defended the bloated and self-congratulating *szlachta* and denied that their rule had brought the country to ruin. He trained himself not to use the less sophisticated Lwowian dialect, but to speak a pure, classic Polish. He traced in his blood a direct vein of greatness. Though he was far enough out of the nobility (and cognizant of family failures: Julian) to know he had to work for his success, he was high enough above the common Poles to grow up imagining that diligence (not financial security, connections, or luck) was all there was to it.

But his arrogance was mitigated by his generosity, his seriousness by his mirth, his grinding scientific bent by his love of poetry and music. These traits held true, with some rare and sad exceptions, to the end of his life.

This nascent nonconformist learned above all how to get his own way, through the force of his intellect and will. But his strength was not forged on an anvil of adversity; it was allowed to crystallize and harden in the mellow and privileged atmosphere of fin-de-siecle Galicia.

The hammer blow was due, and fell in August 1914: the First World War. Within one month after his twentieth birthday, with only a semester to go at the Polytechnic, he met for the first time this force greater than his own, which knocked him off his self-prescribed trajectory to the top of his field. With the Russians entering Lwow, Tad encountered the cold and unforgiving world.

CHAPTER TWO

KIEV

1914 - 1918

It was early one morning in the third week of August 1914. The armies of Czar Nicholas were drawing closer to Lwow and the armies of Emperor Franz Joseph were having no luck stopping them. The Sendzimir family was leaving Lwow for the safety of Austrian-held territory. Tad would stay behind.

In the mirrored and chandeliered second-class waiting room of Lwow's train station, Kazimir and Vanda sat on one of the soft leather couches. The children huddled in close by the family's trunks. Hundreds of Lwow's citizens pressed around them, surging and boiling through the doors and passageways. They were boarding trains heading west, away from the advancing troops. On the wall, the life-sized portrait of arch-prince Karol Ludwig, in full officer's uniform, looked down upon his countrymen in the act of evacuation—a representative in oils of the old order mutely surveying the birth pangs of the new.

Tad had come to see the family off. His student deferment so far had kept him out of the Austrian army. If he were to flee west, he would certainly be drafted, and few Poles went willingly to die for Austria. It was safer to remain in Lwow, try to finish his last semester at the Polytechnic, and take his chances with the in-coming Russians.

Kazimir told Tad once again that they'd be back in a few weeks. The Russian army would be defeated quickly, everyone thought, and all this would be over. His remarks were meant as much for the younger children as for Tad. Aniela, eighteen years old, was anxious for the return of the days when Tad would go to concerts with her and introduce her to his friends. Zbigniew, however, was looking forward to this adventure. He was glad to be getting out from under his brother's shadow, but he was also envious of Tad's independence. Terenia, almost nine years old, sat on a trunk and cried. Her marvelous big brother was not coming with them.

Tad was pacing, smoking, glancing at his watch, stroking his short beard. Handsome and tall, thin but robust from a month of hiking in the Tatras, even in his nervousness Tad held his head high. His prominent aquiline nose and wide forehead slant upward on the same forty-five degree slope, zigzagging briefly at the brow. His eyes are keen and gray as the tungsten steel points of two drills. What a setback, he must have been thinking. No, a catastrophe! *He* should be the one leaving for Vienna, in another year, to get his doctorate.

But in another year, the Great War was far from over. Kazimir, Vanda and the children were still refugees in Prague, and Tad, no diploma in sight, was working in a car repair shop far behind Russian lines in Kiev. In the seven hundred miles between them the armies of Germany, Austria and Russia squatted in their trenches, playing poker and swatting flies.

* * *

The length and brutality of the First World War stunned some Poles, like Kazimir, who expected a swift and orderly resolution. But many Poles realized, and hoped, that this upheaval of empires would bring an end to their century-long imprisonment. In the decade prior to 1914, nationalist sentiments had been flooding Central and Eastern Europe. Tensions were rising, in Lwow no less than in Sarajevo.

In Galicia, while nationalist Poles agitated against Austrians and Russians, nationalist Ukrainians were agitating against Poles. In 1906, a Ukrainian school teacher in Lwow shot the governor of Galicia. In the following year, Ukrainian and Polish students clashed over the Ukrainian demand for their own branch of the university.

Polish nationalists also took to the streets, their hopes for independence rekindled by the 1905 Russian Revolution. The two strongest nationalist parties were divided over whom to ally with, Austria or Russia—depending on which state they thought would be more willing to make concessions to a free Poland. The National Democrats (ND), led by Roman Dmowski, believed that a pro-Russian stand would prevent Russia and Germany from making a deal at Poland's expense. Their activities concentrated on cultural and educational work. On the opposite side—both in strategy and tactics—was the so-called Socialist Party under the strongly charismatic Jozef Pilsudski. Pilsudski was an authoritarian—if not indeed totalitarian—populist who is righteously revered as the father of his country. He organized paramilitary units in Galicia, the Riflemen, whose aim was to join Austrian forces in opposing the czarist armies.

Neither group raised so much as a bead of sweat on the brow of the Austrian government in Galicia: the ND were able to freely distribute Dmowski's articles and pamphlets, citizens could argue volubly about independence in Lwow's cafes, while Pilsudski marched his rag-tag Riflemen openly through the streets. One afternoon in 1912 when Tad was crossing town to Uncle Tolloczko's lab, he heard drum rolls and saw a large crowd gathering in the park across from the Parliament building. He made his way into the throng and saw Pilsudski standing on the steps, straight and stiff in bearing as his signature thick moustache, impervious and persuasive as a howitzer. Before him marched in formation the several hundred men of his army, saluting as they passed. This was the first parade of the Riflemen. Only the officers wore the blue tunic and trousers later adopted by Pilsudski's League; there weren't enough funds yet to put the troops in uniform.

Dmowski's National Democrats sought reunion and independence through gradual evolution. But the ND's nationalist ideal had its anti-Ukrainian and anti-Semitic undercurrent. By 1910 the ND had gained a large following among Poland's middle class, landowners and peasantry. The party was seen as a stable, conservative force promoting Polish independence, and Kazimir Sendzimir typified its mostly passive membership.

The National Democrats played only a minor role in the Sendzimir household on Saint Teresa Street. Despite the relatively high level of political agitation in Lwow, for most Galicians the atmosphere of an immutable status quo prevailed. "When I was a teenager, and even in my twenties," Tad said, "the situation seemed to be so fixed. Nothing could undermine it. It was all still blocks of concrete." Kazimir did not go to party meetings or lectures. Strategies for Polish independence were discussed, but as one among many topics at the dinner table, or with his friends at the bridge games he liked to host.

Tad agreed without dispute to his father's political ideas. The political activities taking place around him in his youth shaped his patriotism as much as did the epic poems of Mickiewicz. But while he was predisposed to the line of the ND, such things mattered little to him. He already had a cause: science, and his own advancement. It was only many decades later, when his personal goals were comfortably met, that Tad took up, as a philanthropist, the plight of Poland.

*　　*　　*

In August 1914, Galicia's turmoils were subsumed, and Tad's goals submerged, in the continent-wide conflagration. The news of the outbreak of war came as a shock at Saint Teresa Street, as it did to most homes of the Empire. More alarming still, soon after, were reports of the rapid advance of the Czarist armies. The Russians' ill-equipped and disorganized forces in the North were about to be pulverized by the Germans at Tannenburg. The Russian generals were sending their big guns and large divisions to the South instead, toward Galicia, against the weaker Austrian army. By the end of August, General Nikolai Ivanov's South West Army Group was bearing down on Lwow.

Kazimir had been evaluating the situation for days, discussing the options with Vanda, listening to the rumors caterwauling through the halls of the Parliament building. At supper on a hot August night, he explained the plans to his children: Lwow was in danger, they must leave and get to safety, away from the front. The family would move to Czeslaw and Malgorzata's in Wilamowice, a small town southwest of Krakow near the Czech border. But they'd be back soon.

By September 3, 1914, when Ivanov's Russian soldiers entered Lwow, Kazimir, Vanda and the three youngest children were in Wilamowice. Czeslaw could not house them for long—he had four children of his own—so in November Kazimir took his family to Prague. They spent nine months in the safety of Prague, living off savings, then moved to Bielsko-Biala, where the Galician salt department was resuscitating itself. The family only returned to the vacant house on Saint Teresa Street in 1916, a year after the German-Austrian counteroffensive had brought Lwow back under the control of the Central Powers. Tad had by then fled east to Kiev.

Tad stayed at home on September 3, 1914. The neighborhood was quiet; the entire city was quiet. The Austrian army had vacated Lwow days before, slipping quietly out the front door and leaving the back unlocked and ajar. The residents watched silently as the Russian troops marched down Lwow's central boulevard.

The population was not hostile to the incoming Russian army, Tad recalled, as long as they behaved themselves. It was on the contrary the civilian Russian administration, pouring in hot on the heels of the Army, that created havoc. The victors treated the newly occupied territories as permanent annexations to Mother Russia. The civil liberties Galicians had enjoyed were suppressed, the Ukrainian separatists trampled, and swarms of priests descended to forcibly convert the Uniate Christians to Orthodoxy. In the Polish expression, Lwowians began to live "as mice under a broom."

Tad, on the other hand, more closely resembled a fox. He was not rooting for one side or the other. He wanted to get through the war in any way he could without fighting: "For very good reason when the war started I declared myself as an adherent of Russia. I had no intention of being taken to serve in the Austrian army. Why should I have been fighting for Austria, which was the hated country?" As a member of the ND he might have favored Russia over Austria in the abstract, but, more to the point, the Russians were not going to draft him.

So when the Russians reopened the railroad repair shops and advertised that they needed men, Tad had no qualms about applying to the occupying power for a job. (Was this collaboration? In wartime, in a war-related industry, yes. He soon realized that he could be shot as a traitor if the Austrian or German armies re-took Lwow. A year later, when they were doing just that, it was fear for his life, as well as fear of the draft, which put him on a train to Kiev.)

Tad took the twenty-minute streetcar ride down to the railroad yards, and presented himself to the general manager, Mr. Szelbitski, a Russian who knew Polish. Tad claimed to be a young engineer whose favorite hobby was automobiles and who knew how to dismantle engines. He was hired on the spot. On the third day, Szelbitski came and asked him to organize an automobile repair shop. Tad had never laid a finger on an actual car engine in his life. He'd never even *driven* a car. But without a thought, he accepted. "Nobody of sound mind would have agreed like that," he said, years later. "But for me, with my ambition, goodness, why couldn't I do it? Surely I could."

He was not entirely unacquainted with the texture of grease and the obstinacy of spark plugs. For two years he had been nursing a Belgian motorcycle that had a four-cylinder engine, exactly like an automobile engine, but without clutch or gears. It was, alas, a hypochondriac. He'd had to dismantle the engine and regrind the valves four or five times. So when Szelbitski mentioned auto repair, Tad did not hesitate.

He set to it, in one empty hall of the railroad yards. He went about collecting the machines he needed from shops around Lwow, because one of the first things he discovered was that spare parts did not exist. Every broken piece had to be fixed or fashioned from scratch.

Tad knew how to handle machines. But Tad was now a manager and now he had to handle men. Two Russian fitters (machinists) were put under his command. They spoke no Polish, and he no Russian. They assumed he knew what he was doing, so they never asked questions, and his air of authority and determination was able to mask his initial ignorance about how exactly one fixed a car. He had only to set the fitters into action; they had to struggle with the dirt and details. But Tad wanted, as always, to learn. He quickly picked up some rudimentary Russian, and made friends with one of the Russian foreman. "I learned quite a lot from him," Tad remembered. "I already knew how to dismantle a car, and I knew how to put it back together. But if there was anything to repair, that I had not the slightest idea."

Soon after the shop opened for business, Szelbitski came in to see how things were going. Tad vividly recalled the day. They had fixed their first car, a Ford Model T. Tad folded up the hood for his boss and displayed the loudly clattering engine. Szelbitski nodded. Then he opened the passenger door, sat down and asked Tad to show him how the car worked on the road. Tad paled. He climbed into the driver's seat, saying to himself "This can't be too hard. It's just like my motorcycle, but with a steering wheel and gears." He put the Ford into first gear, and slowly let out the hand brake. The car jerked forward and out the door of the garage. The street, thank God, was empty. He swung the steering wheel around to the left, then straightened out and held it steady to the corner. Then, left again, around the back of the garage. Pigeons scattering, the engine screaming to get out of first gear, Tad's knuckles white on the wheel, he turned another corner, and one more, and at last back into the shop. He had never shifted to second gear. The general manager stepped down, shook his hand, and left the shop satisfied with his new employee. Tad pulled out his handkerchief, wiped the film of sweat from his forehead, and returned to his desk.

The cars they fixed came from the front, and no two were alike. An Overland and some Fords from the United States, an Opel and a Benz from Germany, a Fiat or two from Italy, a Bugatti from France: an imbroglio of broken axles and busted valves. Once in a while something interesting would roll in, like the American Hupmobile with its low design Tad admired very much, and a car from Berlin whose entire crank shaft of the four-cylinder engine was on ball bearings. Everything had to be rebuilt from scratch. A car came in with its carburator dismounted. They couldn't get a replacement for that make, so Tad designed his own. The Russian fitters built it, installed it, and it worked.

By June 1915, Tad had learned more on his feet than he would have by sitting in the Polytechnic's library for his last term to earn his mechanical engineering degree. And in June he did, in a way, matriculate, but not with cap and gown. With, instead, a small suitcase, crowded aboard a Russian train evacuating Poles from Lwow to Kiev, as the German armies advanced like brushfire across Galicia.

The first assault on the Tarnow-Gorlice line had come in mid-April. By the middle of June, the railway yards in Lwow were once more in a frenzy of evacuation. Tad remained calm, he claimed, but he knew that "since I was friendly with the Russians, and I didn't hide that, when they were leaving Lwow I had to leave with them." Kiev was the closest city considered safe. He packed a small bag, stopped to take one last look around his room—his books piled on Grandmother Octavia's desk, his mother's paintings above the doorways, the framed photograph he had taken of Aniela and Terenia—and left to board a train filled with repairmen and car drivers who had been working in the yards.

The combined German and Austrian armies entered Lwow on June 22, 1915, and stayed until the end of 1918. Tad would not return for eleven years.

*   *   *

Tad, as one of so many Polish and Ukrainian refugees pouring into Kiev that spring, would not have been given the traditional Ukrainian welcome: a huge, fragrant loaf of rye bread topped with a container of salt, presented on a white linen cloth. No one in this city more than twice the size of Lwow even knew or cared who he was as he stepped off the train.

Kiev would hardly have noticed this flood of people; the city was accustomed to guests from out of town. Since 988 Kiev had been the Jerusalem of Russia. Thousands of Russian Orthodox pilgrims flocked to the city's domed, frescoed, mosaic-lined cathedrals, churches and shrines. As Tad walked from the railroad station to the center of town, he passed the seven glittering domes of the Byzantine-style St. Vladimir's Cathedral. He looked forward to the chance to visit the shrines—for their art, not for their religion, which hardly interested him. But now he needed a job. He had inherited this trait from his father: he was as nervous as a geiger counter whenever he found himself without a source of income, no matter how much money he had in his pocket. The nonremunerative aspects of life could wait.

He got hold of a newspaper and responded to an ad for a room on a small street climbing uphill off the Kreshtchatik, Kiev's Times Square and Fifth Avenue. Two middle-aged Russian women had a spare room in their apartment, and they accepted the well-mannered Polish refugee as a tenant.

He immediately set out to find a job. The flood of refugees had still not satisfied the city's wartime hunger for skilled workers. Several auto repair shops needed men, Tad saw in the newspaper, and he noted down their addresses. But then he spotted something interesting: the Russo-American Chamber of Commerce was looking for a secretary. Here was a chance to move into the world of business. He hurried down to their office, and presented himself as a Polish engineer fluent in Russian and English. Tad's grasp of Russian was less than a year old, and confined to words like "throttle," "driveshaft," "accelerate," and "dismantle." But English he knew. He had been studying it on his own for at least five years, in hopes of opening a door just like this one. He was hired.

It was a small job. Once a week in the evening he would go to their meeting, take notes and type them up. The potentates of Kiev's export interests—sugar beet seeds topped their list of concerns—were quite satisfied with his abilities, especially as it turned out that most of the board members were of Polish descent. His Russian improved quickly, as did his understanding of the world of commerce. No one seemed to mind that Tad was better educated than the lot of them, and he didn't so advertise.

Tad then went looking for work in the car repair shops. The ads listed one shop just up the hill from his apartment. He found the number on the front of a three-story building, but to his surprise it was a private house. As he pushed open the tall wooden door to the courtyard, he was relieved to hear the unhappy rattle of misfiring engines and the steady clang of mallets meeting metal. A score of disabled and dismantled automobiles filled the large, enclosed yard, and above the din Tad could hear the familiar buzz of drills and lathes coming from inside the building. A greasy thumb pointed him toward the office. There a familiar looking face glanced up from the cluttered desk, and greeted him in Polish. The face belonged to the garage manager, Eugene Porembski, an engineering student at the Lwow Polytechnic one year ahead of Tad. He hired Tad immediately as his assistant.

The Regional Motor Car Repair Works was run by the Society of Landowners, *Vcerosyjskij Soyoz*, a benevolent organization similar to the Red Cross. The shop repaired the cars they used on the southwestern front, bringing in food and medical supplies and carrying out wounded. The government had requisitioned this private house for the Society to use as its garage.

Tad and Porembski ran the administration of the shop and became good friends. Tad had a somewhat higher status than in the railway yards in Lwow—he even was consigned the organization's uniform, sand gray with a little saber, which he wore on official occasions. But the problems were the same, multiplied in scale: many different makes of cars, no spare parts. It often took two or three months before a car could be sent in working order back to the front. And the cars of those days were delicate beasts. "Every five thousand miles," Tad said, "you had to open the cylinders and regrind the valves, otherwise you lost compression. If you went a hundred miles and didn't have to change a tire, that was a miracle."

Every so often someone important would have car trouble and appear at the shop. Tad said that General Anton Denikin, whose fiancee lived in Kiev, came in more than once. This stocky, beetle-browed general with the booming voice and triangular white beard was briefly put in charge of the southwestern front, but then arrested for conspiracy in August 1917. He escaped from prison in December and became the commander of the White Army in southern Russia during the Civil War.

Once he had settled into his rented room and his two jobs, Tad was able to look around at Kiev, as pleasant and as green a city as one could want to wait out a war in. He spent his free time walking up and down the city's steep, chestnut-lined streets. He ate in small restaurants on the Kreshtchatik, prowled in the large Polish bookstore, and had an occasional pastry at the Semadeny cafe, reading over the Polish newspapers that could be bought there. Tad joined, as often as he could, the boisterous crowds at the opera (an art form enjoyed in Russia as much by the hoi polloi as by the high and mighty). When the July temperatures hit 100 degrees, he escaped the heat by swimming in the Dnieper, along with the rest of the population, most of whom, men, women and children, had no belief in bathing suits. Tad remembered that despite the war, Kiev had pockets of plenty: "There were three or four luxury shops selling only honey, maybe forty or fifty different kinds of honey."

Tad ran into some friends from the Lwow Polytechnic, Stanislaw Tomasik and Roman Rusienkiewicz. Tad had known Rusienkiewicz and his father quite well back in Lwow. The father had been the general secretary of the University; his son was a romantic sort, but nevertheless a good engineer. Tomasik was a few years older than Tad or Roman, and not so high in social status; in Lwow, he had had to work to put himself through school. The three became close friends, swimming in the Dnieper, smoking in the cafes.

As an attractive, educated young man, Tad was in demand in the parlors of well-off Poles whom he met through Porembski. But apart from the occasional soiree, and outings with his close friends, he kept to himself, cherished his solitude, and was happiest walking in the parks accompanied only by his thoughts.

*   *   *

In 1917, these thoughts turned increasingly to war, as the peace of Kiev was rent by food shortages and fatigue after two and a half years of fighting. And, no less, by the momentous events taking place in St. Petersburg.

The February Revolution against the Czar passed bloodlessly in Kiev, but the revolutionary ferment galvanized the Ukrainian nationalists into action. By the end of March 1917, a Ukrainian Central Rada (or governing council) had been formed, to attempt to establish an independent Ukraine. The Provisional Government in St. Petersburg was forced in June to grudgingly accept the Rada's proclamation of an "autonomous Ukrainian republic," federated with Russia.

But the ship of a Ukrainian independent state was a somewhat leaky barge with few oarsmen and a swarm of school teachers wrestling with the helm, while waves rose higher over the bow. Only a small minority of the population actually supported the movement: the Ukrainian peasantry was more anti-Polish and anti-Semitic (the landowners and the merchants, respectively) than anti-Russian; the scant proletariat was primarily of Great Russian, not Ukrainian, origin, as were the families who ran the industries. The Ukrainian nationalists did manage to conduct large demonstrations for independence in the streets of Kiev and smaller cities, but it remained a movement of middle class intellectuals and teachers, allied more with the same class in eastern Galicia than with the local population. Lacking broad support, the movement had to turn for help to foreign powers, thus undermining its credibility as a popular native cause. These political difficulties were further complicated by the powerful economic interdependence of Russia and Ukraine. The Ukrainian nationalists were trying to tear away a region with one fifth the population of Czarist Russia, containing its most fertile land, its most modern industries, its tremendous coal and iron resources, all dependent on, and necessary to, the markets of Great Russia.

Public order gradually broke down. By the eve of the October Revolution, the separatists had gained the upper hand against the Bolsheviks and other parties. But the chaos only deepened over the winter months: the government changed again four times.

In February 1918, the lid blew off this boiling kettle. On the eighth, delegates from the Rada signed a separate peace treaty with the Germans. That very same day, Soviet armies were entering Kiev, and within a few days the Rada was overthrown and a new Soviet government put in its place. This government was to last less than three weeks. The German armies, with the green light of their treaty with the Rada, were marching quickly east across Ukraine toward Kiev.

*   *   *

Tad did not look to the advancing German army—his nemesis from Lwow—with any kind of relief, even though he abhorred the Bolsheviks and he was fed up with the incompetent Ukrainians. As he explained it, "After the Russian Revolution the Ukrainians felt, 'All right, it's our city, time to get independence.' But it happens that the Ukrainians were totally unprepared to be the rulers. They made one mistake after another." The Germans, on the other hand, might restore order — but in the process he and his Polish friends might be hanged for treason.

Kiev life had descended into anarchy. Deserters from the army streamed through town. Policemen no longer patrolled the streets. One day on the Kreshtchatik Tad remembered passing a small angry crowd. He heard a shot, and saw a man fall to the ground. The crowd dispersed, leaving the dead man lying on the snow-covered sidewalk. "He was a spy," someone said as they shuffled past. No one was arrested, no questions asked. On another day, late in January, Tad was trying to make his way over to the Chamber of Commerce office when suddenly shooting erupted from both sides of the street. Tad hid with two other men in a doorway. Five minutes later the shooting stopped and he continued on his way.

Tad stayed off the streets as much as he could, going out only to get something to eat, and to pick up any newspaper that could tell him how close the Germans were. In the middle of February he quit his job. The fall of the Bolshevik government in Kiev and the entrance of the German army were a week away. When the Germans came, Tad was sure he would be court-martialed and hung.

Tad took the trolley down to the train station and pushed his way through the raucous crowds of returning soldiers to the large timetable mounted on the wall. He calculated a route that, winding north and east from town to town, changing trains often, would get him across the Urals without going through Moscow, where there might be trouble. His goal was Chelyabinsk, where he could board the Trans-Siberian Railway and get out of Russia by going east, away from the war.

He left the station and hurried over to the apartment of Tomasik and Rusinkiewicz. They'd be hanged if they stayed in Kiev, he told them. They should leave with him, the next day. They agreed to meet at the station. (He said later that without his initiative they would simply have stayed put and prayed.) Tad returned home, packed his small suitcase, tucked in his Austrian passport and his Russian work card, and collected what money he had—half in Russian rubles and half in the recently coined Ukrainian money (good, almost immediately, only for lighting fires).

The next morning the three men found each other at the station. The platforms were jammed: unshaven soldiers trying to return east to their villages, Poles trying to move their families west back to Poland, Cossacks making their way south to their farms along the Don, Great Russians moving north up to Moscow and out of the path of the Germans. In between the tired and anxious groups came peasants selling hard bread and, if you were lucky, eggs.

A train whistle screamed in the distance. An engine appeared, drawing behind it a length of freight cars, and one or two passenger cars already overflowing. Its sign read "Moscow." Half the crowd surged forward and began to board before the train came to a full stop. Tad and his friends followed a dozen other men up the ladders to the roof of a car. They found some metal handles to hang on to and huddled together for warmth. Next stop was Chernigov, over 50 miles to the north; from there they could catch a train going east. The train pulled out from the station. It soon began to pick up speed. White smoke from the engine came streaming down the line of cars, over the scores of men clinging to the roofs. God granted one little favor to Ukraine in February 1918: a mild winter. They might all have frozen to death before reaching Chernigov.

They stayed up there for two days. The cold wind bit their faces, but they felt safer on top than below, where AWOL soldiers bragged to each other of killing this person and that, and dispensed their own justice in the crowded cars. A story made its way along the roof: "I didn't witness that," Tad said, "but they say that a woman found one hundred rubles missing from her pocket. They suspected a young boy, and then they just twisted his head off. One of the soldiers did that."

When they reached Kursk, they found room inside a freight car. They squeezed in with forty or fifty people and the few possessions each could cling to. At every town they would get off, look for the next train going east, find a spot on the floor of a freight car, and move on, north-northeast: Voronezh, Tambov, Penza, Syzran, Simbirsk, Kazan, Ufa. Up and over the spruce-robed Urals, past the sign post telling them that they were leaving Europe and entering Asia, and finally down to Chelyabinsk, where they met the Trans-Siberian Railway heading across Siberia and out to the Pacific.

The chaos of the Revolution did not pass as easily over the Urals as did the trains. The Bolsheviks were in control, the Civil War was months away, and so some order prevailed. One could buy tickets in the Chelyabinsk train station, and get seats in third- and fourth-class cars, instead of having to crowd pell-mell onto any piece of rolling stock. But the war was still on: no more the fancy dining and parlor cars, the upright pianos and the shelves of books that adventurous European travelers had enjoyed while crossing the monotonous steppe. Tad was happy enough to be inside a car with seating compartments, sitting on his own hard wood bench or curling up to sleep in the luggage rack overhead. The 1914 edition of *Baedeker's Handbook for Travelers* claims that the trip from Moscow to Vladivostok could be completed in eight and two-thirds days. In March of 1918, it took Tad and his friends one month.

After the week spent inside or on top of freight cars, Tad, Tomasik and Rusinkiewicz settled exhausted into their seats in the dark-green third-class carriage. There was little to do but watch the white birch forests, thin black branches against the snow, run slowly, endlessly past the train as it pulled across western Siberia. In every compartment Russian soldiers passed the time engrossed in card games. "There were mostly peasants on the train," Tad remembered, "and many, many soldiers running from the front back to their villages. There were no other foreigners. We tried to keep a low profile, staying away from the soldiers. We didn't want to have anything to be remembered by." They searched for any scraps of newspapers that might come aboard which could give them news. "We were all eager to know what was happening ahead of us. For instance in Vladivostok, if there were some bloody upheaval. And also, back of us, if there was a counter-revolution in Moscow."

As each new kilometer separated Tad from the war, he breathed more easily. If Vladivostok was clear, he could get out of Russia, and, perhaps, even get to America. He could relax a little now, and congratulate himself. And he had cause to. He'd been on the brink of three successive battle fronts and escaped unharmed. He hadn't had to fight in anyone's army, nor face any of their firing squads. He had broken free of the anarchic rubble of Kiev. He was on his way out of Russia.

History had knocked him briefly off course, but he missed hardly a beat finding a new one. While he still lacked a diploma, the war years had not been unkind to him. He knew almost every car manufactured in the world, he could contrive their parts from virgin metal and pull together the people and pieces to put the cars back on the road. On the side he picked up some business skills from the Russo-American Chamber of Commerce. He became fluent in Russian and English, to add to his Polish, Ukrainian, French and German (and of course, Latin and Greek). He'd been lucky, but he'd also been savvy. He had what it took: ingenuity, a will of iron, chutzpa—the mechanic who'd never touched a car engine, the repair shop manager who'd never driven a car—and a certain talent for self-preservation. He'd made from life's lemons lemonade.

His friends may have noticed a different Tad than the young man they had known in Lwow: less the idealistic admirer of the Romantic poets, the scholar ensconced in his lab, the student of logic and philosophy. This was a tougher individual. His determination and inventiveness had sharpened. And his idealism, the clear-eyed goals of his ancestors, had softened and clouded like sea glass beneath the exigent tide of war. This thin, twenty-four-year-old great-grandson of a nobleman had survived.

In one week they made it to Irkutsk, a city of over 100,000 just west of Lake Baikal. The birch forest had given way to snow-covered hills and meadows, and, closer to Irkutsk, flat pine forest. The relative quiet of the past few days allowed Tad's adventuresome spirit to get the better of his practical side. He decided—when would they ever be back in Siberia?—to stay and see Irkutsk for a few days. They found a hotel and went immediately for a long bath.

They passed the next three days as curious tourists, walking along the wooden board sidewalks half a yard above the muddy street. They visited the gold smeltery and the museum of the Imperial Russian Geographical Society which had an exhibit of mammoth remains. The houses, the churches, the commerce of Irkutsk impressed them as distinctly Russian. Yet here they were three thousand miles east of Moscow, less than two hundred miles north of the Mongolian border. This was the Siberian Denver, Billings or Cheyenne. Tramping across the sidewalks were tow-headed Siberian trappers, farmers and miners; silk-robed Mongol traders from Ulan Bator; and Oriental, black-haired Buriat herders from the mountains beyond Lake Baikal.

After three days they left Irkutsk on a train going east to Vladivostok. Soon they were weaving in and out of the tunnels on the southern edge of Lake Baikal: the mile-deep, storm-swept, fresh water sea that cuts a blue, primeval trench in the barren mountains. They stopped again briefly in Chita, where the route to Vladivostok branched. Tad asked at the station which train to take. One could go directly southeast, the agent told him, on the Chinese Eastern Railway through Manchuria; or one could go north up along the Amur River. The latter route was twice as long, the track in places newly laid so the trains ran slowly. But, travelers on the former were advised to carry revolvers.

Tad returned to his friends with this trenchant summary. They boarded the slower, safer train.

The thickly forested mountains along the Amur gave way to pleasant, rolling prairies. With each town passed, greater numbers of Asians filled the streets: Chinese, Koreans, Japanese. Finally, at the end of March, the train came to the banks of Amur Bay, rolled slowly down the western edge of a long peninsula, and came to a stop under the high brick arches of Vladivostok's immense railway station.

The three men grabbed a taxi for the nearest hotel. They would stay roughly a week, subsisting on...red caviar. "There was a shortage of food," Tad said. "You couldn't get bread. You couldn't get meat. But curiously there was any amount you wanted of red caviar. It came in big barrels. So I was delighted at first, and then I had enough because it was very salty." Vladivostok was like the mirror-image (with the Pacific to its *east*) of San Francisco: located on the tip of a peninsula; hills sparkling with golden domes and white stone navy barracks; Chinese and Koreans, the latter in long white garments and stiff black horsehair hats, running the kitchens and washing the clothes and carrying the freight for the white population—Russian, German, British, French, American—over 100,000 in all. Chinese junks awaited unloading in the harbor, engraved against the distant blue mountains of Korea.

At that moment, the Bolsheviks happened to be in control of Vladivostok, but Japanese, British and American warships sat in the harbor. On March 25, the Soviets had put an end to several months of bickering on the local city council by seizing the post and telegraph offices. They remained in power even through the landing of Japanese and British soldiers on April 5, and were deposed only in June.

The Russian commercial fleet was on strike, so no boats were leaving port. While waiting for the strike to end, Tad tried to obtain a British visa for Hong Kong. He was determined to leave Russia—for anywhere—but he carried only his Austrian passport and his Russian work card, and the war was still on. The consulate turned him down. Go to Shanghai, they suggested. Shanghai was an open city—you didn't need a passport or visa. Just find a boat.

The strike of the commercial fleet ended. The first steamer out, the *Simbirsk*, was bound for northern Japan. Tad was on it. Tomasik stayed behind (but turned up a year later in Shanghai). Rusinkiewicz got war fever when he heard from refugees about the formation of a Polish Army under General Haller in Paris, and he made his way back there to fight. They both came down to the dock to see Tad off, at the end of their five-thousand-mile journey together. Not one of them knew what his next step would bring.

The *Simbirsk* landed in Japan the following morning. Tad caught a train running south along the coast to Nagasaki, from where a boat made regular trips across the East China Sea to Shanghai. He spent a couple of days in Nagasaki waiting for the next departure. He passed the time looking around the hilly city, one of the few in Japan accustomed to the sight of foreigners. Would he have been surprised to find out that this small country, four decades later, would develop a voracious appetite for his inventions? Probably not.

One morning, early in April 1918, Tad boarded a steamer for Shanghai. He was to remain in China for eleven years.

CHAPTER THREE

SHANGHAI BOOM

1918 - 1924

As Tad's ferry drew near Shanghai, he could see the granite towers of banks and trading houses, and imagine, with astonishment, that he was approaching a European city. But when he looked down on the water, a sweaty, exotic scene chased off that Occidental mirage. The river surface was pulsating with cargo junks, fishing trawlers, night soil boats and long trains of sampans (linked tail to nose) bobbing and snaking between ocean liners and warships from the United States, Great Britan, France and Japan. The scene lacked only the classic opium hulks—the barges, done away with a decade before, where the drug had been stored and bonded.

Tad entered Shanghai in the same way as every round-eyed invader, trader and adventurer who had come before him, sailing the twelve miles up the Huangpu River from the wide brown estuary of the Yangtze—like thousands of tiny, parasitic worms floating along a vein to the heart.

The Europeans had first come in the 1840s, up the coast from Canton, to this then second-rate town of perhaps a hundred thousand souls. Shanghai could boast of no lacquered imperial palaces or crumbling, moss-covered shrines; it was a young settlement, by China's standards, a collection of huts on marshy soil walled off against Japanese pirates only in the sixteenth century. Shanghai's claim to fame was only, eminently, location: the port of entry to the vast Yangtze River valley, home to almost half of China's population. Shanghai was the door to China, a fact of geography easily grasped by the rapacious nineteenth-century European traders. They seized the key to this door in the Opium Wars; the signing of the Treaty of Nanking in 1842 allowed the British to open five treaty ports, Shanghai the most important. The French quickly moved in alongside and established their own zone. The British and Americans combined their jurisdictions to form the International Settlement, and by 1870 Shanghai was China's premier trading post. It became, in the words of one historian, "a city for sale."

The Europeans brought industry on the heels of commerce: ship builders, flour and cotton mills, silk filatures, chemical works and machine shops sprang up along the river banks, stretching north and east as the boundaries of the International Settlement spread. Chinese peasants, fleeing destitution and calamity in the countryside, found grueling employment in and around the foreign settlements; by 1915, the population of Shanghai had swelled to one and a half million.

Only the constant influx of peasants from the villages could compensate for the heavy toll exacted by disease, poverty and industrial carnage. Whole families came to occupy single tenement rooms in labyrinthine alleys, noisy with hawkers and squealing children, lined with night soil pots, shaded by canopies of hanging laundry. Thousands more lived on the pavement under reed mats or oil drums. Each month hundreds died in the squalor of the streets or in the factories; corpses, often fished out of the canals, were placed in wooden caskets and stacked beside open fields to wait in the humid air for burial.

The streets were filled with the penetrating odors of fish and melons rotting in market stalls, of cottonseed oil smoking in cooking pots, of sandalwood incense wafting from small temples, and of the "honey carts" making the rounds each morning to empty the night soil pots. Yet these smells could still be overwhelmed by the stench from a silk filature. In huge vats silk cocoons were boiled, giving off clouds of foul-smelling steam. Young girls with swollen red fingers stood for twelve hours over these vats, their arms scalded by the foreman as punishment for threading a spool incorrectly. Innocent-faced boys of twelve and thirteen would be sold to factories for four-year "apprenticeships," during which they worked fourteen-hour shifts and were given only a greasy cotton quilt to sleep on, on a plank above their machines. Factories opened in dark tenements; the inside walls would be knocked out, and machinery crammed in. Exploding furnaces, broken stairways, sealed-off exit doors—such nuisances were settled by a small fine, or a payoff to an official in the court. Wages were kept at rock-bottom due to the overwhelming supply of labor pouring in from the countryside.

But this was not the city the Europeans would acknowledge as their spawn, and most lived out their days as if this unsavory Shanghai did not exist. In the residential enclaves they built villas behind high brick walls, with wide verandas facing south to catch the breeze and the aroma from the purple wysteria climbing trellises in their gardens. They passed to and from the business district in their long cars down avenues shaded by elms and willows. They surrounded themselves with the familiar: neo-Gothic churches and heavy stone buildings with arched windows and slate roofs. They had their polo field, their race track, their social clubs and their cricket matches. The wide green lawn of the French Club was kept in trim by a line of a hundred Chinese women on their knees, inching forward, snipping the grass. Orientals were not allowed in the European clubs except as servants. The Europeans constructed their ponderous palaces of commerce along the Bund, the wide roadway beside the Huangpu river, busy with electric trams and expensive cars. The Chinese had compelled the English to leave thirty feet between the edge of the river and their mushrooming buildings, so downtown Shanghai was spared a waterfront knit with dark, forbidding wharves (the usual fate of working ports). The highest and the lowest could promenade along the Bund's embankment, to escape the dense streets for a whiff of air, up to the Public Gardens at its northern end, where the famous (perhaps apocryphal) sign read "No dogs or Chinese allowed."

* * *

A small crowd of Europeans was waiting on the dock when Tad's ferry landed. As he stepped off the boat he quickly recognized, with surprise, the words they were calling out. The language was too familiar: Russian. These relatively new residents, quite often poor, came to meet the incoming passenger boats to offer their services to newcomers—hundreds of whom, at this moment in history, were fleeing the Revolution. A man approached Tad and asked if he needed a place to stay. He offered him a room in his family's apartment, and Tad accepted. They went off together up the Bund, across Soochow Creek to the district filled with White Russian immigrants.

Crossing over Garden Bridge, they passed into Hongkew, a densely packed district where Shanghai's Japanese community lived cheek by jowl with Chinese and poor Europeans, often Russians, who could not afford the more fashionable, more spacious neighborhoods. It was one of the few areas of Shanghai which housed such an indiscriminate mix of foreigners and natives (packed in among scrap iron dealers, pawn shops and vegetable stands), and for this reason was looked down upon by better society.

As they chatted about the world he had just left, Tad was meanwhile observing with awe the world he had just stepped into. Coolies ran down the narrow street, balancing two heavy baskets fore and aft on a bamboo pole across their shoulders. Middle-aged and elderly women, Tad noticed with horror, tottered on tiny, bound feet along the alleys. Merchants stood in the doorways of their open-front shops, their goods spilling out into the street. Bare-chested coolies pulled and pushed wheelbarrows piled high with furniture, wooden crates, chickens in bamboo cages, steamer trunks, or bales of iron wire. They chanted sing-song phrases to keep their pace and alert wayward pedestrians. (Tad was instantly fascinated by the Chinese wheelbarrows: "I put a question to myself then: That wheelbarrow was developed over the centuries. If I wanted to improve on it what would I do? Absolutely nothing, you couldn't improve it.")

They turned a corner and walked past the great Hongkew Market, the city's largest. Baskets of vegetables leaned against the walls, next to barrels of fish and crates of chorusing ducks stacked five feet high. The aroma of cooked food came from baskets carried by coolies selling meals on the street. Of all the unusual sights seen on his arrival, Tad remembered most vividly this abundance: "My very first impression is that I came after four years of war, where there was no white bread, many articles were missing from the shops, and so on. And all of a sudden I find myself in a city where food was everywhere, you didn't see any war, anything you asked for in a shop you could get. Sort of as if you came from another planet. War was by telegraph and the news in the newspaper."

Tad settled into the spare room of the apartment of a Russian Jewish family. They were not Orthodox in practice (and so caused this young Polish aristocrat no social discomfort). Tad fit in as any fellow European refugee in a sea of Chinese.

*   *   *

Tad was sympathetic and, for a European, quite respectful of the Chinese. He could enthusiastically explain the steps of the Chinese process for extracting soybean oil, and how in 1800 Chinese industry was more advanced than European. He admired the gyrodynamics of their wheelbarrow, the intelligence and industriousness of their workers, the richness and variety of their markets. Yet he had no Chinese friends, and he lived through the most tumultuous decade in Shanghai's history entirely unaware of the political chaos around him. His obliviousness came less from a European arrogance about race and Western Civilization, and more from his nature: the absent-minded inventor, the single-minded entrepreneur. This was the period in his life, the swelling and bursting stretch of his thirties, when, through difficult, absorbing mental and physical toil, he came to realize his calling. Nothing else mattered.

*   *   *

Tad stayed with the Russian family about a month, but very soon had cause to regret having settled in that neighborhood. Almost immediately after his arrival he went down to the American Consulate to apply for a visa. Any reasonably astute and ambitious young engineer, especially a Polish one, had his eyes set on America: the land of Edison, Ford and the Wright brothers, not to mention Kosciuszko and Pulaski. An official at the Consulate greeted him, took the paper Tad had filled out, and asked where he now was living. Tad told him the name of the street, and the American's brows lowered slightly—the cheap side of town. A few weeks later, Tad learned his application had been denied.

Meanwhile he found a job at the Eastern Garage, an American-run car repair shop. But they didn't take him to fix cars; they needed instructors to train hundreds of Chinese to drive Ford Model T trucks. Nearly 200,000 Chinese were sent to Europe and the Middle East during World War I for work battalions, as their country's contribution to the war. The drivers trained at the Eastern Garage were being shipped off to France to clear battlefields.

It was hardly a job for an engineer, but Tad fell into his task with characteristic enthusiasm. He discovered that the other instructors were teaching their students one at a time. "I didn't like that at all," he remembered. "It was too slow. So I said to myself, 'Never mind what the others do. I will do it logically, my way.'" He took several students in the truck and, sitting behind the wheel himself, drove back and forth around the lot, explaining (in his few words of Pidgin English) how to handle the truck's two gears and reverse. Then one after the other he let each student take the wheel, in that small lot, going forward and backward and around. On the second day they took the truck out onto the street. In four days he had trained a dozen drivers.

When not at work, Tad scouted around the International Settlement for better opportunities. He met people in the communities of Polish, Russian and Czech emigres, and through them found out that the president and vice-president of the Russo-Asiatic Bank were Poles. He went down to their offices on the Bund to pay his respects. Count Jezierski, the president, and Zygmund Jastrzembski, the vice-president, were Polish businessmen in their fifties who had come to Shanghai some years earlier. They received Tad cordially, eager to hear his first-hand news of the revolution and the war. They took a liking for him. He left with their promises of help.

Around the middle of May, Tad met a man from Holland who was living up in Tsingtao, on the coast, and wanted to open a garage there. He asked Tad to come immediately to start and manage it. Tad took the next steamer to Tsingtao.

*   *   *

In Tsingtao, Tad was in for another surprise. Just when he was getting used to the bustle and smell of congested Shanghai, he arrived at this seaside resort and shipping community of clean, tree-lined avenues, and newly built, green and red tile roofed buildings. Not a temple or slum or upcurving roof in sight: it was like a paper and matchstick village constructed by a meticulous Prussian schoolboy in his attic.

Tsingtao sits at the tip of the Shantung Peninsula, on the eastern edge of one of the best natural harbors in northern China. A substantial junk trade plied these waters for several centuries before the Europeans arrived. In 1898, the Germans occupied Tsingtao by force and wrote themselves a ninety-nine-year lease on the bay, the surrounding territory, and all rail and mining rights. They didn't simply move in; they levelled the Chinese village so they could start fresh and unimpeded. The Chinese were excised to the far side of the peninsula, out of sight behind the hills, and with Teutonic efficiency the Germans built a model city. They laid streets out in irregular patterns, to cut down on the dust, and set flat granite blocks next to the sidewalks for the slow-moving wheelbarrows, to get them out of the way of carriages and rickshaws. They built their European-style houses facing south for the winter sun and surrounded them with gardens; they erected government and commercial buildings on the slope overlooking the harbor entrance; and they put a hotel and a string of summer cottages along the fine, crescent-shaped beach.

Such tranquillity could not survive the battles fought in Europe, nor the expansionist desires of Japan. Japan declared war on Germany in 1914 in order to grab Tsingtao, which they seized in November of that year and continued to occupy until 1922. When Tad arrived in May 1918, the French and English summer residents were still crowding the beaches and the race track, the Germans sat in their beer halls and their shops (the social relations between the Germans and the other Europeans were icy, though not overtly hostile), but the policemen on the streets were Japanese. The Japanese kept a low profile. They left the Europeans alone, and tried to build up an image as a civilized nation, in anticipation of future collaboration. They were drafting their capacious territorial demands for when the war ended.

Tad easily found a room in the house of a German family, who were delighted to have a German-speaking boarder. "I was not particularly friendly with the Germans, but they were very, very friendly with me," he said. They thought of him as an Austrian (that's what his passport said), and took pride in introducing this handsome young engineer to all their friends.

The job at the garage differed not at all from his work in Lwow and Kiev, except the workmen were Chinese and the language of instruction Pidgin English. On his days off Tad swam in the Yellow Sea, visited his German friends, and spent hours walking on the beach or along the roads leading out of town. He was reasonably content, he was earning good money, but he was not challenged. On his walks he let his mind ramble over physics and chemistry and engineering problems that the mundane garage could not supply to his hungry intellect, or his ambition.

Toward mid-summer Tad got a letter from Jastrzembski in Shanghai. They knew a fellow who had some ideas for starting a factory. Could Tad pay them a visit on his next trip to Shanghai?

In Jastrzembski's office, Tad met a Russian merchant, an outgoing man named Heyman, who had come to China years before to make his fortune. Heyman explained that among his many ventures was the supply of parts to the Chinese Eastern Railway. The railway needed untold quantities of bolts and nuts, Heyman said, which he had been purchasing from Europe. He thought they could be made cheaper here. It would be the first machine-made bolt factory in China, and Tad was the man to do it. The bank would supply the capital. Tad would start up and run the factory. It would be called the "Sendzimir Mechanical Works."

Tad paused less than an instant. He knew nothing about bolts and nuts, nor about trade in the Far East, nor about production conditions in a semi-tropical climate. What he did know was that he could figure it out, that he was bored with running a car garage, and that he liked the sound of "Sendzimir Mechanical Works."

*　　*　　*

"I had never even *seen* a bolt factory," Tad liked to boast, in describing how he started up his shop, "but I imagined very well how bolts should be made." In September of 1918 the war in Europe was still on, and one couldn't get those jaunty Acme Bolt Headers that winked at you from the pages of American machinery catalogs. So he went around to Shanghai's machine shops and bought up a few simple presses, the kind used for stamping sheet iron. He hired some draftsmen and fitters, and set them to work redrawing and converting the presses to churn out bolts.

Tad could not remember whether any families had to be evicted from the three houses on Fearon Road that he purchased for his factory, but given the density of this neighborhood north of Soochow Creek, we can assume so. He couldn't remember how the partitions separating the buildings were knocked out, or how he hired his handful of draftsmen, fitters and laborers. But within a few days, he claimed, the buildings were gutted, the machinery rebuilt and put in place, and the offices set up on the top floor. With two machines to start, Tad said, "We began production almost immediately." The Sendzimir Mechanical Works—Sendzimay Chi Chi Chung, in Chinese—was in business.

While the images of people were dim, the machinery remained, characteristically, sharp and clear. What Tad did remember, in exhaustive detail, is how he made his bolts.

Four-hundred-pound bundles of iron wire, imported from Belgium or Holland, lay stacked up in the alley outside the shop, their garish orange patina of rust gleaming in the sun. A hoist would lift one bundle from the top of the stack, and a man fed the tip of the wire into the descaling machine, which kneaded the wire this way and that between rollers to loosen and crack off the rust coating (in itself valuable iron that was swept up and sold as flake scale). The rebundled wire, restored to its original slate gray color, then was carried over to be cleaned. The bundle was plunged into a pickling bath, to poach for two or three minutes in an acrid-smelling, simmering solution of hydrochloric acid. The now pure iron wire was then lifted out and the acid rinsed off. The dull gray bundle was next dipped into a thin soup of lime and water, emerging with a white frosting, and set to bake dry over a hot plate. Once dry, the white wire was dredged through a box of fine, powdered soap. The lime and soap formed a tough, slippery skin, so that the wire could pass smoothly through the wire-drawing machines.

The iron wire, cleaned, buffed and powdered, now had to be drawn, to reduce the diameter and in the same process toughen the metal, whose crystals elongated and strengthened as they were pulled through the tungsten carbide die. Wire for nails was drawn three or four times, as nails need to be thinner and far stronger than bolts. Bolt wire went through but once, and then was ready for the bolt header. This machine delivered a series of hammer blows to the tip of the wire, forming the particular shape bolt head required. The wire was then pulled forward slightly, and chopped off to the length of shank necessary for that type of bolt. The bolt dropped into a basket, the newly severed wire tip pushed forward, and the hammering and chopping continued (at 300 bolts a minute) until the machine had chewed up the entire bundle of wire like a string of licorice.

One last machine cut the thread on the shank, a process Tad designed himself after studying some machine tool catalogs. One by one each bolt was heated, then placed in a clamp. The threading die screwed into it, cutting the thread as it went, then unscrewed, and the threaded bolt was released. The bolts were tumbled briefly in sawdust to give them a shine, then coolies carted the boxes of finished bolts to the storeroom and bagged them in hemp bags labeled "Sendzimir Mechanical Works." The factory later produced nails in the same way (with similar but simpler machines), and sold them by the keg.

The redesigned machinery was primitive. But still it was better than anything operating in China at the time. Tad's innovations did not revolutionize boltmaking; he simply mechanized it, through determination and ingenuity, in a place where modern methods were beyond reach.

*   *   *

While mechanization improved the quality of the product, it did nothing to improve the working conditions. When his friend Tomasik arrived in Shanghai looking for a job, a year after Tad had said good-bye to him in Vladivostok, he found his respected friend in circumstances little different from all the other hot, crowded machine shops thick on the ground in the International Settlement.

Tomasik located Tad via the grapevine of Polish immigrants. He hired a rickshaw to take him out to the factory. Fearon Road ran up the left side of a tiny canal jammed with sampans. As Tomasik pulled up to Tad's shop, a score of small children scampered across and up from their sampan homes to entreat this new foreigner.

Tad was pleased to see his friend, and proudly showed him around the factory. The ground floor was hot, steamy and dark—low ceilings and small windows sealed the heat in and the daylight out. Fans strained to move the stuffiness about.

Twenty men in dark blue shirts and pants were operating the clamoring machines. The same number, but in long coats, were carting supplies, hauling and bagging bolts, and tending the hoist and pickling tank. Tad, shouting over the din, explained the hierarchy: coolies, in long coats, were at the low end; fitters, as semi-skilled operators, were paid a little more and wore pants because they had to crawl around their machines, where long coats would get in the way.

The machines stretched in a line the length of the shop, powered by pulleys running from a single drive shaft along the floor (the ceilings were too low to run it overhead). Tad told Tomasik sadly about an accident that had happened a month before: It was against the rules for coolies in their long coats to step over this shaft, which was rotating at about 270 revolutions per minute. But to save steps they often did. One man caught his coat, and was instantly killed.

Tad took Tomasik upstairs to his office. The roar of the machinery diminished slightly, but was replaced by shouts and clatter from sampan traffic on the canal. The wooden floor was crowded with large tables, where two or three Chinese draftsmen spread out their machinery drawings. Tad introduced Tomasik to a Russian engineer who was working briefly as his assistant. They walked over to the far corner, from where Tad ruled the roost at a desk all but invisible under piles of drawings, letters, files, scrap paper, newspapers, magazines and catalogs. The lighter material was prevented from sailing out the open window into the canal by ashtrays, tea cups, broken machine parts and a telephone.

He offered Tomasik a job as an engineer. The shifts ran for ten hours, seven days a week, with frequent night shifts to finish a special order. At seven a.m. the foreman opened the shop and set the men to work. When Tad arrived an hour or so later they would go around the shop together to greet each worker and check on the production. Tad developed a fond relationship with Ah Chang, the blacksmith, an older and experienced man with whom he talked over problems on the floor. Tad thought highly of all the men who worked for him: "The Chinese were excellent workmen. They were very hard working, trying to do the best. They picked new things up very quickly and were very cooperative. And they were all devoted to me personally."

He paid slightly higher wages than similar Chinese shops, and handed out bonuses for good work and at Chinese New Year, when most had a three- or four-day holiday, the only vacation of the year. He established a system rewarding workers with small pay hikes for each consecutive week they showed up, penalizing those who didn't by putting them back to base pay on their return. "This was my dirty trick," he said proudly, to get the workers to remain on the job.

Tad said that he did not take on fourteen-year-old apprentices, nor did he hire any women, nor did any of his employees sleep in the shop above their machines. From his own stories, he was a kindly but shrewd factory manager, reasonable, responsible, and well-liked. "You were the best boss I ever had," an elderly Chinese told him with tears in his eyes, when Tad met him again in Shanghai sixty years later. In the 1920s, Shanghai averaged well over fifty strikes a year, some encompassing the entire city. His workmen never walked out, Tad claimed. When he left Shanghai in 1929, all the workers came down to the dock to see him off.

But stories from later on in his stay in Shanghai (his harshness with household servants, for instance), stories from employees in Poland and the U.S., and stories from family life show another side. Tad was not a mean or cruel man, but he was often insensitive to the feelings or needs of others; he was determined to have his way and usually succeeded; and his generosity rarely extended into business relations. I don't doubt that his employees in Shanghai revered him. But his portrait of his trouble-free shop, in those difficult times, run on diligence, mutual respect and brotherly love, is hard to swallow whole.

Yet as a businessman, Tad held his own. He had a small catalog of his goods printed up, and with it expanded his sales to all the hardware merchants of Shanghai and beyond. He went with his secretary to visit other machine shops to order parts made, and their Chinese proprietors came once in a while to Fearon Road to talk to Tad, for he had developed a reputation around town as a man who could find solutions. He frequented the scrap iron dealers on Peking Road, their merchandise rusting peacefully on the sidewalk, to rummage for useful items. The manager would be sitting in the back of the shop, half asleep from opium smoking, while his clerk attended the customers in front.

Tad's secretary served as guide and translator, and would point out interesting sights as they went about town. Once, as they were walking back to the shop, Tad asked him to stop a wheelbarrow coolie, so he could see how that fascinating contraption worked. His secretary hailed a man pushing a load of cotton bales. The coolie, perhaps frightened, perhaps amused at the request from this tall, scrawny Round-Eye, stepped aside. Tad took hold of the handles and pushed slightly. The wheelbarrow instantly tipped over, the bales of cotton rolling down the street. Tad apologized, thanked the coolie in Pidgin English, and gave him a coin. He and his secretary walked away, his respect for wheelbarrow dynamics and for the sweating coolies now doubled.

What interested Tad most in the shop were the mechanical details—to solve problems, to redesign machines for new uses, to come up with new products from old machines, to make gems out of junk. This was what occupied his creative mind, what he chewed over on his walks along the Bund. He was gradually coming to realize that he had a special talent, and the makings of an inventor. "For me it was a good school," Tad reminisced, "I have been observing, drawing my own conclusions, testing and so on. Finding the technical solutions, how to produce it best, and cheapest, gave me training in machine design. I educated myself as an inventor, because each problem had to have a special solution."

But he did not resent his job as a manager and businessman. Unlike the scientist or artist who wants to devote himself entirely to the creative process, Tad liked the balance of the two jobs. He enjoyed the responsibility, power and control.

The trouble was he hadn't much control. In his naive eagerness to set up a business, he found himself in a dead-end trade. He could solve problems of engineering within the walls of his shop; he could not solve the problems of economics within the boundaries of Shanghai. Indeed, he ran the only mechanized bolt factory in China, and had the advantage of cheap labor. But his competitors were not the Chinese blacksmiths who were hammering out hand-made bolts. His race was rather against the giant factories in England, Scotland and Belgium, which used modern, fully automated machines and paid a negligible five percent duty on their products. Certainly no foreign power in Shanghai would protect local industry by levying higher import taxes—on goods coming in from their own countries.

Tad was to spend eleven years struggling to make a success of it, improving one detail after another, without grasping the overview: the situation was hopeless. His meager profits, churned immediately back in for improvements, were made simply on his advantage at being a local supplier, when the shipments from abroad were delayed, or came in a cent or two above his prices.

Why did it take so long to figure this out? For one thing, he felt duty-bound to his partners, Jezierski and Jastrzembski. For another, in 1923 he got married, with a new son arriving in 1924, and his financial obligations kept him longer than if he had been free. He might have quit, say, in 1925, after giving the factory seven years of his life. He might at that point have gone to the United States, then enjoying its post-war boom. He might have found a backer there to help him develop his inchoate ideas about galvanizing. Such a backer couldn't be found in 1930, just after the stock market crash, when Tad finally landed in New York.

But in those first few years, the post-war period, the prospects were looking bright for industry in Shanghai. Tad was young and energetic. He had a challenge. He would not be licked.

*　　*　　*

A mad clanging of bells and honking of horns from speeding fire trucks awoke Shanghai's international community on the morning of November 12, 1918. The Armistice had been signed in Europe (where it was still November 11). Miles of bunting and triumphal arches materialized on rooftops and doorways. "Victory," in bright red lights, flashed in English and Chinese characters from a dock across the river. Tad followed the military parade out to the flag-draped race course, on one of the three days set aside for celebration, and took pictures to commemorate the event.

Just as World War I had spelled the end of an era in Europe, so in Shanghai the golden age of the tai-pan and the tea-sipping colonials was now over. Local industry had blossomed during the war years, due to the cutback of foreign imports; with the end of the war, Shanghai's economy boomed from the fresh influx of Western capital and the heavy Western demand for food and raw materials. Expensive new commercial buildings sprouted along the Bund; new factories and housing blocks spread across the outskirts of town. Shanghai became an industrial city. The Sendzimir Mechanical Works had been born at a most propitious moment.

But all was not so well outside the gates of the foreign settlements. China had come into its "warlord era," when extortionist generals with private armies waged almost constant civil war for the spoils of the feeble Republic. As the Chinese government drew from forty to fifty percent of its revenue from Shanghai customs, control of this area was vital. Reinforced barricades were thrown up around the foreign settlement when the fighting came closer, as it did in 1924: the settlement's Municipal Council declared a state of emergency, the civilian militia was mobilized, parties of marines came ashore from the warships, and the Europeans read the unsettling headlines in the *North China Daily News*, next to the announcements of missing dogs, bridge club parties, and polo ground openings. And another 200,000 refugees came pouring into Shanghai from the besieged countryside.

The civil wars and the boom in industry gave a new and modern face to the native population of Shanghai. At the top of the ladder, opulent warlords retired to mansions in the French Concession. Down a step or two, a small Chinese bourgeoisie began to emerge, enriched by the industrial boom and dependent on the foreign community—yet stirred by a nascent (and often economically motivated) nationalism. On the lower rungs, Shanghai's laboring population was becoming, truly, an industrial proletariat. In 1918, some 15,000 workers went out on strike in Shanghai. In 1922, some 65,000. In July, 1921, the Chinese Communist Party held its first national congress in a two-story brick house in the French Concession. And on the streets, off the ladder rungs completely, the poorest still slept under reed mats and died in droves from cholera each June when the watermelons were ripe.

The most momentous event in modern Chinese history that occurred during Tad's early years in Shanghai was the May Fourth Movement of 1919. In 1915, China's anemic government had been forced to accept Japan's Twenty-One Demands, reducing China to a virtual Japanese protectorate. The news from Paris in early May 1919—that Japan was about to be granted Shantung province, wrested during the war from the Germans—sparked the protest. It began with student marches in Peking, where bystanders were so moved by the slogans that many wept silently as the marchers passed. The movement easily spread to Shanghai, where a sweeping boycott of Japanese goods began. The broad-brimmed straw hats worn by every student—made in Japan—disappeared overnight and were replaced with white cloth caps; the major department stores took all their Japanese merchandise from the shelves; strikes were called, and businesses, theaters and schools voluntarily closed on May 9 to mark the Day of National Humiliation, the fourth anniversary of China's acquiescence to the Twenty-One Demands.

Had Tad ventured out of the foreign settlement, he would have seen the long angry banners and closed-up shops. To his credit, he disapproved of the ban on Chinese from the European clubs and parks, and he was on friendly terms with his Chinese workers and with many Chinese businessmen in Shanghai. But, as typical of most foreigners, he never went to the Chinese city and had no close Chinese friends. The International Settlement was an ostrich head, buried in a manicured, fortified hole in the sand. Shanghai to the Westerners was simply a delightfully exotic European metropolis, eight thousand miles from The Continent.

In the early Twenties, Tad lived in a boarding house in the French Concession. The Concession had developed as a secure residential enclave, for Europeans as well as for rich Chinese, Koreans, and the leaders of the underground and the underworld, while most of the international community's business and industry spread through the British- and American-run International Settlement to the north. As the French municipality had little industrial revenue coming in, it sought its income from licensing opium dens, brothels and gambling houses. While arms shipments were interdicted by the British, the French were known to look the other way. Six hundred sixty-eight brothels were operating in the International Settlement alone, but it was probably the French Concession to which the missionaries referred when they claimed that, if God let Shanghai endure, He owed an apology to Sodom and Gomorrah.

Tad claimed ignorance of all this. "Quite possibly that was there," he said. "But I wouldn't know where. I knew only the French Club and the residents. I wouldn't even know where to look to find those things, like opium dealing and gun smuggling." He swam in the large pool at the French Club, met friends for drinks on the Club's veranda, enjoyed the status of living in the approved section of town, but it was to him only a bedroom community. He did remember at least the preponderance of tattered White Russians who gravitated to this district and sat in their small restaurants, licking their wounds and reminiscing about old St. Petersburg. Tad had few Russian friends, but he went more than once to the Russian restaurant called, with unintended irony, Renaissance, where men in frayed Cossack uniforms sang and played the balalaika. The Russians clung to the lowest rungs of the European social ladder: the men worked as bodyguards or riding instructors, the women as hairdressers, dance hostesses and, in quantity, prostitutes.

Tad spent more of his time in the International Settlement, but he participated little in the genteel hedonism of the British—the copious eating, drinking, dancing and gambling, attended by scores of faceless servants. He went to movies and concerts ever so often; he took walks along the well-trimmed paths of the Public Gardens, and stayed occasionally on a summer evening to hear the orchestra. Once in a while he had need of a new shirt or a razor and he made his way down to the overflowing shops and department stores on Nanking Road.

Once he moved to Madame Tapernoux's boarding house in the French Concession, he settled into the relentless routine of an ambitious Western industrialist. The other boarders, and Madame Tapernoux herself, a jolly, gray-haired widow juggling and cajoling her fifteen or twenty boarders with the help of half a dozen servants, scarcely knew him. It was an international group, mostly French with some English and other nationalities, living in this three-story home near Avenue Edward VII.

By 1922, Tad's efforts seemed to be paying off: the Sendzimir Mechanical Works needed to expand. Tad drove out to the eastern section of the International Settlement, a still undeveloped area of small vegetable plots and a few Chinese houses. He found a piece of property on Linching Road, half a mile from the nearest large building. Jastrzembski loaned Tad the capital to buy the land and construct a new factory. Tad first put up a long narrow brick building with a pitched roof. This was all he could afford to build, but he needed more space. He erected a tremendous bamboo hut, a typical Chinese temporary construction—their answer to the circus tent—of thick bamboo posts covered with matting. In one week, the Fearon

Road shop was dismantled, wheelbarrow coolies had hauled the one-and-a-half-ton machines over three miles of infrequently paved streets to the new location, and the factory was again in business.

Tad was also plotting for expansion. With the new space, he began making nails, using the same wire drawing machines and slightly altered bolt cutters. He found out that the Belgian factories were only making nails out of scrap wire, and using good wire for galvanized fences. So he too began making wire net fences, and he set up the hot, smelly, time-consuming process of coating the wire with zinc. This diversification, a small improvement like all the others to eke out a tiny bit more profit, was to prove momentous—the single step at the beginning of the journey of a thousand miles. For Tad soon discovered that he didn't like this galvanizing process. There must be a better way to do it.

CHAPTER FOUR

SHANGHAI BUST

1924 - 1929

In 1922, the granite-domed Hong Kong and Shanghai Bank building held a gala opening. A stream of men in white suits and straw boaters flowed up the steps between two bronze lions crouching at the door of the Bund's newest display of imperial puissance. Later that year Tad had occasion to walk through that marble lobby and take the elevator up to the office of Bisset & Company, his broker, to have lunch with Bisset's partner, Hathaway. As they were walking to the Shanghai Club, Hathaway told Tad about a small venture the firm had put some money into: a mechanized laundry. The laundry had failed, but the brand-new building had a large apartment on the second floor available rent-free if Tad was interested in living there.

The year 1922 can be identified as a watershed year in Tad's life—perceptible, as watersheds will be, only from a distance. In 1922, Tad started a small galvanizing sideline at his new, larger factory; ten years later he revolutionized the process and came up with a product no one in the world could match. In 1922, he was offered a new apartment, and moved in with a dapper White Russian engineer; a year later, he married the engineer's sister. A year after that, she bore him a son. The ramifications of these events are still being felt.

Nicholas (Kola) Alferieff called such a fateful sequence "Madame Tapernoux Complex," after the owner of the boarding house where he and Tad met. Nicholas was the brother of Barbara, who is the mother of Michael, who is the first son of Tad. Kola explained to me, in his musical Russian accent, his philosophy of how our families' destinies became intertwined. "Madame Tapernoux Complex is just this: given sufficient time, any small event becomes really very important. Before the event happens, there are so many possibilities, billions upon billions. Then, bang, at one moment something happens, and one of the billions is fixed into reality."

Nicholas, engineer cum metaphysician, was, like Tad, one more well-groomed 1920s Continental: clean-shaven but for the small, cropped moustache; dark hair combed straight back from a high forehead. Where Tad was tall and thin, Kola was of medium build. He wasn't particularly handsome, but the twinkle in his brown eyes exposed an understanding of the whimsy of life. He was the first son of a high-ranking civil servant family in Russia. The Alferieffs came from the charmed town of Tsarskoye Selo, outside of St. Petersburg, a Russian Versailles swaddled in parks for the czar and his family's summer amusement. Kola's father had lived briefly in Harbin in Manchuria before the Russo-Japanese War, when he was head of the railway department. In November 1917, the family moved from Tsarskoye Selo to Harbin and settled in one of the grand houses built for the Czar's bureaucrats. (Harbin was a Russian military base and headquarters of the Russian-operated Chinese Eastern Railway. The White Russians living there were generally of a higher class than those who drifted down like sediment to Shanghai. For a few years after 1917, Harbin was the largest Russian city outside the Soviet Union.) Kola was briefly involved in the Civil War, then came down to Shanghai to find a job.

For Kola, the first Madame Tapernoux Complex "event" came in 1921, when he moved from his shabby lodgings to the much nicer boarding house in the French Concession run by Madame Tapernoux. There he met Tad. One day Tad knocked on his door (the next "event") and asked him if he'd be interested in sharing an apartment in the International Settlement. He accepted.

The next day, Tad and Kola went to take a look at the flat above the laundry. Tad drove them out to a sparsely settled part of the

International Settlement, north and east of downtown. A few Chinese houses were scattered about, guarding obedient rows of cabbage heads and parsley stalks. The aroma of nightsoil presided over the neighborhood. Tad and Kola easily picked out the modern two-story building from the ramshackle houses nearby. The ground floor was empty: the laundry had never opened for business. They climbed the stairs and found a spacious apartment, with two bedrooms and two baths, a dining room, living room and kitchen. A cook, a "boy," and a coolie had already been hired. Tad and Kola agreed to move in immediately.

The temperaments of these two Slavs could hardly have been more opposed. Kola was the carefree bachelor, who, though professing to be a loner, took leisurely lunches, played tennis at the French Club, flirted with the secretaries and debutantes, and drank with his expatriate friends in the clubs and ballrooms. Tad thought of little else but work. Despite their differences, the two became good friends and shared an amiable life together. They had some mutual friends; they ran into each other at the French Club, Kola coming back from the tennis court, Tad on his way to the pool; they went together to the Paramount theater to watch silent films. After the movie, Kola remembered, Tad would "invariably want to visit his factory. Even at three o'clock in the morning he would insist on driving out to check on some experiment, or just to see what the night shift was doing."

Tad looked after the affairs of the house. "That was characteristic," Kola said. "He wanted to go into details and have everything the way he liked." He ruled over the servants like a petty inquisitor. If, during dinner, the salt shaker was missing, Tad would call in the "boy." He wouldn't then simply say, "Please bring the salt"; he'd say "What's missing?" and let the poor servant shift nervously and stare at the table until he could figure it out. The same happened with the car driver: everything was a test, a fussy, annoying demonstration of Tad's superiority. (These stories from Kola call into question how kindly and patient Tad had really been with his factory workers.)

Kola nonetheless developed a great admiration for Tad—for his discipline, for his drive and concentration, for his sense of humor.

But he also thought him a little odd. Kola recalled how this had first vividly struck him. Tad had asked Kola to teach him to play billiards. They met at the French Club one day after work, and went up to the huge billiard room, served by an army of white-robed boys, the markers, who stood beside each table. "I told him the principles," Kola remembered, a smile playing at the corners of his mouth. "If you hit half of the ball, naturally then your ball will go at a forty-five degree angle. If you put less, then it will go at less of an angle, and so on. So I played my ball, and I said, 'Now it's yours, see what you can do.' And he looked at the table, where the balls were, and where the pockets were, and he got out his slide rule and started calculating. The markers thought that was hilarious. They never saw a billiard game being played with a slide rule. Other markers came over and we had thirty or forty of them standing around, watching Tadeusz studying his slide rule."

The two housemates didn't talk much at home—during dinner Tad would barricade himself behind a copy of *Popular Mechanics* or a machinery supply catalog—but Kola said that Tad got him interested in Polish poetry and classical music. They even went on a vacation trip together to Tai Hu Lake, west of Shanghai, where tourists could rent fully-staffed houseboats for a week to float on the lake and escape the heat of the city.

The one topic Kola did talk to Tad about was his "beautiful, wonderful" sister Barbara. The talk was innocent, just a proud elder brother going on about his favorite sister, whose picture sat on his desk: a pretty brunette with large dark eyes and good legs. No one was more surprised and horrified than Kola when Tad returned from a vacation trip to Tsingtao, when he and Barbara first met, and announced that they were going to get married. "What a mismatch!" he thought. "They wouldn't fit at all. Because she wants everything her way, and Tadeusz certainly wants everything his way." Kola wrote to Barbara, and by way of explaining the potential conflict, told her the billiards story. How could *she* ever get along with a man who used a slide rule to play billiards?

Barbara was just twenty when she met Tad, and she was bored. Back home in Tsarskoye Selo she had been pampered, but she'd also received a fine education and developed a skill for writing and a deep love for Russian literature. She might have become a poet. But in 1922 she was living with her family in Harbin, where young women were at a premium. Her nervous, spoiled, sprightly nature fit in well (far better than did her literary persona) with the gay parties and *apres nous le deluge* spirit of the White Russian community. She basked in the frivolity and the attentions of men.

Tad didn't know what hit him when he met Barbara in Tsingtao, where she was vacationing with her mother. He had danced with many young girls in Lwow, but his romantic experience with women had been, if anything, long-distance. He suffered a slight affection while in Gymnasium for one of Aniela's friends, Maria Petzhold, and during his years in the Polytechnic he kept up a sweetly florid correspondence with a distant cousin from Warsaw, whom he saw but once a year during holidays in the mountains. He couldn't recall any romantic affiliations in Kiev. Throughout, he seems to have sublimated most tender yearnings into the pursuit of the perfectly purring machine and the elegantly designed widget. But now, on the eve of his twenty-ninth birthday, he became instantly infatuated.

For her part, Barbara saw in Tad a handsome, dashing—even sophisticated—and successful young man. No doubt Kola had extolled his roommate at length in his letters home. A friend claimed Tad and Barbara were the most beautiful couple in Shanghai. Barbara also saw a new adventure, and an escape from the family and provincial Harbin.

Barbara's parents hoped that the marriage would make Barbara settle down. They would have liked Tad even without the advance recommendations they had received from Kola. Tad got along especially well with her father, an educated man who was fond of discussing mathematics and astronomy, and who, with his broad nose and full beard, resembled Tolstoy. Barbara's two youngest brothers, Michael and Eugene, were away at school in Paris; Barbara's older sister Natasha still lived at home, as did her brother Alexander, a lively, irresponsible young man who started smoking opium and was finally packed off to America by his father.

The courtship was brief, at Barbara's insistence. They met in

Tsingtao in the summer of 1923, and were married before the end of the year. Tad didn't even have time to exchange letters with his parents about it.

Natasha and Alexander represented the Alferieffs at the wedding in Harbin. Kola was working in Shanghai and so could not be there, and by Russian Orthodox custom, the parents of the bride do not attend the ceremony. Tad had to return immediately to his factory after the wedding, so the couple postponed their honeymoon. He had found a house for them in the International Settlement, the home of a British family on temporary leave. There was a veranda with flowers, and, inside, a very large drawing room which Barbara, when she first laid eyes on it, easily imagined filled with party guests.

Very, very quickly Barbara got bored, and restless. She was, after all, twenty-one years old. It's not hard to imagine about what a day might have been like for her: Tad would leave for the day right after breakfast. Barbara was left to give orders to the cook, and write letters to her mother and family. After lunch she might go down to Nanking Road to see if the department stores had any new merchandise from Europe. Then she'd take a rickshaw to the Renaissance, for a cup of tea and a chat with some of those handsome young Russians who spent the afternoon there. Maybe she and Tad had arranged to meet for a swim before supper at the French Club. She'd arrive at the Club and find a message from him: he was delayed again at the factory and would have to miss supper. She'd stop at the club's bar to pass the time talking to some of Kola's friends. One might gallantly offer her a ride home, and kiss her on the cheek at her door. She didn't mind; he was kind of cute (and maybe Tad would see and then have to pay attention to her). But Tad had still not returned. Barbara would eat her supper alone, and go to bed with a Turgenev novel.

Six months after the wedding, Barbara wanted to return to Harbin. She'd had enough. "I lost," she said to Tad. "The factory won." Tad was not surprised; from her behavior, he had already formed his damning opinion: "She didn't mean to marry me and be a good housewife. She married me to have one more fellow."

In retrospect, Tad admitted that he had gotten involved too hastily, too blindly. He'd had very little experience with women; his iron will power was softened by Barbara's feminine wiles. "She made me want it," he said, like an accusation—and then went on to concede, "I was very deeply in love." But he thought he could rein her in. "I did hope that when we were married that I would gradually influence her."

But before Barbara could leave Shanghai, she became pregnant. A glimmer of hope appeared. Tad thought a baby would domesticate Barbara; Barbara thought a baby would give her something to do, and make Tad spend more time at home.

Michael Sendzimir was born November 21, 1924, at the French Hospital in Shanghai. Tad left the hospital at three a.m., an hour after his son's birth, and in his excitement ran into a milkman's truck as he was driving home. A short period of domestic peace followed, as everyone doted on the baby. They hired an amah, a fifty-year-old Chinese woman, to take care of Michael. She always wore the traditional blue cotton pants, reaching down to her bound feet, and greeted Michael unfailingly with, "Hello, baby darling!"

The baby was not able to reunite his parents' hearts and temperaments. Michael was, however, the cause for Tad and Barbara to reunite, briefly and fraudulently, in the eyes of God. In the midst of their quarreling, they went through the motions of a Roman Catholic wedding ceremony. Tad had not been to Mass in ten years, but he wanted Michael baptized; the priest he found refused to do it because the parents hadn't had a Catholic wedding. That was the price, and Tad was willing to pay it—to prevent his son from becoming Russian Orthodox. Barbara was on the verge of walking out, they couldn't live together, neither could stand the other's way of life. But they went through with the ceremony, and Michael was baptized by the rather unscrupulous agent of St. Peter.

Soon after, Barbara packed up the baby and left for Harbin.

Over the next five years, she seems to have spent half her time there, half in Shanghai. When she did return to Shanghai with Michael, they lived in the same house with Tad, but there was never any pretense of patching things up. She had boyfriends, and several offers of marriage, but she and Tad couldn't agree on a divorce.

Barbara wanted to keep Michael, but this Tad would not accept: why should he give up his son just because she wanted other men? She also wanted money, and Tad didn't have much to spare in those days. She used Michael, he claimed, as a tool: "Barbara stuck to Michael like some lioness would do. She loved him very dearly — but there was little more. Just the same as, for instance, the Poles were Catholic for centuries. But with the Russian persecution, Catholicism was also a political weapon, against the Russians."

The stories are often contradictory. She wanted a divorce, she dated other men, but she'd return to Shanghai (and later to Paris when Tad was there) and live for brief periods with him almost as husband and wife. Sometimes it seems she wanted him back. Barbara would not agree to tell me her side of the story, but I can easily imagine her bitterness over the situation. What twenty-year-old will eat supper by herself night after night? There were lots of other men around. And she certainly could not leave Michael with this distracted and irresponsible man. As one story goes, she came home one day and the baby was gone. The amah told her, "Master took the baby." She called Tad, and indeed, Michael was at the factory. She came in to find him sitting on top of a machine, exposed gears and bundles of sharp wire all around. Tad: "Oh, I told him not to touch it."

The tug of war went on for another eighteen years. At last in the early 1940s Tad was doing well financially, he wanted to remarry, and Michael was coming into adulthood. They agreed on the terms of a divorce in 1942.

The marriage resulted in a longlasting bitterness in Tad toward women, which hadn't been apparent before. Forty years after their divorce, his descriptions of Barbara would still bite. "What did she look like?" I asked him, wanting to know what physical images remained vivid. All he could think to say was, "She was a flirt. Whenever she saw a man, she always wanted to make an impression. But I must say that is characteristic of some Russian women." My mother, though French, was as far from a coquette as one can imagine, but still it took four years of courtship before he managed, with some explicit conditions, to propose. And this was after twenty years of his second bachelorhood. As a child, I was encouraged in sports, in reading, in schoolwork, but never in dolls, dresses or things feminine. Barbara's ghost haunted our house.

Still, Tad was no tender-hearted young gallant. As he described his first marriage, his emphasis was almost legalistic: we are told of a broken contract, not a broken heart. "I am not an emotional man," he would say. But this wall of opacity was erected with care.

* * *

Bitter or not, Tad kept his shoulder to the plow throughout this domestic turmoil. He drove off to the factory in his 1920 American Maxwell at seven each morning; he swam, went to concerts, and ate dinners in the homes of business partners, whether Barbara was there or not. His friends at the French Club commiserated with him. "I can see you have a difficult situation here," one murmured to Tad, on observing Barbara flirting with other men at a dinner party. The Sendzimir Mechanical Works labored along, half a step ahead of the competitors one day, half a step behind the next. The riots and strikes that shook Shanghai through the summer of 1925 seem not to have affected Tad or his factory. He didn't remember any of it, although all Japanese and English factories were struck and it was unsafe for a white man to show his face on the streets.

By 1926, Tad had the operations of the factory enough under control that he began to consider a trip home to Poland. Through these years he had been writing boastful letters to his family and sending them small gifts—fans and silk robes and the like. He had sent a telegram to his parents when he got married, and also on the birth of Michael. The sudden marriage had been a shock and disappointment for his parents. Barbara was not Polish; worse yet, she was Russian. And they had not even met the girl beforehand. His mother finally wrote to Tad that "it was a long time later that I began to be happy about it."

Tad wanted to return home as a flawlessly successful young businessman, husband and father. It wouldn't do to add another injury, or to show that he had made a mistake, that he had been foolhardy. So the fiction of the marriage continued. Tad easily persuaded Barbara to come along, as she was always eager for adventure and new sights.

In the middle of August 1926, they took the boat and train from Shanghai to Harbin. In Harbin, they left tiny Michael in the care of his grandparents, and traveled north to Chita, where they boarded the Trans-Siberian Railway bound for Moscow. There was no need, as when Tad fled in 1918, to skirt the Soviet capital. The guns of revolution and civil war had been quiet for over six years; Moscow was as safe for the foreign traveler as London or Paris, and perhaps (lacking beggars) more so. They arrived in Moscow in a week. Tad was anxious to get home—in her last letter, Vanda had told him that Kazimir was quite ill—so they went immediately on to Warsaw and from there to Lwow.

Tad and Barbara took a cab from the Lwow station to Saint Teresa Street. Tad had wired ahead, so the family was expecting them. Of the children, only Terenia remained at home. Aniela had married in 1920 and was living in Torun; Zbigniew had gone to America and gotten a job building cars in Detroit for Mr. Ford.

Terenia met the couple at the door. What a sight for her spirited imagination, cooped up in this provincial town: Tad, tall and elegantly dressed, arriving from China, his beautiful dark-eyed Russian wife on his arm, standing among suitcases concealing fancy presents. Terenia kissed them boisterously, then hurried them into the bedroom, where Kazimir lay. Vanda was sitting at his side by the bed.

"Look what a Lazarus you have come to meet," Kazimir said as Tad leaned down to embrace him. His skin was pallid, his flesh loose and flabby beneath it, his formerly calm and jovial eyes now turbid and tired. He had been in bed for six months, suffering from an enlarged heart and, recently diagnosed, cancer of the blood. But here was his first born, whom he hadn't seen for twelve years, now a successful businessman with a new wife. Pride and excitement brightened Kazimir's eyes. He pulled himself up in bed, and the two men chatted for five or ten minutes before Vanda shooed the newcomers out so he could rest.

Tad was eager to show Barbara Lwow and give her a taste of Polish culture. After supper that evening, he, Barbara and Terenia went to see a play in town. On their way back, as they were nearing the house, the concierge ran out into the street to them, crying, "The Master of the house is very, very ill!" They rushed inside and found Vanda in tears. Kazimir had died in his sleep while they were at the theater. His weak heart, it seems, had been overwhelmed by the emotions of his son's return.

The funeral took place three days later. Kazimir was buried in the Jasklowski family plot next to his father- and mother-in-law, Karol and Octavia.

In telling this story, Tad remarked sorrowfully that "If I had not come, he might not have died." But it's certain that Kazimir wouldn't have lasted much longer—it's almost as if he hung on just for Tad's return. Vanda had spent the past two years caring for her steadily weakening husband. Tad and Barbara's presence was if anything a blessing. Tad helped with the funeral arrangements, and Barbara made herself useful around the house. She was kind to Vanda, so Vanda's heart softened toward her new daughter-in-law.

The couple spent only a few more days in Lwow. Tad visited Uncle Tolloczko's lab, and tried to look up friends from his Gymnasium. Glad as he was to see old familiar faces and walk through old familiar parks, he did not consider coming back to settle in Poland. He felt no surge of patriotic joy upon returning to his native, and finally independent, land. He had by now taken on the attitude of a citizen of the world, a "large-E" European, making his career wherever opportunity lay. While the difficulties of his business were certainly evident, still Tad felt bound to his factory. "I went to Poland," he said, "always with the intention of returning to Shanghai. I had the ambition: I will fight through and it will be all right."

Tad and Barbara left Lwow, stopped briefly in Krakow, then boarded a train for Berlin. They were headed for Paris, to see the sights and visit Barbara's brothers, Michael and Eugene. On the way they stopped for a day in Cologne, where the firm of Meyer, Roth and Pastor manufactured their nail-making machines. While Barbara visited the famous cathedral, Tad visited the famous machines. He ordered four or five in different sizes to be sent to Shanghai, where, on his return, he would faithfully copy them to make a few dozen more for his shop. After a week in Paris they headed home.

On their return to China, Barbara remained in Harbin, and Tad continued down to Shanghai, where the most savage period in the city's history was about to unfold. Within eight months, up to 10,000 men and women were slain in the streets and alleys of Shanghai, their blood on the hands of Chiang Kai-shek.

*　　*　　*

Tad had seen Chiang some years before in the halls of the banks, buying and selling shares for the stock exchange. "The stock brokers were a race by themselves," Tad said. "They went from one bank to another selling shares. There was no stock exchange. So they went around—'you buy,' 'you buy,' 'you buy,'—on the run, upstairs, downstairs, all the time. Mostly they were foreigners. I remember Chiang Kai-shek because he was the only Chinese doing that."

This seedy and violent little general was known around Shanghai long before his Kuomintang army came through in 1927. He was tight with Shanghai's underworld, especially the powerful, right-wing Green Gang, for whom as a young man he'd committed extortion, murder and armed robbery. In the early Twenties, the Green Gang leaders took him under their wing and set him up as a broker in the stock exchange, a way to make a fast buck.

In the fall of 1926, the Kuomintang (KMT) army was advancing north from southern China, battling warlord armies and seizing territory in slow progression toward Shanghai. The Communist Party, still in tenuous alliance with the KMT and Chiang Kai-shek, had been growing stronger in the city, and began a series of strikes and demonstrations in anticipation of the army's triumphant arrival. In mid-February 1927, with the KMT less than twenty-five miles from the city, a tremendous general strike began. River traffic ceased, trams stopped running, the post office and stores shut their doors, factories closed down.

Tad's factory, he insisted, remained open. In the tense quiet, he drove back and forth to work past troop trucks and manned barricades set up to protect the International Settlement. One hundred twenty-five warships and 20,000 troops from ten countries had been amassed to defend the property and interests of the trembling Europeans. Tad turned a blind eye to the higher rate of absenteeism—his workers had to come on foot, pass through barricades and skirt demonstrations—and he scaled back some operations, relying on local suppliers and the raw material he had in stock until shipping resumed in late April.

As the Europeans quivered in anticipation of a Red Terror, a White Terror commenced. In February, police and the mercenary army attacked the demonstrators and strikers in the streets, beheading them on the spot. Severed heads were displayed on poles or strung up in bamboo baskets hanging from lamp posts. Chiang stalled his troops outside the city while his "allies" were being butchered. For a brief period at the end of March, the leftists, led by Chou En-lai, were finally able to seize the Chinese sections of Shanghai. They kept shaky control with their limited forces, many still imagining reunification with the KMT. The KMT arrived at last—as soon as the fighting was over.

Three weeks later, Chiang made his move. At 4 a.m. on April 12, Chiang's most trusted troops and armed squads from the Green Gang blasted into homes, union halls and Communist Party offices in every section of Shanghai. The fighting on the first day left over five hundred dead. Fleeing demonstrators were chased down alleys, dragged out of houses and bayoneted. Thousands more were slaughtered in the following days.

The White Terror brought peace to the hearts in the European community: the Red Peril had been vanquished. The garrisoned soldiers were sent home, shipping traffic on the Huangpu resumed, the *North China Daily News* smugly reported on how Chiang's troops mopped up the last of the labor movement, and life continued.

*   *   *

With the troubles over, and Barbara and Michael out of the house, Tad could throw himself full tilt into work at the factory. The nail-making machines came finally from Cologne, and he set his machinists to work making copies. A special prize arrived from

America: Tad had mustered the capital to purchase a genuine bolt-header from Acme Machines in Cleveland, Ohio. Coolies hauled this precisely forged, polished, seven-ton beauty from the docks and placed it on a specially-built concrete foundation in the bamboo shed, like a Ming vase on a carved mahogany pedestal.

Over 150 men were working for Tad by 1927. A few years before, he had changed the name of the firm to the General Forge Products Company of China. Now he put up another building, on an adjoining lot, for his battery of new nail-making machines. Tad was selling his products to hardware merchants in Shanghai, as well as to his original customer, the Chinese Eastern Railway. Shanghai's hardware dealers often came asking Tad if he could produce specialized items. He hired an agent, an Englishman named Elliston, to handle the sales on commission from his offices downtown. They became good friends.

As Tad's reputation as an innovator spread, his problems and products grew more intricate than the lowly bolt and nail. He got an order from the Chinese government's arsenal, for special blades to cut smokeless powder. He did some silver plating and zinc plating. The telephone company wanted metal swan-neck arms, to hold the wire traveling from pole to pole. Tad designed a jig to curve the iron into shape. The company was pleased, and came back to ask if he could also make the wooden sections holding the porcelain insulators. Wood! Well, he was not a carpenter. But he designed a small machine to cut and drill the wood, and began churning them out, two a minute.

During these last few years Tad lived in China, he traveled more than in the past, impelled equally by business and by curiosity. In the early twenties he had seen Peking on a brief vacation trip. He passed through the cities of Dairen, Mukden and Nanking on his business trips, and once with Kola Alferieff went for a weekend to the park-like city of Hangchow, south of Shanghai. Several times he took the five-day boat ride down to Hong Kong, and once from there to Canton, ninety miles inland from the South China Sea. He found the Cantonese merchants hospitable, but more arrogant and ambitious than those in Shanghai. Perhaps it was an arrogance of history: this southern city had been in existence since around 1000 B.C. All he remembered of the young city of Hong Kong, at that time no more developed than Shanghai, was the beautiful sight of the mountain on approaching the harbor: "The English built their houses high up, because there it's cooler. So when you came by boat at night, it was a beautiful sight. All those houses lit up—it looked like stars imbedded in the mountain."

In 1927, Tad's brother Zbigniew came to live in Shanghai for a year or so. He had not been satisfied with his job at Ford; he quit, had trouble finding another job, and wrote to his brother that he was out of work. Tad invited him to come to Shanghai, and sent him money for the ticket. When he arrived, Tad found him a job supervising a construction crew.

At that time, Kola had moved in again with Tad, and Barbara and Michael were coming back and forth from Harbin. Zbigniew joined the household. Kola, at least, found Zbigniew pleasant company; the two bachelors went around to the clubs together. "Zbyszko was a nice man," Kola remembered. "I liked him. But of course, he was no intellectual. Tad didn't have very much respect for him. He used to say that his center of gravity is a little bit too low."

Before he left Detroit, Zbigniew had made some friends among Poles who worked for General Motors. One was an upper class gentleman in a management position. GM was looking for new markets in the late Twenties, had the idea to open an agency in Poland, and appointed Zbigniew's friend general manager. When the friend got to Warsaw, he sent Zbigniew an invitation to come over as maintenance manager. Zbigniew shuffled, dawdled, tossed and turned. Here was a great opportunity. But, Poland was still so poor. Only, wouldn't it be great to live in Warsaw? Those Polish girls never could get enough of him. Finally Zbigniew came to Tad for advice, and Tad told him, with exasperation, "Zbigniew, this is your life chance. Go ahead!" And he went.

When Barbara and Michael came down from Harbin, Tad took his four-year-old son for drives along the outskirts of the city, but he ignored the comings and going of his wife. Michael's first and most vivid memory is of the cartwheels and bright lights he saw when his father carried him on his shoulders to a Chinese Luna Park, a sort of amusement park.

At the factory, Tad's interest turned more and more to the problems with the wire galvanizing operation. He hadn't liked it from the beginning. All that smelly work—pickling in acid, rinsing with water, the flux bath of zinc ammonium chloride, then finally the zinc bath—just to get a piece of wire that, yes, will not rust, but bend it twice and the zinc peels off. All galvanizing was done like that, in the modern factories of Europe as well as in the antiquated shops of Shanghai. All galvanized products would begin to oxidize at the first bump or scratch, when the silvery skin would flake away and leave an open wound.

The problem was the bond: how to make the zinc bond with the iron and stay there. He realized that the zinc couldn't bond if the iron wasn't pure; it was bonding only with the impurities on the surface, the thin layer of iron hydroxide produced by the air and humidity. He had to figure out how to make the iron pure, and keep it that way. It was, to him, just a matter of logic.

Tad conducted most of his work in his head. He labored in this select laboratory as he took his daily walks; as he swam in the French Club's pool; as he drove himself to work and back; even as he dined with Elliston and his wife, taking out his small leather notebook distractedly and making a sketch or two between courses. He studied articles from the small library of scientific journals he had been accumulating, and from the papers of the Iron and Steel Institute of Germany, which he had joined in 1926. But he kept to himself. He didn't seek out the opinions of local engineering professors, or discuss his ideas with the metal shop owners who came to him with their problems. At last, he began some small experiments at the factory. They showed promise.

Meanwhile Tad was still struggling with the problems of the factory, problems that wouldn't succumb to scientific logic. His frustration over small profits was mounting. The little innovations and new products kept him only ten seconds ahead of the competition. He wanted to be farther than that. He wanted to make his mark on more than just a better way to turn a screw. The depressing realization came slowly through the dense heat of Shanghai: there was no future in this.

But he didn't give up yet. He got the idea that if he brought in an experienced manager—someone with authority and a little pull at the banks—the company could perhaps take off in a more profitable direction. In the middle of 1929 he went over to a ship-building company he'd worked with to talk to the manager, John Buchanan Mauchan. Mauchan was a burly, dark Scotsman, a naval architect in his late fifties. Tad had been selling Mauchan rivets for his ships. They were on friendly terms, although Tad had heard rumors of this Scot's nasty temper. He sat down in Mauchan's office and explained his offer. He wanted to make his firm into a limited liability company, where he, Tad, would continue as general manager, and Mauchan would come in as president.

Mauchan knew Tad had been running a reputable operation. The offer was generous, impossible to resist: he would suddenly be president of a company. And the business couldn't be too complicated. He took the post.

The new partnership was established. Then, within a few months, Mauchan turned on Tad. Mauchan went to the stockholders to try to oust him. According to Tad, Mauchan thought it was a simple operation, this bolt factory. With all of his managerial experience he could certainly run it better by himself. Who needed this eccentric Pole? Mauchan won the trust of the principal shareholders and succeeded in convincing them to let him get rid of Tad.

Mauchan hired an Englishman as Tad's assistant, and Tad saw immediately that Mauchan meant for this man to replace him. They had already been quarrelling. This Englishman showed not the slightest glimmer of imagination. There was more to it than good management; Tad's success was built on his mercurial touch with any sort of technical difficulty. Not anyone could do that.

But wait, Tad hesitated: Why fight it? Mauchan had double-crossed him, but at the same time Mauchan was handing him the opportunity to escape. Here was the chance to jump off this leaky barge and get onto solid ground. Tad swallowed his anger at

Mauchan's perfidy with the sly contentment of the cat swallowing the canary. He quit.

His only regret was that he hadn't demanded severance pay. His vindication came four years later, when he received a letter from friends. General Forge Products Ltd. had gone into voluntary liquidation. Mauchan had failed.

As soon as he handed in his resignation, Tad lost no time. Finally he could go to America. He closed his accounts, got a U.S. tourist visa (with no difficulty this time), and booked passage on the *Asama Maru* heading for Tokyo, San Francisco and Los Angeles.

Barbara and Michael were at that time in Harbin. Before leaving, he sent to Michael a box of toy cars. Michael remembers that moment with an intensity that serves as a floodlight: "Oh, that was something! From my own father. Tonkin, all made of lead. But it came from my father. I was up on top of the world."

Tad knew that his move to the United States was essential, if risky. His galvanizing idea still had bugs, and maybe no potential—it might prove too costly or too complicated. The papers had been full of stories of the crash on Wall Street in October, just over a month before. No one was sure yet how serious the problem was. Tad collected names of contacts in the U.S. from Elliston and other business acquaintances. He hoped that there was in that land of opportunity and innovation some investor or factory owner who would let him try out his ideas.

He packed several suitcases with his scientific journals, his latest camera, his better suits, and his bathing trunks. He said good-bye to Elliston, to Hathaway, to his friends at the French Club, in the bank, and around town. On the evening of his departure he hired a wheelbarrow coolie to bring his bags down to the dock. He went by rickshaw, the last he was ever to take in his life.

As he approached the dock, he saw an immense crowd waiting beside the ship. He paid the driver, heard his name called out in a high-pitched Shanghai accent, and was immediately surrounded by a small group of smiling Chinese. Ah Chang, the foreman, and a dozen or so of his factory workers had come to see him off. They pushed their way to the edge of the dock and began setting off rockets and firecrackers. Suddenly, more fireworks erupted from the ship and along the dock, and a lusty cheer went up from the crowd. The Chinese were delighted: Mr. Sendzimir is so famous! But nobody was looking their way. Tad looked over to the gangway, bleached white under floodlights, and saw Mary Pickford and Douglas Fairbanks walking up to the deck, waving to the crowd. Tad's little farewell celebration was drowned by movie fans, whose idols were boarding Tad's boat for the same journey.

Christmas was celebrated mid-Pacific. Tad nodded politely to the celebrities if he passed them on his circuits of the decks, but he spent most of his time contemplating galvanizing, writing a few letters to his family, and conversing with a young Chinese scholar about facets of Asian history. Tad stepped ashore in San Francisco with the tolling of the New Year.

Kazimir and Vanda on their wedding day, 1893.

Left to Right: Tad, Zbigniew, Vanda and Aniela, around 1906.

Aniela, Terenia and Vanda, 1911.

Tad in self-portrait with his home-made camera, 1912.

Tad and Michael in Shanghai, 1929.

Barbara (Alferieff) Sendzimir, 1930.

Ignacy Moscicki, President of Poland (in white hat), visiting the galvanizing line in Kostuchna, around 1934. At far left is Kaz Oganowski. Next to him is Tad.

Setting up Tad's cold rolling mill in Maubeuge, France, around 1936. Tad is at far right.

Tad, Berthe, Stanley and baby Jan Peter.

Berthe Bernoda and Tad in Middletown, Ohio, 1945.

Tad and the author, 1956.

Michael Sendzimir with a group from the Iwai trading company, in the 1950s.

Michael Sendzimir, President of T. Sendzimir, Inc.

Reception at the Kosciuszko Foundation in 1976 for Cardinal Karol Wojtyla, two years before he was elected Pope. Tad is on right.

Stanley, Berthe, Tad, Jan Peter and the author on Tad and Berthe's fortieth wedding anniversary, 1985. Scar on Tad's forehead is from removal of a skin cancer growth.

Tad lecturing on the Z mill to engineers in China, 1984.

July 15, 1989: Tad talking to Harold Tong while opening his ninety-fifth birthday presents.

May 4, 1990: Celebration of the re-naming of Huta Lenina, Krakow.

CHAPTER FIVE

NEW YORK, POLAND

1930 - 1931

Tad arrived in San Francisco three years before work was to begin on the Golden Gate Bridge. It would have delighted him to be able to watch as its iron spans shot out into mid-air from the California cliffs. But in January 1930, San Francisco—from the barrenness of its hills to the drabness of its citizens—fell abruptly short of Tad's expectations. He was coming from the land of lacquer and silk, temples and warlords, a land where every white man was a king.

"My first impression of America was that the cars were all dirty. I was used to Shanghai, where labor was cheap, almost everybody could afford a driver, and the car was kept spotlessly clean by the driver. But apparently nobody cared in San Francisco. The cars were all full of mud."

Tad's second impression of America was that there were no aristocrats. "In Shanghai, the white man was *ipso facto* an aristocrat, something very special. Coming to America, it looked to me so dull. There is nobody outstanding. Everybody is mediocre."

Tad had been reading and dreaming about the United States since he was a boy. The Polish people have an emotional connection to America, starting with Poland's military heroes Tadeusz Kosciuszko and Casimir Pulaski, who served in the American Revolutionary War, through the millions of refugees who escaped Poland's nineteenth-century decimation for the promised lands of Chicago,

Buffalo and Bridgeport. Tad happened to land in America's most beautiful city. That he did not extol its features and his good fortune at being there says only that he had grown used to the privileges and opulence of Shanghai.

Tad's ship had a day and a half layover in San Francisco before it continued on to Los Angeles. Tad took a trolley from the busy docks to visit his friend Malewinski, a Russian he knew from Shanghai. Malewinski welcomed him and took him around in his car to see the sights. Typically, what Tad remembered best was not a monument but a machine: Malewinski could only get the car up the steep hill to his house by driving in reverse.

Over dinner, Malewinski told Tad about the economic situation. It was all very confusing. The crash had happened three months before and the stock market was still in a slump. People were losing their jobs. But President Hoover kept saying not to worry.

The next morning, Tad bought a copy of the San Francisco *Chronicle* from a newsboy in front of the Ferry Building. The stories were indeed equivocal. He boarded the *Asama Maru* frowning, and took his place outside in a deck chair, despite the chilly wind blowing in from the Pacific. As the ship sailed south to Los Angeles, he watched the California hills drift by, green with January rain. What, he must have wondered, lie for him beyond those hills?

He knew *un*equivocally three things: The first was that, at thirty-six years old, with a wife and child depending on him, he couldn't waste any time. He'd wasted plenty in Shanghai. Now he was here in the land of opportunity and he had to make a success of it. The second thing he knew was that his galvanizing idea was good. Maybe very good. If he could make it work, it would completely change the metal-coating process world-wide. And, he'd be rich. All he had to do was find someone who was galvanizing wire the old way, and let him prove it. Weren't the Americans crazy about new ideas?

And he could do it. That was the third thing he knew. Hadn't he kept his bolt factory afloat through his own genius, will power and hard work? Hadn't he recognized this galvanizing problem and worked out a satisfactory, even brilliant, solution? Hadn't he already endured and survived hard times? A fall in the stock market couldn't be worse than the Great War. But still, the economic news was troubling—a wild card in the deck he thought he had stacked. All he could do was hope for good luck, and work like hell to get it. He'd done it before.

He pulled his notebook from his inside breast pocket, jotted down the day and date of his departure from San Francisco and the expected time to dock in Los Angeles, and rose to take his morning perambulation of the deck.

Another passenger on board the *Asama Maru* was the Spanish consul in Chicago, vacationing with his wife and sister. The consul was planning to drive from Los Angeles back to Chicago. He invited Tad to come with them and share expenses. Tad grabbed with pleasure this opportunity to see a bit of the country.

After a couple of days in Los Angeles, Tad and the consul's family set off across the California desert, driving east through Arizona, New Mexico, Texas, Oklahoma and up to Chicago. The scenery must have had an alluring effect on Tad only subliminally; he later could remember little about that trip, but he returned to those canyons and deserts with great joy many times in his later life. His clearest impression in 1930 was still that of the sameness, the averageness, of these Americans. "The overwhelming thing was that this was not a place for anybody special," he recalled. (He said this with a mild contempt, as the great-grandson of a nobleman. He did not say this, or recognize this, as an indication of hope, as the key to the "land of opportunity," for this new immigrant with big ideas in his head and little cash in his pockets.) But his memories of this part of the trip were dim primarily because he was growing more and more worried about his future, and was contemplating not grasslands but galvanizing.

Tad stayed only a day or so in Chicago, then boarded a bus for New York.

*   *   *

In October 1929, one and a half million people were out of work in the United States. By the time Tad arrived in New York, three months later, the number had jumped to four million. In another nine months, one year after the Crash, the ranks of the unemployed would double again.

Early in 1930, however, most people were still unclear as to exactly what was happening. The barons of business and government concealed their dismay with optimism. For the millions of Americans worried simply about feeding their children and paying the rent, the grim figures seemed unbelievable. Wasn't America a *rich* nation? The 1920s had brought cars, radios, refrigerators and talking pictures into the common vocabulary. America was, as Will Rogers noted, "the only nation in history that ever went to the poorhouse in an automobile."

Opportunities in the steel industry were quickly evaporating when Tad came to New York. The rate of new investment—his only hope—was plummeting. Twice the number of banks failed in 1930 as in 1929, while half the number of cars and trucks were produced. The auto industry slump hit the steel makers hard, as did the precipitous decline in the construction of railroads, pipelines and large buildings. And it was going to get worse. By 1932, the steel industry was operating at less than 20% of capacity.

Tad was beginning to realize even before he arrived in New York that it might be impossible to find a job. In January of 1930, the Depression was not yet so visible to the eye as he crossed the continent, but even a man with Tad's pin-point preoccupations could see that something ominous was going on. "It was only starting," Tad remembered. "Everybody was shocked. No one knew what was happening." Indeed it was another Great War, whose battlelines would be breadlines, whose trenches would be shanty towns, whose artillery would be eviction notices, plant closings, and bank failures. The begging children Tad saw as the bus made its way to the New York terminal gave witness. These were white children, Americans, not wretched Chinese on the streets of Shanghai.

*   *   *

Tad had seen his first skyscraper in Chicago, where the phenomenon was born. In Manhattan, before the Depression could slow them down, skyscapers were sprouting like concrete and steel exclamation points—punctuating New York City's bulletin to the world that it had become the planet's capital of commerce, wealth and modernity.

The tall buildings loomed shoulder to shoulder, block upon block, hugging the sidewalk straight up to the sky. Still, Tad was unawed by New York when he alighted from his bus; it did not seem so large as he had imagined. He soon changed his mind. He had been told by friends that hotels in Manhattan were very expensive, so he crossed the river to Brooklyn Heights, a fashionable area of that unfashionable borough, and found a clean and modest room. That evening he went for a walk, down to the river's edge close by. An ice cold disk of a January moon shone on the forest of giant buildings across the water. The lights from the buildings and from the streets contributed their own glow in the bitter air. He could make out the fishing boats docked at the South Street Pier, and to his right, the web and chunky towers of Brooklyn Bridge. The lights kept going up the river, unending. The city and its sentinels that at first had not seemed so big became significant in the moonlit winter night.

The next morning, Tad pulled out his list of contacts. The name at the top was Fred Wonham. Tad's friend and agent in Shanghai, Elliston, had written a letter of introduction to Wonham, who ran an import-export business from his small office on Battery Place. Tad took the subway into Manhattan and made his way to this office.

Wonham, an aristocratic Canadian in his early sixties, listened with interest as Tad spread out machinery drawings on the desk. Tad explained each detail in his thick Slavic accent, his long fingers pointing and darting across the page, his intelligence and enthusiasm brilliant in his gaze. Here was a man who was going somewhere. Wonham was converted. He became one more in a long line of men—we can already count Szelbitski, the Russian railyard manager in Lwow, and Jezierski and Jastrzembski, the Polish bankers in Shanghai—whom Tad was able to convince to give him support. Every major leap in Tad's career took place from the shoulders of a man who believed in him, and who sometimes suffered through years of trouble and disappointment before seeing his reward. This capacity to win people over is often cited, by those who knew him, as Tad's greatest asset, the key to his business success. Wonham was the first of this line, however, who was won over to a specific idea: the galvanizing process. Tad now had a product to sell besides himself.

Wonham agreed to put up money to finance Tad's stay in New York and his trips to visit wire companies in the East. Tad made out a patent application with the help of a patent attorney, but the attorney cheated them and never sent the patent in. (This turned out for the best because the process he was then trying to patent was incomplete, as he found out by doing experiments. He also discovered some prior patents with similar ideas, which he was then better able to work around.)

Tad could not remember later in the 1980s, of what exactly this first fumbled patent application consisted. His critical insight in Shanghai in 1929 had been that the steel must be kept assiduously clean, and away from oxygen, before it is dipped in the zinc. The essential feature in his eventual galvanizing breakthrough in late 1930 was that after cleaning the steel would pass through a sealed box containing hydrogen gas, where no oxygen could get in to contaminate the steel's sensitive surface. But he had, there in New York, many hours of research still to do on similar patents and on the uses of gases in a vacuum, before he could perfect this idea. Nevertheless, off he went to the wire companies with a technique that was still only partially baked.

This was the first instance of another pattern (closely related to his ability to garner support) played out often in his career. He had an idea, even a very good idea, but the details weren't quite hammered out. He had an overriding (and often illusory) confidence in the ability of his brain to puzzle through every tiny facet of a process or machine before it was even drawn on paper. Then, according to Tad, it simply had to be built and turned on. Nothing so distressed him as the suggestion that deep in the heart of his scheme this widget couldn't possibly turn that widget. "Never mind such details! I know it will work." Two decades later, when he'd made a name for himself, he was able to convince people with this line. In Depression America,

Tad Sendzimir had no such reputable name, and few companies were willing to take such risks.

He visited a dozen firms—one in Chicago, one in Cleveland, three in Pittsburgh, the rest near New York. None bit. The demand for light steel products, such as wire, strip or tin plate, remained relatively steady in the Depression, in contrast to the fall in demand for girders and heavy rail. But fear and caution prevailed. Tad blamed his failure on management's shortsightedness, but undoubtedly the state of the economy had something to do with their reluctance to sink money into this Pole from China with the strong accent and the strange ideas.

He was able to convince a wire company in Massachusetts to let him try some experiments. The shop foreman, however, refused to cooperate, and the results were inconclusive. Tad returned to New York discouraged. But the tests had given him a clear idea of the research he needed to do. With Wonham's support, he settled himself into the New York Public Library for the summer of 1930.

It must have been a pleasant interlude. The coughing and grumbling from the souplines, the shouted headlines about bank closings, the rumble of buses down Fifth Avenue—all could be shut away behind the swish of the library doors. Tad would head for the Science Reading Room, settle himself beneath one of the tall windows overlooking Bryant Park and spread his papers out on the worn-soft oak table. Sometimes he'd cross the hall to the Patent Room and spend a few hours scanning the dry, succinct prose of patents for pickling and coating metal.

The studies Tad found most relevant described research done by Irving Langmuir at General Electric. (Langmuir would win the Nobel Prize in chemistry in 1932.) What interested Tad was the work Langmuir had done in perfecting tungsten filament lightbulbs, in the course of which he found that it was the oxygen remaining in the bulb that caused the filament to so quickly disintegrate. He experimented with other gases in a vacuum, most notably hydrogen, and was able to produce a long-lasting tungsten filament bulb. Tad immediately made the connection: "..[Langmuir] needed to investigate to find equilibria between metal oxide and hydrogen and its partial pressures at various temperatures. Those papers firmly established that my new conception of my galvanizing process, namely annealing [slow heating] in a hydrogen atmosphere, then partial cooling and finally dipping in a molten zinc bath, was OK. The New York study gave me at least a more scientific base that the conception was correct."

It is doubtful that Tad would have shouted "Eureka!" in the quiet Science Reading Room. More probably a smile would be playing at the corners of his mouth as he read through the reports, and his step would be quicker as he strode up Fifth Avenue at the end of the day. He'd find himself suddenly in Central Park, having tracked seventeen blocks lost entirely in thought. He'd look for a telephone, call Wonham to give him the news, and Wonham would invite Tad over to dinner to hear more about it.

Outside of the library, Tad spent most of his time walking, visiting the Wonhams or a friend he had known in Shanghai, or seeing movies, which still were cheap. He went to hear Rachmaninoff play in Carnegie Hall. Tad would stroll down Fifth Avenue to Thirty-fourth Street every so often, to marvel at the Empire State Building rising at what seemed like a floor a week. The Chrysler Building, just four blocks down Forty-second Street from the library, was completed that year, also with Tad's sidewalk supervision.

From Brooklyn Heights, Tad could see across the harbor to the low flat buildings of Ellis Island, where so many of his compatriots had come, changing or shortening their names to fit the American tongue. (The only such accommodation Tad made was to insert an "n" in Sendzimir, to retain the Polish pronunciation. The Poles spell it "Sedzimir," putting an accent mark under the "e" that calls for an "en" sound.) Tad did not, in 1930, make any effort to contact the Polish emigre community in New York, though he did so when he returned to the States later in the decade.

By the fall of 1930, Tad was finished with his research. He would have liked to stay in America, where opportunities had to be greater in the long run, he felt, than in Europe. The Depression was growing worse in the United States—but Europe had not yet been hit. He thought perhaps, with his relatives and school contacts, he'd be able to find something in Poland. He bade Wonham good-bye, promising him that he'd continue working on his invention, and Wonham would see his faith and his investment rewarded. In October he set sail for France.

*   *   *

He did continue, he did pay Wonham back, and well. Five years later the galvanizing process had proved a complete success and Tad was signing a fat contract with one of America's top ten steel companies. Simultaneously he had turned his attention to the mills that roll steel strip down to the thin gauge necessary for galvanizing. By 1935, six years after he had left Shanghai with little but a hunch, Tad Sendzimir's name was established as an important industrial inventor.

Tad's first invention, the galvanizing process, came about because Tad was familiar with, and thought in terms of, not only metallurgy and mechanical engineering, but also chemistry. Most inventors operate like this: they combine ideas from assorted fields, and they think not linearly but laterally across disciplines. They leap the boundaries of approved and specialized knowledge that constrict the thinking of us lesser mortals. The process has been compared to the art of metaphor: seeing the similarities no one else has noticed— similarities between divergent fields, and similarities in the way things work. Thomas Edison, for example, equated a water system and a telegraph: he designed his quadruplex telegraph using the analogy of pumps, pipes, valves, and water wheels.

A changing and variable work environment is known to promote the quick and flexible thinking needed for inventing. Tad had plenty of opportunity in Shanghai to sharpen his skill at finding unorthodox solutions to sundry annoying problems. But his work in Shanghai— before the galvanizing invention—reveals the difference between inventing and innovating. Jerry-building machinery to outwit the weather and the poor quality raw material is simply clever innovation. A true invention is not just improvement. It is more than a simple combination of elements, an extrapolation of the past. It is almost a work of art. A true invention makes one plus one equal three.

Tad's galvanizing invention was not an Einsteinian upheaval in the concept of steel making. Someone was bound to realize that hydrogen gas could be used to prevent oxidation on steel before it is galvanized. That insight was long overdue: hydrogen gas as a "reducing atmosphere," an atmosphere free of oxygen, had been known for some time. Similarly, his first cold rolling mill was a replica of a German mill in use at the time—but he made the crucial modifications. It then became "revolutionary."

Inventors tend to be individualists and non-conformists, and Tad was both. They will not listen to what their colleagues insist is "reason:" they will not listen when they're told "It can't work." The plant owners Tad met in the U.S. in 1930 shook their heads when he tried to explain his new galvanizing idea. "At times I found myself in opposition to the whole world," Tad said. And these individualists like to work alone; to make a success out of such solitary endeavor they must have an immoderate supply of optimism, self-confidence, and stubbornness. They are (as Tad was) without apology unconventional in their ways and in their thinking.

As Tad worked with the conventional galvanizing process in Shanghai, he thought, "Surely this could be done better." While often uncritical of their own ideas, inventors characteristically are critical of much else in the mechanical world. When they notice a machine that is clumsy, impractical, dangerous, or simply inelegant, they want to improve it. The itch to improve is tied as well to their voracious curiosity; they are fascinated by how things work, and unsatisfied until the last screw has been pried loose to reveal its secrets.

Of all the traits of inventors, the most important is imagination. They see the unapparent, and they often have a unique ability to visualize, to conceive of things in great detail that have never existed. Many famous inventors—Leonardo da Vinci is the most obvious—have also been artists or poets. What separates the inventor from the artist, in many cases, is quite mundane: an early, incorrigible fascination with mechanical and electrical devices.

Inventors need expertise, but that expertise must be both theoretical and nuts-and-bolts (literally) practical. Tad's boyhood spent in Kaczmarski's machine shop, and then in his Uncle Tolloczko's chemistry lab, were as important as his lectures and exams at the Polytechnic. But formal education can also be a hindrance; schools reward conformity and can extinguish the inventive spark. "Education, the more you have, the more you know that it (a novel idea) cannot be done," Tad insisted.

Inventors are motivated in their work by those traits of curiosity and the need to improve things. Inventing is almost a chronic condition, not necessarily stoked into action by that "mother of invention," necessity. Countless needs go unmet; countless inventions have no urgent purpose. Nevertheless, some needs do serve as a stimulus, or as a signpost pointing out a direction to take. Henry Bessemer described how he came to invent the first practical method to convert iron into steel in the mid-nineteenth century. He had been told by officers in the army that stronger cast-iron guns were needed: "...I had no idea [how to] attack this problem, but the mere fact that there was something to discover was sufficient to spur me on. It was like the first cry of the hounds in the hunting field."

Once a need is perceived, most inventors begin by inquiring about past attempts to solve the problem. Tad, alas, would not. He often threw himself merrily into the fray and came up with a solution, only to find that someone else had already figured it out. (He wasted a lot of time this way, but he of course would not consider it wasted, even if no viable product came about.) Still, for Tad and for any inventor, the burst of inspiration comes not from the clear blue sky. Inspiration comes after gradual and laborious mental industry, chewing through the aspects of the problem like a sluggish computer chews through its bytes. Experienced thinkers know how to position themselves to think best: during naps, taking baths, sketching on paper, and so on. Most need solitude. Tad took long walks, and he recommended deep breathing. His galvanizing idea took shape as he strode along Shanghai's Bund and up and down Fifth Avenue in Manhattan.

After the flash of insight, the inventor then will visualize his construct in detail, working out much of its operation in his mind's eye. Tad swore by this method, as did Nikola Tesla, the flamboyant pioneer in high-tension electricity, who claimed that building actual models only got one bogged down in the details and defects, where one could lose sight of the underlying principle of the design.

But, of course, there *are* details and defects. Tad and the engineers who worked with him might spend months and years perfecting an idea before applying for a patent. Many inventors are glad then to move on to something new, and leave the commercial exploitation of their invention in other hands. Here Tad differed, significantly: he wanted to keep commercial control, and he built up a prosperous business on his inventions. He also admitted to never quite letting his designs go, never giving up the tinkering: "My inventions are like my children. I like them all around me, and I go through occasionally and see if I can improve anything or modify anything." (Indeed, in his nineties he claimed to still be considering some alterations on galvanizing—a line he'd been out of touch with for fifty years—and likewise he never gave up on my brothers and me.)

* * *

In October 1930, Tad landed in Cherbourg, France. He arrived but a few months ahead of the eastward-sweeping winds of economic disaster. The Depression began to be felt in Europe in the spring of 1931. The crushing blow was to come six months later, with the crash of Vienna's largest bank, financial panic in Germany, and Great Britain's abandonment of the gold standard. The steel industry in England and France had enjoyed a post-war boom between 1924 and 1929; by 1932, production was down by half. This time, Tad didn't bother knocking on the closing doors.

He was headed back to Poland, but he decided to stop for a week in Paris to visit Barbara's brothers Michael and Eugene. Paris was still tense and hot with artistic and intellectual excitement—fed by Picasso, Stravinsky, Joyce, Hemingway, Stein, Cocteau and many more on the Left Bank. In cafes on the opposite bank sat the businessmen, thumbing nervously through their stock reports. The City of Light of the 1920s was about to darken—with unemployment, and the violent clashes between Right and Left in the 1930s.

Michael and Eugene Alferieff had introduced Tad, on his visit in 1926, to one of their Russian friends, Theodor (Fedya) Bostroem. Bostroem was six years younger than Tad. He had been studying mechanical engineering. Tad welcomed this news when he met him again in 1930; he asked Bostroem to help him with his galvanizing patents.

Bostroem, a lively and suave young man with a square face framed by short cropped hair and a crisp bow tie, was the son of a former Russian admiral. His parents were living outside of Paris, and he brought Tad to meet them. As Bostroem recalled, "I don't remember any strong impressions of Tadeusz at that time. But my father knew graphology, and when he saw his signature, he said he was a complicated person. 'He's a very talented man, but you will have your troubles sometimes with him.' And it was very true."

Tad, out of cash, needing help and anxious to return to Poland, made Bostroem a generous offer: a fifty-fifty share in the profits if he would file patents for the galvanizing process in the industrial countries of Europe—England, Germany, France and Belgium. Bostroem agreed, borrowing money from his family and friends to do so. The patents were written in both their names, though Bostroem contributed nothing to the idea of the invention itself. He filed the patents in 1931.

So began a relationship that lasted over fifty years, ending only with Bostroem's death at age eighty-seven. Due to his serendipitous access to cash and know-how at that moment in 1931, Bostroem lived well for the rest of his life on the rewards for his then-slender efforts—a fact that, despite his fondness for Bostroem, stuck in Tad's throat like a small, sharp bone. But Bostroem's prodigious and critical work were still to come: people say that without his loyal help in Poland (Tad asked him to join him in 1933, to help start the first rolling mill) Tad's inventions might have been abandoned for scrap.

Tad left Paris by the end of October and returned to Poland to his mother's house in Lwow. Vanda was alone by then on Saint Teresa Street: Terenia had married and was living near Katowice; Zbigniew was in Warsaw and Aniela in Torun.

While he was in Shanghai, Tad had kept up with Poland's

fortunes—and lack thereof. He had read carefully the small bits and pieces of Polish news covered in the Shanghai foreign press: that independence had been gained with the fall of Austria, Germany and Russia in 1918; that a parliament (Sejm) had been formed; that the Versailles Treaty had established the borders with Germany, but that the eastern frontier with Russia was only settled by a war with the Bolsheviks. He did not know much about the squabbling between the many political parties in the Sejm. But he'd read with interest about Pilsudski's coup in May, 1926, remembering that afternoon in 1912 when he'd seen the rigid and resolute officer surveying the ranks of his rag-tag followers in a park in Lwow. Tad was sympathetic to Pilsudski's strong-arm tactics, and considered him a great patriot, as did most Poles. He believed that had Pilsudski not died in 1935, Hitler would never have invaded Poland.

Tad on his return found Lwow a different place. Walking along the streets near the *rynek*, he noticed the small shops and vegetable carts bearing signs in Ukrainian. He passed a group of old men on a street corner who also were speaking that language. After his years in Kiev and Shanghai, Lwow's "orientalness" now struck him—a flavor from its Ukrainian population he had ignored as a boy. "Poland looked to me kind of exotic," he said. "[The feeling was that] I came not to my old home." He felt no sense of relief on his homecoming; indeed he did not even view it as such. He would have preferred to stay in New York or Paris. Lwow was a provincial town, a temporary stopping place. He knew he had to move on quickly, at least to Krakow or Warsaw, and probably to Katowice, in the steel and mining region of Silesia. He was running out of money.

Broke and rootless as he was, soon after he got to Lwow he did something he promptly regretted. Taking some of what little money he had left, he wired it to Harbin and asked Barbara to bring Michael and join him in Poland. Did he hope to patch things up? He said maybe. "I did hope we could get together, but I would say that at the time I may have been thinking too much about Michael. I was afraid that Barbara would flirt with somebody and then marry him. And then Michael would be under her and I will lose him as a son."

Barbara's brother Kola was shocked by news of the move, because their mother was getting old and needed Barbara's help in Harbin. He got a letter from Barbara saying "My husband is going to Poland, and I must go too." This seems like an uncharacteristic swelling of wifely devotion. Life in Harbin must have been getting tedious.

Michael learned to skate that winter in Lwow's parks. Tad settled his son and Barbara in with Vanda, and Barbara at once began asking for money, increasing Tad's already urgent search for an income. After several months, Barbara and Michael moved to Zakopane, the resort town in the Tatra mountains.

Before he left Lwow, Tad visited Uncle Tolloczko at his chemistry lab. Tolloczko was quite happy to see his prodigy, now a grown man, but one as thin and tense and driven as ever, and bursting as ever with ideas. Tad explained his galvanizing concept, and his uncle let him do a small experiment on a counter in the lab. Over a burner, Tad brought a small pot of zinc to the melting point. He constructed a crude but airtight box for the hydrogen gas. Taking a piece of wire, he cleaned it in acid, fed it into the box, and from there into the molten zinc bath. To his joy, the zinc stayed on the metal: "It was wetted! It was a full victory, on microscopic scale, in theory and in practice."

Tad set off with rekindled confidence. He was by then desperate for any kind of job, for any source of immediate income to feed himself and family. But he kept his eye out for investors.

*　　*　　*

Tad couldn't have chosen a less propitious environment. Poland's industry was barely breathing. Before World War I and independence, Austria and Germany had kept their Polish provinces (with the exception of Upper Silesia) in a state of agricultural backwardness. Russia had developed some industry in Russian Poland, but kept it weak in fear that Polish nationalists might seize the factories and begin making guns. Russia also had stifled private initiative, and prevented the construction of railroads and other municipal services. At the beginning of World War I, Russia carted off much of the industrial equipment in her territories. What was left, the invading Germans sacked and carted off in the other direction. Polish industry suffered approximately two billion dollars worth of damage. From 1914 to 1918, heavy industry in Western Europe grew to meet the demands of the war; Poland meanwhile was just a battlefield, its labor force decimated by mass deportations. After the Armistice in 1918, Western Europe began to rebuild, experiencing a boom in 1919-1920. During those boom years, Poland was still at war with Russia.

Peace and independence finally came in 1920. But there was nothing left: no plants, no workers, no capital. Not even, at first, a common currency. Western creditors were far happier to invest in the industrious Germans than in the desolate and argumentative Poles. U.S. loans to Germany in the Twenties amounted to $21.60 per capita; to Poland, $5.63 per capita. Poland had to rely on its own crippled resources. Its development was stymied also by protectionist trade policies in the West.

Trade and capital loosened up in a brief, bright period between 1927 and 1931. Poland made rapid progress. The onset of the Depression then killed it off.

In 1921, Poland acquired from Germany the relatively more industrialized region of Upper Silesia in the southwest, and so got a fledgling, albeit ransacked, steel industry. The Germans left with everything they could carry, from electric motors to floor slabs, and severed the ties of service and customers that had kept the industry going. Poland's poor quality iron ore and coke further hampered the steel industry's development. The slow process of rebuilding then was struck by the Depression. It was 1933 before faint signs of improvement began to appear. When Tad was looking for work in 1931, the outlook was bleak.

*　　*　　*

Tad first went to Krakow, hoping that a relative who was president of a bank would help him out. But even a bank president could find nothing for him. He then took the train to Warsaw, where several men he knew from Lwow and the Polytechnic held posts in the government. They would perhaps have contacts in the steel industry. He stayed with his brother Zbigniew.

Zbigniew was working as technical director at the General Motors office—the job Tad had urged him to take when they were in Shanghai. Although the office was losing money, Zbigniew was still paid a good salary, and on it was enjoying briefly the life of a *bon vivant:* parties, nice suits, money to spend on the ladies. For once in their relationship, Zbigniew was the brother with cash and standing, Tad was the supplicant. But money in Zbigniew's pocket did not induce resolve in his character. During this period Zbigniew became engaged to a girl from a good family from Lwow. The arrangements were made. The wedding date arrived. The guests and bride's family filled the church. Tad was best man. Everyone waited...Zbigniew didn't show up. "I had to make apologies to the family," Tad remembered. "Zbigniew was scared."

Once in Warsaw, Tad set out to contact friends in the government. His first attempt dealt a well-remembered blow to his pride. Joseph Beck, then Minister of Foreign Affairs, had been Tad's close friend in their first year together at the Polytechnic. Tad followed Beck's later rise in the Polish government, and when Tad came to Warsaw Beck was the first on his list to see. On the day of his appointment, he put on his best suit and took the trolley over to the minister's office building in the center of town. When he arrived, Beck's secretary informed him that her boss apologized, but he had been called to an urgent meeting with the Prime Minister. Such things happen, but Tad took it personally: "He didn't leave a message that he'd like me to come tomorrow, or something. So I never tried again. As foreign minister, he was a very important figure and I was still nobody." Tad's ego—despite that strong will and self-confidence— was easy to bruise. And just then, given his meager, needful situation, it was easier still. These months of searching for a job were the lowest point in his life.

He had better luck, eventually, in the offices of another close friend from school days, Tadeusz Kudelski. The Kudelski family had been neighbors of the Sendzimirs in Lwow. Now the son was financial adviser to President Moscicki. Kudelski greeted Tad warmly. Because of his position, he knew many people in industry and government. He promised Tad that he'd look around.

Tad finally got a job in Katowice through his sister Aniela, who had friends there. Tad was hired as assistant to the president of a new engineering trade school. This job ended in a month, when he quit for a higher paying but temporary post with a man who was liquidating a company. Tad was in charge of the auction, and made several hundred dollars for a few days' work.

He held on to his galvanizing idea. Kudelski told him the name of a company that produced galvanized sheet, in the town of Bedzin, in Silesia. The firm of Furstenberg was Poland's largest producer of galvanized sheet, sold almost exclusively as roofing material. Tad's process had been designed for galvanized wire, but he saw no reason why it couldn't be done on flat sheet as well. He went out to Furstenberg's factory and explained his idea to the boss. Sorry, he was told, they had just installed a new kettle. They had quite enough capacity for their present production.

But that's not the end of the Furstenberg story. Zinc in Silesia was controlled by something of a monopoly. Two families, Furstenberg and Inwald, shared the business by long-standing agreement: the Furstenbergs produced galvanized sheet; the Inwalds produced zinc white, the zinc oxide powder used as a base for paint. Neither strayed onto the other's side of the plate, and so the pie was sliced for several generations. Now, however, this Furstenberg who had just installed a new kettle decided also to start making zinc white, and abridge the family agreement.

Zygmunt Inwald was not the man to take this lying down. Inwald possessed a quick, warm and dynamic character, and eyes that his friends claimed "bore right through you." He had been injured when a block of wood fell on him at a construction site, and so walked with a markedly hunched back. As with many handicapped people, his disability served only to intensify his energies. When he found out about Furstenberg's perfidy, he quickly started up his own galvanizing line at his zinc white plant in Kostuchna, a small town near Katowice. But the line was inefficient and he was losing money on it. He was looking for help when he received a call from a man who had gotten his name from Kudelski. "I have invented a process that will revolutionize galvanizing. It is more economical and the product is far superior in quality," said this Pole from Lwow.

Inwald and Tad met for breakfast in a cafe in Warsaw, sometime around the end of 1931. Tad told Inwald about his process, and Inwald was tremendously interested. Inwald wanted the galvanizing line built at once. But Tad wanted to be careful. "No, Mr. Inwald, I will not," Tad told him. "I have it only in theory; I haven't done it yet. I must first make a test line for three hundred millimeter wide strip." Inwald didn't like this delay, but he saw the logic.

Tad set up his experimental line in a large unused hall of the old German factory in Kostuchna where Inwald ran his galvanizing operation. For the first time, Tad was able to fully discover the problems—and there were problems—with his invention. "My first tests were full of difficulties, which all centered around making the furnace sufficiently air-tight, the atmosphere completely reducing." The tests ran on expensively for several months, inducing dismay and disapproval in the board of directors of Inwald's company, who were not so open-minded as its president. They grew angry. Finally, Tad remembered, they had a director's meeting, "and they had already decided to say, 'Sendzimir go to hell.'" Inwald, still on Tad's side, had been stalling them.

The morning of the meeting, Tad fired up the newly-caulked furnace and ran some steel through his process. The zinc held. At last he had produced a properly galvanized sheet. As soon as it cooled he grabbed it and ran over to the board meeting. They passed it around, flexed it back and forth, and looked at one another in astonishment. They voted unanimously to let him build the line.

CHAPTER SIX

KATOWICE, ROLLING AND GALVANIZING

1932 - 1935

First he needed strip. Thin in gauge, wide in width, steel strip, in long coils that could be unwound, slip through the hydrogen atmosphere, into and out of the molten zinc bath, up into the air to dry, in a continuous flowing band. Then only would that ribbon of steel be cut into eight foot lengths, or sheets.

But at the moment, there were no long coils of strip; there were only sheets. Men galvanized them one by one, dipping them painstakingly into the zinc, lifting them out and setting them to dry on a cylindrical rack studded with long spikes, named after the animal it resembled, a porcupine. No one in Europe made steel in coils to the fine one-third millimeter gauge Tad needed, and his process couldn't use steel in sheets. The whole point was to produce galvanized steel in long coils: a process that would be much faster and more economical—and previously unheard of because of the fragility of the zinc coating. Now, with Tad's galvanizing invention, the world *would* have coated steel that could be shaped and hammered into useful, rust-resistant goods, and the zinc wouldn't peel off in the hammering.

But he had to find that steel strip first. When he couldn't find it, he decided to make it himself. And so Tad got into the business of rolling steel. By 1945, the cold rolling mill he invented in the early 1930s had rolled steel so thin that radar devices made from it were light enough to be mounted on airplanes in World War II. This mill would then revolutionize the making of stainless steel strip. Today, ninety percent of stainless steel produced world-wide is rolled on the grandchildren of Tad's first mill in Poland.

*　　*　　*

The cold rolling of steel is the easy end of the enterprise. They insist you wear a hard hat, nowadays, to cushion the blow if a steel coil slips off an overhead crane. The rolling itself is relatively safe, clean, quiet, and, let's say it, dull. Only a wizened operator can get excited by a machine that, in one pass, squeezes 0.05 millimeter more out of the thickness of a strip of cold steel. Only he knows that's quite extraordinary.

Indeed the whole process of making steel is extraordinary. Cold rolling is just the back end of the complicated, dramatic and dangerous job of taking raw iron ore and making the material that built the twentieth century: from the huge black blast furnaces that produce molten iron, to the fiery drama of the steel-making furnaces that cook that iron into hard steel, to the burly slab mills that pound that steel into thick slabs, to the hot rolling mills that squeeze those slabs into long coils of steel strip.

After hot rolling comes cold rolling. The steel is again rolled, at room temperature, into very thin gauge strip. Cold rolling makes the steel stronger and harder, and gives it a smooth and lustrous finish on its surface. But cold rolling has a disadvantage: with increased hardness comes less ductility—the metal's ability to be shaped into a final product. So most cold rolled strip has to be annealed, often several times. Annealing, a process of slow heating in an enclosed box, softens the metal without harming its strength or finish. A major advantage of the mill Tad invented is the superior strength it makes possible. The strip, hard and tough as it is, could be squeezed down to very thin gauges without having to be taken off the mill and re-annealed every three or four passes through the rolls. Thus the excitement of those wizened operators, watching a strip hard as diamonds get thinner and thinner...

Cold rolling became an increasingly important part of the steel industry in the 1930s and 1940s, contributing to (and no less induced by) the boom of the auto and appliance industry. Now it was possible to get strong, good-looking steel sheet that was ductile enough to be stamped into auto body parts, refrigerators, toasters and washing machines. Before the improvement of cold-rolling and annealing techniques, such deep stamping would have cracked the steel sheet like a dried leaf.

Cold rolling was not born in the 1930s. It had first been tried in the mid-eighteenth century, and through the nineteenth century was used on narrow strip to make clock and watch springs and wire for hoop skirts and corsets. It was done in the same way as hot rolling—passing the cold steel back and forth between two large, heavy rolls. This is called a two-high mill, one roll on top of another. But it was soon discovered that small diameter rolls are much more efficient than larger ones at biting into the sheet, as a sharp knife cuts steak better than a dull one. But small rolls bend easily, and so must be reinforced, or "backed-up," by heavier rolls. Thus the four-high mill—a design Leonardo da Vinci had suggested four centuries earlier—came about: two small "work" rolls (the rolls through which the steel is passed) sandwiched between two larger rolls. (See diagrams on following page.)

Still, in the early part of this century, all this rolling was done on individual sheets of steel fed through the mill by hand. Only in the United States and Germany, in the late 1920s, did mills begin rolling hundreds-of-feet-long coils of steel strip. The material Tad found available in Poland in 1931 had been fed by one man, as a sheet, into the mill, and removed from the other side by another man. They sent this through several times, while a third man screwed the rolls down closer for each pass. When the rolls could pinch no tighter, the sheet would be folded onto itself, and the process would start again. After several folds, finally the desired thinness would be reached, and the men would take this steel—squeezed together like strudel dough—and laboriously pull the sheets apart with tongs.

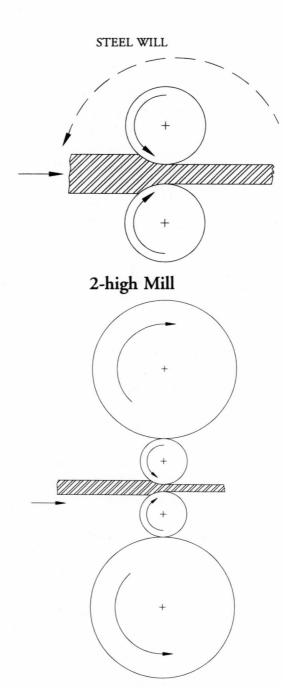

2-high Mill

4-high Mill

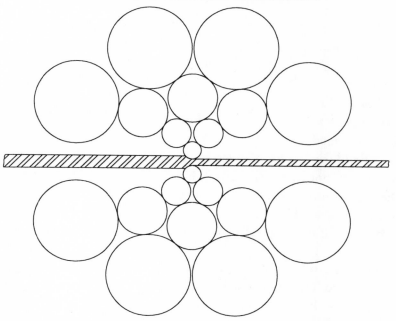

Cluster Mill

The edges would be trimmed, and the sheets sent on their way—to be, for example, galvanized.

For Tad, of course, this sheet by sheet business just wouldn't do.

*　　*　　*

Zygmunt Inwald, Tad's boss, could get steel in wide sheets from Huta Pokoj ("Huta" means "steelworks" in Polish), a mill in nearby Katowice. But Inwald needed it not three millimeters thick as it came from the mill, but one-quarter millimeter thick. This was the gauge he could sell for galvanized roofing material—and so steal the market from Furstenberg. But such thin gauge at that wide width was almost inconceivable: the long work rolls needed for wide strip would bend — slightly, but critically — in the middle.

Tad and Inwald set off for the biggest mill builder around, the Krupp works in Magdeburg, Germany. Krupp's four-high mills were state-of-the-art in 1931, and he was justifiably proud of them. Inwald told Krupp they needed a mill that could roll down to one-quarter millimeter. Krupp—who might well have laughed at this hunch-backed Jew and his vainglorious Polish sidekick—said his mills could roll down to one and a half millimeter, but no further. "I told him right there," Tad remembered, "'*You* cannot do it, but I *can*.'"

Tad had been reading in *Stahl und Eisen*, the German steel industry magazine, how mills were being built to solve the bending problem. He discovered the work of Wilhelm Rohn, an engineer in Hanau, near Frankfurt. Rohn had designed a mill where each work roll was backed up not by one large roll, but by two rolls, side-by-side, and these in turn were strengthened by three more rolls, side-by-side, on top of the two. This was called a cluster mill. The pressure of these two layers of back-up rolls greatly reduced the bending of the work rolls.

Tad went to Hanau to see Rohn, but he still wasn't satisfied. Rohn was only rolling narrow strip, and while he had cut down on the bending, he hadn't eliminated it. Nevertheless, the cluster of rolls idea had merit. On his way back to Poland, Tad began to formulate three important concepts that, together, might make the difference.

First of all, the rolls of Rohn's mill were held in place by bearings on either end. In his head, Tad moved those bearings *above* (and below) the work rolls: "What if the work rolls were backed up not by two rolls," he was thinking, "but instead by hard steel roller bearings, spaced out on a heavy beam along the width of the work roll?" He imagined thick, fat bearings, two inches thick and nine inches in diameter—like giant steel hockey pucks. These would be much stiffer than a long, cylindrical roll. His second idea was about the mill's housing, the two pieces of cast iron that hold the work rolls in place. "What if I made the housing solid, from one piece, completely rigid? If I cast it in steel and fixed the bearing supports up into it, no amount of rolling pressure would budge those work rolls." Lastly he added the concept of tension. He knew that the work rolls do a better job if the strip is held taut, like a sail in a stiff wind. The strip then can be rolled even flatter. "I thought that instead of a ten percent reduction in gauge on each pass, I could maybe take fifty percent!"

Inwald responded with unflinching faith to Tad's mill idea, and they set off, back to Germany, to find someone rash enough to build it. This time they went to Dusseldorf, to the mill building firm of Schloemann, where reigned one of the industry's prophets, Dr. Ludwig Loewy. Again they were turned down.

They took their business elsewhere, down the road to a small shop that had been building quality rolling mills for four generations: Walzmaschinenfabrik August Schmitz. Dr. Peter Schmitz was now the proprietor, and into his office came the hopeful Poles. Schmitz listened politely to Tad's explanations, looked over the rough sketches, looked back up at Tad and Inwald and said, "Hair will sooner grow on the palms of my hands than this machinery will work."

But Peter Schmitz was a broad-minded man, and he apparently had some time on those hands and enough of a penchant for the precarious to offer to build a small model, just to try it out.

Inwald returned to Katowice, while Tad settled into a hotel room in Dusseldorf. To save time, Tad simplified the design. The model was inexpensive and quickly built, and soon they were rolling brass as a sample of what the mill could do. Tad telephoned to Inwald to come and look.

Inwald came with another Polish industrialist, Swiecicki, who ran a galvanizing plant in Warsaw. They had agreed to go into this mill venture together, in order to get strip for both their galvanizing lines. The small mill was running. The operator rolled a strip of brass down to the thinness of foil; Tad cut off a piece and handed it to his patrons. Inwald and Swiecicki examined the strip closely, bent and twisted it, and rubbed its gleaming yellow surface. They turned to Peter Schmitz and placed an order on the spot for an 800 millimeter mill. Schmitz said that was the easiest sale he ever made.

During the next eight months, in 1933, Tad stayed almost constantly in Dusseldorf. The workmen at Schmitz had never built such a mill, so it required Tad's constant attention; the rigid one-piece housing, the precisely-forged roller bearings, the four-inch-diameter work rolls—all were unique. Tad quickly realized that he needed help, especially in making the complicated drawings to be used by the mill builders. He called Fedya Bostroem, his Russian friend in Paris who'd filed the galvanizing patents. Bostroem arrived in Dusseldorf and set up a drafting board in his hotel room. After six weeks he was dispatched to Katowice to oversee the preparation of the plant to receive the new mill. He knew about ten words of Polish.

Inwald arranged for the new mill to be installed right in the Huta Pokoj plant in Katowice, about fifteen miles from his galvanizing factory in Kostuchna. Huta Pokoj had been hot rolling steel for one hundred years; the buildings were of brick and wood, held together by soot. Inwald and Swiecicki formed a separate company, Walcownia Sendzimir SZOO (Sendzimir Rolling Mills Company, Limited). Tad was given one separate hall for his mill. The director, Bruno Absalon, became friendly with Tad, even though he later was to complain to the workers about the terrific noise the mill made. But it was his mill manager, Stanislaw Borkowski, who, by running interference at each stage, greatly assisted in the long toil that eventually got the mill going. Bostroem did most of the hiring, as he needed help, while Tad was held up in Dusseldorf. Unemployment and poverty were still severe in Silesia; many men were desperate for work, and the quality of those steelworkers was high. It is said that they were the descendants of those who had come to Silesia from a village near Krakow where for centuries smithing had flourished: iron was in their blood in higher quantities than in ordinary men.

*   *   *

The problems encountered in Dusseldorf were minor compared to what lay ahead for these workers in Katowice. Bostroem spent six months setting up the plant for the mill. Once it was installed, another six months went by before they produced satisfactory strip. It was, in Bostroem's peppery French, a "periode heroique," and most of the workmen expressed their desire never to live through such a thing again.

First they had to build the most singular aspect of Tad's design, his fanciful (and ultimately abandoned) winding system. Most steel strip is rolled on "reversing" mills. The strip is passed back and forth between two tremendous winders, spools really—exactly like tape in a cassette player. Tad conceived instead a method to roll the strip in a continuous closed loop, always in one direction. As the metal was rolled thinner and thinner, the strip would grow longer and longer. So a complicated system of pulleys, and a carriage mounted on a long railtrack, had to be constructed to take up the ever-lengthening loop of strip. Bostroem built a track system in a long wooden tunnel, running in a straight line out of the building for about fifty meters.

The mill needed a motor, and Tad found an enterprising electrical contractor, Maniura, to help. Maniura discovered that Katowice was changing from electrical street cars to trolley buses. He bought some of their old electric substations and installed one of these in the mill.

With the carriage/pulley system built, the pickling tanks constructed, the motor found, and the foundation prepared, Tad and Bostroem turned their attention to making the long loops of steel to feed through the mill. To get a long strip, they had to weld ten sheets of steel together lengthwise, like gluing a deck of cards together end-to-end. This "strip" would then get threaded through the mill, around the tension rollers, the pulleys and the carriage, and back to where the ends could be welded together to make a closed loop. But Tad soon realized that ordinary acetylene torch welds would tear and the sheets break apart—and down the drain into the Vistula would go the entire enterprise. Then, Tad recalled, "I remembered something from my New York stay. Langmuir had been developing a welding system where the electric arc was acting like a flame to melt the steel. The arc would make a neat clean weld as soft and ductile as the rest of the sheet." Such a welder was found in Berlin, installed, and the men trained to use it. The welds held, but made a frightful bang! bang! bang! on the first pass of the strip through the mill.

Most of this set-up work was done by a handful of workmen, Bostroem, and Bostroem's assistant, Stanislaw Grazynski, a small, strong and wiry man who might in other circumstances have taken a bantam-weight boxing title. Tad was thus freed from the innumerable mechanical annoyances and could keep his mind focused on the big picture. That certainly was his style, and the style of many inventors: the details are too trivial and discouraging. Yet his success was due not only to his genius, but in equal measure to the men who over the years labored valiantly over his frequently intractable ideas.

Unfortunately, Tad seemed little aware of this. His aristocratic, self-made-man self-image prevented him from noticing the efforts of others. And those efforts were prodigious, because Tad was gradually losing his feel for the gritty reality of machines. After his hands-on experience as a small boy in Kaczmarski's machine shop, all his work, throughout his career, was done not with his hands but with his head. At the car repair shops in Lwow, Kiev and Tsingtao he was telling others what to do. In his own factory in Shanghai, he was designing those re-built screw machines, but he wasn't the one tearing apart the old presses and constructing the new ones. How a set of gears and screws and shafts fit together harmoniously became more and more vague, as some of his own fanciful notions replaced the laws of physics and engineering. As an inventor, Tad came up with grand designs that often were impossible to build, say the men who worked for him from 1932 on.

Bostroem maintained that Tad's ideas were the driving force, and that he himself merely smoothed over a bump or two in that "periode heroique." Others from that era give Bostroem more credit, both in the content of his ideas and the style of his management. What was obvious to all was Tad's attitude to those above and below him. To those above, he bordered on the obsequious: bowing and addressing Inwald and Absalon with great courtesy and formality. To those below, he was removed, and sometimes cold. "Tad was a mixture of extreme roughness and a very kind heart," Bostroem said. On the one hand, a story is told of how Tad gave a job to a man who came begging for work, saying he had a child to feed. On the other hand, one story has it that he forbade a young man to get married: "Well, for a month he's going to do nothing!" (Bostroem took the man aside and urged him to go ahead: "Look, Sendzimirs there are many, while your wife is only one." Tad was of the opposite opinion.)

Grazynski's first contact with Tad set the tone for the cool relationship they had through the start-up of Tad's first three mills. "I had heard all about the 'Big Boss,'" Grazynski remembers, "so I had a lot of respect and some fear at our first meeting. I was standing near a machine, ready to introduce myself when he came by. He came walking through the building, inspecting the work we had done. He saw me and said, 'Why are you standing! You have nothing to do? Take a broom and sweep the floor!'"

Tad spent those six months traveling back and forth to Dusseldorf, and checking in both at Katowice and at Kostuchna, where another crew was constructing his galvanizing line. He also went to Zakopane frequently, to see Michael. Barbara and Michael had moved from Lwow to this resort in Poland's Tatra mountains in 1931. When Tad began making money, he bought a small plot on a slope in town and commissioned a three-story apartment building of brick and stone. Barbara and Michael moved into the top flat. Michael became a skier, and perfected his Polish on the lifts and in the local grammar school, while his mother made friends and dabbled in writing articles for the newspaper. Tad would drive down to Zakopane in his green Ford roadster and take Michael for hikes in the mountains or for tours around southern Poland. He would also make the short trip to visit his mother, who had sold the house in Lwow and was living for a time in Krakow.

When the mill was finally delivered from Schmitz, Bostroem and company took several weeks to install the motor, hook up the carriage and pulleys, and attach the tension rollers. The mill stood over eight feet high and seven feet wide. The solid, square, one-piece housing could barely be seen beneath the array of tremendous gears, attached to the housing on all sides, like a clock mistakenly built inside out. (Regulations later prohibited such exposed gears.) The fantastic machine squatted peaceably on the floor of the shabby brick building—a cast iron toad ready to roll out its tongue of steel strip halfway into the yard beyond to snatch a fly.

Tad was on hand for the start-up. The workers took one of the coils of welded sheets and threaded it through the mill. They welded the ends together, and Bostroem adjusted the pressure on the loop in the tension rollers. Maniura was ready to start up the electric motor. Tad took his place at the controls; Bostroem, Grazynski and eight or ten workmen surrounded the machine, each watching closely this or that piece he had spilt blood for. Would it now work?

Maniura started the motor. Tad threw the clutch for the work rolls. Slowly the strip began to inch into the rolls. Bang, came one weld. Bang, another. They held. The strip rolled on. Tad increased the speed slightly. Bang, bang, bang. The carriage started moving, pulling its end of the loop away from the mill. Suddenly, just as the men were ready to exhale, a loud crunching noise came from the mill. Tad shut it down. The strip had crept over to the left side, instead of going in a straight line through the rolls. Its edge was making "cabbage" against the gears.

The men climbed over the mill to find out what was the problem. They'd never seen such a thing. On a conventional mill, the strip is guided through the rolls by the winders on either side. It cannot stray right or left. Here Tad didn't have that control. The strip had to be yanked out of the rolls, and the entire roll assembly dismantled and reassembled before they could try again.

It took six months to solve the problem. Many meters of steel found their way into the scrap pile. Tad finally found a solution in using two flat planks, above and below the moving strip, pressed together so that the rubbing friction generated some back tension. "So," Tad remembered, "I connected [the lever that pressed on the planks] with a small steering wheel, like a motor car. One steered it just like a motor car, except that the road [the strip] was moving, not the car."

Finally, indeed, the planks seemed to be working. The strip was kept from crashing into one side or the other by a man at that steering wheel. The mill was at last able to build up speed, and could now begin producing strip for Inwald. Tad was irritated that one additional operator, on that steering wheel, had to be employed. He asked Grazynski whether that man couldn't be helping with something else also. By then, Grazynski had lost some of his fear of the "Big Boss." Grazynski came in the next day, after giving the idea some thought, and said, "Give him a broom and tie it to his backside and let him sweep the floor at the same time."

When Tad felt confident with the operation of the mill, he called the directors to come and see for themselves. Inwald, Swiecicki, Absalon and several guests from the steel industry showed up. The guests picked up the sample pieces and found their faces reflected dully back at them. They had never before seen such thin, smooth steel. In fact, the finish was uneven, the surface a bit scratched and pitted—but the paper-thin gauge was a great improvement over a hand-fed mill, and the strip could easily take a layer of zinc. The mill was rolling those three millimeter sheets down to one-third millimeter strip in under twelve passes, without having to anneal it in between. It was, there in that small industrial town in Poland, the first in the world ever to do so. Inwald was ecstatic.

The mill went into full production at once, for Inwald needed all the strip they could roll. After half a year, they would put on three shifts to meet the demand. The mill produced over four hundred tons of strip every month in those first years; with improvements, that total reached one thousand tons a month before the outbreak of the war.

Tad could now turn his full attention to Kostuchna, where workers under a quick and sympathetic foreman named Szewczyk had been building the galvanizing line, and were now waiting impatiently for strip.

*   *   *

Iron plus oxygen becomes iron oxide: the flaky or powdery red substance that eats our cars from the tires up, and returns the aged tractor, abandoned on the edge of the cornfield, to the earth from whence it came. Rust. The strength of iron can be vanquished by the air we breathe, by frank and guileless molecules of oxygen in a moist atmosphere.

Zinc does not react to the air in such a self-defeating manner. As zinc is plentiful on this planet, easy to melt and relatively inexpensive, metal workers discovered long ago that coating iron with a thin layer of zinc (a process called galvanizing) would protect the underlying metal from corrosion. And so were born, or vastly improved, all those sturdy devices of daily life that are called upon to face the elements: roofing, siding, culverts, drain spouts, hay loaders, watering cans, chimney flues, laundry tubs, storage tanks, garbage cans, mail boxes, minnow buckets, manure spreaders...and the many assorted parts of the automobile, from mufflers to rocker panels to under-bodies.

Why not use paint instead? Zinc has more to commend itself for a coating material than mere paint, or even other metals such as tin or lead, which are also sometimes used. Zinc on iron produces what is known as a "cathodic effect." Rusting is an electro-chemical action between iron and oxygen (the term "galvanizing" comes from galvanic currents). When the surface of a galvanized product is scratched and some iron is exposed, the zinc, not the iron next to it, will interact with the oxygen and decompose. The exposed iron won't rust; the neighboring zinc "sacrifices" itself, electro-chemically, instead.

Such magic is limited in scope, and limited further by the tendency zinc has of not binding firmly with the iron. A scratch may be protected, but that zinc could soon begin to chip and peel off. On a galvanized sheet, many micro-thin layers of zinc-iron alloys form between the pure iron and pure zinc; these layers weaken the bond. The less clean the metal surface to begin with, the more alloy layers appear. In the standard galvanizing process, the sheet was pickled first to remove scale and impurities, but then it was left out in open air—even just for a few moments—while waiting to be dipped in the zinc bath. An invisible layer of iron oxide had already formed instantly. Several remedies — adding aluminum to the zinc, spreading a layer of flux of the zinc — had been found, but they only slightly improved the process.

Tad knew the problem was to improve that zinc-iron bond, and he knew the ways and means of fluxes and fumes and the shoddy product they produced. He knew the scope for improvement came in devising a more efficient way to clean, and keep clean, that iron surface. He realized also that the hand-fed operation of dipping the iron sheet into the zinc, even when done by highly skilled operators, could never be as accurate and controllable, or produce as much, as a mechanically operated continuous strip process. But to make it a continuous strip, you had to have that tight bond between the iron and the zinc, because the resulting galvanized strip will face a future of molestation and abuse: it will be hammered into shapes, or unrolled and tacked onto roofs, or cut and riveted into objects—all processes that will chip off the zinc if it's not in a firm embrace with the iron.

And so, between his wire making operations in Shanghai, his thought-filled walks along the Bund, his experiments there and in the United States, his hours of reading in the New York Public Library, and his scribbled designs and formulas on the pages of his small notebook, he came to the essence of the solution: annealing the strip in hydrogen. He could describe it best:

> I preheat the strip in ordinary atmosphere to oxidize it, by putting it over an electric stove. You can see the temperature without measuring, because the metal changes color, from blue, to yellow, to brown. I want to go right up to the brown color, to get steel sheet covered with a microscopic layer of iron oxide, perhaps one ten-thousandths of an inch thick. That's up to about 400 degrees F. The strip is oxidized and degreased, all at the same time.

This preliminary oxidation was a crucial step—but not, as we shall see, for chemical reasons. Tad goes on:

> Then I take it into an airtight box containing the hydrogen atmosphere. I make a little slot for the strip to enter the box, and out of that slot I blow excess hydrogen [so that no air can enter the box]. There it goes up to about 800 degrees, and the iron oxide is reduced. The hydrogen will suck the oxygen from the iron oxide, and make water out of it. (The water stays as water vapor, which I have to pump out through a kind of refrigerator.) And what remains is pure iron. In this place it is soft annealed, by the hydrogen atmosphere at 800 degrees.
>
> Then I make like an elephant's trunk, a long enclosed chute at the end of the compartment and there my strip cools to about 400 degrees, and enters into the galvanizing pot, the molten zinc. The pot of molten zinc is resting on fire bricks, on top of a furnace. You have to melt the zinc before you start, but then you can shut off the furnace, because as the hot strip goes through it keeps the zinc molten, and will also melt the zinc bars you have to add as the zinc is used up. This is another way my process saves costs.
>
> The strip goes into the zinc bath and is wetted, the zinc adheres. It comes out, and I must draw it up quite high. The

zinc must be completely cool and crystallized before the strip touches the pulley above. I draw it out at about three meters per minute. The problem they used to have of drying the sheets without smearing the zinc is eliminated. When the strip is cool, I can either cut it into sheets or coil it up.

Tad's process was faster, cleaner, cheaper—and made a far superior galvanized sheet. "It was so stupidly simple," Bostroem remembered. "And the base material would disintegrate before that zinc would fall off—unheard of!" Not only did Tad's method produce a pure steel surface before the zinc bath, but they could again add aluminum to the zinc for better adherence, since there was no need for the flux. Almost as a by-line, Tad had simultaneously invented "bright annealing." The conventional method of annealing was to slowly heat coils of steel in an enclosed box—a giant, gentle oven—a process that could take a week. With Tad's bright annealing method—the strip passing through the heated hydrogen atmosphere—a coil could be annealed in minutes. The mechanism was the same as for galvanizing, but without the final plunge into molten zinc.

The first step of Tad's galvanizing process, the oxidation, turns out to have been "something of a trick," he confessed to me. During his research in New York, he'd found a 1907 patent from an English inventor, Cowper-Coles, describing a system almost identical to the one Tad had in mind. Cowper-Coles hadn't developed his technique or put it into production, but nonetheless there was the patent: in the way. So Tad decided to create a diversion: "It was spoiling my patents. I couldn't get a royalty. So I have introduced there one step, which was a fictitious step. You could get the results even without it, but everybody repeated it and never changed it. My first step is to heat it, to cover the strip with the thin coat of iron oxide. And then I get into the hydrogen. So my system was based on the fact that you have to first produce a thin iron oxide, and nobody checked to determine if you can get the results without it. (A suit between Armco Steel and US Steel in the 1950s, when US Steel was using Tad's method and Armco—who by then owned the patent—challenged them, hinged on just this point: the oxidation step. US Steel's lawyers would have gone to town with such a confession from the inventor.)

In Poland in 1932, that prior patent was resting quietly in someone's drawer a thousand miles away. Tad had come up with the same inspiration on his own and now was taking it off paper and putting it into production. Many inventions, dreamed up by theoreticians, lie sleeping in the files until someone with an entrepreneurial bent has the will to wake them up and get them to perform. This trick was the only way Tad could see to do that.

*　*　*

The galvanizing process may have been "stupidly simple," but building the first production line in Kostuchna was not. Inwald had given over to Tad one large hall of the long and low brick building where the sheet galvanizing work had been done. A sign reading "Cynkownia Sendzimir" (Sendzimir Zinc Works) was placed over one door. The foreman who ran the old operation was a tall, muscular fellow in his early thirties, Szewczyk, who knew his galvanizing, Inwald flew in and out, fanning the experiment with his wings of authority and enthusiasm. "Inwald was everywhere where you needed him," Tad remembered.

The line was one hundred twenty feet in length. The annealing furnace was a long steel box lined with fire bricks. To save time Tad decided to fit the bricks together dry, without mortar, which would have taken months to become completely dry (not a molecule of water vapor could remain in the unit).

Tad's next problem was finding a source of hydrogen gas. Hydrogen could be bought in high pressure tanks, but it was expensive, potentially dangerous, and always contained a tiny bit of water vapor. "Here again my knowledge of chemistry proved very beneficial," he boasted. "I looked into synthetic ammonia, the foul-smelling gas that is three-quarters hydrogen, one-quarter nitrogen. I needed the two gases separately, and here I remembered my studies of the General Electric experiments. They had built an apparatus for splitting ammonia into the two parent gases, called the 'ammonia dissociator.' I found out later how they did it, but then I had to experiment on my own. I took a steel tube, filled it with iron filings and heated it electrically to a high temperature. All the ammonia smell disappeared, which meant that the two gases were completely split. With this last problem solved, I was ready to start as soon as I got the strip."

The strip came, finally, from Huta Pokoj. The start-up took place without incident, and the line was soon producing a smooth, wide strip glittering with the icy spangle of zinc. Inwald put his rolls immediately on the market, where they caused a minor sensation in the building trades. Rooftops across Poland began to sport these wide galvanized strips, so much easier to unroll and tack down than the short, narrow sheets. Tad and Inwald's *coup de maitre* came with the refurbishment of Krakow's famous Sukiennice (Cloth Hall), the fourteenth-century covered market which yawns and stretches across the city's central square. The 328-foot-long roof was given a new robe of Sendzimir's galvanized strip.

Inwald's brother began selling the coils to Switzerland; roofs in Zurich were soon being draped in galvanized strip from Poland. The fame of the strip reached the ears of the Polish government, ever on the lookout for a local success story; President Moscicki, with a bevy of reporters, came down to Kostuchna for an official visit. He had been a professor of physical chemistry before taking office, so he knew the mess and smell of galvanizing the old way. "This isn't a zinc factory," he exclaimed when he saw Tad's operation, "it's a sanitorium!"

A photograph survives of this official inspection. Moscicki, a tall, white-haired man in a heavy coat with fur collar, is standing and talking to Tad while they look into the zinc pot. Tad is turned toward Moscicki, listening seriously, his profile showing his signature sloping forehead and nose, his tiny brush moustache. Standing respectfully behind him is a handsome young man who was in charge of the line that day, wearing a suit and tie, and thick leather gloves—Kasimir Oganowski.

Inwald had hired Kaz Oganowski a few months before, directly after his military service, to oversee production as plant engineer. The galvanizing line needed someone to keep it running. Oganowski consulted with Tad when Tad dropped in, usually once a day, but otherwise managed by himself. Tad wasn't satisfied, however, to leave things be. He wanted to try the method on aluminum coating, and tin plate, and perhaps brass. As the production unit couldn't be shut down for such experiments, Oganowski built a small laboratory line, working on strip about four inches wide.

Tad's process was not without limitations. Many articles needing galvanizing, such as pipe elbows and heavy equipment pieces, still had to be dipped in zinc one by one. Materials with a high alloy content, which contain oxides that are difficult to reduce, could not be used. Steel with severe scale on its surface needed additional treatment before it could be put through this system. The galvanized strip from Tad's method was very slightly more rigid than steel galvanized in sheets. Finally, Tad's process tolerated no slacking off: it required care and precision to operate (a characteristic feature of each of Tad's major inventions). Swiecicki built the second production galvanizing line at his plant in Warsaw, but the quality of his strip was never as good as what was coming from Kostuchna, because he didn't pay enough attention to his leaky furnace. This goose demanded pampering or she wouldn't lay those galvanized eggs.

Nevertheless, word was making its way across Europe by 1934 that a quite revolutionary product was coming off that small line deep in...where? Poland!? Don't they only make ham in Poland? Such might have been the thoughts of Bob Solborg, vice president and general manager of the Paris office of Armco International, the international branch of Armco Steel of Middletown, Ohio. Solborg was a short, stocky man who paid careful attention to the cut of his cravat. He also happened to be my mother's boss. Solborg figured that since his firm's specialty was coated steel sheet, he ought to catch a train to Katowice and find out what those Poles were up to.

CHAPTER SEVEN

MIDDLETOWN, PARIS

1935 - 1939

Tad was celebrating his fortieth birthday in 1934, when his efforts of the preceeding four years began to receive notice beyond the rooftops of Silesia and Poland. At forty, his career was about to accelerate into the global arena. This development was surprising to Tad only in that it had taken so long—twenty dry and frustrating years had passed since he left the Lwow Polytechnic. At last, no more drafty car repair shops, no more sweltering nail factories, no more big shots breaking off appointments or laughing at his ideas. The name Sendzimir, by the end of the decade, was enough to open doors in the steel industry (even if just from curiosity) across the industrialized world. The galvanizing process put that name on the map; the rolling mill, as he developed it over the next fifteen years, put that name in every text book.

The first notice came from France. A small steel maker in the town of Maubeuge, Joseph de Beco, had heard about Tad's remarkable galvanized sheets and was interested in producing the same. He called his friend and confidante in Paris, Bob Solborg of Armco International, and asked him to come with him to Poland to see this new invention. De Beco wanted Solborg's advice; Solborg was himself interested, for his U.S. parent company, Armco, did a heavy business in light coated steel.

Solborg and de Beco came to Kostuchna in the summer of 1934.

De Beco, a man who did not need time to think things over, signed a contract with Tad at once. Tad was to install a mill and galvanizing line at De Beco's factory, Fabrique de Fer de Maubeuge, in the coal mining region close to the Belgian border. Solborg cabled his report on the new material to Armco's office in Middletown, Ohio, and got a return wire asking him to send five tons of galvanized strip over for testing. Solborg also spread the news to the British steel company John Summers & Sons, an affiliate of Armco. Summers sent Kenneth Younghusband out for a look, and soon another mill and galvanizing line were in the works for the Summers plant in Shotton, south of Liverpool near the Welsh border, where England's steel belt meets the Irish Sea.

Armco's research lab in Middletown found the strip they received from Tad superior not only to their own galvanized sheet, but to any other sheet on the market. It was imperative that Armco sign up this Pole before one of their competitors did. Solborg arranged for Tad to come to Middletown in early 1935.

*   *   *

In the winter of 1935, a note in the appointment book of George Verity, the founder of Armco, is said to have read, "Today I met a very interesting Polish engineer. His name is difficult to remember, but it sounds like 'Send him here,' and they did!"

George Verity had himself started up a very interesting company, to make rolled steel, thirty-five years before. Verity was one of the first to think of controlling the quality and supply of his raw material by cooking it up himself instead of buying steel ingots from a supplier. His operation began with an open hearth furnace, a bar mill, four sheet mills, a galvanizing plant and a factory for making sheet metal products. When the American Rolling Mill Company poured its first heat of steel in Middletown in 1901, Verity was in the business almost from soup to nuts: the addition of just a blast furnace would have made Armco the world's first fully-integrated steel plant.

Verity also saw the need to control and promote technological progress: Armco was the first (and for a long time only) steel mill with its own research lab. Over the years, Armco developed more grades of flat-rolled steel and stainless steel alloys than all the other domestic steel companies combined. Armco made its name on its innovative products and processes. There was the special-purpose electrical grade steel Armco developed with Westinghouse for the nascent electrical industry; and Armco Ingot Iron, Armco's most famous product, a 99.84% pure iron that's almost rust-proof. It was used around the world for culverts and other highway construction products; Tad saw the material even in Shanghai.

The spirit of innovation, the specialization in electrical and corrosion-resistant steels, the relatively small size of the firm—all made Armco a salutary match for Tad. A far different scenario might have taken place had Tad been lured to Pittsburgh instead of Middletown.

Tad was greeted at the Cincinnati train station by Earl Emerson, the debonair middle-aged president of Armco International. The small city of Middletown lay an hour's drive north, on the flat eastern bank of the Greater Miami river. On the road through southwestern Ohio's low hills—draped, in those cold winter days, in corn stubble under snow—Emerson chatted with Tad in French about Armco's history and present position. The first years of the Depression had been tough, but there had been an upturn in 1933 due to the relatively steady (and steadily growing) demand for light, flat-rolled steel. They projected that sales that year, 1935, could be higher even than in 1929, before the Crash. On their way into town, Emerson pointed out the construction under way at Armco's new and expanding Eastside Works, a growing agglomeration of blast furnaces and giant, windowless, expressionless buildings spreading across a flat plain to the south and east of the city. Emerson drove through town to show Tad Armco's main offices and some smaller finishing operations still housed nearby, stretched down either side of tree-lined Curtis Street. Before dropping Tad at the hotel, he pointed out a building an American might have mistaken for the local high school: the white columned, three-story brick structure with its wide steps was Armco's General Office building.

The difference between Tad's reception at Armco in 1935, and his factory visits in the U.S. in 1930, when he was an unknown, is as day to night. "I was received by Armco very graciously," he recalled. "They invited me all over. They wanted me to stay with them, to become a member of the Armco family. It flattered me. Here were people who wanted to have my cooperation."

Tad gleaned from his tour of Armco that the executives he was about to face were running a fairly healthy company that was eager to stay ahead of the flock. His galvanizing process could guarantee their lead in coated sheet. Their backing, in turn, could guarantee him the financial security to pursue his other ideas, especially his cold rolling mill. But he knew that his position was far from secure: "Forty years old is still young for a businessman to face a large company. Armco had a good reputation. They were not trying to cheat me. But still I was all alone and I had to make an agreement with them. I was a little bit scared. I had only my own senses to protect me, my own brains; I was my own lawyer."

But Tad ran into luck. When he met the head of Armco's legal department, Ed Correa, they took to one another as if they'd shared a tent in the last war. They were very much alike. Correa was a handsome man, a charming and sophisticated lawyer, born in Colombia and educated in Europe. Their close ties—business and personal—lasted till the end of Correa's life in the early 1980s. When Tad climbed the granite steps and entered the General Office for his meeting with Armco's executives—George Verity, Charlie Hook (Verity's son-in-law, who was then president), Dr. Anson Hayes (Director of Research), and Calvin Verity (Vice President and son of George)—Correa was there as Armco's lawyer, but also as Tad's ally.

The one stumbling block to Tad's success came in the form of what was then the company's pride and joy: the world's first continuous hot strip mill. This mill, developed in 1925, was perhaps the most revolutionary innovation in steel technology since the open-hearth furnace; it was to steel what the cotton gin was to cloth (and what, ironically, Tad's galvanizing line was to coated steel sheet.) John Butler Tytus, whose family was in the paper business (Middletown's other big industry) had watched how paper was made on a series of adjoining mills. He applied the concept to the hot rolling of steel. Tytus came up with a process where a continuous strip traveled the length of a football field through ten individual stands of mills, each rolling faster than the one before as the strip grew thinner and longer.

At that moment, Tad was not in the business of hot rolling steel (he only stepped into that field, with his planetary mill, in the early 1940s); he had only his galvanizing line and his cold rolling mill. But the Tytus mill, or, rather, the mill's inventor (high in Armco's hierarchy) stood nonetheless in his path: Armco was not interested in any new mill that might take the spotlight away from Tytus' hot mill. They were keenly interested in Tad's galvanizing process; they were keenly uninterested in his mill. The issue at the negotiations became what to do with that mill—and what to do with Tad.

Tad came to Armco at a time when the work of inventing was shifting out of the hands of the lone, independent genius, and into company-run research labs, stocked like ponds with specialized (and all but anonymous) scientists and engineers. Technology was getting too complex for isolated individuals to master alone. And large companies realized—as George Verity had—that there was profit in performing and controlling their own research. Big business began to swallow up young inventors, who were seldom heard from again.

Tad managed to avoid this. Simply, he was not one to be swallowed, and Armco was too near-sighted to appreciate all he had to offer. Instead, they cut a deal: Armco got the galvanizing, Tad got the money and his independence. He signed over to Armco all rights to the patents—for galvanizing *and* for the cold rolling mill. He was to get royalty payments of forty cents on each ton of galvanized sheet produced (a quite generous sum). But Armco didn't really want his mill, so a separate company (later called Armzen) was established to develop and exploit the mill. Armco owned 51% of it, Tad 49%. In this way, Tad got help and resources for his mill, and the freedom to go off on his own with it, as Armco was a decidedly lax partner. Finally, Armco International was to sell licenses for Tad's galvanizing on the world market (with royalties also going to Tad), and Tad would set up his own operation in Paris in the Armco offices.

This young and relatively inexperienced Pole was able to claim, for the rest of his life, that he had walked into the offices of this American steel giant and walked out with everything he asked for. "I could have taken my galvanizing to one of their competitors. They had to take the whole package as my condition," he would boast. Pride and short-sightedness turned Armco's executives away from what Tad later developed into an industry leader. But Armco turned Tad's galvanizing into an industry leader, and left Tad behind. He got the fortune, but little of the fame.

* * *

During the next twelve months Armco engineers visited Poland, tests were run, and memos criss-crossed the Atlantic. It is interesting to note, in light of Tad's habit in later years of making grandiose claims about his inventions, that in these early days his attitude seemed to be quite humble. Bob Solborg mentioned in one memo that it wasn't "absolutely necessary to verify and check Sendzimir's statements, as we have not found them to be unduly optimistic, nor colored, in our experience with him so far." Tad was being careful to tread lightly on the not yet solidified foundation of his reputation.

Armco wanted Tad to come to the U.S. to get their first galvanizing line started, but Tad was busy with the Shotton and Maubeuge rolling mills. He suggested that Armco take instead the bright young engineer who was running the Kostuchna line, Kaz Oganowski. Oganowski arrived in Middletown in March 1936. He came with an armful of drawings and the several dozen words in English he'd gained command of on the boat ride over.

The new line was to go into Armco's factory in Butler, a small city in the hills of western Pennsylvania. In that plant Armco was already producing light cold-rolled coils of steel, which now sat waiting for their skin of zinc. Oganowski settled into a hotel, and went each day (and many nights) for four months to work with the crew. They too had trouble making the furnace air-tight. Finally in July it seemed to be holding.

That first line cost ten times what Tad had originally estimated (over $110,000, instead of $11,000). But Armco and their customers were thrilled with the strip. Armco named the material "Zincgrip."

They began using it to make their "Hel-Cor" pipe (helical corrugated metal pipe, as used in culverts), and so produced a cleaner, higher luster, and more easily made pipe at almost half the cost. Armco's sales department sent samples to their customers—makers of gutters, downspouts, roofing, structural sections, tubular radio aerials, steel rolling doors, playground equipment—and all asked to switch to Zincgrip immediately. Armco sold Zincgrip as far away as Uruguay: several thousand tons to be made into locust barriers.

Oganowski moved from Butler to Middletown to set up an experimental galvanizing line in the new, modernistic research building in 1937. Armco wanted to test other coating materials, and to establish the basis for the U.S. patents, which were granted in 1938 and 1940 (in Tad Sendzimir's name, but owned by Armco). Armco made significant improvements in the process.[Appendix, 1] More lines were built in the 1940s and '50s, in Butler, in Middletown, and in Ashland, Kentucky. And Armco began selling licenses to other U.S. steel producers for use of the process.[Appendix, 2] By the 1960s, lines licensed by Armco were common world-wide.

Armco became the domestic leader in continuous galvanizing. The boom in sales came only after 1945; the few years before the war were a developmental stage, and during the war tonnage was controlled by the government. (Nevertheless, the Army ate its share of strip, in Quonset huts at least. A company in Tennessee sent Zincgrip into battle in the form of five-gallon gas cans attached to every Army vehicle.) After the war, the Sendzimir process blew open the field of applications for galvanized steel. One retired Armco employee is convinced that his company would have gone under in the early 1980s steel slump if not for its coating business. In 1988, Armco alone sold 620,000 tons of hot dip galvanized strip. (Of course, the patents had expired and Tad was no longer receiving forty cents on each of those tons.)

In the 1990s, a modern galvanizing line bears as much resemblance to the simple steel furnace box Tad built in Poland as a Harley-Davidson does to a bicycle. But at its core you will find the same physical and chemical process. For five decades, Oganowski and the engineers in Armco Research continued to make improvements.

Oganowski started twenty-two galvanizing lines across the globe, won several awards, and eventually became Director of Coating Research.

After signing the idea over to Armco in 1935, and designing their first line and a couple of lines in Europe, Tad had little to do with it. He made one or two trips to the U.S. between 1935 and 1939, and while there he consulted with Oganowski occasionally. Tad's time and thoughts were bent instead on the cold rolling mill—improving it, selling it, and establishing a business with it in Europe and America.

His contribution to galvanizing is acknowledged and respected. He received the Golden Cross of Merit in Poland in 1938, the Bronze Plaque for Fundamental Achievement in Galvanizing from the American Zinc Institute in 1949, and the Bablik Gold Medal from the International Zinc Institute in Paris in 1964. People in the business know his name. Still, that name is attached only to his rolling mills. In textbooks and dictionaries, in the technical literature, you read about "Sendzimir mills," not the "Sendzimir galvanizing method." (In Europe, however, they do call it the "Sendzimir Process.") No one thought to call it "Sendzimirizing."

Tad could certainly have been more active. Armco didn't close its doors; Oganowski didn't refuse his calls. I believe there are several reasons why he did not pursue it (although he kept playing with galvanizing ideas for the rest of his life). First, Tad was always more of a mechanical engineer than a chemist—he liked machines better. Second, the galvanizing was on its way. He sold to Armco a complete and self-contained process, which Armco showed great enthusiasm and ability to develop. They didn't need him—his baby would survive in their nursery. The mill, on the other hand, was barely out of the incubator. It *did* need him. It was something to grasp, develop, and make his name on. It was still a challenge.

*　　*　　*

The large, modern steel plant in Shotton, England, sat in the mud flats of the River Dee, three miles up from Liverpool Bay. The surrounding countryside supported farmland, leading off in one direction to Wales, in the other to the ancient town of Chester. The building in which Tad's cold mill and galvanizing line were to be installed was a new one, all steel and glass like a hangar—a far cry from that dilapidated brick shed in Poland.

Tad spent many hours in that building, and in the home of Kenneth Younghusband, as well as in the company of Henry Summers, son of the founder and at that time the firm's aging chairman. Summers' basement had been transformed into a clock factory, and there H.S. spent much of his time hand-building clocks in graceful wooden cases. While this elder Summers may have received Tad just as gracefully, he was less so about Tad's mill and its problems. At one point H.S. wrote a memo saying the whole thing should be shut down: "We cannot have our key men wasting their time on a machine which does not possess the first essentials of any kind of success."

Work nonetheless continued. Younghusband's daughter Frances remembers Tad's stay, and what her father told her about the struggle with the mill (as she related in a letter to me):

> ...the installation was not without its problems...and half the time your father was sitting on the floor inventing modifications and making drawings as the need arose; feelings were torn, I think, between awe and respect for his genius, and amusement—and some exasperation—at his personal foibles.

Exasperation was one of the emotions Stanislaw Grazynski felt on that site, the others being anger and despair. He had been sent over from Katowice to install and start up the mill. He does not remember Tad "sitting on the floor inventing modifications." Far from it. After Grazynski had been in Shotton for about a month, working with engineers in a language he could barely understand, the mill was ready. With an audience of twenty, Grazynski started the mill. Tad was at the controls. The strip began moving, and almost immediately started to drift to the left. Grazynski warned Tad, who shouted back impatiently for him to continue. In one second, the strip crashed into the side of the mill.

"You should have seen my face." Grazynski told me. "I felt a hundred times worse than an 'ulan' [a Polish cavalry officer] when he falls off his horse. Then I said, 'Mr. Director, I think I will now dismantle the machine and take a look.' Mr. Sendzimir said, 'Yes, yes, that's OK.' He went off to the telephone, and everyone left. He came back in a few minutes and said to me, 'Mr. Grazynski, I'm in a hurry, I must go to Paris. I trust you can find a way out.' And he left. Well, it was like the general, who had just lost the battle, had given over command to the corporal."

In three days Grazyinski found a solution. The mill began rolling in earnest by early 1937 to everyone's relief. Among other things, the forty-inch wide steel strip was used in the construction of air raid shelters during the war.

The mill at Maubeuge had far fewer problems, but Bostroem, who had been dispatched to France by Tad, had to build the facility from the mud up. "It was just a marsh," Bostroem remembered. "Water hens were running on the terrain where we put the mill." The mill itself started up without difficulty. Grazynski came over to train operators, and Bostroem moved down to work in Tad's Paris office. The Sendzimir Division became the pride of Fabrique de Fer de Maubeuge. Another mill for the plant was in the design stages when the war started, but the town of Maubeuge was erased from the map by Hitler's bombs.

Both the Shotton and Maubeuge mills had been built by Schmitz in Dusseldorf, larger but of the same design as the mill in Poland. Schmitz built two additional mills before the war. One, for Swiecicki's factory near Warsaw, was never delivered; the mill housing was used as a bomb shelter in Dusseldorf during the war. The second went to another Armco licensee in France, the firm Chatillon, Commentry & Neuves-Maisons, which specialized in alloy steel in Isbergues, near Dunkirk. The Isbergues mill was the first of the second generation of Sendzimir cold mills: Tad made the work rolls smaller, and introduced another set of rolls—two intermediate rolls between the single work rolls and the four backing bearings, which gave his mill the first real appearance as a "cluster" mill. The set of intermediate rolls improved the performance of the mill, and eliminated a mild streaking problem on the strip. (This mill is classified, in the nomenclature developed for Sendzimir mills, as a 1-2-4 mill: one work roll, two intermediate rolls, four sets of backing bearings, top and bottom. Over the next ten years, various configurations of 1-2-3 and 1-2-4 mills were built, when finally the best combination proved to be that of 1-2-3-4, the classic Sendzimir cold mill. After 1950, almost no other variety was built.)

The Isbergues mill was also the first of Tad's mills to be a "reversing mill:" it used winders (large spools) on either side of the mill to feed out and take up the strip. Abandoned at last was the elaborate, elongating loop of strip Tad (alone) had been so fond of on his first three mills, and which had caused all those steering problems. The strip in the Isbergues mill wound and unwound neatly between its spools. It strayed neither left nor right.

*   *   *

"When Poland became too narrow, too cramped for my inventions, I set out into the world," Tad told a group of Polish scientists in 1983. He was referring to 1935, when he moved his base of operations to Paris.

Tad had come several times for business discussions to Armco International's office, in the Seventeenth Arrondissement near Place Pereire. On one such trip he set out on foot through the neighborhood to find a place to live, and soon was introducing himself to the concierge of a small apartment building. This district, to the north of the Arc de Triomphe, was once an assemblage of small, narrow-front private homes of respectable but diverse description. Their middle class occupants would tell each other they were "going down to Paris" on the old railway line. Then the Metro was built and Paris came to them. The neighborhood's tranquility drew an influx of artists, who were gradually driven out by rising rents, their domains taken up by company offices and government departments. Armco moved in 1932 to Avenue Gourgaud. The secretaries lingered by the windows to catch a glimpse of Maurice Chevalier when he came to see one of his mistresses who lived across the street.

From his small apartment Tad could walk to the Armco office, or over to and up the tree-lined Champs Elysees. Paris was still a city of the eighteenth and nineteenth centuries, a city of old-fashioned facades and street lights—its cheeks rouged with few neon signs, its hair pinned up with no skyscrapers except the Eiffel Tower. Modern times were just starting to encroach, the mansions along the Champs Elysees one by one were being replaced by noisy clubs and brightly lit movie houses. For his evening walks, Tad preferred the crowded avenues near the city center, around the Opera. Sometimes he'd go as far as the Ile St. Louis and visit the Hotel Lambert. This seventeenth-century mansion had been bought by Prince Adam Czartoryski, who in 1834 organized in its grand rooms the unofficial Polish government in exile. (The Hotel Lambert became synonymous with the aristocratic, not to mention artistic, wing of nineteenth-century Polish emigration; both Adam Mickiewicz and Frederick Chopin spent time there. The Polish Literary and Historical Society, which Tad joined, established itself around the corner.)

Tad's first office was in an atelier, near Armco International, where he set up drafting tables and his desk. Soon he moved into larger quarters at the Armco office, with Bostroem and a small staff.

Tad spent much of his time traveling from one mill site to another—over to Shotton, up to Maubeuge or Dusseldorf, back to Katowice. In Poland, he cut quite a figure now: the successful inventor, driving up to the Huta Pokoj plant in his large French Berliet. ("He had a passion for convertibles," his son Michael remembers.) Grazynski, in a letter to me, recalled the impression Tad made: "At times, Sendzimir would dress eccentrically, drawing the attention of the children near the plant. He wore a long, rust-colored fur coat, leather gloves of the same color, and smoked thin yellow cigars. The coat made a big impression because he wore it with the fur on the outside. In Poland only women, or mountain men from Zakopane, wore their coats like that then."

Tad's energies in Paris were devoted mainly to improving his inventions, both those under construction on the ground and those under construction in his head. He also managed the business aspects, with the help of Armco International, which paid him a salary as well as royalties. He was on good terms with most of the American officials there: Earl Emerson, who came over from the States to visit both the office and his mistress in town; Bob Solborg, the vice-president, and Hal Pape, Solborg's assistant. Tad's closest friend was Paul Parent, who ran Armco's French subsidiary. He was the son of the master of a French foundry. "Paul had iron in his veins," Tad remembered fondly. "He just loved to argue for argument's sake, but his friendship gave me a lot. When we traveled together to visit our French customers, he told me about France and French food and French customs."

Armco International was supplying auto body sheets to Renault and Citroen, through its French licensees, as well as selling silicon sheets (for transformers) and a variety of machinery, from huge continuous hot mills to motor boats and washing machines. In addition, they eventually realized that they had to keep an eye on Sendzimir. This, Armco in Middletown believed, was a full-time job. For it they sent over Alexander Saharoff, son of a Russian clergyman who'd been educated in America, a tall, humorless, self-made man fluent in engineering and five languages. "Armco didn't quite trust me," Tad explained, "so Saharoff was sent to check if the mills I built would be working, to see if anything from the angle of engineering was not correct. Nobody ever told me, and if I thought they had sent someone to watch over me, I would have cried bloody murder."

But Saharoff's criticisms were pointed and accurate. They will echo throughout Tad's career. From Tad's own notes: "They claim my promises to customers are too far reaching." Other criticisms included "Non-practical engineers," "Poor management," "Not enough thought given to suggestions." Clearly Armco had something to worry about.

* * *

"Tad was considered kind of wild," Bostroem recalled, "and Armco thought they should send Saharoff to tame him. So they sent Saharoff to tame Sendzimir, and instead of taming Sendzimir, he fell in love with Sendzimir's wife." (Barbara, just as untamable as her husband, did fall in love with Saharoff, but only much later. They were married in the 1950s.)

Barbara would come to Paris, from her home in Zakopane, for

weeks at a time. By 1937, Michael was in boarding school in Switzerland.

Zakopane had become passe, so Barbara settled into Tad's apartment. It was she who chose the elegant furniture there. (But it was he who chose, and designed himself, his hand-crafted desk. Its sides were vertical sheets of stainless steel, supporting a polished walnut top.) Barbara and Tad lived together, so to speak, and maintained the air of a respectable married couple, but supper conversation over the fat French cheeses must have been lean. Tad was frequently out of town.

On trips back to Poland, Tad would visit his mother in Krakow and take her to concerts. On one such trip, in 1938, Tad brought Vanda up to Warsaw. He had been summoned by President Moscicki. In a private ceremony in the Presidential Palace overlooking the Vistula river, Moscicki presented Tad with the Golden Cross of Merit for his galvanizing invention. The memory of this must have comforted Vanda during the difficult years ahead, the last years of her life, in that labor camp in Kazakstan—her famous son, so far away. Safe.

Michael was in school in Switzerland. His relationship with his father remained close. Tad would take the day's drive from Paris to visit him, or Michael would come to the city by train on holidays. Tad was notorious even then for, as one person put it, his "nerve-wracking genius for arriving at the very last second to catch a train or plane." Kola Alferieff remembered Tad depositing him and Michael on an already moving train: "Tad was very particular about not wasting any time. He would always come at the very last moment so as not to waste even the last five minutes at the station."

*   *   *

With the slightest encouragement, Berthe Sendzimir, my mother, will tell anyone the story of what happened when she first met Tad. Berthe Madeline Bernoda was Bob Solborg's young and very capable secretary. One day a tall and dignified Polish engineer came into the office to see her boss. In perfect French delivered with a thick Slavic accent, like a croissant washed down with a ladle of borscht, he introduced himself as Tadeusz Sendzimir. She already knew who he was. Solborg had been talking about him, and she had typed reports by Armco engineers who had visited Poland. She asked him to please take a seat. While Tad waited for his appointment, Berthe had trouble keeping her eyes on her work.

For the next few weeks—this was before he had his own office— Tad spent a lot of time at Armco, and even occupied one table in Berthe's office. They spoke to each other politely. Once in a while he would give her a blueprint and ask what she thought of it (she had never studied a blueprint in her life). Outside of work, she talked of little else. One day she was walking with her father in the Bois de Boulogne, and her father said, "Who is this Tad Sendzimir? You can't stop talking about him." And the words that came from her mouth shocked them both: "You know, I think someday I'm going to marry him."

She was immediately horrified by what she'd said. Tad was twenty years older (she was twenty-two at the time). He was married and had a son. The idea was absurd. And so it seemed for the next five years, when Tad on just one or two evenings took Berthe, along with one of the other secretaries, out for a meal. He would occasionally bring her flowers or a box of chocolates. Nothing more. (He himself remembered little of this; she says oh yes, even then he was aware that she was somebody.) Nothing more...until much later, after the war began, when these two Europeans found themselves in the small and very American city of Middletown, Ohio.

Berthe Bernoda could have been an atomic scientist. As a child she was fascinated by the work at the Pasteur Institute; she had the drive, the keen intelligence and the love of learning that could have gotten her in. But her family didn't have the money for an academic high school. When she was finished with grammar school, her father said she must attend the public high school that trained young girls in accounting and secretarial skills. She must learn to earn her keep.

She could have become a top executive in a company. She left the business school one year early and got a job at Armco at sixteen in the typing pool. In four years, at twenty-one, she was already secretary to the boss. She was not the kind to have made it into that position by any means but skill. She was pretty, but in a simple, even severe way; her clothes modest and plain, her long black hair pulled back and tied, her lips thin and barely painted. Only her very round and very warm brown eyes softened the image of this strait-laced French girl. But French girls weren't then taking over large businesses, especially as the Code Napoleon still forbade women to have bank accounts, to buy or sell property, or to travel without their father's or husband's consent. She couldn't have risen much higher. And she wasn't given to questioning that.

When she eventually married Tad in 1945, she left behind the chance to use those skills or to develop that potential (more of a possibility in the U.S. than in France). But while her professional training went to waste, her psychological conditioning more than adequately prepared her for what was to come. With certain critical differences, her father and her husband were cut from the same cloth. With only four years of independence in between, she jumped from domination by one to domination by the other.

George Bernoda also had craved schooling, but had gotten very little of it on the farm where he was raised. When he fled the army after a fight, he wound up in Paris, around 1900, and cadged a job in a pharmacy. He made his living as a pharmacist until he was laid off in the Depression. He married my grandmother, Madeleine, who was working in a candy shop, in 1911. Their daughter Berthe was born two years later.

Berthe's only taste of home rule came in her first six years. The First World War took her father off into the army, and he soon was taken prisoner in Germany. Berthe ruled the house until she was six; when her father returned from the war he very quickly let her know who was in charge. And he *was* in charge. He supervised every purchase with the eye of a French tax collector—no unauthorized items of clothing; one pair of shoes was enough every couple of years, no books (he read the paper every day but never books). He taught her to read in two weeks flat, using the back of his hand, when she had to get into a new school for first grade. If she came in other than first in her class, she'd get a drubbing. When she was older, he never allowed her to go to the theater or cinema, and rarely even to dinner with friends.

Her mother put up with all this. George was handsome, intelligent, she sweet and meek, and she loved him. But she put up with even more. His stern disciplinarian ways fell by the wayside, every day, on the way to the tracks. He gambled—obstinately, fruitlessly, incessantly. He used up all his own money, all the household money that Madeleine didn't hide away, and, when she died when Berthe was twenty, he went right on (he was unemployed by then) and gambled away Berthe's earnings.

Berthe remembers being furious at her mother's weakness, at how her mother would suffer from his verbal and psychological abuse, and cry about it only in private, to her. "Why don't you *tell* him? Why do you let him do this to you?" she would scold. But when Madeleine died, Berthe filled her place without a word. She also loved him. She also found him fascinating. From when she was very young they would take long walks together in the parks of Paris. George would point out flowers and trees in the woods, which he seemed to know everything about. Though Berthe recognized and suffered from his faults, she remained devoted, and unwilling to escape.

Perhaps Berthe did not subconsciously seek out Tad's tyrannical habits. But in the way an alchoholic's daughter will find herself married to one, being comfortable and familiar with the patterns, Berthe was comfortable and familiar with living under the thumb of a very intelligent and strong-willed man. She was comfortable being dictated to. Tad seemed to her, in fact, to be the exact opposite of George, (and in this one sense it is true): Tad had stability. He did not gamble. That for Berthe made all the difference.

Of her parents, Berthe remembers: "He was like an island. But she was a very warm person, very sweet." I can say exactly the same of mine.

What Tad saw in Berthe was most certainly that warmth, which came from her heart like his mother. How different from the brand of warmth—the manipulative flirtatiousness—of Barbara, which had captivated, struck him down and embittered him a decade before.

Both women were attractive and intelligent, but just as Tad was not a gambler, Berthe was not a flirt. That for Tad made all the difference. Did Tad also realize that he could dominate Berthe as he could not Barbara? Probably he did, over the course of their courtship in Middletown, and that too set his reluctance, his enmity, toward women, in this one exception to the rule, aside.

*   *   *

Tad enjoyed his stint in Paris. He remembered those years, 1935 to 1939, with fondness. Lwow and Kiev were more familiar to a Slav, Shanghai more exotic; but his subsequent homes in Ohio, Connecticut and Florida pale miserably in comparison to the City of Light. Professionally, however, Mohammed had to go to the mountain. The United States steel industry was like a great lump of iron tugging from across the Atlantic on Tad's tiny magnet. He made the trip by boat at least twice in those years. And while he denied that it affected his inchoate plans for moving to the U.S., the atmosphere of hatred, fear and belligerence that was spreading over Europe made America all the more alluring. By the late 1930s, talk of war could not be ignored.

In Poland, on his frequent visits, Tad heard the terrified tones in the press and in conversation. The Poles had as much if not more to fear from Germany's rearmament as the French did. Poland's government was more stable than that of France, due simply to the work Pilsudski had done tearing away most of the constitutional power for the executive branch. The result was a near-totalitarian and militaristic state that Latin American generals might well have used later as a model. Another result was that when opposition parties were curtailed in Parliament, the tensions between the Polish Catholics and the country's large minority populations were forced out into the streets. Anti-Semitic groups, with national stature and acceptance, began violent attacks on the Jewish communities.

Tad was disgusted by such violence, even if his sympathies lay with the Poles. His anti-Semitism was as drilled in and doctrinaire as anyone's from the Polish nobility (and as unremitting: even as an old and otherwise tolerant man he would speak of a person as "That

Jew...," with a slight curl of the lip, and perfect naivete). But his Jewish business acquaintances were truly friends, and bloodshed was not for him a solution to the "Jewish problem."

Tad was in Dusseldorf in 1933 when the Nazis burned down the Reichstag in Berlin. National elections were to take place a week later; Hitler's troops were staging mass rallies, bonfires and torchlight parades across the country. While in Dusseldorf, Tad read in the newspaper about the fighting that broke out in the city between the Nazis and the Communists. Within a few months the fighting, along with all opposition, ceased. The courageous were on their way to concentration camps. Tad grew more and more fearful on his trips across Germany, between Paris and Poland: "Sometimes I went by train, and I remember how I was with boys, eighteen or twenty years old, and you could see that if they could they would murder everybody. They wanted war. Near the frontier those Germans, you saw them, they were just like wolves."

In the autumn of 1938, Tad visited his mother in Ligota, in Silesia. She had moved there from Krakow to live with Terenia and her husband and two children. The family also had a small cottage in the mountains, in the village of Rabka. Tad urged Vanda to move there if war broke out; he felt they would be safer among the Polish peasants than in a city. Terenia's husband, however, wanted the family to get as far away from the German border as possible. In late August 1939, Terenia and Vanda and the children moved east, back to Lwow, figuring the Germans would never get that far. What they couldn't have figured on was the document signed that very same week: the German-Soviet Non-aggression Pact. Lwow and all of eastern Poland was being deeded over to Stalin.

In March 1939, Tad took Michael on a spring vacation to the Cote d'Azur. Tad remembered the conflicting moods of the French vacationers: "There was news that Hitler had made a conciliatory speech, and everybody was happy and gay. Two days later there was a new speech with an ultimatum to the Czechs, and you could see everybody on the beach was sad."

When he returned to Paris, a week later, he found a telegram from Chicago waiting for him. The Signode Steel Strapping Company agreed to order a Sendzimir cold rolling mill. During his trips to the United States, Tad had been casting among steel manufacturers, trying to interest them in his mill. This was the first bite. The mill was to be built by United Engineering in Pittsburgh; Tad would have to come at once to finish the designs and oversee production. He was very excited about this breakthrough, and not at all unhappy to leave Paris, which was flooding with refugees and defeatism.

Tad arrived in the United States in May. He stayed a few days in New York to visit the just-opened World's Fair ("Poland had a very nice pavilion," he remembered above anything else, "and a monument of King Jagiello on a horse."). Then he took a train to Pittsburgh. He spent the summer between Pittsburgh and Middletown, with an occasional trip to Chicago. United Engineering was being less than cooperative; they didn't believe in the mill, and Tad had a fight over every gear. It was enough to keep his mind off Europe. On September 1, 1939, he awoke in Middletown to the radio announcer's voice: six hours before, at daybreak, Hitler's tanks had begun rolling over the border into Poland.

CHAPTER EIGHT

MIDDLETOWN, WORLD WAR II

1939 - 1945

Two days after Hitler invaded Poland, Tad tried to enlist in the Polish Army. He and Kaz Oganowski said their good-byes in Middletown and boarded a train for Washington, D.C. "We went right over to the Polish Consulate," Oganowski told me, "but they didn't want us. 'Thank you very much,' they said, 'but the last thing Poland needs right now is manpower. You stay and contribute whatever you can from here.'"

Contribute Tad did. The galvanizing royalties were starting to make him rich. He was able to send packages to his relatives, support Polish organizations in the U.S., and still remain in—and even expand—his comfortable circumstances in Middletown. Tad helped Poland, but he spent his emotional capital during the war fighting for himself: fighting to promote his cold rolling mill and fighting to establish his name and his place in the steel industry. As ever, these "fights"—with men and with machines— were conducted in the manner of a Polish gentleman. A Polish gentleman with vertebrae of steel.

He came out ahead, and on the way made significant contributions to America's industrial prowess and to the technology of making steel. As he said later, on reflection, "The war was a stimulus to my imagination." America needed what that imagination had to offer.

* * *

When Tad returned to Middletown from Washington, a cable from Paris was waiting. It was from Barbara, asking for money to come to America. This cable had crossed his own, the one he had sent with tickets for her and Michael on the morning the war broke out. Michael had spent the summer of 1939 in Paris with his mother. The two had been touring Brittany in Tad's car. Barbara seems not to have been in the habit of reading the newspapers, where she would have learned that war was coming and Poland was the likely victim. In mid-August she decided it would be nice to take Michael there for a visit. Fate intervened at the Bureau d'Auto in Paris: Barbara's driver's license had expired and she failed the test for a new one. They couldn't go to Poland. They almost certainly would not have returned.

Hitler's armies moved into Poland on September 1. Through a friend Barbara was able to obtain two U.S. visas. She and Michael sailed from Rotterdam on September 5, and Tad met them in Hoboken nine days later.

He piled them into his new Chrysler Royal sedan and drove across the river to Manhattan, where he'd booked two rooms at the Lexington Hotel. At dinner the first evening, Tad set the agenda: they had to find a school for Michael and a home for Barbara. Middletown would not do. Barbara wasn't keen on settling into a small town, especially one that was also occupied by Tad (only Paris had been big enough for both of them). On this they agreed. Tad then said he'd show them around. They set off on a whirlwind tour of the Northeast and the Midwest, and landed finally in Middletown, where they reached an agreement. Barbara would live in Pittsburgh, where she had friends; Michael, soon to be fifteen, would be enrolled at a military academy in upstate New York, and come to Middletown on holidays to spend time with his father.

* * *

Tad had been able to quickly bring out of harm's way what he cherished most in the world, his son Michael. But that was the extent of his powers. Over the next few months, he had to witness the loss of much that he held dear.

He sat close to his radio, head in hands, listening to broadcasts about the German obliteration of his homeland. When he arrived in New York to pick up Barbara and Michael, he found a discarded copy of the *New York Times* from the day before, September 12. He winced as he read their correspondent's report: "The Germans are today crushing Poland like a soft-boiled egg." He paid his dime for *Life* magazine at a curbside newsstand, and saw the first fuzzy wire photos of Hitler being congratulated in the Reichstag, and German soldiers on the march near Danzig. The following week's edition had a large map showing how far they had advanced: two hundred miles in seven days.

Tad's mother, his sister Terenia, and Terenia's two children were in Lwow, far to the east. How soon, Tad wondered, till the Germans got there? On September 17, he heard the news on the radio. The Red Army had invaded Poland. The Germans didn't need to get to Lwow; they had signed a pact with the Soviet Union dividing Poland between them. Lwow was in Soviet hands. On September 27, Warsaw surrendered.

Six months later, the Russians began shipping out thousands of Lwow's Polish residents, including Vanda, Terenia, and the children, Eva (ten) and Jacek (six). They left in mid-April and spent three weeks in a railroad cattle car. They arrived finally in Semipalatinsk, Kazakstan, at a labor camp by a brick factory.

While Tad waited to hear from his mother and sister, his attention was focused, with the civilized world's, on Paris. The German push into France began on June 5, 1940. Nine days later they were marching into Paris. They had no need to decimate the city from the sky, as they had Warsaw. Within weeks, however, the Germans occupied many buildings and apartments, including Tad's. He learned a few months later that he had lost everything: the family portraits (many from his own camera), his prized stainless steel desk, his 1938 Cross of Merit from President Moscicki, and, most painful, the gold medal given by Prince Poniatowski in 1809 to his great-grandfather Stanislaw.

Tad finally got word that Vanda and Terenia were in Kazakstan. Terenia had gone to work in the brick factory. Later on the whole family, even six-year-old Jacek, would earn a bit more money for bread by knitting sweaters. Vanda related the grim conditions in a letter to her sister:

> The filth here is horrible; we live as if behind a car speeding through dust on a dirt road. The dirt makes its way into every crack and crevice, into every glass of water and bread, and the flies and bedbugs fall from the walls and ceiling. We don't open the windows.....It is very hard to get food. We haven't seen fruits for a long time. We sell what we can. The weakened strength and stomach problems added ten years to our ages.

Tad and Zbigniew milked every contact in foreign offices in the Soviet Union to try to get them out, without success. They could only send packages and letters of encouragement. One from Tad survives, from August 1940, and is characteristic of his sanguine tone:

> It is very important for all of us who left our country...to know how to adjust to new conditions and a new environment, and how to get along with people and to try to get to know the better side of them. Furthermore, one should never lose faith, even in illness, inconvenience and suffering. Let us leave everything to chance and see what will happen. I think that much of what is evil has collapsed, and hopefully everything will soon be resolving, even here in the West.

In August of 1940, evil was just shifting into third gear, and Tad, who read every little piece of news from Europe, was aware of it. He wrote to console and encourage, as the family patriarch. The letter also reveals Tad's secular, passive philosophy toward human events. Any problem with technology, with a machine, must be seized and resolved. But a problem with men, with governments and power, must be left to chance, to "see what will happen."

In Kazakstan, Terenia helped to keep the family alive, and Vanda helped to keep the camp alive. Terenia told me of her mother's efforts one Christmas.

When the Polish Army was formed in the Soviet Union, it was recruited mostly from people who had been arrested earlier and put in concentration camps. My mother organized this Nativity play during Christmas for those soldiers. There was a manger, and a little Lord Jesus lying on hay. We painted it on a newspaper. Angels had their wings made from the same newspapers. There was one room, pretty small, and we had all the Poles there, and all the soldiers, and the prisoners. We had quite a crowd. And we sang Christmas carols and watched the play. We had communion, and later my mother gave this wonderful and uplifting patriotic speech. The whole thing was her idea.

And so they waited out the war.

*   *   *

In the fall of 1939, Tad realized that he had to settle down in Middletown, now that the war had (with finality) sealed off his Paris base. Middletown had escaped the worst of the Depression. By 1935 Armco was almost back to full capacity and was expanding into its enormous Eastworks site. At the end of the decade the entire steel industry was feeding well off the mushrooming U.S. defense budget and the British and French orders for munitions, tanks and planes. Most of Middletown's roughly 30,000 citizens worked for Armco, or Sorg, the largest of several paper companies, or Lorillard, the chewing tobacco maker. Downtown was spared the rotting stench of the paper mills along the riverbank, thanks to the prevailing easterly wind. It was only after the war, with the expansion of Armco's plant, that on a still night the residents would fidget and dream of volcanoes and dinosaurs under the thick, burnt aroma of the Eastworks' coke ovens. The town had a golf club, a swimming pool, a sparsely staffed symphony orchestra, and one very small movie theater. The establishments lining Middletown's Central Avenue petered out after four blocks. You had to take the train down to Cincinnati to spend any real money.

The 1940-41 city directory reports that Middletown was "American-born—96%." Middletown had not drawn its labor force from the southern or eastern European springs that fed Pittsburgh, Cleveland and Chicago. What remained of the community's ethnic identity was mostly German, like Cincinnati, coming from an earlier and now fully assimilated wave. The Lutherans and Episcopalians Tad came to know worked hard, married young, measured success by material wealth, played bridge and golf, ate fried chicken and corn on the cob every Sunday during the summer, drank. On all counts but the first, Tad couldn't have fit in less. Nor, still less, did he care.

He was on good terms with Armco's top brass, even among them John Tytus, the inventor of the continuous hot rolling line (who opposed any new mill ideas coming from Tad.) The tall, aging Tytus could be found every evening—all evening—in the bar of the Manchester Hotel. Tad had a drink with him once or twice. The only executive causing Tad any trouble was Calvin Verity, the founder's thin, bespectacled son who was then Vice-President. "Calvin Verity and I didn't fight," Tad said, "but I didn't like him much, and that may have been reciprocal. I made a joke once, on the Latin saying *'In vino veritas'*: when you drink wine, you tell the truth. So I said, 'Here it would be *In CALvino Veritas*, but he didn't like that."

Tad started out with a small office in the research building. His closest ally was his immediate superior, Dr. Anson Hayes, the research director. Doc Hayes, keen eyed, broad chested and balding, kept a pocketful of coins at a constant jingle as he argued with a clutch of engineers, or peered over a drafting table, or inspected the tension gauge on an experimental mill. Those jingling coins were his own tension gauge. Doc Hayes believed in Tad and Tad returned the admiration; he was one of the few men Tad ever sought out for advice since he left the lab of Uncle Tolloczko.

Tad found himself in an enviable position at Armco. As the tide was shifting from the inventor working alone in his garage to the inventor working with others in a company lab, an argument developed over which of them, after all, can be the most creative and productive. The solitary inventor has the alertness and flexibility, the freedom to take risks, the faith and drive to see his own ideas come to life. He needn't wage battle with the legions of company bureaucrats whose eyes never stray from their ledgers. Many of this brethren also suffer from "NIH": the "Not Invented Here" syndrome. Good ideas fall on barren soil. John Tytus fought and won his case against Tad's rolling mill in part because of "NIH."

But a large company's research office can be a rich estuary of talent and ideas. It can also provide resources—and protection—unavailable to all but that rare sub-species, the well-known and well-off inventor. Few independent inventors can bear the financial burden of the patenting process. Standards may also be higher in large firms: years later, Tad's efforts suffered from lack of quality control. And projects of the magnitude of a steel mill are nigh impossible to rig together in one's basement (although Tad would never cease trying.)

Tad's position in the early 1940s was perhaps the best of both worlds. As an Armco employee, he had available the Research Office's considerable resources. But Tad was also Vice-President of Armzen, the joint venture company he'd created with Armco in 1935 to exploit his rolling mill. Armco was but mildly interested, so Tad took off with it, his initiative and will power unslighted and undiminished.

Tad worked on his own in research, consulting with Doc Hayes and occasionally asking for this or that experiment to be done in the lab. He kept to himself. Inevitably, he developed a reputation among these Midwesterners as an eccentric. Or as, less kindly, "that nut." Oganowski said that, "...Tad was never 'one of the boys.' He was always very considerate, very polite. But he gave the impression that he was unapproachable."

Tad was preoccupied. He never felt a sense of isolation in his new environment. Nonetheless, to his good fortune there arrived in Middletown another European who, like Tad, didn't quite fit in. Conveniently enough, she was already in love with him.

*   *   *

Berthe Bernoda left her home and took the train out of Paris in October 1940, four months to the day after the Germans had marched in. Work at the Paris office of Armco International had ceased. From the beginning of the war, her boss, Bob Solborg, had been working for the British and French intelligence services (he was an American). Berthe had helped translating and typing documents for him, but she didn't want to commit herself any further. "I stopped working with the intelligence service," she told me, "because I felt that as a woman, when you work in intelligence, you have to, you know, 'befriend' the enemy. And I didn't think I would be any good at that."

Solborg offered to send her to Middletown, since there was no work for her at the office in Paris. Armco sent her a visa in July 1940. It took her three months to get an exit visa from the Germans, on the pretext that she was going to Marseilles to visit her sick parents. She spent another two months in Marseilles waiting for a transit visa for the trip through Spain to Portugal, from where she could board an American ship. By the time she got to Lisbon at New Year's, with ten francs in her pocket, her U.S. visa had expired. The new visa came within a few weeks, but she was delayed in Lisbon for another two months because so many people were trying to leave Europe. Through February and March 1941, only U.S. citizens were allowed passage on American ships. Berthe finally arrived in Middletown at the end of April 1941, six months after she'd left home.

Berthe initially felt at odds in the all-American atmosphere of southern Ohio—the first names and the football games and the narrow-mindedness. Middletown didn't even have a bookstore. But she was a good-natured and curious 27-year-old. She had worked for Armco since she was sixteen—this was Armco headquarters and she considered herself an "Armco girl." As such she was received warmly by everyone from top to bottom, something that never would have happened in France.

She soon became the secretary of Hal Pape, who'd known Tad in Paris, and who was now running Armco's Mexico division from the second floor of the old administration building. This square brick house, gathering dust opposite the new General Office building, looking the wrecker's ball in the eye, had been pressed back into service for the duration of the war. Two rooms on the first floor— George Verity's original office—were eventually given over to Tad for the offices of Armzen. Thus Tad and Berthe came to be spending their working days under the same leaky roof.

*   *   *

Tad was able to establish a private office for Armzen only after his first American-built rolling mill had survived hand-to-hand combat with the conservative and incredulous mill builders of Pittsburgh. This is the turmoil that had brought Tad to the United States back in the spring of 1939, and kept him there through the onset of war. It was a replay of the early 1930s: the initial skepticism of the mill builders, the faith and endurance of the mill owners, and the final triumph, after much hard work, of this peculiar, peevish, powerful mill (and its pertinacious inventor).

The order from Signode Steel Strapping in Chicago was Tad's breakthrough into the U.S. rolling mill market. This mill, this standard bearer, must work. Signode wanted to roll 1/8 inch thick hot rolled steel down to 0.020 inch strip, to be slit into narrow bands for strapping, to bind huge coils of steel like twine around a roll of hay. Using Tad's mill, they could roll right down to this thin gauge without stopping to anneal it. The president of Signode, John W. Leslie, the works manager Fred Marsheff, and the chief engineer Everett Magnus championed this mill through its coming battles.

United Engineering in Pittsburgh built rolling mills for Armco. With great reluctance, they agreed to put together this newfangled Sendzimir mill—for the sake of friendly relations. "But," said Tad, "they definitely didn't want my mill to be a success." UE signed the order with Signode, and added a rider: if the mill doesn't work, they'd take it back and give Signode, for an additional amount, a regular 4-high mill. In effect, "they wanted to kill the Sendzimir mill," Tad said. "So they would have said, two days later, 'You see, the Sendzimir mill doesn't work. Here is our order, let's take it off.' Then they would have put it back in their warehouse and said to any new customers: 'You want a Sendzimir mill? Here, we have one. Nobody wants it.' The mill would have died right there."

Tad Bijasiewicz, an engineer who worked at Armzen later on, was at United Engineering for five years. He says the industry was conservative, but honest: "A lot of things were done on a handshake. Deals were made at the Duquesne Club, the famous club where steel people always meet, in Pittsburgh. My personal suspicion is just that people were very conservative. So when they installed the Signode mill, they were unhappy and trying to discredit it. They simply didn't think it would work. Why would anyone want a new mill when the old ones did the same thing?"

The point, in fact, was that this mill did *not* do the same thing. Signode could have produced its low-carbon steel strapping on a 4-high mill—less efficiently, more expensively. But the Signode Sendzimir mill began to make history when they started test-rolling silicon steel, at the insistence of the MIT Radiation Laboratory and the War Department, and this mill did what no 4-high ever could.

* * *

By the autumn of 1941, the steel industry in the United States was booming with arms manufacture for the Allies. The material in demand, however, was heavy plate metal, for guns, tanks and ships—not thin sheet steel from a mill like Tad's. But then it was found that such micro-thin steel was indeed strategic.

America was still two months away from entering the war. Many American scientists, however, had for at least a year been "drafted" to work on the development of new technologies of warfare, to aid Great Britain in its now lonely fight. The severely outnumbered Royal Air Force had already trumped Hitler's Luftwaffe in the Battle of Britain—a victory many ascribe to the network of radar antennas placed along the English coast in the 1930s. Radar was then still a large, primitive, inaccurate device, using long, low frequency wavelengths—a heavy pair of tongs instead of a tweezers. In the summer of 1940, British scientists developed a method to greatly shorten those wavelengths. The Multi Cavity Magnetron generated microwaves; these made a narrow beam which could distinguish between objects. An additional advantage was that it was much smaller: the transmitter-receiver using the magnetron with a dish antenna could be installed on aircraft. This invaluable instrument was shipped in the fall of 1940 to the United States for further development, to the quiet and secure shores of the Charles River in Cambridge, Massachusetts—to MIT.

When this powerful and accurate radar was eventually put on Allied planes, the invention made the difference, many believe, in the air and naval combat against the Germans in World War II—in locating German U-boats blockading Great Britain, for instance, and in the pinpoint Allied bombing of German defenses prior to the Normandy invasion. Fighter planes could lock onto enemy bombers, and even destroy ground-launched "buzz bombs."

In October 1940, recruits began arriving to work on this still top-secret project, at the newly instituted MIT Radiation Laboratory. The Rad Lab would by 1943 grow from a handful of scientists to a workforce of 4000, tinkering across fifteen acres of MIT floor-space—this being but one indication of how important radar became in the war.

One aspect of the development of the Multi Cavity Magnetron was the intense electrical power it required. The Pulse Transformer was invented for this—a new kind of electrical transformer made up of very, very thin sheets of silicon steel. The Pulse Transformer needed steel sheets .002 inch in thickness—two-thirds the thickness of a human hair. With that steel, the transformer weighed only two pounds, the whole radar transmitter set less than fifty pounds. If made from heavier steel, the transformer would have weighed over 400 pounds.

But first the scientists at MIT had to find someone who could produce those thin silicon sheets. In the 1940s, Armco was the world's top supplier of silicon steel for the electric industry, mostly to Westinghouse. MIT first approached Westinghouse, who directed them to Armco, who in turn directed them to Tad. As Tad sat in his office in Middletown one morning, a gentleman from the MIT Rad Lab walked in, introduced himself, and explained that his project needed very, very thin silicon steel—.002 inch. So far, everyone had told him the mill didn't exist that could roll such steel. Tad's eyes fairly drilled through the fellow. "*I* can make strip that's .002 inch thick," he told him. "If you want, I'll even make it *.001* inch."

*　*　*

Tad had never tried to roll silicon steel. It was true that there wasn't a mill yet built with the teeth for such work, teeth—rolls and backing assemblies—strong enough to cut like diamonds. Silicon steel's hardness is formidable. What that hardness meant, for rolling, is just this: "When you roll it, it gets brittle," says Bill Trettel, a compact, thoughtful mill operator who worked on Tad's first mill in Middletown. "It just cracks when it goes over the mill. It breaks so many times. But they had to get the reductions [in thickness] *before* they could anneal it, to get the special properties of the steel. They couldn't just roll it down to some gauge and re-anneal it and start again. They had to take it down to the gauge to break that grain size down, for the electrical properties."

The Signode mill was not designed or built for this. It was built for the job of rolling soft and agreeable low-carbon steel (The British don't call it "mild steel" for nothing). But the Signode mill was the only Z mill—as the Sendzimir cold rolling mill had been christened—in the United States. So off to Chicago went a young engineer from Armco Research, Charlie Smith, with 2000 pounds of Armco's silicon steel, to send it through the Signode mill and have it come out at .002 inch thick.

Of course the mill broke, more than once. Smith and the chief engineer, Magnus, spent weeks rebuilding the mill and improving the rolling techniques, until finally some strip was extracted at .002 inch gauge. It wasn't easy, but it was possible. And Signode slowly began rolling out this fine, thin steel. The steel was used in the transformers, which put radar onto the planes fighting the war. (Signode later earned a special medal from the War Department, but the mill's inventor was never so recognized.)

The steel sheets were shipped to Westinghouse, the company making the transformers. Those in charge at Westinghouse, and those in charge at the War Production Board, were unhappy with the fact that only one little mill in Chicago was producing this strategic material. Westinghouse began pressuring Armco for another source of silicon sheets. Armco's resistance to purchasing its own Sendzimir mill began to crumble.

*　　*　　*

Calvin Verity was against it.

Westinghouse put it this way: "Either you build a Sendzimir mill, or we'll buy one and produce the sheets ourselves."

John Tytus, the story goes, balked: "As long as I'm in charge of the Armco rolling operation, there will be no Sendzimir mill in Armco plants."

Doc Hayes phrased it another way: "Put a Z mill in or find another Director of Research."

Gurney Cole, an Armco manager and one of Tad's champions, kept pushing. John Tytus said to him: "Gurney, you're a nice man, but you're making an absolute *fool* of yourself over the Sendzimir mill."

Finally Charlie Hook, Armco's president, stepped in to overrule Tytus' men—who thought the Z mill was a toy. Because of the Westinghouse deal, Armco had to have this mill.

Unloved, begotten with threats, the Armco mill became the granddaddy of all succeeding Sendzimir mills. Because this mill's job from the start was to roll hard silicon steel, it had to be designed from the start to do that. Tad made two of his most important innovations on this mill and they were immediately successful. The first was that instead of driving the work rolls (powering them directly), the intermediate rolls were driven and the work rolls were left to do their business by friction alone. Because the work rolls weren't hooked up to the motor, they were much easier to take out and replace. The roll changing process on a 4-high mill can take half a day; on the Z mill it could be done in half an hour.

More importantly, Tad decided to add one more story of rolls, to make the roll formation 1-2-3-4 (one work roll, two intermediate rolls, three second intermediate rolls, four backing bearings—top and bottom). This configuration greatly strengthened the mill, and allowed the work roll to be made much smaller: it was no longer powered, and it was now reinforced with two sets of rolls behind it. The essence of Tad's mill had always been that small work roll, cutting like a sharp knife instead of a blunt one. Now the work roll was smaller still, and its bite that much more trenchant. This formation became the classic Z mill design. Dr. Nicholas Grant, a specialist in steel at MIT, told me that "[The 4-high mills then in use] were very mundane. His was a couple of orders of magnitude more sophisticated. It made a tremendous difference in the steel industry."

The mill assembled itself in Tad's imagination and was carefully drawn out in detailed specifications by John Eckert, a young Armco engineer who'd been working evenings at Tad's house. Eckert was a gifted engineer, amiable but resolute, tall with a receding hairline and a plain-spoken manner. He came on full-time in 1942. Tad signed a contract with Waterbury Farrel Foundry, a mill builder in Waterbury, Connecticut. But their shop was already loaded with high priority war work, especially a large Russian order for nut and bolt makers to replace those lost at Stalingrad. Armco sent a man to the War Production Board in Washington to finagle clearance for the Z mill.

Eckert worked closely with Waterbury Farrel 's design department. This time there were no fights—Waterbury Farrel was not, as United Engineering had been, philosophically opposed to this new mill. But Jim Young, an Armco engineer, told me he had to take several trips up to Connecticut to importune machinists who'd never done anything like this; Waterbury Farrel had been building rough-and-ready bolt makers, and here what Sendzimir wanted was virtually a Swiss watch. The mill was installed at the Armco Research Lab in 1944. It was an almost instant success. No one had seen a mill like it; no one had seen a mill do what this one did.

The mill's purpose was to produce those silicon sheets, and it served its purpose well. Armco is said to have made a fortune with it. They weren't slow in taking credit, as boasts their 1944 Annual Report:

> One of the latest examples of Armco achievement is the volume production of ultra-thin steel sheets for use in radar apparatus. Thinner than the paper on which this is printed...these sheets help to account for the superiority of American radar over that of our enemies, and post-war they will facilitate the development of commercial radar, radio, and television as well as many other segments of the promising electronics field.

Similar but catchier prose graced a full-page ad in the *Saturday Evening Post*, under a large picture of the Sendzimir mill. We might credit Tytus, or the beagle-like tact of the publicity department, for the absence in either spot of the name of the inventor.

The mill was simply a phenomenon. Many industry people came to Middletown to see it, and they brought with them samples of other metals—silver, brass, copper, steel alloys—to roll. Tad was showing off, trying to get orders, succeeding.

*   *   *

By 1944 the Armzen office in the old building on Curtis Street was well established: Tad in George Verity's former office, his secretary with John Eckert and the drafting tables in the room adjoining. Tad's first secretary had lasted only a few weeks. Fed up with trying to decipher Tad's turbid accent on the dictaphone rolls, she ran off to Los Angeles to be a welder in a shipyard. (Armco itself didn't put any women onto production lines during the war.) Betty Walters, blond, slight and spunky, then got the job, with the help of her friend Berthe Bernoda. Berthe was working upstairs. Berthe by then knew Tad more than a little, and had told Betty, "If you can hold on for six months, you'll be all right. He won't trust you for six months." Betty survived, and even came to enjoy it.

He'd come in on a morning with a restaurant placemat full of sketches from the night before. Or with his three inch by five inch notebook pages, his tiny script crammed to within a centimeter of the paper's edge. These he'd give to Walters to type. "He used the dictaphone an awful lot at home at night," Walters says. "It would just be murder when he'd bring in those dictaphone rolls. A lot of them were details of the inventions. I would listen to them, and get just as much as I possibly could, and then I had to go up and get Berthe. She'd listen, and she could pick up what I couldn't."

"Mr. Sendzimir was difficult to keep up with," she goes on, "because he was always so far ahead of everything and everybody. He'd often say to me, 'I'll do the big things and you do the little things.' I laughed and said, 'Well, that's all right with me.' Because the big things were making out all these inventions, you know. He was always a gentleman, always very well-mannered. But there was never a dull moment."

There weren't many dull moments for John Eckert either, which is why he quit Armco to work for Tad full-time. He remembers, at the start, being somewhat in awe: "I was a young kid to be working with a man like this. It was a whole different approach from what I was doing at Armco, day to day drudgery engineering. Here was something way off in the wild blue yonder—conceptual work, not just grinding out details." Eckert became Armzen's chief engineer.

By 1945, Tad needed more help. He hired Charlie Smith away from Armco, for his background in metallurgy and his experience operating the Armco Research mill. Smith became the man to get the new mills going once they were installed. The Z mill could turn a company's production process upside down, while increasing their productivity two- or three-fold; Smith was on hand to help them streamline and re-organize. Tad also needed help with his new ideas, especially the so-called "planetary" mill, the hot-rolling mill Eckert had spent time "in the wild blue yonder" sketching. Tad got a fellow who'd been a designer for a lathe company in Cincinnati, the tall, lanky, slow-talking Jim Fox, who says it felt like he slept more nights with the planetary mill over the next fifteen years than he did at home. One of the most important people at Armzen in those early years was Tad's friend Eddy Correa, the head of Armco's legal department who'd helped Tad get a better deal back in 1935. Correa became a vice-president in Armzen, as well as its legal counsel.

The mill orders started coming in the mid-1940s: one by one, four or five of the eventual four hundred Z mills sold around the world—the first drops of rain before the quenching downpour. Armzen had put out a twelve-page catalog in 1942, showing pictures of the Isbergues and Signode mills, and some fanciful sketches of ideas that never made it beyond the glossy pages. Tad suffered from an allergy to paid advertising. He got his orders by sending interested parties to visit the Signode and Armco mills. Potential buyers saw those mills in production, and came back to sign an order. Waterbury Farrel went on building mills: for rolling molybdenum, aluminum, brass, bi-metals, low-carbon steel, aluminum alloys. Then, in 1946,

Washington Steel Corporation in Pennsylvania ordered a mill for rolling stainless steel. And with Washington Steel—and the realization that the Z mill could roll stainless steel, one of the hardest of alloys, as if it were pizza dough—the Sendzimir cold mill hit its stride.

*   *   *

Tad's work took up the greater portion of his waking life. With the rest he walked, he flew, he built, he planned, he wooed. His work didn't limit or exhaust him—it energized him.

In 1940, he learned to fly. He gathered ten Armco men, including Kaz Oganowski and Doc Hayes, and formed the Middletown Aviation Club with a small plane and a schedule for sharing it. But he soon tired of having limited access, and bought his own Piper Cub. He flew for enjoyment and for business: to Chicago, to Waterbury, to New York (and in the 1950s, back and forth from Connecticut to Florida). The trains were too slow, not half as much fun, and Tad was always uncomfortable when he had to mind someone else's timetable. With his plane, he just had to mind—still with reluctance—the timetable and rules of the sun and weather. Eckert flew with him once and from then on managed to find an excuse. As did Charlie Smith. Only Jim Fox enjoyed it, although he told Betty Walters once that "It scares me to death. He puts that thing on autopilot, and he starts working on one of those inventions, and he pays no attention." Tad would dip the plane over and say, "Jim, read that sign on the ground down there and find out where we are."

Fox remembers those days in the air, and that side of Tad, with great fondness: "One night, first or second trip I took with him, we were coming in to Waterbury, and as we turned to go into the pattern to land, here was the sunset. The fog was starting to fill the valleys, and there was silver and gold and red. He said, 'Did you ever see anything like that?' We took—it was getting close to dark, the sun was setting, we had come in on a seven-hour trip from Middletown—we took about a 45-minute trip riding around Connecticut, just looking at the scenery."

Eckert, Smith and Walters would also avoid having to ride in Tad's car. Walters can laugh now: "The way he turned corners, the weird things he would do, would scare you to death. He'd park anyplace he wanted to. He just wouldn't bother to look at the signs. And he'd come back with all these tickets. The police got so they knew him. I think they recognized the car."

That wouldn't have been hard. By then he'd sold the Chrysler Royal and gotten himself something to look at, a twelve-cylinder Lincoln Zephyr convertible. "I pressed the button and the roof was going up," he said. "Everybody was looking at that." Tad throughout his life was something of a small boy about his vehicles. He always had the best he could get. If they had enviable new gadgets, all the better. He skippered a succession of Cadillacs, but he also had an unrepentant fondness for the French Citroen, even though the only mechanic willing to touch it was in a town an hour away. The Cadillacs were for the comfort and the status; the Citroen was for the novelty. No one else had one, which is why Tad did.

No one else in Middletown had a house made of steel, which is why Tad ordered one for himself. He'd scouted around in his Lincoln Zephyr, found one hundred acres of land for sale in the rolling farmland west of town, and set out to make a modest development. He had the brook dammed and created a two-acre lake, then put in several roads and gave them names to his liking—Emerson Road after Earl Emerson, Shotton and Sheffield Roads after the home of his Z mill in England. He sold half-acre lots and christened the whole thing Cascade Lakes. (The second of the planned lakes never materialized.) On his own three-acre lot, on the hill overlooking the lake, he put up his house. Armco was then manufacturing and distributing galvanized and painted steel panels for housing construction, called Steelox. Tad said that Armco was quite pleased when he ordered a house from them himself. The external white walls of the house gave off a metallic shine, against the black shutters and wrought iron entryway. Cozy on the inside, from the outside the house was small, boxy and crude.

Tad invited his friends to the lake for swimming in the summer and skating in the winter. To the house he invited Berthe, who would come and cook supper for him. They went for long walks in those hills west of the river. He'd take her once in a while to Cincinnati, to a concert or to dinner. Forty-five years later, Tad could distantly recollect what was there to begin with: "Berthe represents something in her erudition, in her background. I could talk to her. And American girls in Middletown, maybe there were some who were intelligent, but they weren't very cultured. And she helped me, making the proper arrangements, acting as hostess when we received guests. She was also quite tolerant with my dietary somersaults, like for instance making carrot juice."

They would dine on black bread, butter and garlic cloves, as Betty Walters, who would sit across from Berthe the next day, can attest. Berthe liked the carrot juice, but got violently ill from a small glass of raw onion juice Tad once plied on her.

She knew of course that he was married. She ignored the fact for two years. But then, as he made no mention of getting a divorce, she started seeing someone else. She called that off after a year when she realized she just wasn't in love with him, as she still was with Tad. She went back to Tad even after Charlie Hook, Armco's president, had called her into his office to tell her that Armco was a strict company and they didn't like her dating a married man. She said she was sorry, but it was none of their business.

Meanwhile Tad *had* gotten a divorce, back in 1942. He hadn't mentioned this to anyone for fear of hurting Michael. Michael had been coming to stay for several weeks during the summer and holidays. (He and Berthe struck up a warm friendship; she was only eleven years older.) Tad took Michael to Colorado one summer, where the two transplanted mountaineers could get alpine air back into their lungs. Michael's Uncle Zbigniew would come down to Middletown from Chicago, and annoy Tad with his affectionate jollity over his nephew. Michael tells the story of going with Tad to pick Zbigniew up at the Cincinnati train station. Michael took the backseat, and Zbigniew, sitting down in the passenger seat, reached up and turned the driver's mirror so he could see Michael. "What are you doing?!" cried Tad. "Well," said Zbigniew, "I want to talk to Michael!"

Barbara herself seldom came to Middletown, much to Tad's relief. (Kaz Oganowski said that Tad "gave him hell" once when Barbara was in town and Kaz had taken her to the country club as his guest. He told Kaz that "When she is here, I don't want to publicize, 'Here is Mrs. Sendzimir!'" He didn't want people to see the genuine item.) By 1942 it seems they had mutually decided enough was enough. Michael was in the Army and all but an adult by then. They reached a settlement for a flat sum paid to Barbara, $15,000. She agreed to this because it put immediate cash in her pocket, and at that time Tad's income was not so substantial. But the sum paled in comparison to what Tad was, eventually, worth. Three years later, when Tad wanted to marry Berthe, she came back for more.

* * *

In his nineties, Tad could scarcely remember the gas rationing and food shortages of the war years. His memories were not of deprivation but of opportunity. "It was a stimulant," he said, "very definitely. Each war has brought marked new inventions, new processes. To me, war invariably means progress. I saw that the war was bringing a lot of problems to be solved, and that would give me a chance to have a bite."

His Z mill was such a bite. He toyed also with ideas for other inventions, but the majority of these, as usual, he didn't pursue past the sketches and comments in his notebook. A score of these "bibles" (as the notebooks were dubbed) survived him, most with worn leather covers, edges rounded, some just the pages themselves bound with a dessicated rubber band, all the same three inches by five, all filled with the same tiny script (with the invention of ballpoint pens, this script began to appear in red, blue and green). There rest the myriad and multiform ideas which floated from his mind onto paper over ninety-five years.

The war was certainly a stimulus for Armco. While steel plate for shipbuilding was the product in most demand, Armco did a good business with its flat-rolled steel (not least the silicon steel for radar from the Z mill). Armco produced shell containers, powder cans, drive shafts and parts for Liberty Ships, and specially designed hangars that could be shipped in sections and erected quickly. Armco drainage pipe (the Hel-Cor pipe produced with Tad's galvanizing method) was used in road building in China and Alaska. With copper and zinc in short supply, the Research Department developed a steel to substitute for brass in cartridge cases.

Armco took ten percent of everyone's salary and put it into War Bonds. Berthe knit socks and sweaters in the Bundles for Britain program; the ladies of Middletown went down to the hospital to be nurses' aides. Tad's flying was in fact curtailed by gas rationing, and tires were in short supply.

*   *   *

On June 22, 1941, Tad's attention had been drawn once more to the battlefields in Europe. Hitler had turned on his Soviet ally and invaded Soviet-held areas of Poland. In less than three weeks, the German armies had pushed east almost to Kiev. Their progress was slowed at this point, but by November 1942 they made it to the outskirts of Stalingrad.

Semipalatinsk, and the labor camp where Tad's mother and sister were held, lay another fifteen hundred miles to the east. Hitler was after oil fields in the Caucasus south of Stalingrad, not the dry Kirghiz steppes. But Tad knew as well as most of the Soviet citizenry that if Stalingrad fell, the rest of the country could not be far behind. He searched for every scrap of news of the war on the Eastern Front, more difficult to come by now that U.S. soldiers were dying in Western Europe and in the Pacific. In January 1943, he was relieved to hear that the Soviet Army had prevailed at Stalingrad. They began to drive the German troops west out of their country.

The victories of the Red Army had no effect on the general misery in the Soviet labor camps, except to increase it with the addition of great numbers of German prisoners. In 1944, in Semipalatinsk, Vanda died from exhaustion. Terenia and the children remained for another two years. They were released when the Poles were granted "amnesty" in 1946 and shipped back to Poland. They could not return to Lwow—Eastern Poland had been annexed by the Soviet Union. Tad's hometown, basted in six centuries of Polish history and culture, was being swallowed by Russian nationals and regurgitated as one more industrial city in the Soviet Ukraine.

*   *   *

During the war, Tad deepened his contacts with the Polish emigre community in New York. Now that he was financially secure, he began his long career as a philanthropist. He helped such American causes as the YMCA and the Boy's Club, but the bulk of his beneficence always went to Poles. He first joined the Polish Institute of Arts and Sciences, which had been founded in New York in 1942, on the pattern of French and Russian scholarly academies. The founders intended that the PIAS be re-established in Poland after the war, and in the meantime serve as a symbol that Polish scholarship hadn't disappeared under the Nazis. The Institute's mansion on 67th Street near Park Avenue became a gathering place for war-era Polish emigres.

There existed not a little animosity between the earlier wave of Polish immigrants, who'd flowed through Ellis Island after the turn of the century, and the World War II contingent. The earlier Poles felt the latter had it easy, in comparison. But the latter, mostly middle class, took a greater fall when they came here. The earlier wave looked upon the PIAS as the aristocracy, even though most were simply university professors. The university professors looked upon their predecessors as peasants. Indeed, Tad never had any contacts with the Polish bakeries, churches and clubs leavening working class neighborhoods in cities of the Northeast and Midwest. The antagonism has declined over the past forty years, and been diluted by the several waves—the latest an escape from Martial Law in 1981—to have washed ashore since.

In the 1940s, Tad stopped in at the PIAS whenever he came to New York. His name appears on the post-1945 letterhead of a group calling itself "Warsaw of To-Morrow, International Planning Committee for the Reconstruction of Warsaw." He provided seed money for the Polish daily newspaper in New York, *Nowy Dziennik*; he joined the Polish engineer's association, Polonia Technica; he later supported Alliance College, a small Polish college in Pennsylvania;

and in the 1960s he became involved, financially and personally, with the Kosciuszko Foundation. And he hired, over the years, many, many Poles. (One former employee quipped that there must have been a large sign with an arrow posted on the New York docks: "Engineers for Sendzimir—This Way.")

After the war, a fight ensued in the emigre community over the Institute's relations with the Communist government in Poland. Many said Polish Americans should have nothing to do with any Polish government body. The PIAS' position was that to help Poland you had to stay in contact with Polish institutions, like the universities. Tad deeply disliked the new government, but his reasoning always returned to how he could best help Poles, and so he remained a PIAS supporter.

* * *

In late 1944, returning to Middletown from one more trip to Waterbury, Tad decided that he must move there. His company, Armzen, had little business in Ohio (Armco was a very silent partner), while the mill builder in Connecticut, Waterbury Farrel , regularly needed to consult with his designers. John Eckert and his wife moved first, then Jim Fox and Charlie Smith. Tad took a room in the Waterbury Club, and began to think about settling down.

Thirty-five years later, in 1980, Tad wrote a very rough draft of his memoirs. Several pages were inserted into that manuscript, added as an afterthought to the recounting of his successes. (I don't know if he needed prompting, or if, glancing at Berthe doing all his typing, he realized on his own that he'd left something out.) The addendum reads:

> Berthe succeeded in getting a transfer from Middletown to the Armco New York office, and so we saw each other frequently, sometimes making long excursions to Cape Cod and other places. Our friendship culminated in a wedding on the twenty-second of December 1945, and that changed the lives of both of us very considerably and very much for the better. Now, almost forty years after that event, we have only pleasant memories of the past with our three children, all grown up....

179

"Only pleasant memories," indeed. Not one of those three sentences remotely reflects the difficulties involved.

First Tad decided he'd finally found a woman he could trust. But he didn't want a big wedding, which it would have become because of all the people they knew in Middletown. He asked Berthe in the spring of 1945 to move to New York, to be married there. She moved, took a post in Armco's New York office, and then spent eight months waiting.

She was waiting because Barbara had gotten wind of this marriage, saw red, and tried to cancel the divorce. She could see that Tad was getting richer, and that if he got married and had children, Michael might be short-changed. (Michael was in the Army in the Philippines, and knew nothing of either the divorce or the pending marriage.) Barbara took Tad to court, but then failed again and again to show up on the trial dates. Tad was anxious that nothing should jeopardize his relationship with Michael, so he proceeded gingerly. (Simple openness with his son seems not to have crossed his mind. Michael only heard about his father's remarriage eight months after the fact, when he returned from the Far East, and then not from Tad but from a family friend.)

Finally in December Tad's lawyer told him he might as well go ahead and get married. The trial was delayed again for a year, and if Tad was remarried, the court would find it awkward to cancel his divorce. Tad called Berthe and asked her to come up to Waterbury for the weekend. He made his formal proposal, with two conditions: that she love Michael as her own son, and that she never bring cats into the house. (Later she regretted that she'd made no conditions of her own.)

Neither of these foreigners (they only became U.S. citizens in 1946) knew that getting married in America wasn't so simple. They got the blood test, and the doctor sent it off to Hartford. He told them that since Tad was fifty-one, and so probably knew what he was getting into, the five-day waiting period could be skipped; they could drive the two hours up to Hartford to the lab and pick up the results themselves. It was snowing that day, hard. The tire chains broke twice on the way. When they finally arrived in the late afternoon, the lab was having a Christmas party and wouldn't let them in. At last the staff relented. The two returned to Waterbury. The next morning they went to City Hall for the marriage license. They expected to make the noon train to New York. They got the license, and were stunned to hear that there was more to it: they had to find a judge (it was Saturday); they had to have an actual ceremony; they had to have witnesses. After three or four calls, they found a judge. For witnesses they enlisted the town clerk's secretary and called Jim Fox over from Tad's office. As John Eckert remembers, "City Hall was somewhat agog. This wasn't the usual couple." A fifty-one-year old Pole and a young Frenchwoman, whose thirty-first birthday had been nine days before. Finally it was done. They caught the noon train.

CHAPTER NINE

WASHINGTON STEEL, WATERBURY, ARMZEN

1946 - 1950

Tad sold his Lincoln Zephyr convertible early in the war, in 1942, when he realized it would take him less far per rationed gallon than would a more humble vehicle. He bought himself a Willys. "I can easily pick up another Lincoln when the war is over," he told Berthe as they rattled around town. He was chagrined to find, in 1946, that he could not.

Thirty-six thousand people a day were being discharged from the armed services in that year, and they *all* wanted cars. And washing machines, and stoves, and refrigerators, and even, just available commercially, television sets. The ethos of Depression and war-time austerity evaporated like a bad dream. Tad had to settle for a black Plymouth sedan he procured with some inside help. The nationwide thirst for modern amenities may have temporarily cramped his style, but it catapulted his career. For what washing machines, stoves, refrigerators and cars need is steel—rolled flat sheet steel.

Steel built post-war America. Science had made this most versatile metal into the muscles, sinews, bones and skin of the modern world: it was hard enough to cut glass, yet pliable enough to bend into a paper clip; it was springy enough to cushion the tender loads borne by mattresses, yet strong enough to pull 500,000 pounds per square inch; it could be pounded into thick girders for skyscrapers and bridges, or rolled into strip (with the Sendzimir mill) one- hundredths of an inch thick for a shiny veneer. The pubescent world of commerce gobbled it up for office buildings and what filled them: telephones, dictaphones, typewriters, desks, tables, chairs and filing cabinets. The transportation industry stamped it into shapes and put it on wheels: barrels, tanks, drums, automobiles, buses, trolleys, trucks, and railroad cars. Civil engineers spread it from one ocean to the other: pipelines, culverts, signposts and guard rails. And back at home, two to four tons of it materialized in that "average American household."

The steel plants in the late 1940s couldn't knock out their product fast enough. More rolling mills were needed, and Tad was eager to comply.

Many new businesses sprouted up, fertilized by talents and energies released from the war. One such talent was a young man from a steel family in the southwest corner of Pennsylvania: Tecumseh Sherman (Tom) Fitch, named after his grandfather, General Sherman, the nemesis of Atlanta. Tom Fitch was a lean man with black hair and sympathetic, hooded blue eyes. He had asthma. His condition had kept him off the battlefield and put him on the War Production Board as a Dollar-A-Year Man (a federal appointee receiving only a token salary). When the war was over, Fitch looked around for an outlet for his excessive gusto and ideas. His uncle's company, Jessup Steel, was too strait-laced. Fitch met Tad through a mutual friend at Armco. He came out to Middletown to see Tad's mill, and what he saw—he was the first to do so—was that the Z mill was to stainless steel, that so difficult alloy to roll, like a sail is to wind, like a turbine is to steam, like a rake is to autumn leaves—the consummate tool for the job.

Harry Brearly of England won the Bessemer Gold Medal in 1920 for his discovery that adding chromium to iron made a very hard steel that resisted corrosion. He took the prize and coined the term "stainless steel," although several other scientists had preceeded him in the development of this metal, beginning nearly a century before.

Stainless steel's resistance to corrosion has made it indispensable in the industrial tasks that involve metal-eating substances: chemical and drug manufacture, petroleum refining, pulp and paper processing, the mixing of dyes, varnishes and lacquers. Stainless steel tanks and drums then are used to ship these corrosive materials. Its smooth surface and heat resistance make it ideal for kitchen and hospital equipment that needs to be sterilized: trays, counters, scalpels and needles. Stainless' "toughness" also means that it's strong for its weight. For its lightness, strength and resistance to heat, stainless has been used in aircraft exhaust systems and combustion chambers, as well as on the skin of rockets and missiles. For its smooth and durable beauty, it's formed into decorative (and easily cleanable) surfaces of buildings, as well as shaped into cutlery and tableware, from polished knives to tea services. Lick a piece of clean stainless steel and you won't taste much.

It's a safe bet that all the stainless steel mentioned above was rolled on a Sendzimir mill, and that is all because of Tom Fitch. Fitch saw, back in 1945, that a mill that could roll hard silicon steel like so much putty could do the same for equally tough, and far more in demand, stainless.

In 1946, Fitch tried to convince his uncle, the president of Jessup Steel, to buy a Sendzimir mill and roll stainless steel. His uncle, an alumnus of the old school, would have none of it. Fitch then badgered his wealthy mother and her financial connections in Pittsburgh. With her money he started his own company in Washington, Pennsylvania, a small city you bump into on your way south from Pittsburgh to Wheeling. The sole purpose of Washington Steel was to produce stainless steel strip on the Sendzimir mill.

Fitch became one of Tad's best friends and admirers. A photographic portrait of him was given a permanent place on the wall in Tad's office. Fitch was also best friends with almost everyone in Washington, Pennsylvania. He knew every name, and every child of his employees got a present from him at Christmas. One night a week he'd be in the stands at the ballpark, selling peanuts and popcorn at the Pony League baseball games. When the mayor died two days before the election one year, the city commissioners asked Fitch to stand in; he won, and worked the job for, again, a dollar a year. He and his wife raised seven kids. Fitch named his first Sendzimir mill after one of his daughters. (One hopes that she gave him less trouble than her namesake.)

The Sendzimir mill, and Washington Steel itself, owe their eventual good health and long life to the immutable faith of Tom Fitch. The company nearly went bankrupt in its first couple of years from the problems with that mill. Fitch never abandoned hope, gave in to reason, or altered his words of encouragement to the engineers and operators struggling at their task.

The job of making this mill work went to Armzen's engineers and the engineers at Washington Steel. These men sometimes did and sometimes didn't listen to what the operators, the guys who day and night wrestled and cajoled the mill, were trying to tell them. This mill was brand new, much wider than previous Z mills, and doing a job—rolling stainless—that had only been done experimentally a couple of times before. No one really knew how far to take the mill, how fast it could go, how much it could bear, how hot it could get.

Bill Trettel got to Washington Steel via Middletown, Ohio, where he'd been working as a helper (the operator's assistant) on Armco's experimental mill. A sharp-eyed, methodical kid fresh out of high school when Armco hired him, he'd kept a small notebook for himself and recorded data on each run. Forty years later he still has it, along with a file of vintage articles, ads and promotional pieces about the Sendzimir mill, a piece of machinery he refers to not dispassionately as "my life's work." He was one of the first operators on the Washington Steel mill.

"Today I can pick up a fault right away," Trettel says. "I hear that sound, and I dive for the emergency bar—what they call the panic button, the little red button. You can't see the problem because there's ten feet of strip hidden in the housing. You don't see it until the damage is done. It takes the experience of hearing it, that little sound above all the racket. You just don't find these things out in a day or two. It's not something you can read out of a college manual. And the job is nerve-wracking. In the early days, you had so many cobbles, so many breaks, you were just higher than a kite, you were so tense. Many times I'd walk out of there talking to myself."

Within a couple of years, the process and the problems resolved, the mill began rolling such high quality stainless steel that the company had to buy two more Z mills to keep up with demand. No four-high mill could touch them. Some big steel firms started bringing their own stainless over and asking little Washington Steel to roll it. The other plants couldn't produce that thin gauge at such low cost, with such accuracy and uniformity.

"If it wasn't for the Sendzimir mill, we wouldn't have had satellites. We wouldn't have had the Atlas missile." A little hyperbole from Ed Frank, a former manager at Washington Steel. "The tank for the rocket booster was stainless steel; they needed the accuracy of the Sendzimir mill. Washington Steel rolled it—every other mill had turned the job down. We didn't make much money on it, but we got a lot of prestige. We rolled steel for the nose cones too. Every inch had to be perfect."

The Z mill itself was the rocket booster for Washington Steel as a company. And Tom Fitch was the rocket booster for the mill. Armzen sent visitors to Washington Steel from all over the world, and Fitch welcomed them: "Ask me anything. I'll tell you anything." Other plants were very secretive; Fitch was showing off. These visits produced orders, one by one into the dozens.

Washington Steel's newer mills are now fixed up with digital controls and color computer screens in padded and glassed operator booths. They roll 40,000 pound coils at a thousand feet a minute, twenty-four hours a day, six days a week. But way back at the end of the building the Number One mill still cranks out light gauge stainless for hub caps at a leisurely two hundred feet a minute. The control panel is quaint, analog—knobs, buttons and a couple of dials, some with numbers someone painted on by hand. This mill is nursed by tall, white-haired Art Garbart, who's been in attendance for fifteen years. "This one will go to the Smithsonian when we're done with it," he says, and it sounds like he'll carry it there himself.

*   *   *

When Tad moved to Waterbury, Connecticut, in 1946, the bloom was already off the city's rose; in a few years the petals would begin to fall. Waterbury had been in its glory at the turn of the century, when it called itself "The Brass Capital of the World." Yankee craftsmen started making buttons in their home workshops in the early 1800s. By 1843, three companies were rolling brass for buttons, hinges, snap fasteners, clocks, lamp fixtures, and artillery shells. By 1890, the work had spread to towns up and down the Naugatuck River valley. The area was then producing seventy-five percent of all U.S. ammunition cases. The people who worked in the brass factories, and lived in the brick tenements and asphalt-shingled triple deckers embracing Waterbury's eight hills had come like the Naugatuck River floods, with each decade, from England, Scandinavia, and Germany, then Ireland, Italy, Eastern Europe and Russia. (Waterbury did not, however, develop such a sizable Polish community as did other Connecticut towns like New Britain and Bridgeport.) Later, they came from French Canada, Cape Verde; and, after the First World War, African-Americans came from the South and immigrants from Puerto Rico.

And then came plastic. And aluminum. And no one had much use for brass anymore—certainly not the tons of it that had been putting food on Waterbury's tables for over a hundred years. In the early 1960s, the city's roughly 100,000 souls witnessed in bold relief the decline and flight of manufacturing that had been pockmarking New England cityscapes since the turn of the century. The family-owned brass companies surrendered to large corporations. The corporations refused to retool for the alternative materials; they let the plants run down and finally closed them.

By the late 1940s, Tad was selling his mills to the brass industry in Connecticut, but the reason he moved to Waterbury was just to be near the company building his mills, Waterbury Farrel Foundry. The economy of the city was still strong. Downtown was clean; new shops and department stores were opening on East Main and Bank Streets. The populace lived in neighborhoods roughly but firmly sketched by ethnic origin. The Pope was the most popular guy in town. Atop Waterbury's highest hill, a rocky promontory skirted by an eight-lane highway, stands a sixty-foot high cross, glowing yellow like a neon pencil. Beneath it an Italian immigrant attorney spent his spare hours and finances building a three-acre, waist-high, plywood, tinplate, tile and plaster replica of the Holy Land.

Armzen quickly grew out of the second floor office Tad had rented downtown. He got a loan to put up a two-story brick building out on the Flats, an area of small manufacturing shops near the river. The rooms of this building soon filled with drafting tables and steel desks and filing cabinets, and the men and women attending to the company's boom.

The boom came from Tad's rare combination of inventive genius and business savvy. First of all, he had created a mill that sold itself. It had virtually no competitors; if you rolled steel, especially the hard alloy steels, you had to have one. Then Tad used his charm and his genius to make allies—and practically salesmen—out of his customers. It's unusual for steel companies to allow outsiders to poke around in their plants, but this is just what Z mill owners did for Tad time and again. They did so because of his gentlemanly charm and the respect he engendered, which grew with the sales of Z mills worldwide. He was, impressively, the Inventor, and in that part he never disappointed.

He wasn't a hard sell. He was soft-spoken, gracious. But he was not humble. The mills to him were model children: they could do no wrong. He could not acknowledge that perhaps, in some difficult cases, the Z mill wasn't perfect for a job. As it was perfect for most jobs, so be it. When he started selling his more experimental machines, this courtly bravado got him into trouble.

The mills kept right on selling despite Tad's insistence on charging the customers' royalties (the bulk of which accrued to himself as the inventor, not to Armzen) on the tonnage they rolled on his mills. He could do so because he had a monopoly: his patents were in force until 1956. Any mill owner winces at paying royalties—an insult added to the injury of the purchase price. Some companies bought 4-high mills instead of Z mills to avoid this tithe.

*   *   *

Orders for Z mills came not only from the United States but from Europe (and, by the mid-1950s, Japan). Demand for modern steel technology in Europe, abetted by the Marshall Plan, was bottomless; they were building their industries up from rubble and charred ground.

Tad found it much easier to converse with the Europeans than with the Americans. In Europe he was back in the Old World, where big business was run by what he considered to be a more refined class of people. He was in his element, an element that would sometimes overwhelm the American engineers Tad brought over to help. After one seven-course dinner in France, John Eckert remembers being left behind "to settle all the nitty-gritty details of how these parts we were making in America would fit into these parts they were making in France. It was a considerable problem. I didn't speak French and the fellow I was working with didn't speak English. Everybody else went back to Paris. Well, we were both engineers, so there was really no problem. If we had understood each other's language, we probably would have goofed something up. But because we didn't, we were extremely meticulous."

Ted Bostroem had revived the Sendzimir office in Paris immediately after the war. Another office was opened quickly in London and grew to some stature by selling mills not only in England and Scandinavia, but everywhere in the former British Empire: India, Pakistan, Ceylon, Australia, New Zealand, and southern Africa.

The Paris office covered the rest of continental Europe. To the men in the Paris office, Monsieur Sendzimir was "The Big Boss." Claude Martin was a very young draftsman in the early days of this office. He later became its manager. When Tad came to Paris, Martin remembers, "it was like a theater. We had to leave on the boards all the big drawings. We never knew when he'd come in, because he always was working late, and we were sure he was coming to see what we were doing. It was like in the Army, everything done for inspection. It was completely different than in the States. I found out in Waterbury a lot of people called him by his first name, which I would never allow myself to do."

Tad appreciated a culture that produced such sentiments.

In France after the war, Tad also dipped briefly back into the galvanizing business (he still held the European patents). He sold the license to a French furnace building company, Heurty, and they, like Armco, proceeded to develop the technology far beyond Tad's 1933 designs. Tad participated by cashing his royalty checks.

Tad's business in Europe remained west of the Iron Curtain until after 1956, when the U.S. government slightly eased the restrictions on trade with the Eastern bloc. Poland could finally purchase a galvanizing line and Z mill in 1957—two decades after serving as their cradle and nursery.

*   *   *

Back in Waterbury, as if there wasn't enough to do, Tad started up one more business: Precision Methods and Machines (PM&M), a machinery shop for building the Z mill's inner rolls and backing assemblies. Armzen was just an engineering firm—purely white collar. The staff would sell the customer a mill, draw up the detailed designs, pass them on to Waterbury Farrel, and there the machinists massaged the chunks of iron and steel with their lathes and grinders, and persuaded them to fit together to become a mill. Tad quickly grasped the benefits of running his own machine shop: "My mill depends very much on the precision and quality of the backing assemblies. If a company buys my mill from the cheapest bidder, then the backing assemblies might not hold the pressure or be accurate enough. And the Sendzimir mill would lose its high reputation. So I preferred to have the control myself. And, I could make a profit."

PM&M was incorporated in 1946, with capital from Tom Fitch, and with it Tad became an industrialist. PM&M also gave him, in its shed across from the Armzen office, a workshop for exploring his new ideas. The company lost money hand over fist for the first several years. But in 1950, Tad hired a man who turned it around. PM&M's lathes began, as it were, to spin gold.

Our family knew him as Zig; the engineers at Armzen called him Ziggy; his naturalization papers read "Zigmund Protassewicz." Short and solid where Tad was tall and lean, hot where Tad was cold, he and Tad, two strong-willed and self-opinionated Poles, were bound with the glue of love and hate, admiration and antagonism, profit and loss. They brought to life the Polish expression "when a scythe hits a stone." Tad was steely and immovable; Zig loud and fiery. Zig was an excellent manager, a risk taker, sometimes a bully, a loud and non-stop talker. It was said that Zig had no need for the telephone: he'd just open the window and shout. Under him, PM&M began to reap a fifty percent profit on the Z mill backing assemblies.

Zig became very bitter in his old age over a falling-out with Tad. But still I'm told that in earlier days, his reminiscences of working with Tad were second only to those of fighting Cossacks with a saber on horseback in 1919.

*   *   *

In addition to the Americans he had working for him in the late 1940s, Tad started hiring Poles. Some came from old loyalties: Andrew Beck's father went to Gymnasium with Tad; Jan Tomczycki's mother, Maria Petzhold, had been Aniela's girlfriend and Tad's dancing partner in Lwow; Jan Swiecicki was the scion of the Warsaw family who started the galvanizing line there in 1935. All the rest, and there were many, held, besides some technical experience or an engineering degree, the principal qualification of being Polish.

The Polish engineers Tad hired benefitted because, fresh off the boat and speaking little English, they could hardly have gotten a better or more prestigious job. Tad sincerely wanted to help them make a start in this country, as he had. But it was Tad who benefitted most. He got (usually) well-trained engineers for peanuts: he paid them half what he should have. And many employees were surprised to notice that while he was gracious in hiring the Poles, he was far rougher on them once hired. Sendzimir was a famous name in Poland; they came to him a bit in awe. And they were accustomed to (would put up with) his European—paternalistic, sometimes tyrannical—ways.

Many people enjoyed working for him. In the early, heady days of Armzen, there was a feeling of family, of a team. You could see him as Attila the Pole, or as a challenging, dynamic and fascinating man to have as a boss. He could be cordial, gentlemanly. Vera (Kallaur) Lundberg, one of his secretaries, says, "Mr. Sendzimir, when he came in each morning, he would say hello to everyone, even the person sweeping the floor. That was a very un-Polish thing to do." He would go around to each of the drafting tables (at one point there were forty or fifty) and check on the work, remembering exactly at what point that person had been the day before. He freely issued advisories on health, and prescriptions for carrot juice instead of eyeglasses. In the 1960s, luckless clients invited to our home for business lunches were served a dark green, viscous concoction of raw vegetables Tad composed at the table in a blender. He fasted one day a week, which put him in a sour mood. His secretary would call Berthe in the morning and ask, "Is he fasting today?" They wanted advance warning to stay out of his way.

He could be stern and serious, but his wit leaked out like steam from a cast iron boiler. He was known less for jovial stories (although he had a few) than for droll quips, puns and asides. Coming in one summer morning, he noticed that his secretary, Doris, had painted her fingernails dark green. Walking through the office she shared with another secretary, without slackening his pace, he said, "Good morning, Gina. And Merry Christmas, Doris."

Tad could be harsh in the office, but those who made business trips with him said he loosened up on the road. Andrew Romer, a tall, lanky man with a rubbery face and high, wheezy laugh, was for many years Tad's chief assistant. He recalls one visit to France: "One afternoon, on our way to Paris, we drove through Amiens, which has a famous cathedral. I said—I dared to say—'Mr. Sendzimir, could we stop for half an hour?' Mr. Sendzimir growls, you know. He growls, but he says 'OK, I'll do it.' We stopped. I took my half an hour, and I was ready to go. Well, he spent three hours there. He was so happy, looking at all the details. But, you know, he considered his duty above all. He did not want to permit himself to look at a cathedral."

Those who stayed at Armzen did so because they liked the challenge he imposed and the respect they earned from customers and others in the industry. Many bright but under-skilled individuals got a chance to make something better of themselves: draftsmen and car mechanics became respected engineers—as had Tad from his lowly (albeit well-educated) beginnings in the car repair shops of Lwow and Kiev. And Tad himself was always fascinating. "He could talk about anything," Jerry Jablonski, one of his engineers, remembers. "I learned many things from him. About languages, culture, geography, health. He knew everything." Many people, inside the company and out, described him as a "Renaissance man," a "Jules Verne."

But as a boss, Tad was far less successful than as an inventor. The tight-fistedness and rough treatment were felt not just by the Poles. He was impatient with men who weren't quick enough to follow his train of thought, and angry with those who dared to challenge it. He'd jump on people for mistakes, and sometimes blame others for his own. Praise was seldom mentioned. He was still, even in well-fed middle-age, as thin and taut as a bow string. His scrub brush moustache and long, graying eyebrows could barely soften the effect when he pointed his gun-barrel eyes at you.

Tad found it next to impossible to delegate authority. He believed that no one was as competent as he himself. Tad Bijasiewicz (a feisty Polish engineer who *was* competent, and alas knew it too well for his own good) felt that, "...if you did something, it wasn't because he delegated it to you, it was only because he couldn't do it himself, so therefore, 'Oh my God, I have to give it to him.' My theory is that he figured that when you work at one hundred percent of your competency, that's only about forty percent of his. He never realized that if someone was working full time on a project, that person ought to know more about it than he himself did, or the person should be fired."

Tad's stinginess with salary was renowned in the industry. He couldn't admit that his ideas required adept and intelligent handling to take them from paper to shop floor. Such intelligence costs money, and commands respect; Tad offered little of either. He had to run the show. Top engineers are seldom willing to sit quietly on the sidelines; at Armzen, that was the only seat available. He lost some good people, and he got stuck with some lemons—men he hired simply because he could pay them less. Tad may have been rough on his employees, but he found it very difficult to fire them.

His parsimony was more than petty; it was sometimes reckless and self-defeating. The engineers in his research workshop were building heavy industrial equipment using motors purchased from Sears Roebuck. Such tight-fistedness can be traced to the profligacy of Tad's grandfather, the modest means and poor investment decisions of his father, and the hard times he himself went through early on—the war years in Kiev and Shanghai—when he prided himself on jury-rigging complicated equipment out of crude machines, and finding bargains in scrap heaps. It was his way of life. But still, people expected from this wealthy and successful Polish gentleman a little more largess.

Outside of the office, he could be quite generous, on a personal and often touching level. He'd go himself to the Five and Ten to pick up items his relatives in Poland had asked for—reading glasses, pins, buttons, nylons, cosmetics—and bring them back to the office for his secretary to pack up. He'd invite young Polish engineers far from home to spend weekends and Christmas with our family. He helped and encouraged his secretary, Vera Lundberg, to take a sabbatical at the Sorbonne.

One cannot disentangle Tad's merits as a businessman and inventor from his merits as a boss and manager. His stinginess as a boss was in effect a poor business practice: paying less than adequate salaries meant getting less than adequate levels of talent. His stinginess in constructing his models meant that many of his inventions were never built well enough to prove their worth, and so never sold. His inability to delegate authority meant, later on, that no one was trained and responsible enough to develop and sell his new inventions.

On the other hand, it must be said that some rough behavior on his part may have been necessary. A successful inventor doesn't accept the pooh-poohing of ordinary mortals. A successful negotiator doesn't take "No" for an answer. He was a tough nut and he had to be. Would he indeed have gotten as far had he more the skin of a peach than that of a coconut? He outlasted and outshone most detractors.

*   *   *

Tad became, in 1946, for the second time, a husband and a father. As such, he was both far more and far less than desired. His second marriage continued for forty-three years in relative contentment, until his death. Berthe has some harrowing tales, but only a few regrets. Tad had none. He began, at fifty-two, a second lifetime.

They bought a house on a hillside in Bethlehem, Connecticut (ten miles from Waterbury), a small community of Lithuanian farmers and Holstein cows. "House" is a nice way to put it. It was little more than a log cabin in the woods. Its charm lay in the large, high-ceilinged living room with its warm knotty-pine paneling. With each child, an addition was built. Berthe got into trouble when she spent money on landscaping (a few rhododendron bushes and a lawn) so the place would seem a bit less rustic. She furnished the house by packing baby Stanley into the car on Friday afternoons to comb the Connecticut countryside for auctions, looking for old oriental tables and chairs nobody in those days much valued. Tad, on the weekends, would disappear atop his tractor to clear trails in the forty acres of second-growth oak and beech forest behind the house, between the stone walls Yankee farmers had assembled two centuries ago before they abandoned that thin, rocky soil in disgust.

Berthe enjoyed the chance to get out of the woods every couple of weeks to go into town to get her hair done. She found Waterbury more cultured than Middletown, but less friendly: "There was no bookstore in Middletown; you had to order from Cincinnati. But Waterbury had a bookstore and it was a luxury to go there and look at the books. On the other hand, people in the Midwest are very warm. They are not sophisticated, but they are warm. You feel part of a big family. I felt I was alone in Waterbury."

Berthe poured her skills into her new job: wife of the Boss, mother of his children. His tight-fistedness caused some grief, but sharpened her creativity. The rewards of the work were not insubstantial, as the family was, in fact, well-off. She and Tad went together to New York once or twice a year for meetings of the Iron and Steel Institute, and she spent those afternoons on Fifth Avenue (at least she got to look). They held dinner parties at home, for foreign visitors or for office staff. Tad, less the recluse he became in later years, enjoyed mixing the martinis, cutting the roast beef, playing the host.

They met and became good friends with the sculptor Alexander Calder and his wife, who lived in the next town over. Each man indulged and admired the wit, imagination, and dynamism of the other. They shared also a fondness for gadgets, for sheet metal and for things French. Tad and Berthe would come over for Saturday dinner and be put to work, along with the other guests, operating a segment of Calder's famous miniature circus, for instance manipulating the fellow who followed the elephant (sporting tusks of white pipecleaner) with tiny broom and dustpan.

Tad on occasion would enlist Berthe in some aspect of his business. She worked with Andrew Romer on a pension plan. She was in charge of the Christmas cards. Once she was given a small office next to Tad's, and some duties along with it. None of these jobs lasted more than three or four months because Tad would without explanation change his mind and give it to someone else. She grew bitter over this, especially after the kids were gone, and her considerable business skills remained untapped. She fled for stimulation into her reading, mostly of books on nature and on foreign lands and cultures. Her one compensation was that she was allowed to accompany Tad on his trips to Japan and Europe when in his eighties he needed her help. Her resurrection as a businesswoman came only after he passed ninety.

Tad was Chairman of the Board of family life, but that department remained on the lower rung in his hierarchy of concerns. It was Berthe's job to keep it there, to keep home and children comfortable, organized and out of his hair. He stepped in to dictate terms, when he had the time or the whim. One such whim started when we were still in utero. He thought that Berthe, pregnant with Stanley, should walk—"forced marches" would be more accurate. He'd call her at 6:00 p.m. from the office and say he was leaving. She was to start out on foot in his direction. Then he'd make a few more phone calls, and finally pick her up over an hour later.

Stanley arrived a month early. He was in infancy a great success. Tad would come home from the office, unload his pockets of sharp-edged pens and keys, and proceed to the nursery to check on that tow-headed, stocky baby. He carefully prescribed and monitored the boy's intake of solid foods. Stanley was an energetic, curious child; he was the only one of the three of us who, as a toddler, needed to be put on a leash. At home, he had the run of the place.

Tad very much wanted a family—Berthe says that's the only reason they got married; he wanted the chance he had missed with Michael, to see his children grow. But he wanted only the kinder, less active role, not that of a father—who must teach, discipline, encourage, and participate—but more that of a grandfather. "I want to enjoy my children, and have them love me," he said to Berthe when Stanley was very young. "If you expect me to discipline them, when I come home and I'm tired, then they won't love me."

But while the work of raising kids went to Berthe, Tad treated her in that job as he treated his engineers: he gave her the responsibility, but not the authority. He remained the boss. Berthe put up with his uneven participation—due both to his desire to be loved and to his preoccupations with his inventions and business—and she then had to live with its consequences.

When Stanley would beg for any trinket he could find in a store, and Berthe would say no, he'd run at once to his father when he returned from the office. "Tad would come to me," Berthe says, "and Stanley was with him, with a look showing he'd won his case. Smug. Later, not in front of Stanley, I would say, 'Tad, if you're going to do things like this, then I have no authority.' And he would say, 'Oh, I'm very sorry. But the poor boy was so sad.' This happened all the time. I think in retrospect that he was tired, from the office. He'd probably had a lot of trouble, decisions. And this child coming and asking for a ten-cent thing, you know. It was so easy to make this little boy happy."

A year or two later, when Stanley's needs grew beyond ten-cent whistles, Tad's affection and concern and involvement hadn't grown commensurately. Stanley became too much to handle. The demands and restrictions in school came to the boy as a shock, as did Tad's quick reversal from gentle indulgence to anger and frustration when his son didn't measure up. And there arose a tension between Tad and Stanley that poisoned, for many years to come, a relationship that had been close. Tad became furious and exasperated that a son of such brilliant individuals could be failing, but he wouldn't lift a finger to help.

Tad's flesh and blood offspring could be relegated to a loving mother and a nanny; we would grow with just fresh air and green vegetables. His other children, his inventions, were more demanding. But also, in a way, more satisfying, more controllable, more subject to natural laws and logic. It was to these, to improving the Z mill, to making a success of the new planetary mill, and to expanding his business, that his attention was drawn through the next decade.

CHAPTER TEN

THE INVENTOR

1950 - 1956

The workers at Follansbee Steel were probably not sure what to make of this pair who'd just walked in to look at the new hot mill. One, distinguished-looking, tall and thin, with a moustache—he must be the inventor, Sendzimir. But the other one, the chubby guy, is in bedroom slippers! And a smoking jacket!

Carefully considered attire was not one of Alexander Calder's immediate concerns. Tad had flown Calder over from Connecticut early that morning. He wanted to show his friend the planetary mill. They shook hands with Jim Fox and the three men walked over to the mill. Fox was at Follansbee Steel, near Steubenville, Ohio, helping the company get their planetary hot mill started. One of the first in operation, this mill rolled strip only six inches wide. The machinery was nonetheless formidable: a series of furnaces, two big "feed rolls" to push the hot slab into the mill, the planetary mill itself at the height of a man and ten times the girth, more rolls to smooth out the strip; and finally a long run-out table where the dark red steel ribbon would cool slightly before it reached the coiler at the far end. Formidable also was the noise, like a quartet of jack hammers, when that thick hot slab hit the multiple rolls of the planetary. A hissing cloud of steam, from jets of water sprayed across the rolls and the run-out table to cool it all down, lent a particularly infernal aspect to the tableau.

Over the din (for him nothing less than a symphony) Tad explained to Calder how, essentially, it worked: in one end goes a thick steel slab, out the other comes thin steel strip.

Calder watched for a few minutes and then began to look around, slightly bored. It was so uniform and controlled; there wasn't much art here. And then they heard a loud CRACK, and the dark red steel strip on the run-out table lifted itself up into the air and took flight like the tongue of a giant hungry lizard. The operators ran for cover. Someone hit the switches, and the battery of machines stopped dead. The truant strip clattered to the floor beside the run-out table, and then there was silence. Jim Fox glanced at his boss, whose straight shoulders had perceptibly slumped. Then they both turned to Calder.

"That was terrific!" cried the sculptor, who was rapidly making sketches on a pad. "Can we have that again?"

Tad wore with varied enthusiasm the many hats he'd fitted for himself: industrialist, businessman, boss, father. But the hat worn with particular glee was that of inventor. From 1945 to the end of his life, one machine above all others bedeviled the brains beneath that hat: the planetary mill.

When Tad invented his cold rolling mill in 1933 in Poland, he had to weld individual sheets of hot-rolled steel end-to-end to form a strip to put on the mill. He was not fond of this operation. And so he began to think about hot rolling, and how to get hot-rolled steel in a coiled strip instead of in separate sheets. Those sheets, as described in Chapter Six, were at the time being sent through the rollers by hand until they were thin enough to weld together into a strip. John Tytus, at Armco, had made this process obsolete with his continuous hot-strip mill. Tytus put a series of two-high and four-high mills in a long line. A slab of thick and hot steel was sent through this series of mills, each making a substantial reduction. The hot slab would get thinner and longer and thinner and longer, like so much taffy, until finally it was strip to be wound up in a coil.

Tad instead came up with the planetary mill. As the planets rotate around the sun, someone coined this poetic name for Tad's unorthodox idea. The gist of the mill is two large rolls, each surrounded by much smaller work rolls, that spin as they rotate around their large backing roll. Each of the work rolls, as it passes over (or under) the slab, takes a bite, a small reduction. The metal as it meets the rolls goes from a slab three inches thick to strip one-eighth inch thick in a matter of seconds. It's as if he took the small work rolls off John Tytus' hundred-yard-long line of hot mills, through which the slab would have slowly passed and been reduced millimeter by millimeter, and put all those work rolls in a circle around two large backing rolls, so that it happens all at once.

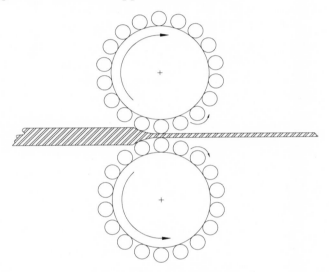

Planetary Mill

In 1935, in Poland, Tad put together a model of the planetary the size of a doll house and rolled some copper on it. The results encouraged him. Five years later, in Middletown, John Eckert's first assignment for Tad was to make drawings of this mill. In 1944, Waterbury Farrel converted an old two-high mill into an experimental planetary. And with this primitive machine, according to John Eckert, "We did some amazing things"—rolling steel, manganese, aluminum, brass and copper. "It seemed to be a good idea." Tad then convinced his old friend at Signode Steel in Chicago, John Leslie, that this was the mill for him.

Jim Fox, who had been working on the pilot planetary mill in

Waterbury, went out to Chicago to start up the Signode mill. Jim Fox and the Signode engineers increased the furnace capacity, rebuilt the gears, improved the work roll arrangement and the use of the feed rolls. This was the greasy work of transforming an experimental machine, a charming toy, into a piece of dependable industrial equipment. Jim Fox became the planetary hand.

By the late 1940s, Sendzimir was a name still not easily pronounced but now not easily dismissed; many people came to see what this Polish upstart was up to. "It scared some of them half to death," Jim Fox says. "They just couldn't imagine what the maintenance would be on a mill like that. It's a high speed thing, with high speed vibrations. You could see it would be a problem." (The Signode mill eventually was bought by Peugeot, and had to be shipped to France. The fellow they sent over to learn about the mill was quite unenthusiastic about it. "I hope nobody drowns," he remarked, "but I hope the boat sinks on the way.")

Some in the industry did see potential; Tad in the first few years sold a few smallish mills, for strip no wider than twenty-four inches. Their largish problems kept Jim Fox living from a suitcase for much of the next ten years.

*   *   *

Tad's firstborn, Michael, had in the meantime become an adult, an engineer, and an employee at Armzen. He'd graduated from military school in 1943, and gone straight into the army—and off to the Philippines. Two thousand men were calling him "Sir" at the end of World War II. He entered Columbia University in 1946. Tad chose all his courses there, and for that Michael reveals no resentment. Michael had inherited from Tad his height and generous nose and eyebrows, from Barbara his keen dark eyes, from both his wit, (and perhaps from his grandmother a solid build—he wasn't wiry like his father). With that Continental accent and those Continental manners, the package was decidedly compelling. He was by 1948 already a husband, and father of a baby girl. And he was aware of his responsibilities. He worked at Armzen and PM&M on the months off from Columbia, either on the drafting tables or at the machines.

During two summers he was given a job at Armco in Middletown, where he learned to operate the Z mill and their galvanizing line. There he was called "Mike," not "Sir," he spent his apprenticeship at the bottom.

By the time he got his degree in Industrial Engineering (with the emphasis more on business practices than on mechanics), he was ready for Armzen, and Tad was eager for him to join. He spent time in the patent department and then went into sales. He worked hard. He was not being carried along to the corner office by limousine—but few had doubts that that was where Tad intended for him to go. Many who've worked with both men say it was a mistake for Michael not to have spent time first in another firm, to gain perspective, self-confidence, and independence, before joining his father. The consequences of this sheltering emerged over the next decade, when Michael was put in the saddle but not given the reins. That is the story of T. Sendzimir, Inc., Armzen's next incarnation.

*　　*　　*

While Tad and Jim Fox had been busy with hot rolling, Eckert and the Armzen engineers had continued, for the most part under Tad's direction, to refine the Z mill. One new trick was to redesign the mill's housing—that heavy cube of metal that entombs the rolls—to shed weight and bulk while retaining strength. Tad enlisted the help of a Polish engineer, a bridge designer who'd worked for Roebling, maestro of the Brooklyn Bridge. He came up with a somewhat hexagonal design—cheaper to manufacture and more efficient—that resisted improvement for thirty years.

The most important innovations came in the rolls. First Tad decided to drive not the first but the second intermediate rolls, which made the mill much more powerful. In detaching the first intermediate rolls from the motor, Tad realized that here he could tackle the scallop problem. On the outside edges of the strip, the rolls inevitably put on more pressure; the edge got "over-rolled" and became scalloped or wavy like a lasagne noodle. Tad came up with the solution one day at Diorio's, an Italian restaurant whose white paper placemats the Armzen engineers often sacrificed for the advancement of science. John Eckert remembered how Tad that day took out his pen and started drawing. "What if I take the first intermediates," Tad said, "and hook on to them at the end? I attach them to an arm, so that I can adjust them, move them one way or the other, as we roll." He drew a rough sketch, showing the roll being moved out or in, the roll's tapered edge set according to the width of the strip. This innovation, Eckert claims, put the Z mill in the big leagues.

Over the next ten years the engineers at Armzen went on making improvements. They made the mills bigger, wider, and more powerful. They experimented with gauge control, lubrication, and making rolls from the new, tougher alloys.[Appendix, 3] There were, of course, problems. Indeed, the mill is a trifle complicated, when you compare it to a four-high. It wants solicitous care and maintenance. The men who run Z mills say, "Treat her nice, she's like a Swiss watch"—precise, beautiful, intricate, demanding—none of which can be said about the four-highs, whose operators doctor them with a sledge hammer and a squirt of grease.

Tad had only a small part in the work of improving the Z mill after the first few years. Nothing was done without his approval; much was done without his participation. It was a repeat of his *modus operandi* with galvanizing; he simply wasn't interested in development—the tedious, studious work of perfecting a machine. He relished the raw ideas, the breakthroughs. The planetary mill was far more tantalizing. This didn't prevent him, however, from sticking his nose in to make last minute changes on Z mill designs that were nearly finished, much to the despair of John Eckert and the mill builders. Jim Fox says that "Some of the things Mr. Sendzimir suggested were real improvements, some were icing on the cake." Fritz Lohmann, Z mill chief at Demag, the West German mill builder, recalled one time when the overdue plans for a mill had finally come in to him from the Sendzimir office in Paris. Tad was in Europe at the time. Lohmann got a call from the Paris office: "Fritz, be careful! Tadeusz is on the way with some other ideas."

It exasperated Tad that he couldn't be in all places at once. While he was tinkering with his new ideas, Eckert had to crank out Z mills, and in the 1950s they were shipping blueprints by the truckload.

Eckert recalled that more than once Tad would come in, look at a blueprint and choke, "What's that?! I don't remember that. You never showed it to me!" And Eckert would say, "This is just a routine thing. It wasn't necessary to show it to you." And Tad would get very upset. Eckert would reply, "If I have to bring every little nitty gritty to you, we won't get anywhere."

First as a designer, and later as Armzen's chief engineer, Eckert must share credit for Tad's success. Eckert's were the eyes and hands and solid engineering thinking that transformed Tad's visions into working machines. His was the stubborn, practical, sometimes heavy-footed logic that evenly—and not without heated arguments—counterbalanced Tad's whirlwind imagination. Tad needed John Eckert in ways Tad was not always willing to appreciate, in ways sadly apparent when Eckert was no longer there. In the way a hot-air balloon needs its bags of sand for a successful flight, or a helicopter needs the vertical propeller on its tail to keep it from spinning into the ground.

"I think Mr. Sendzimir accepted criticism from Eckert much better than from anybody else," says Andrew Beck, an engineer at Armzen. "Later on, there was nobody with the guts, the stature or the independence [to stand up to Tad]." Later on, Tad's chief engineers would fail him because he could ride right over them.

In Eckert's own version, when he's pressed for details, he portrays himself sometimes as the humble facilitator, sometimes as the tortoise to Tad's hare. "During the development of the cold mill, the ideas were *always* Tad's. Some good, some bad. I was the Man Friday who sifted and sorted and changed them, until over the years a basic success emerged. There was a balance between us. I'm a plodder, I'm careful. Tad would have a goal, he'd head towards it, run into some obstacle, go over there. No idea was ever abandoned. If a roadblock developed the idea would be stored away in some remote corner of his brain. It might reappear two years later with a solution. But I had to stay on track."

* * *

While the planetary mill was from its conception to Tad's death (and beyond) the "problem child" of the family—the one of great promise, the one that never really grew up and never stopped pulling at its daddy's sleeve—Tad steadily contrived dozens of other mechanisms and processes. By 1956, he had twenty-one patents to his name in the United States alone.

E. B. Clairborne, head of Wallingford Steel, owned a Z mill and loved it. But he once said to John Eckert, "Sendzimir's a genius, a great character. The only problem is he has so many ideas. Ninety-five percent aren't any good. But the remaining five percent are so good that you forget all the rest."

Some will say that an inventor who is successful with even one percent of his ideas is a genius. Others claim that many of Tad's so-called "useless" ideas may be found, in years to come—when technology is more advanced—to be brilliant, and simply ahead of their time. "It's hard to argue with a visionary," as one of his engineers says. It's also hard to argue with success. Tad hit a motherlode with his galvanizing and his Z mill. The multifarious other visions that passed through his brain and onto paper, model, patent or operating device, were paid for by these first two. Success in inventing, alas, depends not on the merit of the idea in the abstract. It depends, among other factors (one being a good chief engineer), on the availability of the supporting technology, and on whether the idea fills a need. With galvanizing and Z mills, Tad struck at the precise moment in the history of technology when both these inventions were technically possible, and in great demand. For many of his other ideas, neither the technology nor the need were there for him. Who's to judge, then, whether these nascent ideas were brilliant or absurd?

The people who are in charge of making such judgments are employed by patent offices around the world. Tad had seventy-three U.S. patents by the time he died. His ability to garner patents is a testament not only to his unique ideas, but to his unique turn of mind: his way of looking at and explaining his inventions was completely different from how anyone else would approach the subject. Andrew Romer remembers the sessions at the Patent Office: "When we argued with the examiner, Mr. Sendzimir had such fantastic arguments. A normal engineer would think this way, and the examiner would immediately counter that with a normal argument. But Mr. Sendzimir always argued another way, and the examiner didn't know what to say."

But Jacek Gajda, a young engineer who worked with Tad in the 1970s and 80s, insists that Tad's strength was in the *un*patentable concepts. "Sometimes I would sit back, and listen to his ideas. They came from a totally unconventional way of thinking. He would come up with a way of doing something which had nothing to do with the way anyone else had ever done it. He had so many little ideas on accomplishing things no one else could figure out."

Tad never limited his thoughts to the steel industry, either for inspiration or for application. His ideas ranged from the whimsical to the inspired. At one end, there's the "automatic pancake maker," a mechanical device where the batter is put in a small vat, open in a slit at the side, which abuts a heated, rotating drum. The batter oozes out against this hot drum, and cooks as the drum turns. The resulting "pancake" comes out as a long strip, instead of round shape. This machine was abandoned before anyone even had the chance to figure out how to cook the other side.

At the more practical (and lucrative) end of the spectrum, there's the patent Tad sold to Reynold's Aluminum. He'd visited their plant and heard them talking about the problem of making the panels on the backs of refrigerators, for dissipating heat. He thought about it briefly, put it together with his ideas about bonded metal (one of his favorite concepts), and came up with a solution. He spent two hours drawing up a patent application, received the patent, and filed it away. Several years later, he got a call from Reynolds, and they had to hand over $75,000 for the use of it.

A page from Tad's notebooks, dated 1930, describes a pneumatic system for power steering, shifting and ignition on cars. In the 1960s he thought of directing a layer of air bubbles around the hulls of ships, to reduce friction in the water. He came up with a sketch for a toothpick mounted on the end of the tongue, to get those hard to reach spots. In the 1980s, he sent off many letters to NASA to interest them in "collapsible springy strips"—wide, thin-gauge steel strips that roll up, but when extended would be rigid, just like giant spools of measuring tape. As coils they would fit neatly in the rockets. On arrival, they'd be unrolled and put together as the walls of a space station. (NASA said politely, "No thank you.")

His wide ideas reflected his wide reading and interests. An item in the news about a gas tanker truck fire, for instance, got him dreaming of an explosion-proof tank. He read *Popular Science* for relaxation. He wandered through the steel industry magazines, and sometimes, noticing a trend, might apply his thoughts in that direction. He ordered, studied and kept on file patents from around the world. Frequently he went back to his own original patents to make improvements and tinker with pet ideas: casting molten metal, for instance, and galvanizing. "It's like composing music," says John Turley, a T. Sendzimir, Inc., engineer, "the same tunes come back to you, from long ago." And in those tunes, favorite instruments would appear over and over; he liked to play around with differentials in his designs, and with sprockets and chains. No machine was complete without an eccentric gear somewhere. And while real world concerns could inspire him, he might spend months on some delicious mechanism without a thought to its usefulness. He said to his engineers: "First I'll invent something, *then* I'll find an application for it."

He did most of his inventing abroad, or on "vacation" whenever his imagination was let loose from office tribulations. His notebook pages read at the top: "Karachi," "Oslo," "London," "Provincetown," "Stockholm," "Miami," "Istanbul." There he would be, sitting on a bench in an airport, waiting for his flight, shoulders slightly hunched, notebook held open in his left hand, propped close to his chest, near enough to see the thin lines of his pen. Every so often he'd look up and gaze for a moment above the heads of the featureless crowd. His sketches were rough, not clean like those of a trained draftsman. But his pen strokes were sure, deliberate. The image was solid in his mind. He'd been working on that image each day, driving to business meetings, or walking in the streets around his hotel. Many pages from the 1950s and 60s are headed "Delray Beach," the town in Florida where he bought a house and brought the family each winter.

There, walking steadfastly up and down the beach, the details were ground out as the grains of sand ground beneath his determined feet.

But the details, unfortunately, left much to be desired.

There is a vast difference, it must be understood, between an inventor and an engineer. Tad, despite his training, was not an engineer. "He never worried about how things fit together," John Eckert recalls, chuckling. "He could make a design that was impossible to assemble. That didn't bother him any."

"Father was an artist," claims his son Michael. "His concept was to achieve something of beauty, what they call an 'elegant construction.' He loved for example the little Citroen. The fact that you had a pool of oil underneath it every time you parked—totally beside the point. He liked its construction. Other people would design for pragmatics. His objective was to sculpt something beautiful in steel."

As Jacek Gajda explains, "Tad was looking mainly from the theoretical standpoint: 'If I turn this, it should turn.' But the world is not perfect. [Many of his machines] were too flimsy. Overdesigned in some areas, too complicated. In just plain rigidity and toughness, for steel mills, it wasn't there."

It wasn't there because Tad wouldn't give anyone the chance to put it there: there wasn't enough money to build it right, and there wasn't enough time to make calculations and tests. And besides, his ego considered calculations and tests superfluous. "Certain things are by inductive reasoning," Tad boasted to me. "I can design it, build it, set it in operation, guarantee it, without having any previous experience."

Tad wanted entrepreneurs to find him, buy his inventions, and put in *their* capital to make them work. And when he was forced to spend his own money, he guessed and used shortcuts. Machines intended for heavy industrial work were put together with dime store hardware. This gave them problems, and these problems masked the potential of the original ideas. And scared the entrepreneurs off. Add to Tad's stinginess with materials his stinginess with salaries; his refusal to pay top engineers left him with less qualified men to push and transform that dime store quality material into Tiffany-quality machines.

Tad could not recognize his own limitations—either in his time, with his other duties running a company, or in his prowess. If only he'd left the details to his engineers. But for Tad that would have meant letting go, losing absolute control, and trusting others—those others whom he never thought were as smart as he. On the other hand, Tad assiduously avoided the details of development, the details—let's say it, the problems—that arose *after* the machine had been sold. Here was the painful evidence that his mechanical children were not perfect.

Tad's greatest strength was his overweening self-confidence, that force that launched and sustained his career. It was also his greatest weakness. John Turley viewed Tad's attitude with some bemusement: "He reminded me of King Canute, the one who was so obsessed with his own power that he took his throne to the seashore and commanded the tide to go out. Sometimes Mr. Sendzimir would come up with an idea, and I'd say 'Now wait a minute. I don't think the natural laws permit you to do that.'"

When natural laws would *not* cooperate with Tad's way of thinking, he refused to cave in. He'd store the idea away in the attic of his imagination (once in a while going up to peek at it), and months or years later it would be brought downstairs again, maybe wearing a new dress. He simply couldn't admit—even to himself—that an idea was wrong. Later on, this persistence became counter-productive. In the words of Michael: "He was a stubborn person—a trait of Sendzimirs. He never would say, 'I have failed.' Some ideas he pursued beyond the point of normal return. It's not just a question that it cost him money. It also cost him time, before going on to something more successful."

To evaluate and explain Tad Sendzimir's gifts and contributions as an inventor, we have to separate theory from practice, ideas from execution. On the one, he was ingenious. On the other, sometimes, abominable. But the failures can be ascribed not to his limits as an engineer, but to his limits as a human being: his stinginess, his mistrust of others, his egotistical self-confidence. However, just those traits...well, could he have been as brilliant, as driving, as ground-breaking, without them? I don't know.

Nicholas Grant, Professor of Metallurgy Emeritus at MIT, told me without hesitation, "If you went to a thousand people in the steel industry, and in the universities, and simply said, 'Off the top of your head, list five names in the steel industry that come to mind,' you can be sure that Sendzimir would be one of those. Bessemer would be another, and he was over a hundred years ago. Sendzimir would be right up there."

Tad's place in the pantheon has been acknowledged by every award the steel industry can bestow, starting in 1949 with the Bronze Plaque for Fundamental Achievement in Galvanizing from the American Zinc Institute, to the Bablik Gold Medal from the International Zinc Institute in Paris in 1964, to the Bessemer Gold Medal from the Iron and Steel Institute in London in 1965, to what is the engineering equivalent of the Nobel Prize: the Brinnell Gold Medal from the Royal Academy of Technical Sciences in Stockholm, in 1974. As one of his tried but loyal engineers said, after discussing the problems working with Tad, "You know, they don't give so many medals to just anybody."

CHAPTER ELEVEN

THE FATHER

1950s

My earliest memory is of cages filled with giant, drooling St. Bernard dogs, the crisp mountain air of Switzerland, and profound annoyance. It was the summer of 1956. Tad had taken the family to Europe for six weeks. I was three and a half, Jan Peter was six and Stanley ten. The boys got to go up the Great St. Bernard Pass on the ski lift with Tad, while I, too small, had to stay at the bottom with the dogs and my mother.

I was too young then to appreciate what was more unusual than a roomful of St. Bernards: Tad's company. He was for once being a father, in the way he could best. He enjoyed packing the family into a car and carting us all over the countryside. And we enjoyed this man as he was in those times: relaxed (well, relatively), warm, lively, full of facts about geology, history, minerals, clouds, music—whatever might come up on a trip across the Alps. And we quacked and preened like ducklings on a sunny March morning—basking in the unfamiliar glow of having this dynamic person all to ourselves.

But, as always, we didn't; we had to share him. Our itinerary took in only those mountains and villages that lay between the customers Tad was visiting. We were herded into and out of hotel rooms, and while waiting in the car for him Berthe had us practice counting to twenty in French.

"Family" for Tad was a powerful, but unfortunately abstract, concept. His own childhood in Lwow had been storybook, warm and close with siblings and parents. Now with his own brood, he cherished the ideal of family but allotted little time for the practice of it. It's not that he felt himself too old; Tad was still young and energetic at sixty, when I was a baby. He simply applied that energy to his other children: his inventions.

His business drew him away on trips over a dozen times a year. When not out of the country, he worked in the office all day, came home and kissed us on the cheeks, ate supper with the family and then retreated to his study. He'd come back to the living room around nine o'clock to play a few simple etudes on the piano, to relax. On most weekends and in the long summer evenings, when light and weather allowed, he went alone into the woods, clearing trails and thinking. We stayed behind.

Despite his physical and mental absences, his effect on our lives was abundant. We were like a neighborhood of small homes built at the foot of a skyscraper. Some of our windows faced in other directions, but he was always hovering there in back, casting his shadow across the entire landscape.

Tad was an absent, and absent-minded, tyrant. His love for us was balanced with his love for his work and his inventions. His desire to have his children around him was balanced by his need for solitude in order to think. He was impatient and quick to anger, but quick as well to forget. His urge for control, for domination, was balanced by what Stanley calls his "short attention span." His high expectations for us were balanced, were indeed negated, by his absences, and his refusal to teach or guide or even discipline us in any consistent way. "What's puzzling," Jan Peter says, "is how Papa could be so tough with everyone else, but with his kids he couldn't lay down the law."

Tad made some attempts, in the early days, to exert control over his children. Stanley was first in line and received the brunt of it. He was expected, as the eldest, to be mature—and so was blamed when any of us misbehaved. He was expected, as the son of two intelligent people, to excel in school. But Stanley and school were occupying different wavelengths in the hum of intellectual pursuit.

Tad responded not with help or compassion, but with disappointment and accusation. "It deeply hurt him that Stanley had such poor grades," Berthe says. "He'd say things to him like, 'You have the intelligence and you're not doing anything with it.'" Tad's lack of sympathy for Stanley's problems was fueled by his callous and self-congratulatory individualism. For Tad, all failure is failure of will: "He's just lazy."

"I couldn't really respond when he was scolding me," Stanley says. "I was left with a sense of helplessness and shame, of not being capable of dealing with things. With a sense that I was a failure."

Tad's dominance over Jan was less specific, perhaps because Jan was a sensitive and quiet boy. He didn't challenge Tad just by standing in the room, as one gets the feeling Stanley did. Jan also had problems at school, but he tried harder, and was allowed a little latitude. But in Jan's case, Tad's potency bred dependence. Jan claims that his childhood was pervaded by the sense that Tad was always there with the right answer, always knew what to do and could bail you out when you tripped up.

With Stanley, Tad's dominance produced resentment and despair. With Jan, it produced dependence. With me, eventually, it produced rebellion.

In my case, I was shielded somewhat because I was a girl. I wasn't asked to carry the full weight of his expectations, but I also was never thought less capable. I suppose he made exceptions in his ad hoc autocracy, I don't know how else to explain the fact that I always feared him less than my brothers did. Scholastically (and this is what counted in our family), I set out on better footing and so had less trouble than the boys. Waterbury's best school was a private Catholic school admitting girls only. I was a pretty good kid (albeit a smart aleck) until I became a teenager, and by then it was too late to re-assert control—since of the many things I inherited from my father, hard-headedness is probably foremost.

Berthe was caught—she placed herself—squarely in the middle. She played the go-between, the peace-maker, the protector. Protector of Tad from us, and vice versa. "I'll talk to your father." "Let's see what your father says." She might wheedle out the little indulgences, but would not openly question his authority or his sacrosanct agenda, for instance by bringing up the fact that his children needed him.

Jan Peter remembers vividly the one instance of close and loving help from Tad: they built a model boat when Jan was five. "It was very crude, just pieces of balsa wood. It was for kindergarten. But we made it *together*. I remember how he sat down with me and we talked it through, we planned it out carefully. Then we cut the wood, and glued it, and made the little boat. I was so proud of it. Not because I'd made it, but because we did it together, from start to finish. Because he'd taken the time to help me."

There were no more model boats, there were no more lessons or shared projects with Tad. Why should he have been surprised and disappointed, then, when none of the three of us grew up to be engineers? The surprise would have been if we had. Tad's work went on inside his head, or on those beautiful and mysterious blueprints we weren't allowed to touch. No delightfully dirty machines lay in pieces in our garage for us to ask about and get our fingers into. I was twelve years old before I ever saw a steel mill (and even then it was Michael, not Tad, who took me).

But this is not to say that we never saw him. He made time for vacations and weekend outings, and we were squeezed in with his continuing passions for physical activity, for America's open spaces, and for the many varieties of the internal combustion engine. On Sundays in Connecticut we'd be packed into the Cadillac and taken for long excursions. On Cape Cod, where he'd bought a cottage in 1960, he'd have us trek across the sand dunes near Provincetown. In Florida, he had a brief fascination with small boats, and he'd take the family up and down the Intracoastal Waterway. In the mid-1950s, he found and bought a gigantic motorized trailer, twenty years before they became popular as "RVs" (Recreational Vehicles). One advantage to this vehicle was that other drivers could see him coming and get out of the way. (Our enjoyment of these trips was offset by the fear that something was bound to go wrong. We'd be stuck without gas far up a river in Florida, or a tire would blow on the gravel road we'd turned on to because we'd missed the intended road two miles back. His impact as a brilliant and accomplished personage was deflated somewhat by our ready knowledge of Tad as a distracted, ten-thumbed scientist.)

Our distance from him was exacerbated by his foreignness. There was the simple fact that he hardly knew a baseball bat from a telephone pole. He didn't fish. He didn't bond in such American ways with his boys. Berthe at least made a studied effort to counteract the disability she saw in our growing up in this European household; she tried to make us as American as she could. We weren't raised speaking Polish, or even French. But, for me, Tad's thick Slavic accent, his European manners, his eccentric eating habits, his advanced age—all were the cause of anguish.

We suffered, as do most children of an extraordinary parent, in not being (or feeling—there's no difference) qualified to walk in his footsteps. Tad of the overreaching self-confidence raised three children whose paramount difficulty in life has been lack of same. Stanley was belittled, little challenged or rewarded, his legitimate difficulties dismissed. Jan felt Tad was omniscient and omnipotent—a safety net Jan had trouble putting aside. As a female, I had less difficulty, but less of me was expected, so I too expected less.

We lived in that house in Bethlehem until 1959. Tad then bought a large brown brick house in Waterbury on Randolph Avenue. We gave up the comfort of the woods and our rustic, rambling bungalow for the comforts of a middle-class neighborhood and one of the more thoroughbred homes on the block. The house impressed me deeply: it had that cool, pleasantly musty smell of old, thick-walled houses; it had a tremendous finished attic for us to play in, and a crystal chandelier in the front room, just under the boys' bedroom. My mother taught me to play solitaire on the round mahogany table in that front room, as she did each evening while waiting for Tad to come home for supper.

Tad's dogma of individualism was conveyed to us in his stories of his life, many of which fudged the facts a bit: "I've always been my own boss." "I pursued my own path." "I ignored those people who said it couldn't be done." We were to learn by example, not by trying it out at home. But he did encourage in us a healthy scepticism of established facts, and he let us get away with little acts of disrespect and disobedience—talking back to him, for instance—perhaps to promote some of that independence of spirit. None of us were forced, later when we were in college, into a certain career at his whim. His code was: "Pursue what interests you, as I have done, and turn that into rewarding work."

We eventually came around to his odd and eccentric tastes. We each now like classical music, and bear a special warmth for Chopin because of Tad's playing each evening. We drink our carrot juice and eat our yogurt, we take our walks. We've grown into interest in our Polish background; we've visited our relatives and studied the language, and developed a taste for beets and poppyseed cake. He was also successful (unless this is purely genetic) at bestowing upon each of us his sense of humor: his appreciation for the witty tale, the multilingual pun, the play with words, the cackling aside. This merry irreverence grew noticeably as he aged, and replaced in our hearts the memories of the harsher aspects of our relationships with him.

In that house in Bethlehem, which Tad and Berthe eventually moved back to, there remains an entire cabinet full of photo albums. Tad's love for cameras hadn't abated since he'd made his own at thirteen. The home movies and the snapshots show a family together: in the pool, on the beach, in his small boat, in the camper. The pictures show a happy family, and they don't necessarily lie. Snapshots seldom show conflict, turmoil or tension. But such conflict was more prevalent in the next decade, with our reaching puberty, and with America reaching the Sixties. Neither Tad nor Berthe were prepared. Was anyone?

CHAPTER TWELVE

THE BUSINESSMAN

1956 - 1965

Two dozen denizens of the drawing rooms and offices of Armzen and its mill builder, Waterbury Farrel, groomed themselves and gathered at the Waterbury Club one evening in 1955. Tad was hosting a formal dinner party to celebrate ten years of cooperation between the two companies. Speeches were made and anecdotes shared and glasses raised, and a photo and write-up appeared the next day in the Waterbury newspaper. Within a year of this event, Tad had bought out Armco's share of Armzen, and sold, in effect, the whole thing to Waterbury Farrel. He set out again on his own, with Michael and a handful of engineers.

Tad fit into that class of businessmen who become uneasy when the organization they run gets over a certain size. "Trusted managers" was an oxymoron. If he had any concept of an organizational chart, Andrew Romer explained to me, it was: "TS—line—and the mob." By the mid-1950s, the mob at Armzen and PM&M had grown to seventy people. PM&M was highly profitable; Armzen was just entering the Japanese market. Tad stared into the jaws of success.

He stared as well into the jaws of competition: his basic patents on the Z mill were about to expire. Armco, the 51% shareholder of Armzen, had said plainly that they wanted out of this relationship when the patent protection lapsed. The royalty payments would evaporate with the patents. Armzen subsisted not on royalties but on fees charged for designing the mills. By 1956, however, there were entire cabinets full of such designs. The mill builders could practically do it themselves. Tad thought Waterbury Farrel might as well.

What he sold to Waterbury Farrel was the Western Hemisphere, the exclusive rights to sell Z mills anywhere west of Europe and east of Asia. He kept the other half of the world to himself, for his new company, T. Sendzimir Incorporated, and the ongoing offices in Paris and London. (This deal looks, walks and talks like restraint of trade. I'm told, however, that the agreement didn't violate anti-trust laws because there weren't any such laws with an international scope.) Waterbury Farrel got the drawings, and the people who had been working on them. Tad and Michael were given managerial titles at Waterbury Farrel (half-time). In this way, Tad had in effect both his cake and the eating of it: he unburdened himself of the company, but retained some say in its operation and some sway over its personnel.

Why did Tad sell? First of all, in relieving himself of this asset, he got to take home a lot of money; Eisenhower taxed capital gains far less severely than income. He also felt that with his U.S. patents expiring, he ought to bail out on this continent and concentrate overseas. There were signs that the U.S. market had eaten its fill.

But Armzen could have stayed in the ring if Tad had combined it with PM&M. He would then have had an engineering company with a reputable and profitable manufacturing arm, and he might have been able to slug it out in the U.S. Tad was not, however, a slugger. While he was interested in making money and promoting his mills, his game wasn't competition or manufacturing. His game was inventing. So he cut his potential losses, sniffed out what was still available without a struggle overseas, and pared his firm down to focus on new ideas.

A year after that big fish Waterbury Farrel consumed Armzen, it was itself consumed by a whale: the Textron Corporation of Providence, Rhode Island. Textron's founder, Royal Little, was known as the "Father of Conglomerates", that new permutation of Big Business that developed after World War II as a way to grow but still avoid anti-trust laws. Though Little personally hated the word "conglomerate," he earned his nickname by acquiring fifty multifarious companies between 1953 and 1960.

When Tad first heard of Waterbury Farrel's sale, he seized the phone. "What about Bliss? Or Farrel Birmingham?" he asked. "Waterbury Farrel should join a company in the mill building family." Left unspoken was his worry that he himself would lose some control in the depths of such a giant corporation. Then he realized he could collect on Textron's new stake in rolling mills. As even Textron executives admitted, when they bought Waterbury Farrel they were buying a cat in a bag, but the cat jumped out at the last minute. The cat was PM&M. Whenever a Sendzimir mill was sold by Waterbury Farrel, three sets of backing assemblies had to be ordered from PM&M, at one hundred percent mark-up. Textron wanted—needed—to control the whole operation.

Tad had wanted out of manufacturing. Selling PM&M to Textron let him retain his authority and status, unshoulder some responsibilities, and, again, make a tidy profit. One final impetus for the sale, according to Michael, was a lingering yearning for prestige. "Those were the days of...you could call it 'euphoria'," Michael says. "Father wanted to get a seat on the Textron board. He wanted to have a little say in the operation of a big American company."

PM&M continued to do well at Textron despite a few bad investment decisions on Tad's part. He was less careful with Textron's money than he'd been with his own. But eventually the slackening demand for Z mills took its toll. (Japan—the only growing market then for the mills—had arranged its own supply of backing assemblies.) Textron finally merged PM&M with Waterbury Farrel in 1970. This little company, once second from the top of Textron's list in profitability, plummeted to second from the bottom.

By 1970 Tad was spending less than five minutes a week thinking about PM&M. His concerns, through the 1960s, centered around the company he launched in 1956, T. Sendzimir Inc. (In 1964, Textron made an offer to buy T. Sendzimir Inc. also. Tad had mixed emotions, the majority of them bad: "...I fear a certain loss of initiative," he commented in his notebook. But he left the decision to Michael. Michael killed it, having no taste for the dog-eat-dog corporate atmosphere.)

*　*　*

Everyone came to work as usual to that brick Armzen building on the Flats, on the morning after the sale of Armzen to Waterbury Farrel. Pieces of paper had been signed, promises and plans swapped, hats shuffled, sign painters summoned and new business card designs sent to the printer, but all the employees took their places at their old desks and drafting tables on the first floor, as they'd done for ten years. Only the chain of command was different.

Upstairs was T. Sendzimir, Incorporated: Tad, Michael (who in six months was made President, while Tad became Chairman of the Board), Andrew Romer (a V-P and Tad's assistant), Ted Bostroem (in semi-retirement), Rodney DeLeon (the accountant), Tad Bijasiewicz for the planetary, and a few draftsmen and secretaries. As the point of the business was expansion overseas, the work to be done was leg work, not board work (sales, not new designs) so Tad serving as his own chief engineer did not pose immediate problems.

Those must have been a blissful first few months for Tad, as admiral of this trim craft before it hit the open seas. The bluster and barks couldn't hide Tad's boyish delight in his power over this small crew. But on the course Tad had set, Magellan-like, he had no alternative but to grow. Eight years later, he was again in charge of seventy people.

These seventy were busy, through the 1960s, as the business of making, shaping and treating steel continued to expand. The sales staff spread like Jesuits through Australia, India, Eastern Europe and the Soviet Union, and strengthened existing business in every Western European country and Japan. The men on the service staff spent up to four months at a time in those countries, training novitiates and bringing the mills on line. The competition Tad had feared when his patents expired never really materialized. It remained the case that if you wanted to roll thin gauge metal, especially stainless steel—and everyone from Liverpool to Lusaka did—you had to talk to Sendzimir. In 1968, T. Sendzimir, Inc., sold sixteen mills; ten years before they had danced in the aisles over the sale of just one. Michael recalls the Brazilian fellow who came seeking a mill for his brass and copper plant. "He negotiated, this reduction and that one, and then finally, at the end of the day when everybody was exhausted, he comes and says, 'And now the last thing. How much discount do I get if the payment is cash?' Everybody looked at him. Finally the sales manager said, 'OK, five percent.' He opened his wallet and counted the money out, paid on the spot. Maybe $150-160,000."

In the next twenty years, the mills got still bigger and faster—and better in many small ways: improved wipers, winders, gauge control, housing. The T. Sendzimir, Inc., brochure began to appear with strange items on the back pages, as Michael sought to expand the product line: cartridge mills, tandem mills, skin pass mills, turret mills, sheet and plate mills—all variations on the Z mill granddaddy, which itself pure and simple showed no signs of age.

Some mills became tiny. In 1962 if you visited Imperial Metal Industries in Birmingham, England, (if they'd let you in) you'd not be issued the standard visitor's hard hat. Instead they'd give you a white lab coat. You'd not be taken into a cavernous building with a herd of hammering, elephantine machines and stacked-up rolls of greasy, dark steel. Instead they'd lead you into a quiet, sealed and air-conditioned room. On a table in one corner, attended by two men in lab coats and protective eyeglasses, would stand their Z mill, the size of a large toaster, rolling zirconium foil to a gauge accuracy of 0.0008 inch, give or take 0.00004 inch. Some of this foil was shipped for use in a nuclear reactor; the rest landed in the hands of paparazzi for their zirconium-lined flash bulbs. At a similar mill I visited in Hamilton, Pennsylvania, the work rolls were 1/4" thick and would easily be mistaken for expensive ballpoint pens. The foil from this mill is shipped in tiny clear plastic boxes, half the size of a box of straight pins.

The big and brutish sibling of those foil mills can be found in the wine region of central France, at Gueugnon, pressing stainless and silicon steel. This is the sixth of Gueugnon's Z mills, the top of the line of the ZR-21s. Nothing special about it—the inner mill workings look like those of 1960—but this mill is the largest and fastest in the world. To the top of its hoods sucking up the oil fumes, this pea-green monster stands two stories high. This mill's work rolls could not be mistaken, as those of the tiny foil mill, for ball point pens: they're five feet, not five inches, in length.

The bulk of the steel strip coming forth by the ton from Z mills is used for the prosaic needs of the industrialized world: cabinets and hub caps and kitchen sinks and subway car railings. But Z mills also spew out the stuff of scalpels and hypodermic needles, and in the past helped fashion early computer memory cells and rocket nose cones. A plant in Tennessee was rolling uranium on a Z mill. The Pentagon commissioned 350 tons of .001 inch thick stainless steel for the sandwiched layers of the outer skin of a Mach 3, B70 bomber. That foil mill at Hamilton Precision Metals in Pennsylvania used to roll an alloy for flight recorders on jets—the metal tape was thin enough to stamp data onto, and strong and heat resistant enough to survive a crash.

It's fine to say, "This product is terrific for flight recorder tape, so thin yet so tough." But how did it get that way? Imagine the numbing labor required to squeeze an eighth-inch thick piece of metal that's hard as a diamond down to the thickness of the film on your eyeballs. Only Tad's Z mill can do it. Three hundred and ninety-one Z mills have been sold around the world since 1946, and three hundred and eighty-seven of them are still running.

*   *   *

In 1962, not long after we'd moved to Waterbury, I was playing with some kids on the street in front of our house on a windy, stormy, spring afternoon. Suddenly one of us looked across at the hillside to the west. No more than a mile away a long, bent, black finger of cloud was pointing and touching the houses and trees beneath. The twister was studded with large pieces of those houses and trees, and with bright flashes, explosions we could hear above the roaring wind. I ran into the house to get my mother: "Mommy, I just saw a roof fly by!" To my great disappointment, she felt it best that we not go back out to look for more.

I doubt that roof was the same one that came off the T. Sendzimir,

Inc., building. The drawings and blueprints in the drawing room on the top floor were strewn about, but no rain had fallen. Everyone picked up the pieces and a new roof was installed. A week later, in a heavy storm, that roof collapsed and the drawing room flooded. Tad held out through these inconveniences, but a few months later he met finally an irresistible force: a six-lane highway project was being steered right through the center of the building. Tad chose a spot on top of a hill nearby, in a new industrial park, and erected a low, modern office building sheathed with black metal panels against which his chrome letters reading "SENDZIMIR" showed up smartly.

Inside the building, Tad set up his L-shaped office in one corner, looking down the hillside at the spot where his research shed would soon rise. In later years visitors to the T. Sendzimir,Inc., office, if they had the bad luck to arrive when Tad was off in Florida, would get the next best thing: a glimpse of that office. On the walls hung gruesome and humorous masks from Africa, Indonesia and Mexico. (Tad delighted in masks—he probably saw himself in their ancient, fierce, cagey, laughing faces.) There was a Chinese scroll, and behind his desk, award certificates in frames. On top of the bookcases were wooden models of his mills, a Japanese tea set, a globe, and two brass Chinese scholars sitting cross-legged, conversing. On the shelves were back issues of steel industry journals, reference books, well-thumbed machine tool catalogs, and a few small heaps of steel scrap, like piles of apple peelings—samples rolled on experimental mills in his research shed. Between the mounds of memos, correspondence and blueprints on his desk sat a rice paper lamp from Japan, a conch shell from Florida, and several hefty sparkling rocks and geodes he'd bought in Colorado. Plus a model airplane. What usually caught the visitor's eye was the compact but magnificent Samurai headdress, with golden wings, embroidery and silk tassels, perched on the corner of the desk atop its black lacquered box.

*   *   *

On the occasion of Tad's seventieth birthday, in 1964, the occupants of that new T. Sendzimir, Inc., building descended into town and threw him a party. His son Michael always welcomed and generously reimbursed the attentions of a captive audience. Tad's speeches, on the contrary, were succinct, unpretentious and surprisingly humble. Here's what he said that night to the people who worked for him:

> This is a nice cornerstone in my life, if I am to measure life by years and not by achievements. I find that I have been always pursuing some objective, trying to solve some problem, without counting the years, always sure that the solution was just around the corner. And now that the years have caught up with me I find that I have more unsolved problems on my hands than I ever had before. And they are as fascinating as ever.
>
> My consolation is in the fact that I am not alone. If I ever had any luck in life, it was with my collaborators: from the beginning of our pioneering work in Poland, then the association with Armco in Paris and during the War in the U.S., then the years of Armzen, Waterbury Farrel and T. Sendzimir Inc. I would never have passed the first hurdle had it not been for the enthusiastic and effective help of my collaborators.
>
> I see some of them gathered here and it is to them that I extend my cordial thanks and best wishes for future successes.

The gathering rose for a standing ovation, and sang a round of the Polish ceremonial cheer, "Sto Lat" (May He Live a Hundred Years.) His true, kind and diplomatic words were taken as justly deserved. (And justly suspect—these gentlemen basked in the success of their illustrious and indomitable boss, but they'd scarcely heard a word of praise before.)

Sitting across from Michael and his vivacious wife Jane was the quick and capable Andrew Romer. Romer had been hired in 1955 as Tad's "administrative assistant," and that meant for business matters he became second in command. Romer might have thought he could take over, but a family business doesn't work that way. He overestimated himself and underestimated Tad's loyalty to his son. Romer stuck it out for thirteen years. Finally, in 1968, Michael let Romer go, and Tad—who valued his assistant and liked him personally—allowed it. As he told Berthe, "Michael is my son, and if Michael cannot work with Romer, Romer has to go."

Ted Bostroem, veteran of the Z mill from the early Thirties and head of the Paris office after the war, was also there enjoying himself at Tad's birthday party. He and his wife Kyra (who had been Tad's secretary in Paris) had come over to the States to work for Armzen in 1947. He was still living well on the royalties from his small but crucial investment in Tad's galvanizing patents in 1931. (With petty resentment, Tad always begrudged Bostroem those gains—conveniently forgetting how Bostroem's tireless engineering labors in Katowice helped launch Tad's career.) Bitterness aside, until Bostroem's death in 1988, not a New Year's Day would pass without a comradely phone call from him to Tad in Florida.

John Eckert and Jim Fox were at the party with their wives, as was the quiet and diligent Rodney DeLeon, the accountant Tad had hired in 1947 fresh from business school. But Tad Bijasiewicz was in Japan. He was working on a planetary mill for Nippon Yakin Steel—on their payroll, not T. Sendzimir, Inc.'s. He'd finally had enough of butting heads with Tad.

Bijasiewicz had been superceded in Tad's research work by a flamboyant, wavy-haired Czech by the name of Val Janatka. He'd been racing cars at the Sebring tracks in Florida before joining the company. He became Tad's favorite, for he was a man who enjoyed working with his hands and who didn't give up easily. "He was not a theoretician," as Romer says, "but he was practical. He would always find some kind of solution, and that was very pleasing to Mr. Sendzimir. Because whatever crazy idea Mr. Sendzimir had, Janatka would try to build a model of it." He was a brilliant engineer, and a ladies' man. He drove to work in a Jaguar. He was also a swindler.

Tad, dependent on Janatka's skills and verve, was at his mercy. He couldn't fire him even though he knew he was being cheated. Janatka sent in the same expense accounts two and three times over. "Once I caught him," Romer explained, "on a really flagrant story. Janatka was ordering elements for one Sendzimir company at one dollar apiece, then selling them to another Sendzimir company for five dollars apiece. When I brought all that to Mr. Sendzimir's attention, he said, 'I know it, but what can I do? I need him so badly.'"

Janatka had once gotten a job for one of his girlfriends—a model—as Tad's secretary, and was surprised when Tad complained that she couldn't type. "What do you expect, Mr. Sendzimir?!" The secretary then attending the seventieth birthday party was Vera Lundberg, a timid slip of a girl who worked for Tad for ten years. The employment agency had warned her about his work habits before her interview. Vera thought she'd been hired by some combination of Pilsudski and Einstein; this frame of mind only exacerbated her nervousness. Two more individuals at the birthday dinner deserve mention. One was Albin Palczinski, the man who'd been promoted to chief engineer over Bijasiewicz. Not a brilliant engineer, he was instead a brilliant organizer, and he kept the drawing room at a hum. He would quit, in 1965, over one more argument about the planetary mill. He would be replaced by Roy Seeling, a coarse, transplanted Brit who'd been hired in 1962. Seeling was, unfortunately for the operation of the company, disliked, and considered a sycophant. His attitude, according to one engineer, was "Yes, I'll work for T. Sendzimir, but I'm the one I'm interested in." That meant not sticking his neck out—challenging Tad—to solve a problem. Even the excessively reticent Japanese complained about Seeling. Seeling wasn't getting much done, but, from Tad's point of view, Seeling wasn't giving him much grief either. It is, however, well-aimed grief—the hard questions, the risky struggle for solutions—that builds quality machines.

*　　*　　*

Gathered around a conference table in 1958 in a hotel room in Washington, D.C., a November wind tapping at the glass, were five gentlemen representing American know-how, and two gentlemen representing Polish have-not. The mood was congenial, business-like. The meeting had the benedictions of the Export-Import Bank. Loans were available now that—two years prior, in Poland's "Spring in October"—Poland had loosened slightly the collar of its Kremlin leash. Gomulka's government was attempting some mild reforms.

With these U.S. credits, Poland set about modernizing her steel industry. First on the list was the gigantic plant built after the war in a new suburb east of Krakow, and named for a man who spent only a short time in that city but whose influence over the country was in those years exhaustive (in both senses of the word): Vladimir Lenin. When the directors of Huta Lenina, the Lenin Steelworks, wanted a modern galvanizing line, it didn't take much imagination for them to call up the man who'd built its prototype fifty miles away, twenty-five years before.

That's how Tad came to be sitting in that conference room, accompanied by Michael, across from the Polish ambassador and his aide. Tad had enthusiastically assembled the pieces—the U.S. companies and their representatives—to build a galvanizing line. For the sake of the Americans, the conversation took place in English. For the sake of paying tribute to a job well-done, the Embassy later hosted a small reception for Tad and Michael.

The ability to lay a coat of zinc onto a sheet of steel was not a skill that much improved a nation's military capacity. In the opinion of the United States government, the ability to roll a sheet of steel down to a gauge of .0001" did. The U.S. military was using steel rolled on Sendzimir mills in its rockets and advanced electronic equipment, so why wouldn't the Poles, the second largest member of the newly formed Warsaw Pact, if they had the chance? After the galvanizing line was installed at Huta Lenina, the plant directors started looking for a Sendzimir mill—but simply to roll low carbon steel, and silicon steel for common, road-side variety electrical transformers. Because of the Z mill's potential for military production, the U.S. government said no.

Negotiations for Poland's first post-war Z mill only began in 1967, and went on for three years. (The 1933 mill in Katowice was still operating, and still rolling the thinnest low carbon steel in Poland.) "Father was inwardly very proud that his equipment was returning to Poland," Michael says. "I think the mill was a little bit closer to his heart. We hired lawyers in Washington. It had to be cleared by the Commerce Department, which had to clear it with the Defense Department and the Treasury. "Even with the green light, negotiations for the mill proceeded in some secrecy. The T. Sendzimir, Inc., man in Krakow sent this cryptic telegram back to Waterbury with news of the closed deal: "[They] served for dinner spaghetti with Swedish meatballs." This meant that the mill would be built by

Innocenti, the Italian builder, and the electrics provided by Asea of Sweden.

In 1961, Tad returned to Poland after a twenty-two year absence. He'd last visited when the Nazis were about to invade. He had sent packages and money to his relatives through Hitler's occupation, and he continued through Stalin's, despite his vast sorrow that his hometown and half of his native province had been carted off and glued on to the Soviet Ukraine. There were those in the Polish emigre community who called for no traffic with the enemy—that is, the people in power after 1945—but Tad ignored them. He pursued any avenue to help his compatriots, especially through his donations to the Kosciuszko Foundation in New York. In dispensing scholarships and requesting visas for students, the Foundation had no choice but to talk with the *apparatchiks* in Warsaw. Tad disliked but was somewhat fatalistic about the Communist regime—echoing exactly his boyhood sentiments toward the Austro-Hungarian Empire. He felt no qualms that his efforts, for instance in helping to modernize Poland's steel industry, might strengthen or legitimize the Communist regime. To his mind, it was for the greater good of his countrymen.

Aniela came down from Torun to meet her brother. Terenia was living in Warsaw then with her second husband. The two sisters and some members of the Warsaw branch of Sendzimirs stood with bouquets in the waiting room at the Warsaw airport, new but already resembling the inside of an ashtray. The official welcoming party consisted of the Secretary of Steelworks and Foundries, Dr. Francis Kaim, who would later become Vice-Prime Minister in Edward Gierek's government in the 1970s. There were no reporters or fanfare for the return of this world-famous native son. Tad hadn't wanted to make a big thing of his visit, as he didn't know what conditions he would meet or what difficulties might arise for his relatives.

He chatted with the customs official as the man glanced passively at the items in the corners of Tad's suitcase—the mundane bounty of consumer society priceless to those who've seen little of it: stockings and cigarettes and make-up and soap. He asked Tad how long he'd lived in America, and was astounded when Tad told him twenty years. Tad's Polish, the man said, was better than most of what you heard even in Warsaw.

Tad immediately went south to Krakow to see the rest of the family and visit the site of the galvanizing line. His favorite aunt, Malgorzata (Madzia), was still alive and in her late eighties. The extended family gathered for a welcoming party in the garden below her apartment. Tad was given a comfortable seat next to Aunt Madzia. A procession of children and teenagers—the post-war Sendzimir progeny—filed by to be introduced. Later he sat in a quiet corner with Terenia, listening with lowered, moist eyes to her account of their mother's last days at the camp in Kazakstan.

Tad had become the patriarch of the Sendzimir clan, and the classic rich uncle in America. With the checks he was sending—carefully portioned out among aunts, cousins, nieces and nephews—and the clothing Berthe packed up in our basement and shipped to Krakow each year, the extended family achieved a small semblance of comfort in otherwise straitened lives. Tad made these gifts open-heartedly, in stark contrast to his practice at the office. He only came to resent, on each subsequent visit to Poland, the crowds of relatives each with their fresh request. This one would like to come to America. That one needs money to pay a bribe to get a better apartment. It exhausted him. But once there, at those family soirees, he sank happily into the warm, scented bath of those Lwow and Krakow accents. The well-fingered stories of their noble forebears and the cheerful memories from Saint Teresa Street and family holidays in the Tatras. The tattered letters and family documents passed delicately around. The old studio portraits on heavy cardboard postcards brought with the newer snapshots in bundles tied with string. It was always difficult to get him to leave.

In Krakow he met up again with Kaim. They were driven out to Nowa Huta, the gray suburb built to house the Huta Lenina workers, and given a tour of the plant. Kaim, in a letter to me, described how impressed Tad had been with the technological advances in Poland, compared to the primitive state of industry before the war. Tad had tried in turn to impress upon Kaim that the answer for Poland lay in even greater modernization. "Mr. Sendzimir [spoke of] the future development of the country as a base for the development of the steel industry. [Only] the most advanced machinery and the most sophisticated technology...would bring about high quality products competitive in the international market." Tad was as always prescribing success via a wave of that soothingly, seemingly apolitical magic wand: technology. Many in Poland, including the Stalinists, wouldn't have argued with him.

Tad also impressed Kaim with his continuing love for Polish literature and culture. On his second trip to Poland, Kaim presented him with a set of the complete works of Adam Mickiewicz, which for Tad was treasure equal to any Z mill order. (Kaim was ousted, along with all of Gierek's government, by the upheaval of Solidarity in 1980. When I visited him in his Warsaw apartment in 1987, he showed me one of the mementos he retains from his time in power: his business card made of stainless steel, 0.05mm thick, rolled on a Sendzimir mill.)

Tad and Kaim met Huta Lenina's director in the conference room adjoining his office. They sat chatting with him for a few moments on the heavy wooden chairs that, with their matching table, had in sheer bulk no doubt filled the entirety of some furniture manufacturer's Five-Year Plan. (When I visited this same office in 1987, I was told that the chairs had been made massive "so we couldn't throw them at each other.") They left the office and returned to their chauffeured car, and on the way out passed around the giant steel sign at the plant's entrance, visible from one mile down the broad avenue leading up to it: "Huta im. Lenina." Thirty-one years after this visit, in 1990, the sign would be replaced. It now reads "Huta im. T. Sendzimira."

*   *   *

For an inventor, Tad was a superb businessman. But this is a bit like saying, "For a dog, Fido was a superb bicyclist." That he did it at all was remarkable. Considering the lot of most inventors, Tad's wealth and success were extraordinary. The question, according to his son Michael (who is a businessman and not an inventor, and so perhaps overvalues his own strengths), should be: What would the

Sendzimir enterprise have become if Tad *really* had been a businessman?

His success came much from his style. He was charismatic and confident, but not pushy. His customers were sincerely fond of him and held him in great respect. Christmas cards by the cartload came in each year from across the world. The mention of the Sendzimir name would gain your entrance to jealously guarded steel plants across Europe.

But he applied his charm selectively. He cultivated his foreign customers far better than ones in the U.S. He could converse with those European mill owners, who were almost all members of the aristocracy. American plant directors wanted to talk about golf. Tad wasn't a drinker (one martini was usually enough), and he was entirely unmoved by sports. He only once in a while took time to rub elbows at industry conferences and trade shows—a requisite for success in this country. He also was critical of the U.S. steel industry for its conservatism, and sometimes he didn't keep that to himself.

He was persuasive, patient and persistent, and that sold a lot of mills. But he time and again *over*sold mills: those little angels who got straight As and never hit a ball into the neighbor's picture window. When the mills misbehaved, some customers came back with lawsuits.

While as an inventor he was daring, as a businessman he was timid. He wouldn't diversify, or seize opportunities a more far-sighted executive would have. At Armzen and PM&M business was throttled down. He didn't hire enough salesmen, service or design engineers to cover the work coming in at Armzen. He steered away from the profitable joining of Armzen with PM&M. His outlook was cautious, his priorities narrow; his firms grew almost in spite of him. He thought not like a businessman, but like an inventor.

His methods of work reflected these same priorities. He'd tear around in fourth gear overseas, but downshift to first when seated at his desk in Waterbury. "There would be a very important issue," Romer said, "and for days and weeks he would just leave it hanging. He would sit in his office and read the technical magazines, but not read the important correspondence. The only time we could get things resolved was one hour before his departure abroad. Then there would be these evening sessions, you had to stay, and he would go through every paper, every folder, and clean it all up. He would shoot orders right and left, everything decided in one hour."

No doubt the most salient explanation for Tad's success is the factor that in business school they can emphasize but they cannot instill: charm. No matter the headaches his mills might be causing, nearly everyone admired and enjoyed the unique and personable individual that he was. He had the warmth, grace and graciousness of nineteenth century polished mahogany—with the brilliance and quickness of twentieth century alloy steel. The center of attention in any crowded room, he had the aspect of a lightning rod—thin, erect, charged, yet also buoyant. Straight shoulders holding up the thin frame; frame leaning gently forward to improve hearing; hearing and concentration focused and floating on slightly bent knees; balls of the feet balancing the coiled load. He would lean his head forward slightly to hear better, but he kept it high. His gaze was steadfast, intense—he never knew an urge to lower it. He smiled easily. His gray eyes would twinkle with an amusing story, or flash with boyish delight as he explained some unusual mechanical design, aided by a quick sketch on his cocktail napkin. His conversation was ency-clopedic. He often could tell a customer obscure facts about that person's local culture or history that the man never knew himself. If the fellow was indeed knowledgeable, a fascinating and nuanced exchange would take place, Tad guilelessly flattering his host with his keen interest. His dinner conversation was punctuated with witty stories, impeccably timed in any of five languages. It was with regret that his hosts had to put an end to this and bring the subject of business back on the table. When it was finally served up, Tad, with his wide technical grasp and unorthodox point of view, talked circles around them. As one executive put it, "Tad was very intelligent, and often it was difficult for those of us less intelligent to follow his argument." He took a warm and personal, avuncular (and often proselytizing) interest in the people he met. Your name and address would be scribbled into his notebook. If you happened to mention a physical ailment you or yours were suffering, a month later you'd receive in the mail a photocopy of a magazine article prescribing raw garlic as the infallible cure.

Yes, he could be exasperating, but his friends (no less than his family) accepted that as an adjunct to his charm and likable eccentricity. Yes, the planetary mill at Ductile in England had more bugs than a bog in June, but when he visited, he was greeted with unequivocal warmth. Jim Fox describes the routine when Tad came to England:

> He used to come and we'd have a meeting to solve all the problems. And about the time we'd get to a real sticky one, he'd say, "Oh, I have to phone the Continent." And he'd get up and go to the phone. Frank Hall [Ductile's president] would say to Charlie Baker: "Charlie, he's pulling a Sendzimir on you. Now when he gets in here, you tell him to sit down there and you're going to get this thing ironed out!" And he'd be half-grinning at the same time, because Frank was really fond of Mr. Sendzimir. In the afternoon, we'd go over to the mill, and everybody that knew Mr. Sendzimir was glad to see him, problems or no problems. Even on the Continent, people that had mills that gave them trouble, they still liked him.

Frank Hall's successor, Bill Sidaway, liked Tad just as well but hadn't Hall's affection for the planetary mill. He said once, in front of Tad, "Tad is a wonderful man, and he is a good friend. But he makes his customers pay for his research." That is, a customer might get a device that was designed on paper, but had a multitude of problems still to solve. Those solutions came on the customer's time—and so on the customer's dime. While most were eventually rewarded with a successfull mill, Tad's practice, as a business principle, could hardly generate good will.

Tad probably smiled at Sidaway's comment. He would have agreed. But he was by no means the sole practitioner of this method. In heavy industry it's impossible on a practical and financial level to build and test every new idea in a lab. Much experimentation has to take place when the machine is built and sitting in the customer's plant, working with their own crew and their own equipment and material. This is standard in the industry. Tad didn't defy convention so much as recklessly exploit it, and in so doing exploit the bonhomie he depended on.

With Tad the matter was also one of prudence. He cited Edison, who supposedly said that he let his customers do the development. John Eckert says that Tad once had a calculated fear of putting his own money into an invention. Tad told Eckert in the 1940s, "I know that I have an awful lot of ideas, some of which perhaps are not very practical. And if I were to put my own money in them, I'd soon spend all my money because I would do foolish things. If I have an idea, and I cannot persuade a customer that this idea will make money for him, of which he can give me a part, it probably means it's not such a good idea.'"

Such prudence was worn down by the stream of galvanizing and Z mill royalties. Tad later found it impossible not to dip into the accumulated pool to water his own "perhaps not very practical" ideas.

As his company got bigger, and as Michael tried to take over the business aspects of T. Sendzimir, Inc., Tad spent more time on research and less on business. Nonetheless, he always enjoyed his role as an executive. He couldn't be one of those inventors who never ventures from his lab and leaves the making and counting and spending of money to someone else. He had to have control. And he took pride in it. He couldn't stay put—he loved traveling around the world. The negotiations and the pace energized him. But Michael has another story: "The main objective in Father's life was never making money. It was to get the name of Sendzimir to the forefront. In the early days, he *had* to be a businessman in order to get his own personal finances going. Once he sold Armzen to Waterbury Farrel, and he had other income coming in, he was pretty much comfortable, so he didn't need to worry. Then he lost interest in the business."

Tad was only a businessman for as long as it was unavoidable—to accumulate the money and the recognition he needed to continue inventing. He enjoyed some aspects of the job, and he was good at some aspects of the job. But what success he reaped, he reaped far more on his own personality, on luck, and on the brilliance of his two premier ideas, than on business acumen. (And it must be noted that, in his own estimate, the greater part of the money he made over his lifetime came from smart investments in stock and real estate, which of course were made possible with the earnings from his inventions.)

While Tad through the 1960s was concentrating less on T. Sendzimir, Inc.'s, business and more on pet projects, he nonetheless held to firm beliefs about how that business should be run. These beliefs were increasingly at odds with those held by his son, the president of the company.

CHAPTER THIRTEEN

JAPAN

Five thin young men stood stiffly in the entryway at the T. Sendzimir, Inc., building. One of their number, a tall, good-looking man with a squarish face and pug nose, said hello to the receptionist through her sliding glass window. She told him Andrew Romer was expecting them and they should go right in. Fujio Umetani knew the way; by the early 1960s he'd come many times to Waterbury, leading squadrons of steel engineers eager to observe Sendzimir mills in their native habitat.

Romer greeted them warmly. When all were seated, he and Umetani reviewed the itinerary of their tour. Romer then showed the men around the T. Sendzimir, Inc., office, and brought them at the end to meet the inventor of the mills they had come seven thousand miles to study. As they entered his corner office, Tad strode over to enthusiastically shake each man's hand. One pulled out a camera and made a quick portrait of the group. They bowed, looked around in some amazement at the paraphernalia on the walls and shelves, and filed out.

Nearly thirty years later, on the eve of his retirement from the Nissho-Iwai trading company, Umetani explained to me how relations had changed since then: "In the beginning, between 1958 and 1969, when I was in the Iwai office in New York, I coordinated many, many trips of Japanese engineers to the United States, to visit steel makers. The U.S. was the teacher. Then, at some point, the situation reversed, and the United States was sending engineers to Japan to visit Japanese steel makers. Then Japan was the teacher."

241

The Japanese picked themselves up from the rubble of World War II with a concentrated, government-directed effort to modernize. Recovery was sluggish at first. Then, with the outbreak of the Korean War in 1950, it surged. New steel plants were built and stocked with the best equipment yen could buy. The quest for maximum efficiency was the ideological mortar binding each project; the quest succeeded—production costs shrank. New plants, for example, were located at the edge of the sea, so raw materials could be unloaded directly off ships, finished products directly onto them—eliminating pricey land transport. (Japan's new breed of tremendous ocean carriers further trimmed shipping costs.) Where in 1946, Japanese steel production was just slightly over 500,000 metric tons, four years later it was five million. A decade later, it had passed twenty-two million. By then Japan had overtaken France's steel production level and was closing in on Great Britain's.

One of the points of Japan's First Modernization Program (1951-55) was to grant preferential treatment in bringing in foreign machines and technology. Japanese engineers combed the globe to find, study and ship home the newest devices the West had to offer. By 1955, they were already able to increase rolling mill capacity six hundred percent. Then they found Tad. And Tad had what they wanted: the most modern and efficient mill for rolling thin sheet metals. Tad stepped aboard Japan's ascending elevator, in the mid-1950s, when it was just gaining speed.

The gangboss over this foreign technology shopping spree was a muscular and influential government agency, the Ministry of International Trade and Industry (MITI). The Japanese government, through MITI, played a decisive role in reconstruction from the very beginning, first targeting and encouraging certain basic industries—such as shipbuilding, coal mining, steel, and electric power—then turning its paternalistic, nurturing gaze on more advanced areas as the economy improved.

Much has been said, by admirers and critics alike, about the intervention of the Japanese government as the explanation for Japan's success. But much has been said, also as explanation, about the Japanese character. The country's geographic isolation helped its people develop a strong, homogeneous identity. The population, heavily concentrated, could only survive cheek by jowl through collective activity and skilled group organization—in contrast, at the opposite extreme, to what families of European settlers faced, alone, on America's vast prairies. The Japanese combine their collective sense with a proclivity for hard work, both in pursuit of education and in mastery of technical skills. The result at the level of the individual firm is an atmosphere of an extended family: trust, support, hard work and cooperation. The result at the level of the entire nation is familial as well: after the war the Japanese people focused on the collective rebuilding of the country, not on the individual attainment of the new car, house, or washing machine. Everyone—from the top engineer to the day laborer—had shoulder to wheel.

The push for modernization didn't slacken once the economy improved. The "Japanese Miracle" went on unabated; their thirst for the newest technology remained unsated. In the steel industry, basic oxygen furnaces and continuous casting machines materialized in Japanese plants immediately after their debut in Europe, while it took years for the Americans to adopt them. Tad's Z mill sold in Japan like bottles of sake on New Year's Eve.

The first Z mill was sold to Japan in 1953. All foreign business with the Japanese flows through trading companies, gigantic outfits that negotiate sales between Japanese firms and the rest of the world. Trading companies have specialists in each field, and it is they who deal directly with the Japanese clients and arrange all government permits. Tad took up with the Iwai Company of Osaka. In 1968 Iwai joined with another trading company, Nissho, to become Nissho-Iwai, now Japan's sixth largest. They sell everything from jets to sneakers to gold bullion...to Sendzimir mills.

When Armzen's team first landed in Japan in the mid-1950s, conditions were still primitive—little better than what Tad had left behind in Shanghai twenty-five years before. Emil Skulski, then a young Armzen engineer, remembers both the enthusiasm, and the difficulties:

The problems came from their not having enough facilities

yet—cranes, forklifts, etc. Everything was done by human beings. To move a ten ton coil of steel, they had twenty people roll it on the floor to the next operation. With rope. The factories were very simple, only just the roof, no sides. In the winter, the typhoon would be blowing through. Sometimes you couldn't get to the mill because of mud up to here.

They were building new plants, but right away they wanted to produce something. They were very impatient. But they picked it up very fast. Every day we had a meeting to discuss the problems, the plans of what to do next. They were smart and well prepared. In other countries, they just don't care: 'OK, we'll see what happens tomorrow.' They choose the easiest way. In Japan, you come the next day, everything was already prepared. No waiting for this or that.

"Between 1959 and 1960 I was in Japan for almost two years straight, working on four mills at once. Six days with one mill, one day travel to the next, stay a week, go to the third mill, back to the first. Seven days a week, usually twelve to sixteen hour days. In Japan they are not like here in the States: "Let's have a cup of coffee," "Let's leave it for tomorrow," No way.

Michael Sendzimir remembers that the customs were strange at first, hard to get used to. As were the trains, and the tiny beds. "You had to go to each individual client. Get up at 7 A.M. and be at it till 10 or 11 P.M. Breakfast with this client, lunch with another one, dinner with someone else. Talking all day. I remember the Japanese night trains. The bullet train did not exist. And we would fly DC4s to Osaka, to Nagasaki, to all these places. Tiny hotels. One communal bathroom. The only heating in the room was one charcoal pot, on which you could rest your fingers and only the first two joints would defrost. The bedcovers were for people about five feet tall; my feet stuck out. So I had to put my overcoat and everything over me."

Tad made his first trip to Japan in 1956. In Tokyo, he stayed in Frank Lloyd Wright's Imperial Hotel, where the beds were sized for Americans and the building would sway on its mud foundations when the earth sneezed. He went back frequently, in later years bringing Berthe; they shared a heart-felt appreciation for Japanese art and culture, and for the Japanese hospitality. "There were always six or eight people to greet us at the airport," Berthe says, "which is far more than we were used to in other places. They had tremendous respect for Tad." While Tad sat in business meetings, Berthe explored the small shops in the alleys off the Ginza, looking for used silk kimonos and for netsukes, the thumb-sized ivory carvings of animals or figures originally used to tie together the strings of the obi, the belt of the kimono. If Tad's Japanese handlers allowed him a few moments rest, he and Berthe would take a walk through the gardens of the Imperial Palace. Between trips, Berthe collected and read the works of Kobo Abe and Yukio Mishima, and made room around the house for the gifts they received from their Japanese clients—the Samurai headdresses and the snow-white-faced geisha dolls. (Fifteen years later the trips to Japan would leave Tad, by then in his eighties, exhausted. He'd treat himself and Berthe to a week in Honolulu to recuperate on their return home.)

Tad left the legwork to his salesmen and engineers. He went to Japan for the executive decisions on partners and mill builders, and to talk over new agreements and experiments. Once in a while he was directly involved with a sale, to throw in the force of his prestige: a plant president might hesitate...then he'd meet the inventor.

By 1961, sales of Z mills in Japan had reached a level where it made sense to open a Sendzimir office in Tokyo. But Japanese law at the time prevented a foreign company from shipping home its profits if it owned fifty percent or more of a firm. Tad came up with a solution: he formed a partnership giving T. Sendzimir, Inc., forty-five percent and the Iwai company forty-five percent—with the last ten percent going to Hitachi, the company that was building the Z mills in Japan. In this way Tad locked in Hitachi's cooperation in the ongoing venture, and T. Sendzimir, Inc., retained both its influence on designs and engineering, and its share of the spoils. Tad became chairman of the board of Sejal, Sendzimir-Japan Limited. The firm started out in some rooms at the Iwai office, and then put up its own small building in a northern section of Tokyo. In the 1990s, Sejal's now dozen plus employees squeeze onto one floor of this building, and the company earns part of its income—a nice part, considering Tokyo's exorbitant real estate costs—from rents on the other floors. (Another part of its income comes with the purest irony: Sejal sells to small restaurants all over Japan a machine that bakes a thin continuous layer of beaten eggs, for shredding over rice or into soups, or rolling up to form some varieties of sushi. The egg-baking machine, invented by a Japanese, is in design, construction and operation an exact replica of Tad's automatic pancake maker. Tad clearly was not far-sighted enough in his marketing strategies.)

The Japanese greatly admired Tad, and he returned that admiration in equal measure. "They will take risks, unlike the Americans," he'd say repeatedly; "They aren't conservative." He felt vindicated by the Japanese.

"Yes, sure. We must compete with America," says Masaharu Sakatani, Sejal's small, gentle-faced, smiling president, "and with each other. So we are very keen to introduce improvements, to make it less expensive, better quality, and so on. So once we think this can be done, then we are willing to take risks. Even if we know there may be technical problems to be solved, they are minor and can be fixed."

The Japanese did not, however, have blind faith in every notion Tad pushed in front of them. In the late 1970s and 1980s, Tad cast many a line into Japanese ponds, and came up with only a few nervous bites. While the Japanese may be keen on the new, they are also pragmatic (see Chapter 17). But their coolness toward Tad's later, more fanciful ideas did not diminish their esteem for the fancier himself. Of all the companies in all the countries around the world that Tad did business with, it was only the Japanese who showed up—five of them—at the tiny church in Bethlehem, Connecticut, to pay their respects at his funeral.

On June 4, 1990, nine months after Tad died, Nissho-Iwai held a large party in his honor in the elegant banquet room high up in their headquarters in Tokyo. The gray tones of the carpet bring to mind a rock garden, and the view from the windows takes in Tokyo's skyscrapers and the green forest of the Imperial Palace grounds. Fifty men from Nissho-Iwai, Sejal and many of the companies owning Z mills attended; Umetani was one of the hosts, Sakatani was there; Michael, Berthe and I were the guests of honor. Old friends who'd not seen each other in twenty years shook hands delightedly, toasted each other repeatedly, and recounted their exploits—traveling to every corner of Japan to sell mills, flying over to Waterbury to drive around the U.S., visit steel plants, and learn about the Z mill. It was a reunion of pioneers. Each came over to bow and shake hands with us, and tell us stories: "Our boss said if we sell five mills in five years it will be great," recalled one early Iwai salesman, "Then we sold five in the first year!" One businessman handed us his card and beamed, "We have *eight* Sendzimir mills!" and he was not alone. The deep fondness for Tad was palpable, based not only on respect for him as an inventor and as a friend of Japan, but on the personal kindness he'd shown and favors he'd done for several—saving one, for instance, from early retirement from Nissho-Iwai by making him president of Sejal. In Tad was crystallized the Japanese reverence for age and knowledge, a forward thinker who paid tribute to the customs of the past.

The true test of Japan's thirst for and skill with new technologies came not with their use of the Z mills, which gave them little trouble and much profit. It came when they agreed to try out the planetary mill. The planetary serves as an excellent example of how the Japanese take on machinery based on what they see as the potential, not on what they've heard of the actual performance. It is an example of their confidence in their own way of doing things: No one else could, but *they* will get it to work. And they did.

CHAPTER FOURTEEN

THE PLANETARY MILL

Some time ago, when Tad was at the height of his career and too busy to sit down to reminisce, a journalist made a casual inquiry into writing Tad's biography. Tad brushed him off: "Just look at my inventions. My inventions are my biography. That's all you need to know." With this in mind, Tad's most controversial invention—the planetary mill—has much to say.

*   *   *

Mild-mannered Charlie Baker has retired from his post as one of Ductile Steel's chief engineers. He has turned his mechanical avidity and attention to detail upon the heather, daffodils and rose bushes in his garden near Birmingham, England. His hair has thinned but his wit and enthusiasm have not. He describes the hoopla Frank Hall, Ductile Steel's irrepressible president, made of the day in 1953 when their planetary mill went on line in Willenhall, England:

> This was a Wednesday. We had not had one single slab through the mill yet. The Sunday before, we'd had a few slabs down the furnace, but the mill itself wasn't ready for a trial run. But Frank Hall always set a date for such openings—either his birthday, or some other anniversary—so everything was arranged, we got all the notices posted, people were coming from far and wide. So it just had to be ready.
>
> Well, we had a grand opening. Charles Wheeler (who later became Sir Charles Wheeler K.B.E.) was invited to open the mill. We'd done lots of build-up. Lots of bigwigs. Industrialists both from the steel side and the components side, the custom-

ers came. Press and local dignitaries came. I think we must have had two hundred and fifty people.

The paint on the floorboards was still wet, because we'd been working up till six o'clock that morning, to finish the installation. I shall always remember Jim Fox standing at the control desk, as nervous as can be, white as a ghost. The building was very long, to accommodate the mill, but very narrow. We all stood there, on the left side of the mill, all crowded in around the mill and the run-out table to the coiler. Oh yes, the coiler wasn't ready. It wasn't wired. So the idea was to get the steel down to the coiler, stop it, and say, 'Thank you very much. Off you go to lunch.' Which we did. *Perfectly.* The strip emerged from the mill and absolutely went down, went down that run-out table, as straight as a die. Everybody clapped, and then they went off and had a good champagne lunch.

That was the last time the strip went down that table straight again, for many, many months. It went left. It went right. It went up into the roof of the building. And Frank Hall said, "Well, it's amazing to think, if that had gone left or right or up into the air on Opening Day, think of the number of competitors we would have killed off!....But my God, look at the number of customers we'd have lost as well!"

Ductile was one among the array of steel shops that thrived in the English Midlands—feeding on steel slabs and billets from the steel giants, rolling those into thin steel strip, and selling the strip to the equally multitudinous auto components shops, who made the bumpers, hubcaps and headlights the auto giants couldn't be bothered to make themselves. When Ductile started expanding its cold-rolling and tube-making operations, they found they needed more coiled hot strip. Outside sources of such strip were at the time drying up. They then took interest in purchasing a planetary mill to roll their own.

For Tad, history seemed to be repeating itself. In 1931, Zygmunt Inwald needed a technological breakthrough; he came upon Tad's galvanizing process, an invention that appeared at precisely the right place and time. In 1945, Tom Fitch recognized that Tad's Z mill was the answer for rolling stainless steel, in those days the metallic equivalent of sliced bread. The planetary, in the early 1950s, had to be the savior of the small steel companies who wanted to produce their own hot rolled steel for a fraction of the cost of a conventional hot mill. The planetary's output was modest—perfect for the many small independent steel shops—compared to the gargantuan tonnage coming out of a conventional mill. The planetary Era had dawned.

In Frank Hall, Tad found a champion no less steadfast than Inwald or Fitch, and no less colorful. Hall was one of the founders of Ductile Steel, and he, with his partner Charles Batten, made of it a profitable enterprise. Hall was a solidly-built man of bullish frame and manner—but a bull who was as well jovial, enthusiastic and friendly, with none of the British reserve. He also had none of the British reserve about new technology.[Appendix, 4] He was a visionary who died, too young, of throat cancer—before the planetary mill was able to prove its worth to his company. But he never had a moment's doubt that it would. At a formal dinner in Wolverhampton, Hall proclaimed, "Give me Tad Sendzimir and one million pounds, and I will create an installation of the size they've done in South Wales!" referring to a new British Steel plant costing twenty times more. Rumor has it that this boast made its way to the House of Parliament, where more than one eyebrow was raised: "Who was this businessman who says he can do for one million pounds what we've just spent twenty million on?"

Unfortunately, bluster and faith won't start steel mills. The mill was installed in 1953 and didn't begin functioning dependably until 1958. Ductile didn't see a penny of profit till nearly 1960. The problems seemed numberless—"heartbreaking," as Baker put it. And, as at Washington Steel, there was no one to call. There were no planetary mill experts with twenty years of stories, and gray hair to match. There was only Jim Fox.

Tad excused a hefty chunk of the royalties he was due, to compensate for Ductile's losses. And he tried—also against character—to take the advice of Eddy Correa, his legal counsel: Don't say to them, "I know it will do it," Correa said in his letters. Say, "I *think* it will do it." But Tad needn't have worried about a lawsuit from Ductile. Despite the immense problems, Hall found it impossible to get tough with Tad. He was too fond of him.

Jim Fox was seen more around Willenhall in the mid-1950s than he was around Waterbury. John Eckert came over too. Their difficulty lay in convincing Tad that certain changes were necessary, changes to designs Tad was convinced would work—because they did in theory. The four thousand miles between Willenhall and Waterbury gave the engineers an advantage. Fox simply made those changes on his own. Tad, as always, was just not interested in the fine tuning. But Tad was also, Fox says, trying to keep out of the abundant personal arguments among the engineers, who each had their pet solutions.

"It is possible," Tad admitted much later, "that I may have been overly optimistic, saying 'Oh, it works, so I can go somewhere else.' The other thing is that I was always on something brand new. When I had a cold mill, I was thinking of the planetary. When I was working on the planetary, I was thinking of some other new type of mill."

Once the mill got going, it became extremely productive and reliable, if given solicitous attention and the proper diet—as you'd treat a beloved but churlish uncle prone to hypochondria. Ductile's engineers raised the planetary to ninety percent efficiency—better than a conventional mill. They had to run two eight-hour shifts every day to meet demand.

And demand there was. The planetary, once up to speed, quickly dispelled the notion that it was just a cheaper version of a conventional hot mill. It was a different mill altogether. It distinguished itself by producing steel strip to much closer tolerances than the strip from a conventional mill.[Appendix, 5] To compensate and get those closer tolerances, the conventional hot rolled strip had to then be cold rolled. The planetary strip often didn't need cold rolling—an entire process could be eliminated for some applications. And for every ton of strip you got five percent more finished product, a pleasant and profitable effect for Ductile's tube company. Baker and the other engineers also discovered ways to make the strip surface smoother and finer than conventional hot strip. Not only was Ductile flooded with orders, but they could charge higher prices for their higher quality strip. Ductile's strip became so much in demand that at times customers had to wait a full year to get their order. And the engineers became so sure of their prowess that in 1966 Ductile bought another planetary from a nearby plant, Habershon.

For twenty years Ductile reaped a profit on its planetary mills. Then the big guys caught up; they hadn't liked being undercut by this pipsqueak. They started building much wider and more efficient mills, mills with better gauge control, mills that produced hot strip at considerably less cost. By the mid-1970s, across the globe the price of low carbon steel was plummeting. Steel from Japan and Europe came courting the British builders and manufacturers. Ductile was priced out of the market, and finally had to shut its doors.

*   *   *

Few planetary mills were able to match Ductile's success. Of the fourteen production planetary mills built, less than half became as profitable. On those, sweat and elbow grease had as much impact as the high pressure water and oil flow systems.

The first batch of production mills were ordered and built in the early 1950s: Ductile and Habershon in England; Atlas Steel in Welland, Ontario; Magnetics, Inc., in Pennsylvania and General Electric in New York. The last of the early mills was also the largest, a forty-six-inch wide mill built for Safim in Milan, Italy. Then came a lull, and in the early 1960s another burst of activity. In 1962 five mills were built: Henry Wiggin, a small mill in England; Benteler (in West Germany), Hellefors (in Sweden), and Orbegozo (in Spain), all three medium-sized mills; and Norbottens (in Sweden), a duplicate of the large Safim mill. Between 1965 and 1966 came the last three planetary mills: a small one for Hitachi Metals in Japan; and two identical giants, one for Atlas Steel in Tracy, Quebec, one for Nippon Yakin, near Tokyo.

Each mill has its own story, of course: its supporters and detractors, its scenes of pathos, its days of hope and its days of frustration, and, for most, the day it was at last unplugged. They all had the problems of the Ductile mill, and some had peculiarities of their own.[Appendix, 6] Arguments ran on about whether the mill was underpowered, but everyone agreed that the mill was underdesigned. Some went further and said the mill was in the first place ill-conceived.

Tad was asking thousands of moving parts to work in precise harmony, to do a hot, dirty, pounding job better left to the burly and simple-minded thugs of the steel industry, those conventional hot mills. The planetary was a machine that "ate itself up."

But why, in 1966, were the last planetary mills having the same problems as mills designed and built in 1951? The main difficulty was that the planetary mill did work in theory. And that theory was *so* beautiful. How could you not love a mill that cost a fraction of its competitors, and gave you an even better product? You could—not love it, that is—if you were one of the men climbing up to remove and replace seized bearings for the fifth time that week. Tad himself never had to. He cherished the theory of this mill as he cherished the design of his old Citroen—a car that leaked oil like an un-housebroken puppy.

When Tad bothered to occupy himself with solving any of the planetary's nagging problems, he did so by *adding* more moving parts, not by subtracting any; he'd make the mill even more complex. Tad and his engineers did make improvements from one mill to the next. But, as Bijasiewicz complains, they never did an overall analysis of the mill: "If we had taken stock, after that first batch of mills—dug in, made an analysis—and then come up with the next mill, then we probably would have been successful." The engineers weren't given the chance to question or study the fundamental design of the mill, to bring forth a new generation.

A mill that amply contributed to the planetary's reputation of being unsound was the one installed just shy of the Arctic Circle, in Lulea, Sweden, for Norbottens. The Norbottens mill was built in 1962 to give work to lumberjacks during the long, dark winter. But the mill's problems began seven years before and 1500 miles away, in Milan, Italy—for the design of the Norbottens mill was a duplicate of the design of the Safim mill. In the words of Professor Blain, head of the IRSID Research Institute in France, "All the errors committed at Safim have been religiously repeated at Norbottens."

The Norbottens mill came at a turning point, both in respect to the planetary's shaky reputation, and to the new development in hot steel: continuous casting. Continuous casting was just then gaining enthusiasts across Europe. The planetary mill was in Tad's eyes the perfect companion for that new process of forming slabs. If the Norbottens planetary had been an unqualified success, Tad might have been besieged with orders. But he had resisted, again, spending his company's time or money solving the problems, because he felt that was the customer's job. The orders didn't come.

Most terrifying to potential customers was the mill's Achilles heel: maintenance. "You've got thousands of pieces and springs and nuts and bolts," says one of the Sendzimir engineers, "and in a rolling mill, everything that's fastened together somehow or other has a habit of breaking loose." Tad had again designed—like the Z mill—a delicate and complicated machine, but this one did its job under incomparably tougher conditions. Conditions that don't make themselves obvious on the pretty blueprints. Steel plant owners looked at the planetary, and looked at the planetary's competitors, and figured, "Why bother? The product is OK, but we can't afford the maintenance."

The planetary suffered not only from its physical problems. It also had conceptual problems. It fit into a rare, tiny niche—the small steelmaker who wanted to produce his own hot rolled strip—that was closing up. With the steel crisis of the late 1970s, with so many plants consolidating and closing down, with so much excess steel being produced worldwide and turning to rust, the planetary's fragile niche disappeared. The small mom and pop steel plants could buy hot strip for far less than it cost to run their own planetary. The large steel plants perfected their giant mills to make a cheaper and better quality hot strip. Plants like Ductile went out of business.

The planetary's sales brochures bear pictures of the Ductile mill under a cloud of steam, the signature diagram of the mill in cross-section, and a list of the mill's piquant attributes.[Appendix, 7] But the Sendzimir engineers and salesmen were never able to convince the steel industry that the planetary, like its cousin the Z mill, was an indispensible piece of equipment. John Eckert: "The Z mill offered something that wasn't attainable otherwise. But the planetary didn't offer that. It wasn't the only way to get there, if you wanted hot rolled strip." To get such strip, there's more than one way to skin a slab of hot steel.[Appendix, 8]

Despite its breaks and bruises, the planetary mill has no cause to hang its workrolls in shame. The fourteen planetary mills have squeezed out over thirteen million tons of steel—that'll give you twenty-six million Chevrolets. Six mills are still in operation. The Norbottens mill, once free of bugs, produced excellent steel for truck parts. The Habershon mill is now churning out steel in Zimbabwe. The Hellefors mill is in India. With a few exceptions, the planetary mills were put out of business by economic trends, not by mechanical failure or dissatisfied owners.

*   *   *

The largest planetary mills built, for Atlas Steel in Tracy, Quebec, and for Nippon-Yakin Steel outside of Tokyo, were identical twins. The drawings were on the boards in the early 1960s. Nippon Yakin's planetary began rolling hot steel in 1966, within a year of its installation. Atlas only began serious rolling on its planetary in 1972, and it was another ten years before it hit its stride.

The planetary mill's congenital problems were proved at Nippon Yakin, to be not so congenital after all. Examining the two largest planetary mills is like reading those intriguing studies that compare twins raised in separate homes. The examination provides some lessons on mechanics and steel industry practices, and on why Japan is conquering the industrial world without firing a shot. Foremost of these practices is attention to detail.

The company that built the Atlas planetary farmed out most of the components to other firms, and seemed to show little concern for the mill as a whole. "These people did exactly what it was on the drawing," Tad Bijasiewicz remembers. (He had worked as a consultant to Nippon Yakin, and was familiar with the Atlas mill.) "Nothing more, nothing less. Sendzimir engineers stayed away. And this was a disaster." For Nippon-Yakin, the Japanese engineers redrew every single drawing sent from Waterbury, to convert them to metric, and in doing so found and corrected many mistakes and weak points in the engineering.

Jobbing out the mill components was the second mistake at Atlas. The mill housing came from Germany. The gears were made in the U.S., but the gear boxes came from Scotland. The drive spindles came from Sweden. Bob Hart, the engineer at Atlas who finally got their planetary to work, explains: "One problem was that all these independent components came directly to the mill site," not to the mill builder. "There they had to be "field-fitted," often in sub-zero temperatures, to try to make a compatible mill unit." The Nippon Yakin mill was built from top to bottom by one company: Hitachi. They worked closely with Sejal and Nippon-Yakin engineers, re-checking each gear and switch.

Apart from the mechanical problems that hadn't been caught in design, Bob Hart blames the lack of spare parts. They only had one planetary roll assembly to start off; Hitachi had provided Nippon Yakin with four spares.

Atlas management also grossly underestimated the size and complexity of the task. The original work crew was under-staffed, and then was transferred (Hart included) to another job, leaving the mill in the hands of men (again too few) with little experience. Here's how Bijasiewicz describes the start-up of the Nippon Yakin mill: "When Hitachi installed that equipment, they tested each electric motor separately. After that, they connected the mechanical equipment, and they ran all the mechanical equipment. They had thermometers all over the place, to measure whether any heat was developing in bad bearings. Nothing like that was done at Atlas. The Japanese, during start-up, had literally about thirty people, who came there from Hitachi to start up the mill; the builder of the Atlas mill sent only one man."

Each mill had its problems, those typical planetary problems, but Nippon Yakin would have the thing figured out in a week, while Atlas would struggle with it for months and years. And because of Nippon Yakin's superior and conscientious maintenance of the mill, many of the typical problems never arose.

Some of the blame for the poor performance of the Atlas mill can be laid at the feet of T. Sendzimir, Inc. By the mid-1960s, Tad was left with the men he had hand-picked, by default, who were not going to disagree with him. From the sloppy drawings sent to the builder in the first place, to the lack of critical engineering practice, the men from T. Sendzimir, Inc., were not the proud standard bearers the company needed to save the reputation of the planetary mill. They, like Tad, found it much easier to blame Atlas. Tad's comfort came from visiting Nippon Yakin. Here at last was the customer he'd been dreaming of—who simply took his mill and made it work.

* * *

The patents on the planetary mill have expired. T. Sendzimir, Inc., sold its last planetary to Hitachi Metals in 1966. No mills have been bought since because of the ongoing glut of low cost steel available to the small producers, the ongoing satisfaction of the large producers with their high volume mills, and the planetary's ongoing reputation as a finicky and unstable device. A new generation planetary mill could be designed, all the experiences of the past three decades taken into account, newly developed and tougher ceramics, plastics and alloys used for the components—and the original inventor is no longer looming over the engineers to prevent them from befouling his beautiful theories. But no one has the capital or the lack of common sense to conjure this up in a test tube. A real live customer has to show up first with the stamina to order one.

Who might? The planetary mill may yet have a future, in two specific and utterly dissimilar areas: one at the highest tech end of the steel industry—continuous casting, and especially "thin slab casting" of steel; the other at the lowest end—in the Third World.

In some respects, the planetary mill seems ideal for budding steel plants in the developing world, where the niche still exists for the small steel producer looking for a cheaper method to produce his own hot rolled strip (so expensive when bought from Europe, America or Japan). Secondhand planetary mills are in operation in Zimbabwe and India. In 1985, Tad signed a joint venture agreement in Lanzhou, China, to assist a steel company in purchasing a secondhand planetary mill [see Chapter 18].

But there's a catch: all that maintenance, all those spare parts. The planetary remains a highly sophisticated piece of mechanical equipment with an aptitude for failure. You need a jeep for those dirt roads, not a Lamborghini. Still, in the case of the mill Ductile sold to Zimbabwe, Charlie Baker is enthusiastic: "I thought it was a great thing for Zimbabwe. Here they were, a nation spending colossal amounts of money to bring in imported steel strip. They had the iron ore and all the raw materials. They'd got a steel works there, where they could make their own slabs. But they hadn't got a mill to convert it into strip. The planetary was absolutely ideal for them—it would save them millions of pounds on import costs. The only doubt was their ability to run it and maintain it. I arranged for two engineers and two rollers to go down to install it, train personnel and get it going. I met one or two good engineers down there who will be able to figure it out, given the time. We sold them a huge supply of spares which should last them many, many years. You can turn out a lot of the other spare parts in a machine shop, on a lathe."

Tad also had immense hopes for continuous casting. It was as plain to him as the nose on his face that this new machinery, which turned molten steel directly into slabs, should be hooked up to his planetary mill. But those industry giants who could afford to install continuous casting units already had their big conventional hot mills. And they were legitimately nervous about the planetary's problems. It comes down to this: how do you put two processes together, both of which *must* operate continuously, when one of them breaks down with the regularity of a Model T Ford? When you're pouring a hundred-ton ladle of molten steel, and that steel is forming a slab that is moving directly into the planetary mill, and suddenly you hear a bearing seize up on the mill and you have to shut it down—what do you do with the twenty tons of hot metal moving down the chute coming right at you? The unreliability of the planetary gave pause.

But continuous casting units also have downtime; they also need maintenance. A new generation planetary could be designed to be more reliable. The new design might lessen the terrific vibrations that many feel would dangerously jangle the nerves of the continuous casting unit. George J. McManus, a columnist for Iron Age, noted that the frightening prospect of breakdown on such a system may "be turned to an advantage. The penalty for failure can force a maintenance program that prevents failures." The Japanese have run their old planetary virtually trouble free for years on end: they do so very carefully.

Despite everyone's fears, the planetary did hold up its end of the bargain with a continuous caster, right in big steel's kitchen: South Chicago. In 1962, U.S. Steel purchased the Safim mill for experiments with continuous casting. The mill was shipped from Milan to Chicago to U.S. Steel's Southworks plant. Slabs from a continuous caster, five inches thick, were sent first through a conventional mill to reduce them to three inches thick. Then they went right into the planetary and were flattened to the gauge of tin cans.

"We were getting fifty tons per hour, very good coils." says Howard Orr, chief engineer of rolling at U.S. Steel during those experiments. "But we needed two to three *hundred* tons per hour. In the Chicago district, all our ladles were 220-ton. We would have needed six planetary mills, not just one. The planetary mill was just too small for us."

No one seems to know where the ill-fated Safim-U.S. Steel planetary now rests, but in all likelihood it has disappeared into the dusty air of its warehouse: cannibalized for rolls and parts. What has also disappeared is the memory of the mill's success with continuous casting, a job no one since has had the courage to try.

In the 1990s, the world steel industry (outside of Japan and South Korea) can but distantly remember the health and vigor it enjoyed in the 1950s and '60s. Those industrialists not betting the farm on tariffs and price supports (and union busting) are looking to advances in technology to streamline the production process and make it more profitable. Either there's fresh hope, then, for the planetary mill, or the new techniques could leapfrog hot rolling entirely and send the planetary and all its competitors to the scrap heap (to be themselves melted and cast and rolled into hubcaps for little Japanese cars).

The planetary's new hope rests with an advance in continuous casting called "thin slab casting," which creates slabs in much thinner forms. In the United States, all eyes are on a pilot project in Crawfordsville, Indiana, where Nucor Steel has put on line a German thin slab casting unit, developed by SMS Schloemann-Siemag, that produces slabs two inches, not ten inches, thick. These thin slabs would fit quite nicely into a planetary mill. "In terms of speed of casting and rolling, the planetary is the only mill that you can put in tandem with a thin-slab caster," says Michael, echoing the steadfast tone of his father. But all those big mills, and the planetary, may still be made obsolete by even more radical advances in casting: strip casting, spray casting, and metal peeling.

The planetary mill never lost its seat on its daddy's knee. Through the 1980s Tad continued to experiment with improvements and variations of the planetary [Appendix, 9] and with new uses for the mill, such as producing clad metals (for instance, a carbon steel base topped with a thin stainless veneer). His great vision was to get steel from molten metal to spoons and forks in one continuous process. The steel would never touch the ground or wait for a forklift. This plan would use, of course, many of his own inventions: first through the planetary, then right into the Z mill, then coiling up on his spiral looper [see Chapter 17], and perhaps some continuous annealing and galvanizing before or after. This was daydreaming, but daydreaming is where progress starts. Less than a hundred years ago steel was being made by hand.

CHAPTER FIFTEEN

DEVOTION, DISTRUST, DEVOLUTION

1965 - 1974

"He was raised between a steam shovel and a bulldozer."

This was Ted Bostroem's summary of Michael Sendzimir's parents (he'd known both since 1926) and their effect on the boy's formative years. Michael himself prefers the less noisy metaphor of the ping-pong ball. Tad and Barbara were evenly (if fatally) matched, in temperament and will power; Michael grew up favoring neither and fond of both. Despite Barbara's animosity toward Tad, she urged her son to take up the slide rule and go into his father's business. She felt his best chances lay with that insufferable but remarkable man.

"My mother," Michael admits, "was building a negative image in me of Father, but at the same time she was pushing me to work with him. She felt that Father was a fascinating person, that he's going to do something." In 1946, Michael was a handsome, almost burly twenty-two-year-old serving as a lieutenant in the Philippines. And he liked the job. But, "Father had only one son, and he was very much interested to push me. Myself, I felt that [engineering] was a fascinating future. I never even considered an alternative. It was ipso facto, force of destiny."

Ironically, despite the hostility between his parents and lack of daily contact with his father, Michael and Tad developed a bond in many ways closer than what I or my brothers shared with Tad. "Father and I had a unique relationship," Michael says. "In my early days, I saw very little of him. But I had a very good feeling about him. We did not ever clash, when I was young. He saw me so little that the moments we had together, the trips, were all very pleasant. We talked a great deal, he about his inventions, and my mind was open to them." In Shanghai, Tad had brought the tiny boy along to his factory. In France and then in the U.S., he took Michael off on school holidays to swim on the Riviera or hike in the Rocky Mountains. Michael got the concentrated doses of paternal love and attention that Tad never realized his three later children also required. (Michael remained in close touch with his mother even as he was being sucked into Tad's world. Barbara married Alexander Saharoff in 1956. They lived in Switzerland for a few years and eventually settled in a suburb north of New York City.)

In 1946, unencumbered with second thoughts, Michael entered Columbia University to pursue a degree in Industrial Engineering. He joined the sales staff at Armzen in 1951 after he graduated. At Armzen he cultivated his skills in customer relations and diplomacy (a talent already honed in childhood), and augmented those skills with his humor and continental polish. He was affable and hard-working. Six months after T. Sendzimir, Inc., was formed, Tad made Michael, then thirty-two, president of the company, moving himself up to the seat of chairman of the board.

This succession had been Tad's not unpredictable goal from the start, perhaps from the day the toddler had first picked up a wrench. Tad wanted to put aside business conferences and sales trips and return to what pleased him most, inventing. Rodney DeLeon, Armzen's accountant, says that in 1956 it did almost seem that Tad might step down: "He said to me, 'Well, Michael, Andrew Romer and you—you're all doing a good job. I think I can start letting go.' But that didn't last long. Poor Michael got clobbered on that deal. He thought the reins were being handed over, and they weren't." What remained immutable, despite Tad's good intentions, was his outlook on creation: nobody knew better than he how things should be done. Michael had to wait another twenty years.

He even had to wait for a private office. He walked into the T. Sendzimir, Inc., building the next day, Day One of his tenure as president, and took his seat as usual at his desk....at the opposite end of Tad's office, separated from his father by only a long conference table. From his spot in the corner of the room, Michael watched as Tad went on running the company.

With the move six years later to the new building, Michael secured his own office and a bit more authority. He was put in charge of sales, organization, attendance, the accounts, and the engineers and draftsmen not working directly under Tad in Research. The president could be seen, each morning, gazing from his windows out over the parking lot, clocking the comings and goings of the people he was beginning to have some power over. That was one way to show it. Tad still controlled payroll and bonuses—and the respect, fear and loyalty of everyone under that roof.

Perhaps Michael should have started his career somewhere else, to gain independence and authority before joining his father. But that wouldn't have altered the facts at hand: Tad's steel-clad personality and his engraved reputation in the industry. Michael shared the lot of Edsel Ford, or, more recently, Fred Wang, sons yearning to have their voices heard above their fathers' thunder. "Of course TS dominated him," Tad Bijasiewicz says, "one hundred percent. But TS probably trusted Michael more than anybody else in the organization. Michael was trying to prove himself, to show that he was attentive to details, or attentive to management. But when I was there, it was TS we called the tiger, and Michael was the kitten."

Michael was willing to play the hand he'd been dealt. He says, on reflection, that a son following his father into business "has to take the position that it's up to him to coordinate with his father, and not vice versa. The son's attitude has to be for the co-relation, otherwise it's not going to work. What I recognized is that Father, beyond all this, was on my side. We worked toward common Sendzimir goals. Leave the difficulties aside." Michael knew also that his predicament was finite. While no one expected Tad to soon retire, he couldn't sit there endlessly holding all the cards—negotiating every contract, butting in on every design process, haggling over every expense account. And his inventions provided an ever stronger pull away from the table. Michael held on to his pair of aces—time.

Tad's domination over Michael was instinctive, not willfully jealous, spiteful or superior. It was as uncalculated as a monsoon rain. Indeed, he did trust Michael over anyone else. But he often disagreed with him and sometimes doubted, as he wrote in his notebooks and mentioned to Berthe, Michael's methods as a manager and businessman. (Though never as a salesman. Tad always valued Michael's touch with customers.) Tad was profoundly aware that here was the Sendzimir who would carry forward the name into history. His love for and loyalty to his son began slowly to supercede his need for control. The first sign of this shift came in the mid-1960s when Tad took Michael's side in his son's power struggle with Andrew Romer. Tad finally told Michael he could fire Romer—even though he might have felt, but never would have divulged, that Romer was the more competent manager.

Michael continued from there to gain strength and self-assurance. Tad's more and more frequent absences from his corner office at T. Sendzimir, Inc., helped. He was spending his time down in the research shed with his engineers, his planetary mill and its satellites. In 1965, Tad built a new house—to his own design, with a swimming pool smack in the middle so he could step out of his bedroom at 7 a.m. and into the pool—by the ocean in the then-sleepy town of Jupiter, Florida. The week-long escapes had lengthened to four or five months. (And he paid the phone company well for this refuge: he would summon his engineers in Waterbury by telephone several times each day.) He was by then in his seventies, hair battleship gray, the first signs of a slight stoop.

Michael grasped early on that he should keep his nose out of inventing. "Every time I brought a new idea to him," Michael says, "he looked at it and said, 'Let me see if I can make it better.' So, shrugging, I thought, 'Go ahead, make it better.' He was paying me to swallow my pride, that was my attitude. So I made it my policy to stay away from inventing. And that took away the possibility of competition." He concentrated instead on the company and the customers, applying what he'd learned in school about the business end of engineering. He knew every client from Buenos Aires to Zagreb, their birthdays, their children's names, their desires and their difficulties. Like his father, he was congenial, gentlemanly, fluent and witty in five languages, and, despite his long legs, willing to spend much of the year in airplanes. Unlike his father, he was careful and systematic. These traits served him well as the president of a company with interests on five continents.

He was also—unlike his father and almost in reaction to him—quite conservative. And soon the views of father and son began to seriously diverge. It became apparent that the two men had opposing conceptions of those "common Sendzimir goals." Each one's viewpoint, not surprisingly, bolstered his own strengths: Tad's for new inventions, Michael's for solidifying the business.

Michael had been looking on in horror at what Tad was doing: making extravagant claims for his mills, refusing to test experimental devices that looked nice on paper, pushing half-baked ideas onto paying customers. Once when the company almost ran out of cash, Michael had to get serious. "We had to pull in our belts," he says, "and generate our own cash. And I made a promise to myself that we would never be without sufficient assets again." Retaining "sufficient assets" meant, to Michael, digging in. Push and develop only the established products. Look for the quick profit, even if at the expense of long term growth. Don't promote wild new ideas. But wild new ideas were Tad's *raison d'etre*.

The divergence of their visions stemmed in part from the divergence of their loyalties. Tad was loyal to the Sendzimir *name*. To him that meant promoting Sendzimir products (his inventions, new and old) exclusively—push the Z mills, show every customer the new ideas. Michael was loyal to the Sendzimir *business*. Expand the markets and diversify the product line—even if those products might include machines and devices that did not originate with a Sendzimir patent. Tad thought Michael's business decisions would take the "Sendzimir" out of T. Sendzimir, Inc. Michael thought that Tad's inventing practices would take T. Sendzimir, Inc., to bankruptcy court. "I was not against development," Michael avers. "I was against *unproven* development. That was our basic conflict."

Tad didn't seem to appreciate how dire the situation had become. Michael faced competition from Waterbury Farrel and from European mill builders—competition Tad had been shielded from by his patents a decade before. Those other companies had the advantage because they didn't charge the eighteen and a half percent engineering fees for the mill's drawings that T. Sendzimir, Inc., was asking. Ordering a mill directly from one of those companies also put that mill in your shop at least half a year sooner than if you'd ordered it from T. Sendzimir, Inc., Michael says that it was less complicated, cheaper, and the results far more accurate if the builder's engineering department did the drawings. So he began to let the builder make up the mill drawings, instead of having his own engineers do it. Tad hit the roof. What was T. Sendzimir Inc., Tad wondered, if not an engineering company? Where would the company be if the Engineering Department kept having its legitimate work—drawing the company's bread and butter product—taken from it?

Michael found himself unable to sell mills, given the competition, while still retaining the engineering work and fees. In effect he had to undercut his own Engineering Department in order, as he saw it, to save the company as a whole. "I saw what Father was doing in business, and if I was going to run the company, if I didn't take certain actions, we would have no company today. I felt the decisions he made were totally wrong." Tad felt the same about Michael's decisions. In Tad's eyes, there would simply *be* no company if the Engineering Department was starved out; yet at the same time he didn't want those engineers feeding on improvements on mills that were—shades of Armco, John Tytus, 1935—"Not Invented Here." (Or, in Tad's version, Not Invented by Tad Sendzimir.)

But what about those new Sendzimir inventions that Tad's long-suffering acolytes down in the research shed were hammering away upon? What about the spray caster and the rocker mill and the basket cages for the planetary? Michael refused to let the men upstairs in his Engineering Department get near them—because Tad would have swallowed those engineers without so much as a burp. And, sadly but understandably, Michael also refused to sell those new machines. A customer might show up at T. Sendzimir, Inc., to talk about buying a standard Z mill. He didn't want any trouble—just a Z mill, a Z mill he could walk out and buy the next day from one of the firm's competitors. Tad would later hear about this visit and ask Michael, "Didn't you at least *tell* him about my rocker mill?". "I couldn't," Michael would respond, "because then I'd lose the Z mill order. These people want something known and proven, and they can go elsewhere quite easily to get it. We tried the rocker mill and it didn't work." Potential customers were sent down to look in the research shed almost as a novelty, not with serious intent.

Michael faced both stiff competition, and a father who, while claiming to be the more distant chairman of the board, continued to rule as president—leaving Michael with the responsibility but without the authority. Michael took that authority in the only way he felt he could: behind his father's back. There was a flip side to Michael's accommodating tone and his tactful, diplomatic demeanor. The price to Michael's personality of being raised between two strong but thin-skinned parents was a debit in the honesty column. "Devious" is the adjective that came to mind most readily out of the stories of those who know him. Say whatever is necessary to retain smooth relations. No confrontations, please. He would seldom challenge his father directly; it was safer to keep silent, agree, and then do just the opposite. Michael claims that he was open in his dealings, but often that openness came after the fact. Seated between the rock, his father, and the hard place, bankruptcy, he felt he had no choice. And that rock, to add fuel to Michael's disingenuousness, was incapable of hearing an unkind word. Tad responded to criticism with the grace and humility of a three-year-old.

In two letters written before Christmas in 1971, fifteen years into his tenure as president, Michael explained why he was not pushing the unproven inventions. He felt his authority was being undermined. Tad responded with bluster, recrimination and reproof: "You do not give me proper credit! You mention my ideas and the difference between an idea and a mill that performs. But look at the facts..." Michael knew the facts: the many months and years of toil Tad's assistants spent getting those ideas to work, the threatened lawsuits, the loss of royalties, the loss of sales.

Tad clung to a vision, reiterated in this letter, of his company, his inventions, his cooperation with his son, and the rosy future ahead. He'd continue developing new ideas in Research; Michael would sell them to the ceaseless stream of eager buyers. Tad's demands—that only Sendzimir inventions be developed, that the Engineering Department retain its fees—look reasonable in this scenario. But the scenario was based on three premises of 1950s vintage: the superior abilities of his inventions, an insatiable demand for steel and steel-making equipment, and an undying faith in the Sendzimir brand-name. By 1970, with the nearly glutted steel market and the repeated problems of the planetary and other designs of Tad's, these three premises turned to vapor.

After the 1971 letter, Michael went on frustrating Tad's efforts, because he fundamentally disagreed with them. "Michael would have all things as they were," Tad told me, "with only slight improvements. And I had no way to make experiments because his heart was not in it. 'Yes, Daddy, we'll try it.' he'd say. And then one month comes, two months, six months. And nothing is done." And in the process, Michael lost the trust both of his father and of many of his own employees. "Michael was...distrusted," one employee relates, "because he was officially smiling, but you never could count on his sincerity. If he would say something, you never knew if that's the way it would happen, or whether he'll make a 180 degree turn-around."

What he didn't lose was his father's devotion to the concept of Michael succeeding him. Tad had groomed Michael for the job, and then this apple, alas, fell far from the tree. But it was still Sendzimir fruit. He disagreed with Michael's business practices, but he was also weary of the fight. "I hate the way Michael handles things," he'd say to Berthe. "You never know what he thinks—he's not honest. But he's my son. I have to give him a chance. Maybe he will do better than I do."

In tiny, terse notes to himself over two days in June of 1973, Tad seemed to make up his mind:

> I founded TSinc and the substance matter on which it lives: my inventions. Further development program at TSinc is dear

to me, but I also consider it as a family treasure which my grandchildren may continue to develop and get their living from it. But *that* Michael does not understand...

The next day he goes on:

Viewing such management conditions, Michael at TSinc, and willing to sacrifice a lot but avoid drastic steps, I decided, more as an act of despair, to form a Corporation to promote my new developments...The Company's name [will be] Sencor.

In 1974, Tad took his Research Department, left Michael in charge of T. Sendzimir, Inc., and started Sencor. He had just turned eighty. He retained his seat as chairman of T. Sendzimir, Inc.'s, Board, but over the next decade had less and less to do with that company. He turned with relief to his pet ideas—new planetary devices, spray casting of steel, an unorthodox strip accumulator—down in that shed that many still referred to as his "hobby shop." Michael was left to his own devices.

*　　*　　*

Tad found himself with an enemy in 1962: Helmut Benteler of Paderborn, a town a hundred miles east of Dusseldorf in what was then West Germany. Benteler was for over four years a steel-plated mosquito incessantly whining in Tad's ear. The battle with Benteler—remarkably the only lawsuit against Tad that ever went to court—so drained him of time and faith and energy that to the end of his life he spoke of it with a bitterness he harbored for very few: "Mr. Bischoff at Demag...highly recommended Benteler to us as a keen businessman," Tad wrote in his memoirs in 1983, "and did not mean and did not say that 'keen' really meant 'bandit.'"

Benteler was a young maverick who commuted to his office by helicopter. Then in his late forties, he was tall, dark-haired, fit and to the point. He was expanding his steel plant to produce high quality tubes for the chrome-plated furniture then seen in the pages of Italian magazines. But the German tube steel barons refused to supply him with strip for his new operation, to discourage competition. He had to make his own strip. Tad was delighted to oblige:

the first planetary in Germany, a planetary to be hooked up to a continuous caster.

When the German steel suppliers saw that Benteler was going ahead without them, they turned around and offered him all the strip he could buy—cheaper than what would come from his planetary. After a feeble attempt to get his mill going, Benteler quickly tried to unburden himself of it. His method was to sue Tad. He claimed he'd been sold a mill that was underpowered.

That, to Tad, was all there was to it: Benteler was just looking for an excuse to get rid of the mill now that he could get cheaper strip. But there was, alas, something to Benteler's complaint—the mill did have problems. But they were problems provoked as much by Benteler's unreasonable technical demands, and by difficulties with his own machinery. He was, for instance, running his continuous caster at the velocity of a snail. "He reproached us," Michael said, "when he could not roll when he was casting at 1.3 meters a minute. But [at that speed] the slabs coming to the planetary had cooled down completely. They were black, not orange. There was no way we could roll them."

The ill-fated union of the two somewhat experimental machines (the planetary and the continuous caster were each of unique design) came to pass. They were installed, hooked up and switched on without pause for doubt or deliberation. And without test runs. It turns out that Tad and Benteler were equally allergic to testing: Tad because he had such faith in his theories; Benteler because a test run would have forced him to accept results he later might like to challenge. As Michael put it, "He had good lawyers. That was his way of operating, and he sued quite a few companies. He'd just go to court to settle. So a test-run would have been counter-productive for him, because he didn't keep his part of the bargain."

Fritz Lohmann of Demag (the company who built the mill) believes Tad was also a victim of his own naivete—and carelessness—about contracts. Contracts the world over were thickening. "The first Sendzimir cold mills, here in Germany, in '56 or '57, had no big guarantee clauses," Lohmann said. "In '65, still the customer was happy to get a strip mill with a higher production capacity than before, and happy to own a Sendzimir mill. But when we sold a mill in '74, we had to specify exactly this and that rolling program, with this speed and this production, and so on. They became stronger and stronger over the years. Mr. Sendzimir was still in the time of believers: giving orders by hand shaking." Today an agreement is a stack of data with the heft of a metropolitan phonebook; Benteler's order was done on a couple of sheets of paper. "Tad should have concentrated only on existing results, on experience," Lohmann continued. "This thickness I guarantee, this speed I guarantee. But he developed all these ad hoc ideas, and put them on paper."

The gossamer accords of the past had kept Tad from losing his shirt. With Benteler he was at last, and publicly, suffering as the victim of his own recklessness and boasting. Tad's fanfaronade had finally brought him to court.

The case went to trial in Germany. Tad's lawyer didn't have the astringent personality necessary to counter Benteler's advocate, and his expert witness didn't have the clout to counter the experts on Benteler's payroll. Benteler won. As Tad had little material wealth to grab in Germany, his loss was more to his pride than to his pocket. Benteler couldn't get damages, but he pressured Demag to buy back the mill from him, the cost split between Tad and Demag. The mill was in ruins because Benteler had pushed it to near collapse and then—in retaliation—extracted most of its usable parts. It sat for fifteen years in a German warehouse, and in 1985 was packed up and shipped across two oceans, to rise from its ashes in central China.

*   *   *

One late summer afternoon in 1976, en route from Waterbury to Cape Cod, Tad and Berthe drove a few miles out of their way to attend a formal dinner in Belmont, Massachusetts. Dr. Theresa Tymieniecka-Houthakker, a thin-boned, warm and sprightly philosophy professor, had invited a score of well-connected Poles and friends to her home in this polite suburb of Boston to greet and pass bread with a childhood friend who had come to speak at Harvard. This friend had made it big in the world of Polish politics and religion. His name was Karol Wojtyla, Cardinal and Archbishop of

Krakow. Two years later, Wojtyla's dominion spread spectacularly when he was elected Pope. Tad paid scant attention to the skirmishes between party and church in Poland, and his Catholicism was decades in default. The Cardinal didn't know much about rolling steel. But Wojtyla was also, among other distinctions, a poet, a philosopher, a linguist and a mountaineer. He and Tad sat next to each other during the meal and found much to discuss. Tad came away touched and impressed.

They saw the pontiff-to-be again a few days later in New York, at a reception at the Kosciuszko Foundation. A photo from that event stands in a lucite frame on one shelf of a bookcase piled high with Polish books near the dining table in Tad's home in Florida. Tad is on the right, with three other members of the Foundation's Executive Committee, Wojtyla in their midst. (During those years Tad also met, in similar circumstances at the Kosciuszko Foundation, Zbigniew Brzezinski, President Carter's National Security Adviser. We would joke then that Tad had connections both in this world and the next.)

The Kosciuszko Foundation had been at work since 1925 inciting Americans to think well of things Polish. They did so by telling the world about Polish contributions to its welfare, and by encouraging U.S. citizens, especially those of Polish ancestry, to study and appreciate Polish culture, history and language—all in the name of that Pole who came to the U.S. in 1777 to help the colonists rid themselves of foreign rule. Tad's close involvement with the Foundation began in the mid-1960s, when he gave them almost $400,000 worth of Textron shares, acquired through his sale of PM&M.

He has said many times that this gift was a clever way to avoid taxes, and while that it was, the boast is also a bit of bluster to cover what was a philanthropic spirit in full leaf. He'd been supporting the Polish cause since war-time, and in addition had given money to the Boy's Club, the YMCA and other organizations that encouraged young men to "go on the correct course," as he put it to Michael. When we moved out of our first house in Waterbury, Tad gave it to the Waterbury Boy Scouts.

Tad's gift to the Kosciuszko Foundation (to which he added

another $150,000 in 1972) was to be divided equally between that foundation, the Polish Institute of Arts and Sciences, and Alliance College, a very small liberal arts college specializing in Polish studies in the northwestern corner of Pennsylvania. The money was to be used to bring Polish students to the United States for graduate study, and for sending American students, preferably those with Polish surnames, to Poland.

So began Tad's sojourns to the Kosciuszko Foundation's Upper East Side mansion in Manhattan every few months, the storm tide of correspondence and newsletters ebbing and flowing across his desk, the lengthy phone calls in Polish to other board members and the copious notes in his little books on the internal affairs of the foundation. Tad never accepted any official positions, but he didn't shy away from the details of foundation business. At his insistence the Board of Trustees formed an Executive Committee (he became a member-at-large) to keep an eye on things in between the twice yearly board meetings. This committee drew away some of the absolute power the president of the foundation had been able to wield in the six-month stretch between meetings. (Lo, Tad Sendzimir, slayer of autocrats.)

Tad was involved much less with the workings of Alliance College and the Polish Institute of Arts and Sciences. He kept informed and wrote or called in his opinion or advice when the spirit moved him, in a way similar to the sporadic letters he'd dash off to *Nowy Dziennik*, the New York-based Polish daily newspaper, expressing his thoughts on Manhattan taxi drivers or the state of Polish industry. In 1967, Alliance College awarded him an honorary doctorate. From that date those obsessed with titles addressed him as "Doctor" Sendzimir, a harmless misnomer he made no effort to correct.

What did Tad receive in return for his generosity? What all philanthropists receive. Personal satisfaction for helping his countrymen, tax breaks, a lofty reputation in the Polish-American community, the chance to meet big-wigs who came to beseech this constituency (and later the opportunity to boast about having met them). Tad appreciated and made use of all these benefits, but simply helping Poles would have been compensation enough.

Professor Felix Gross, the president of the Polish Institute of Arts and Sciences, bears on his shoulders a large, angular head fringed with white. He recalls that Tad was always a gentleman, and always a Pole. "He was very generous financially, but not only that. He gave with a certain grace. It's not very pleasant to ask for money. Sometimes people make you feel that you are begging. It's especially difficult for a European, where you never had to ask. But he was extremely gracious—he not only gave, but he did so with a generous spirit. He trusted that the money was not wasted.

"He also had a great interest in what is going on with the Polish community," Gross continues. "The easiest thing is to cut yourself off, because it is a tragic problem. He never wanted to cut off ties. He was always proud of being Polish. He had a dignity about it, not arrogance. Something like that in Paderewski, that generation—gentleman-like, in the best sense."

*   *   *

Perhaps after you've received a certain number of honorary doctorates it does become appropriate to be addressed as "Doctor." By the 1980s, Tad had accumulated so many awards and degrees that people felt empty-handed calling this esteemed person merely "Mister" Sendzimir. In 1973 and 1980 he'd been given honorary doctorates from the Mining and Metallurgy Academies of Krakow, Poland, and Leoben, Austria, respectively. The zinc industry had honored him in 1949 (Bronze Plaque, American Zinc Institute) and in 1964 (Bablik Gold Medal, International Zinc Institute, Paris). In 1965, he received the Bessemer Gold Medal from the Iron and Steel Institute in London. In 1982, the American Society of Metals made him a Fellow, and in 1987 the American Association of Iron and Steel Engineers gave him their first President's Award. Poland bestowed on him the Cross of Merit three times—in 1938, in 1972, and in 1983. American civic leaders followed suit. He dined at the White House, got three awards in the state of Connecticut, and in 1986 was among the crowd of illustrious immigrants feted with a "Liberty Award" and a breezy sunlit ceremony in Battery Park on

July 1, at the centennial celebration for the Statue of Liberty (Tad sat next to his fellow countryman Isaac Bashevis Singer.)

Most memorable and significant of all these, if least pretentious and time-consuming in the granting, was the Brinnell Gold Medal, given by the Royal Academy of Technical Sciences in Stockholm, Sweden—an award known as the equivalent of the Nobel Prize for engineers. Tad and Berthe traveled to Stockholm in June 1975, and showed up at the main gate to the Royal Palace, accompanied by representatives from the Royal Academy. They alighted from the car in the palace courtyard and were inspected by the king's black labrador retriever. Ushered inside, they waited half an hour on the main floor and then were brought upstairs to a meeting room. In a few minutes King Carl Gustaf came in. He was then a very young man—it was a year after he'd taken the throne and just before his marriage—with pale blue eyes and dark, wavy, closely clipped hair. The king made a short speech in English. Tad thanked him and reciprocated. The king handed Tad the small gold medal, everyone bowed and the commoners were escorted out. The king's aides-de-camp then led them on a brief tour of a few of the seven hundred palace rooms—the French rococo apartments used by King Oscar II and Queen Sophia at the end of the last century, the immense Hall of the Estates with the king's silver throne—and then brought them back to their waiting car.

The occasion is marked by a characteristically compact note in Tad's notebook from 1975—"Stockholm 6 VI 75, Received by Swedish King Carl Gustaf who handed over to me the Brinell Medal awarded by IVA [Royal Academy of Technical Sciences]." Tad gave a speech at the same time to the Royal Academy about steel industry developments and the planetary mill. Berthe says he was really quite impressed and proud about the whole thing. On his return to Waterbury he showed the medal around to everyone in the office, then locked it away at home in his steel cabinet.

CHAPTER SIXTEEN

FIRE AND FAMILY

In 1964 we moved into a dark brown mansion on nine landscaped acres in the middle of Waterbury. The house on Cables Avenue was just a few blocks from where we had been living. I had ridden on my bike past its tall picket fence many times, wondering who lived in the huge silent house, with its matching carriage house, its small overgrown orchard and wide shady lawn. Now it was going to be us.

The house was perched on the brim of a steep hill. Halfway down the hill stood a line of European beech trees that rose from the bottom of the sloping lawn like a green tidal wave. A curving driveway snaked down the hill between rock and rhododendron to the front gate at the bottom. On one side of the house the owners had built a small Japanese-style garden, since grown shaggy. Berthe soon planted tulip bulbs near the entrance to the house, and later put in their place a feathery redwood seedling, which grew thirty feet in five years. She and Tad would stroll up and down the curving driveway each evening before supper. On dull afternoons, I would bivouac in the Japanese garden and think about boys.

The bounteous funds that went into constructing and cultivating the grounds had been matched nickel for nickel in the house itself. There was an elevator. The front hall and main staircase had been paneled and its banisters carved from glowing oak. The dining room had space for two large tables; the baby grand piano did not crowd the living room. There was a long copper sink for trimming flowers in one of the kitchen's two pantries. Tad put his roll top desk in the

279

corner of the sizable study, which was lined with glass-front mahogany bookcases. Up on the walls went the masks, the pictures of rolling mills and award ceremonies, and the small portrait of his mother as a young girl.

Berthe's domain was the rest of the house. This child of a shopgirl and a pharmacist's assistant attained at Cables Avenue the pinnacle of her career as a housewife. The house was just compensation for her twenty years of scrimping and hard work. "That house was so comfortable," she says. "It was so solid and well built, compared to how matchstick the place in Bethlehem was. Tad loved it. He loved to walk and walk on the grounds. What I loved most was the porch. I would sit there in the evening and watch the bats flying around. And those beautiful trees. It was *heaven*. I remember when we went to Paris when Tad got that galvanizing medal [the Brinell]. We were invited to lunch at this beautiful private club with a sweeping lawn. And I was looking at that and thinking, 'Oh, I wish I were back in Waterbury!'"

My brothers and I spent in that house our—and the country's— most stormy years, but they were sweet ones as well. It was the Sixties. We came of age there. We smoked marijuana in the attic and played Jimi Hendrix and put up anti-war posters. Stanley and Jan grew tall and, in their different ways, handsome; Stanley had inherited the Sendzimir size ten nose, a quick mischievous frown and, from who knows where, his deep, booming laugh (it was embarrassing to sit next to him in movies). Jan was, like Tad, the ectomorph. He got from his mother her brown eyes, from Tad his chiseled features and his demoniacal flair for puns. Stanley and Jan fought the draft board and got deferments. I went through puberty and went to Washington, D.C., to march on the Pentagon and fell out once and for all with the Catholic Church. We castigated conformity, and then dressed each morning in the uniform of the day—beads, bell-bottoms, long hair, sandals. Stanley and Jan went off to college, and I to prep school. We came back in the summers and hung around and got stoned. Tad and Berthe kept their dismay at this behavior to themselves, except in my case (the daughter and the baby, after all) when a few of my friends were banned from the premises.

On the evening of March 6, 1971, this grand house and this exceptional time in our lives went up in smoke.

Tad and Berthe were in Florida. I was in school in western Massachusetts; Jan was in Ghana in a foreign exchange program. Stanley was then twenty-four years old, and studying for a Masters of Fine Arts degree at Sarah Lawrence College in Bronxville, New York. Stanley had gone up to Waterbury for the weekend. He'd invited a friend and our nephew Thaddeus (Michael's son) over that Saturday evening. They went out to a movie. When they returned the driveway was full of firetrucks.

When the trucks finally left, the house was still standing. But its core, starting from the central living room, taking in the master bedroom above it and up to the attic, was no longer.

Tad and Berthe flew up to Waterbury immediately. I drove down to meet them. I remember that the sky that March day was dreary and overcast, an apt illumination for a scene of carnage. The great hulk of a house from the back, as I drove in, looked merely charred on the edges. I remember the air filled with that dank smell of wet charred wood. Walking around to the front, picking my way over wet and still smoking planks and black but familiar tables and couches spread across the snow, I looked up and saw what felt like my very heart—ripped open as if by a giant grizzly's paw, the insides blackened, bleeding soot.

I do not remember much else, except the chalky faces of my parents. Tad was speaking to some men. He was writing in his little book—the name of the fire inspector, the items so far missing, questions. His eyes were hard, shielding. He'd barely said hello to me. That had been his heart too. Not least of what he could see he'd lost, in the damage just in the study, was that treasured portrait of his mother.

The grief was still more Berthe's. She lost in one night her heaven, the one bestowed and the one she'd then lovingly furnished and enriched over the past seven years. She and I tried to comfort each other that morning. But what could we say? Only, feebly, "Thank God no one was hurt."

The hurt was still to come. Tad had to assign blame. When the fire inspector ruled out arson, Tad decided that Thaddeus—the only smoker—must have carelessly tossed aside a burning cigartte, to smolder and ignite the small shaggy rug in the living room. And none of this would have happened if Stanley hadn't been there.

Berthe refused to believe it, and only many years later, in hearing the story of a similar fire caused by an old lamp cord, did she remember that in the living room she too had had an old lamp, and had put the cord underneath the shaggy Polish rug. The fire inspector had noticed a narrow gash, a long thin scar in the floor, directly under where that rug had been. But by then it was too late to change Tad's mind. "Don't mention the fire to me again," he said to her. "I know very well what happened."

Tad and Berthe moved back to the house in Bethlehem. (My brothers and I were away at school and not living at home anymore.) Tad decided not to rebuild the Cables Avenue house because, he told Berthe, it would be too expensive to restore to its original splendor. Berthe, as always, kept her mouth shut: "It was his house, I felt, and his money, and he should make the decision." But she hated to move back to the "matchstick" house in Bethlehem. She lost in the fire not only her hard-won, beloved mansion and park. She also had to watch as Tad trampled over the last shreds of love and respect he and Stanley had for each other.

Tad had plans drawn up to remodel the house in Bethlehem, and in that process Stanley would lose the bedroom he'd grown up in. At the dinner table one evening, Tad told Stanley of this arrangement. Berthe could just sit and listen, the food turning to ashes in her mouth.

"But you're taking my room!" Stanley said, in shock.

"You have burned my house that I loved." Tad replied. "You got me out of there. And now I'm taking your room. And that is the least that I can do."

Stanley started to cry. "Daddy, this fire happened. I didn't have anything to do with it. I'm not responsible for it."

"Well, if you hadn't come that weekend, it wouldn't have happened."

* * *

It wasn't the first time Stanley had been ousted. Tad's response to Stanley's problems in school was not help and encouragement, but scolding and blame—and even that was inconsistently administered, for Tad hadn't the time, temperament or inclination to do more than complain. After Stanley's grammar school principal told Tad and Berthe that the boy was heading for juvenile delinquency, Tad packed him off to boarding school in the eighth grade. When Stanley was at the University of Miami, his adviser noticed his signature high IQ and poor grades. He was sent to talk to the school's psychiatrist, who then said to Tad and Berthe, "There's nothing wrong with your son. He just needs a father." During the summer in Waterbury, Stanley would go out with his friends till past midnight. The next morning Tad would get angry not with Stanley but with Berthe: "Why do you let him stay out so late?!" Why do *you*, said the boy's own father.

In 1970, Stanley did find a father figure, a psychoanalyst, who seems to have helped him over seven years of analysis to come to terms with his anger at Tad. As Stanley wrote in a letter to me many years later, "[Papa was] attempting to deny me the freedom to develop into my own person. This I instinctively...resisted with what will I had. His response...was more restraint and coercion, followed later by a kind of reluctant resignation to my failure to follow the path he imagined for me." But according to Berthe that "path", was nothing more circumscribed than better performance at school— perhaps, to some, a narrow-visioned request, but it was not an unreasonable or unexpected one. Tad was not trying to make Stanley into a brain surgeon, or even so much as an engineer.

Tad found psychoanalysis despicable. In a letter to me in 1973, Tad wrote, "Mummy and I feel exasperated over Stanley's steady and stubborn support of that New York psychoanalyst....It seems that it has become some kind of mass psychosis to invent or to keep thinking that there is something wrong with one's mind that such an analyst may find and improve." "As you can imagine," he went on in a following letter, "patients are for the most part weak (and lazy) persons. The temptation to grab the mind and soul of such a patient is right there." Such was his opinion of the patient in question—his son.

Stanley took up theater in college, then began studying to sing opera. Tad did not object, although the ghost of his irresolute Grandfather Julian, the would-be actor, came quickly to mind. Tad finally did begin to show some concern and interest in Stanley's work. His letters to Stanley critiqued the opera or concert he'd watched the night before on public television, or described the notices of singers he'd read in the *New York Times*. But as the years went by, Stanley, studying under one maestro after another (more father figures), rarely made it up onto any stage. He seemed to be crippled by perfectionism and lack of self-esteem—a legacy bequeathed to their sons by many brilliant and famous men. But poor self-esteem can also, the psychologists tell us, find its source in just such erratic and inconsistent fathering as Stanley had known: fathering that fails to teach about cause and effect, that gives no support to the son's ego and confidence, that ignores the need for steady discipline as well as steady encouragement.

Tad continued—via a combination of blind hope, love, anguish, uncertainty and, notably, if incredibly, lack of will—to support Stanley financially. Tad's checks came inserted in letters pleading with Stanley to look for other kinds of work. One letter in 1987 remarks that "You have an unquestionable singing talent that you have been cultivating to a state of near perfection...Unfortunately, for several years you have found no buyers for your talent and never earned a penny. I am 92 and I hate to think when I shan't be here to provide living expenses for you and your family." Six months later, in an even more depressed letter, Tad recounts his own difficulties between 1930 and 1933 "when I did not know where the money for next month will come from. You were spared such experience. Yet since you never had such anxieties as mine, you did not have a real incentive to get a job for a living."

If only Tad had taken the time forty years before to show the same concern, and to inspire in a fresh young mind that hope, that work ethic and that zest. Tad repeated to us over and over the homily of feeding a man one day by giving him a fish, or feeding him for life by teaching him to fish. Tad the self-made millionaire could sermonize, but he never really taught any of us to fish, so he kept on feeding Stanley year after year.

*   *   *

Jan Peter also spent his boyhood looking for father figures, and weaving fantasies about heroes and omnipotence. He would spend hours lying on his bed constructing and enacting epic daydreams. In prep school Jan found a mentor in the school's biology teacher. He found also in biology an ordered, intriguing, beautiful world, and an authorized excuse to muck about in swamps. He wavered from this path only once or twice in the following several decades. After college he found yet another path, another father figure, and some compelling answers to his questions (or is it questions to his answers?) in Zen Buddhism.

Tad, not much given to spiritual inquiry, nonetheless enjoyed the philosophical banter he and Jan engaged in by mail. His negative feelings about Zen were never concealed. In a letter to Jan from 1976 when Jan was living in a Zen monastery, Tad writes, "Your conclusions worry me a bit. Why would you want 'to suppress a purely intellectual understanding' of things? Whatever brought you to Zen Buddhism, you now can't escape being part of an enormous organization and it becomes just natural to follow the saying 'when in Rome do as the Romans do.' But your individuality, your ego is gone! And that would be a great pity. Maybe I am such an irreconcilable individualist that my own ego finds this revolting."

Tad never made the faintest suggestion that Stanley go into engineering. Jan on the other hand showed some aptitude for the more material arts. He also had a devotion to his father that was more evident than Stanley's in his younger years. In 1977, Tad found himself at the helm of a new company, Sencor, with no one standing behind him should he tire (he was then eighty-three). No one, that is, he could trust—regardless of their qualifications. No one, that is, named Sendzimir. In 1977, Jan was praying in a Zen monastery in South Korea. One of his jobs was to get up at 4 a.m. to ring the first prayer bell. His main job was to meditate and find peace within himself. And he began to. "I wanted to stay five years." Jan told me. But on a brief trip to Tokyo in 1977 he called home. Tad had been asking Jan to work with him at Sencor since he founded the company in 1974. The fact that Jan was something of a poet, a philosopher, a monk—a lover of plants and amoeba, not pistons and alloys—was immaterial to his father. Tad asked Jan again. After a year of this 8000 mile separation from home and from his aging father, Jan heard an extra urgency in that voice over the phone line. "I only have one father," he thought. "I owe him a try."

The try lasted two years and ended in defeat. Jan was overwhelmed and saddened by the helter-skelter way Tad was running his business. He no more could challenge his father than could the other employees who were being chased from project to project. "I felt I was learning failure," Jan says. He quit in 1980 and went back to ecology. This was a bitter pill for Tad. Only slowly did he come to respect and support—with encouragement and financial help—his son's work.

Jan suffered also from lack of self-esteem, as perhaps is obvious from his meandering career pursuit. Even after returning to ecology in 1980, at the age of thirty, it took another seven years before he began to study for a PhD. But his reluctance to throw himself into academic work also came from determination to avoid the mistakes he felt his father had made—in (not) being a father. Jan got married in 1985 and by 1987 he had two daughters. Jan wanted to share more than just breakfast and a bed-time story with his two girls.

*　　*　　*

I suppose that Jesus Christ was the authority figure in my early life, although Tad still loomed persuasively, if distantly. Where my brothers perhaps suffered from lack of discipline, I have no such excuse after ten years under the penetrating gaze of the sisters at the Catholic girls schools. Nonetheless, whether due to genetics or to unorthodox influences at home, I rebelled. Tad and Berthe were distraught at the calls they got from the nuns about my transgressions. But they were also sympathetic.

By the time of the fire in 1971, I was eighteen and my adolescent rebellions were over. Still, that volcanic time of growth, friendships, experimentation, rebellion and search for identity had taken place under the roof and in the garden at Cables Avenue. While I felt shock and sorrow the day after the fire, I did not consciously register how abruptly the door of my relatively innocent youth had just slammed shut. But my body did so register. Six months after the fire I came down with chronic ulcerative colitis. My colon became the battlefield for a clash of wills between my father and myself for the next fifteen years.

The purveyors of medical knowledge are sadly lacking in same about why the large intestine of a person, too often a teenager, will suddenly quit doing its job and develop bleeding ulcers. But while medical practitioners hadn't the cure for my problem, Tad certainly did. I was hounded. "Eat raw garlic." "Go to a spa to fast for three months." "Massage the belly." "Walk five miles a day." "Eat more garlic." "Drink carrot juice." "Eat only green, leafy vegetables." "Quit your job and come home and rest for a year." The only cure not mentioned was a pilgrimage to Lourdes.

I ignored most of these prescriptions. All I heard in his harangues was: "You are to blame that you are sick." He never said that as such, but that's what came through. You're responsible, you're running yourself into the ground, you're causing your own sickness. It was, once more, a simple failure of will power. But he was as much in anguish as I. The genius and successful industrialist helpless with his own daughter. The man who since he was sixteen-years-old had been a devotee of nutritional fads and healthy exercise, who couldn't get that message through to his sick child.

I reached the limit of my patience in 1986. After fifteen years of painful relapses, including one Christmas spent in a hospital bed with nothing by mouth for three weeks, I decided at last to have an operation. Tad's response was less dramatic than I'd feared. He was disappointed—I'd given in to those evil surgeons—but he accepted that I was an adult, albeit misguided, and it was my choice. Still, a month before the operation, he made one last effort: how about eating French clay? He had a bottle of the stuff in powdered form and had been reading about its medicinal virtues. I declined. The operation was a success, and lifted a terrible weight from my shoulders.

I keep a snapshot of Tad on my desk at home. It's a black and white photo of me at four-years-old, Tad standing behind me, leaning forward slightly, his hands on my shoulders. Both of us are smiling at the camera. Those were the days when I was — briefly — a sweet little girl. I know that through all the anger and disappointment I never ceased to be for him what I was then, the apple of his eye.

*　　*　　*

Tad was seventy-seven at the time of the Cables Avenue fire. He had another decade of buzzing about like a hornet before he began to mellow in his mid-eighties. The fire hardened him. He became unreasonable, spiteful and erratic for a time, especially toward his wife and children. He banished us from coming home when he and Berthe were away. In an impassioned letter to Tad in 1973, almost two years after the fire, Jan in his grandiloquent style reproached his father:

> Rather than uniting the family in a common declaration of mutual love which cannot be tempered... by fate, you have cast all your children in the light of reprehensible truants who are not to be trusted. How are you to receive the love of a family to replenish your spirit in a moment of loss when you deny the bonds which make the family?... I have yet to hear, save for a few rapid sentences about how glad you were that no one was hurt which served as a preamble to a litany of new enforcements, of any motion on your part that seemed like an attempt to reunify our family after this tragedy... It does not appear to me that you have appealed to reason in this situation. Rather it seems to me that you have fallen back on the structure of tradition in which you were raised: namely, the absolute, un-bending even in error, authority of the father.

Slowly Tad began to cool off. In 1977 he looked around and it perhaps occurred to him that his nearest child was three thousand miles away: I was in San Francisco, Jan was in Korea, Stanley had moved to Zurich. We had our legitimate concerns in these places; the distance wasn't a response to Tad. (Geographical proximity never even received lip service in our family, whose patriarch and role-model, after all, had left home and lived in Russia and China as a young man.) But he was visibly saddened, each Christmas, when the annual family snapshots showed gaps. He kept up his lengthy correspondence with us, even through the early 1970s when he was so bitter. His letters to Jan discussed religion and philosophy; with me he wrote about my difficulties at college—and my health of course; with Stanley, music, opera, bills and the need to pursue "gainful employment."

The years after the fire were even tougher on Berthe. She remained in the middle, more powerless than ever in the face of Tad's hurt and petty belligerence. She felt the distance of her children more keenly than he did, as he was preoccupied with Sencor and with his new problem child, the spiral looper. Only after another ten years was she allowed to help him with his work. She tried in the meantime to settle back into the house in Bethlehem, collecting from the rubble at Cables Avenue some of her books and mementos, restoring them to life.

I was in Bethlehem one evening for supper, within a year after the fire. Berthe had set out on the shelves of the sideboard some family pictures and a few of her treasured knick-knacks—among them a delicate, miniature ivory swan caught in mid-flight, held aloft on a thin metal rod four inches high on a wooden base. Berthe had rescued the swan from the fire and lovingly polished it, but the ivory retained a brown tint. She had put this swan on the center shelf of the sideboard, where she could admire it as she gathered silverware for each meal.

Tad came home from the office clutching beneath his arm a shopping bag from Caldor's. He put this between the plates on the dining table and determinedly extracted a dowdy white plastic clock. "I must have a clock in this room clearly visible from the table." This meant...on the sideboard.

Berthe was horrified at this ugly thing, about to take its place among her treasures on her nicely arranged shelves. The household, after all, was her domain. "Please Tad, it's time to eat. I'll find a spot for it after supper."

But quickly before she could stop him, Tad stuck the clock up on the shelf and began to clumsily push aside her things to make room for the cord. Down came the swan with a tiny snap as it hit the floor. We froze. My stomach sank down near my toes. After a long second, Berthe wordlessly knelt to pick up the pieces, Tad's sad apologies bouncing off her, and walked out. Tad finished plugging in his clock. A short time later, Berthe returned, sat at her place and began passing around the serving dishes.

CHAPTER SEVENTEEN

STEEL COLLAPSE, SENCOR AND THE SPIRAL LOOPER

1974 - 1984

When Tad in 1974 amputated his research work from the living body of T. Sendzimir, Inc., the new firm, Sencor, went immediately on life support; the intravenous tube leading from Tad's bank account was briefly removed only once or twice over the next fifteen years. The money to pay for the research and development of Tad's experimental machines came not, as is normally the case, out of profits from the sale of established products. Sencor had none. It came instead from the royalties and interest Tad had accumulated over several decades. He was embarking in 1974 on a venture he'd sworn to John Eckert he was too smart to fool with: spending his own money on his own ideas.

And that's because nobody else would. The cataclysmic downfall of the U.S. steel industry was still half a decade away, but the machinery industry suffered its own slump in the early 1970s, and during the 1973 oil crisis one could hear the limpid tones of the trumpeter (he was Japanese) playing "Taps" for the gas- (and, in the making of it, steel-) guzzling American car. By the early 1980s, when Sencor finally did have a marketable product, that market had vanished with the rue and finality of a circus leaving town. Plastics and aluminum had replaced much steel. Cars had shrunk. No one was placing orders for rolling stock or oil pipelines. In 1982, the U.S. steel industry lost collectively over three billion dollars.

Beyond the exigencies of energy and economy (but by no means unrelated to them), Tad's lack of interested investors and the U.S. steel industry's collapse had in common one sad fact: the tortoise-like pace at which American steel producers took up new technology. The crisis of the 1980s had its seed in industry practices from decades past.

Back in 1950 U.S. steel companies believed that the world-wide hunger for their product would never be sated. To meet this demand they shoveled money into expansion instead of innovation. Bigger means better in American parlance, and American steelmakers spent their dollars on more and bigger copies of the same machines that had worked in the past. By 1960, they had increased capacity from 100 to 148 million tons of steel a year. But the cost of producing it had increased just as rapidly.

This phenomenon wasn't universal. On other shores, cost-saving, efficient techniques were being tried and proven. U.S. steel companies continued to build open hearth furnaces when the Germans had proved that the Basic Oxygen Furnace was cheaper by half to install, operated at costs $3 to $12 less per ton, and produced a "heat" of steel in forty minutes instead of six and more hours. The Austrians developed the continuous casting process. This vastly cheaper and quicker way to cast molten steel was adopted throughout Europe and Japan; companies in the U.S. wouldn't touch it for many years because they thought it couldn't handle high volume production. The Japanese then got it to work for the big tonnages. By 1981, still only one-fifth of U.S. steel was cast this way, compared to over two-thirds of Japanese steel.

Americans had the same attitude about the giant sixty-inch-wide Z mills T. Sendzimir, Inc., had been selling like hot cakes...to the Europeans and the Japanese. For only one-third more in price, you got three times the tonnage rolled, and you could close down your smaller, less efficient mills. Every big steel company in Europe had at least one. Even Brazil had two. The U.S. had none. When Amtrak was building new passenger cars from sixty-inch-wide stainless steel sheets, they had to send American dollars overseas to get them.

The expansion of American steel capacity in so inept a manner is due in part to the short-sighted strategy of "rounding out" existing facilities, rather than building new state-of-the-art mills (as the Europeans and Japanese were doing). U.S. steelmakers would add on more machines piecemeal, shoehorning new (and often outdated) operations into their crowded, inefficient plants, making them all the more so. But it's faster and it costs less to round out a plant than to build a whole new one. Which is another way to say, as has been said before, that American steel managers looked with far greater acuity and warm-heartedness at the immediate profit picture than at the long term needs of their industry. By 1959, foreign steel was often cheaper, and better, than what was made in the U.S. In that year, for the first time since the turn of the century, more steel was arriving at U.S. ports than was leaving from them.

Yet the bottom line focus of the U.S steel managers was only one aspect of their pervasive dislike for new technology. Critics have charged that the monopoly control over pricing enjoyed by the giant U.S. steelmakers shielded them from the need to cut costs and innovate. On top of that, however, was their very bigness, their resemblance to giant ocean vessels churning on indifferent to shifting wind and wave, unable to swiftly alter their course to avoid the hurricane. "There is obviously a relationship of some sort between large firms with fixed resources like U.S. Steel and their passivity toward new ideas," explains Paul A. Tiffany in *The Decline of American Steel*. "...the internal administrative routines that prevailed at the major producers were simply not well attuned to quick changes of any kind. It was far easier for managers to deny the efficacy of the Basic Oxygen Furnace than to recommend it."

When Tad started Sencor in 1974, he and his company suffered from the steel industry's aversion to new technology. An adventurous, pioneering spirit had catapulted the United States to the forefront of the technological revolution at the end of the last century. This spirit had apparently choked and died.

*   *   *

Michael Sendzimir responded to the slump of the early 1970s by laying off over two-thirds of T. Sendzimir, Inc.'s, draftsmen, another of his policies that Tad bitterly opposed (for who would be left to do the work when the work came back?) but wouldn't intervene to stop. The Sendzimir office in London was closed in 1973 for lack of sales. In Paris, the Procedes Sendzimir office was weakening and about to expire.

Tad had moved the office in 1964 to a new high-rise in the quickly-becoming tony suburb of Courbevoie, on the far western bank of the Seine. Tad bought an apartment in the same building. He had arrived at the construction site one afternoon and asked to be brought up in the elevator to the open floors. At each level he stopped and walked out to the building's edge to survey the view of the river and central Paris beyond. Eventually he found the floor he wanted, four stories up. From there you could see, above the tall, slender trees on the opposite bank, the roofs of Paris and the Eiffel Tower far in the distance, but still you were low enough to watch barges pass on the river. Tad had a fondness for that apartment perhaps more than for any of his other homes. Berthe would go with her cloth sack and pick up yogurt and cheese, garlic, bread and wine in the tiny shops nearby, just as she'd done for her father thirty years before. Tad, after the meetings with customers and the Procedes Sendzimir staff, had but to board the elevator to get home. He and Berthe would then enjoy their baguette and glass of wine in the evening light.

In 1980 Michael closed the Paris office, retaining only one employee, Claude Martin, to keep up the European business. Michael's closing of the two European offices were steps both difficult and, probably, inevitable. They were steps Tad hadn't the stomach for. He ducked the hard decisions because they were too painful, and because he and his son might clash. He concentrated instead on Sencor.

Michael, released from under Tad's weight, grew into the president's role. He became a confidant and competent businessman, comfortable at last in his job. T. Sendzimir Inc., pared down, survived the steel crisis of the late 70s and early 80s. (Michael claims they only lost money one year, 1984. It helps, of course, if you're paying but one third the number of people.) Sales began to pick up again in the mid-eighties. In 1988, in a benedictory profile in Waterbury's Sunday newspaper, Michael was able to boast of orders that year for seventeen rolling mills, adding up to $195 million. Michael now and then glances over his shoulder at the big guys who might want to buy him out, but he claims to be steadfast in his desire to keep T. Sendzimir, Inc., private. He is content, his position safe, his salary secure, in the small pond.

* * *

Tad ignored the slump in steel when he started in 1974 his brand new company, Sencor. Market forecasts left him unruffled. While in Florida, Berthe would buy him the *Wall Street Journal* every morning at the newsstand on her way to the post office. He would scan the front page and look up the price of stocks he held and notice, no doubt, the dark predictions for his industry. Then he'd toss the paper on top of a towering pile and turn happily to his latest patent application. What mattered was not economic trends but the cornucopia of machines and gadgets tumbling pell-mell around in his head.

Many of these already stood in various states of assemblage on the cold cement floor of the research shed, down the hill from the T. Sendzimir, Inc., office. Tad had built that corrugated metal "shed," the size of a small town's high school gym, after T. Sendzimir Inc. moved into its new office in 1964. All the devices that had been nursed at PM&M and in the garage in Bethlehem landed there and filled the place up until it looked like a rummage sale sponsored by *Popular Mechanics*. These machines were cranked up now and again by Tad's engineers, led in the mid-1960s by Val Janatka. Thaddeus Sendzimir, Michael's first son, worked there over the summer in 1966, when he was fifteen.

"I never saw Dziadzo [*Grandfather*, in Polish] down there. I was reading a lot. I wouldn't hear or see anybody, and then all of a sudden at 1 o'clock Janatka would come screaming down, and say, 'Quickly, we have to do this. TS asked me to do this.' And we'd do something, Janatka would write down some numbers and go back. That was how I knew Dziadzo had asked for some figure on something."

By 1974, only a few aspects of this picture had changed: more machines cluttered the floor, one or two men worked on them full-time, and Tad had put up a homely little office building for the drafting tables, a secretary, a water cooler, and a private office for himself. Institutional olive green paint covered the cinder block walls, except in those places where the walls were dressed up with fake wood paneling. So began Sencor.

Val Janatka had quit in 1971 to start his own business. The research work was then taken over by Jerry Jablonski, a man of large proportions who wore his prematurely white mane in a pompadour. Jablonski had been a swimming champion in Poland, had defected during a meet in France and gotten a job at a plant that ran a Sendzimir galvanizing line. He came to the States and was hired by T. Sendzimir Inc. in 1966. Tad took an immediate, avuncular shine to this man who looked like a bear, swam like a fish, and worked like a dog. Jablonski was a competent engineer who would jump through the hoops Tad threw in his path and not argue over each one. "People accused me of being a 'Yes-Man,' but it wasn't like that," Jablonski avers. "I would sit down and do like he wanted, and then develop my arguments why it wouldn't work, and show him the alternatives. Mr. Sendzimir then could change his mind."

Not wanting to become once more buried in the details of the business, nor wanting to curtail his time in Florida, Tad hired a general manager, Dick Martin. Martin had worked in the 1950s for Zig Protessewicz at PM&M. Martin was a tall, fit man—very straightforward and American in manner, an unusual distinction in Sendzimir employees—whose peppery black hair would turn more to salt over each phone conversation with Tad. Tad had assured him that "I want Sencor to be a profit-making company."

A profit-*less* year after Martin came to Sencor a friend of his, a reporter from *Metal Working News*, stopped by to snoop around. Martin gave him a tour. Most of the machines in the shed and on the drawing boards were variations of or improvements upon the planetary mill.[Appendix, 10] There were in addition a collection of mills and machines not planetary in nature, [Appendix, 11], and some miscellaneous experiments with crown control on the Z mill.

There were the beginnings, in one corner, of the ZB mill, a mill Tad was dreaming would supersede—no, more: would slay and bury—the antiquated 4-Hi mill. In 1973 and 1974 he'd garnered two articles about it in *33 Magazine*, a trade magazine for metal producers. The un-bylined author claimed, with the endemic optimism of the trade press, that the mill was "stirring almost as much excitement in Waterbury as its famous predecessor, the Z mill."

Despite the fanfare and the birth of a rickety model in the shed, work on this mill proceeded haphazardly over the next decade [see Chapter 19]. That was because the reporter from *Metal Working News* on his tour with Dick Martin at last found something that caught his eye: the spiral looper. He wrote a small piece on it for his magazine because it was, well, different. But neither he, nor Martin, really saw the looper's potential buried in that traffic jam of looping and winding steel strip. To this day many an educated engineer will say, even as he watches it in operation, "I still can't figure out how it works."

*   *   *

The first drawing of a spiral looper can be found in a separate notebook Tad kept, labeled "Invention Record," in an entry from 1963. Four years later, Tad obtained a patent. A small and flimsy model was built by Val Janatka and abandoned in the shed, where it awaited resurrection after going public in *Metal Working News* in 1975.

The spiral looper is a machine of the type called generically "strip accumulators." Accumulators are needed when strip is running off of one operation, say a galvanizing line, and has to go into another operation, say a pipe-forming machine. The point is to minimize that profit-eating occurrence: downtime. Without an accumulator you have to wind up the big coil of strip on the galvanizing line, stop the line, take the coil off, carry it over to the pipe machine and load it on there. A strip accumulator gets installed, instead, in between the two. The strip runs off the galvanizing line directly onto the accumulator and feeds out to the pipe machine.

The immediate competitor of the spiral looper functions rather like a watch spring, set on its side, standing vertically. The incoming strip feeds in to the outer edge, the outgoing strip plays out from the center of the coil. The drawbacks are that that watch spring hasn't much capacity, and the surface of the strip can easily scratch, rubbing against itself. But it doesn't take up much space, and with only one electrical drive it is simple to construct and operate.

Imagine instead two coils of strip stacked like pancakes, one on a platform (with a hole in the center) a few feet above the other. The coils lay flat, horizontally, so the strip is resting on its edges. The incoming strip feeds in clockwise to the outside edge of the top coil. The inside edge of the top coil peels off and down (through that hole) and into the inner edge of the bottom coil. The bottom coil is running counterclockwise, and from its outside edge the strip feeds out to the next operation.

Here are the advantages: the incoming strip can be running at a different speed than that of the outgoing strip, since there are two

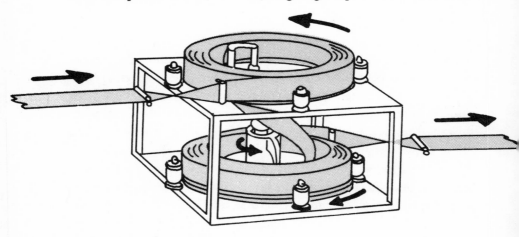

Spiral Looper

separate coils; the capacity runs to miles, not yards; the strip is supported on its edge, not on its surface, so surface scratching is minimal (supposedly).

But sometimes the surface does scratch. And the spiral looper takes up more floor space than a vertical accumulator. The spiral looper also needs a score of electrical drives to push that strip through its paces. And, most curious of all, the coils have to act *not* like coils—each thin layer moving along at the same speed as the one next to it—but like spirals—each layer moving at a slightly slower or faster speed than its neighbor a millimeter away.

As an admiring engineer at NKK Steel in Japan put it, in talking about the big spiral looper bought by them in 1982: "The spiral looper is not a Japanese idea, it's an Anglo-Saxon idea. It's definitely the product of a Western mind." (Tad would have been amused to be mistaken for an Anglo-Saxon.)

The spiral looper was not a breakthrough invention on the order of Tad's galvanizing line. It was superior to the competition on certain scores, inferior on others. It was simply, and in many ways, a good idea.

* * *

The first model of the spiral looper, built in the mid-sixties, ran too fast. In a matter of seconds the strip would spill all over the floor with a great and discouraging clatter. When Dick Martin revived the project in 1975, Jerry Jablonski drove out to the junkyard. He picked up some windshield wiper motors, attached them to the old model, slowed the thing down and got it to work. Someone then came by from the Yoder Company, a manufacturer of tool making equipment. Yoder was looking for accumulators for an I-beam line for their customer, Fruehauf, the people who make trailers for trucks. They came to Waterbury, watched the model of the spiral looper, and ordered four. Four. And Sencor would have to build them.

"Tad was not crazy about this idea," Dick Martin says. "He wasn't crazy about building them, and he wasn't crazy about building four instead of just one. (He wanted to pay more attention to the ZB mill.) 'Let's just develop one [looper],' he said. Which is what he'd always done in the past: put it in production, see what the problems are.

But Sencor took the order. And Tad at last grasped the size and potential of the job, which brought to mind his well-worn axiom: "Nobody can do this better than me." Here was the project to put Sencor on the map. He did not want it placed there on the basis of a machine he'd all but ignored for a decade, a machine he'd been reluctant about in the first place, a machine that someone else—Jablonski—had built a working model of after his own effort had failed. That initial effort had been but a toy, one more fanciful design he'd dreamed up and then put aside. Now suddenly that toy was to be Sencor's flagship. He called everyone into his office the day the Yoder order came in and said to them, "*I* am taking design responsibility." And then the trouble began.

Jerry Jablonski had drawn up a rudimentary and economical design. According to Martin, "Jerry designed four Ford Pintos, and that's what we quoted. Simple design to do the job—no air-conditioning, no power steering. Yoder OKed it." Then Tad jumped in, threw out those drawings, and came up with "four Cadillac Eldorados." (This was the beginning of the end for Jerry Jablonski's tenure at Sencor. Tad's paternal relationship with Jablonski included the down side that Tad found it easy to scold and even humiliate this man in the presence of others. Jablonski quit in 1978.)

Tad did not simply add hood ornaments and fins to Jablonski's Ford Pintos. Where Jablonski had put in something sturdy to do the job, Tad wanted to simplify it, ignoring the immense weight, bulk and speed of the material going through. He took off some controls, again wanting to simplify, when the machine couldn't handle the job without them. On other features, Jablonski's simple designs were made much more complex. As Jacek Gajda, the junior engineer who was to see the Fruehauf loopers to completion, put it: "All of a sudden we ended up with this very complicated mechanism. That's the worst thing you can do with R&D. Because this machine *had* to perform."

Gajda remembers that Tad "wanted to know about every little detail, and he wanted to take every little detail apart. He was concentrating on the little thing here, not the whole picture. We had a timetable. We were delivering four pieces of equipment, to work twenty-four hours a day, high speed. Millions of dollars involved. The whole project depended on us."

The delivery dates neared. The work constructing those loopers took on the aspect of beavers startled by an early frost. Martin, Jablonski, Gajda and several others would disappear into the shed each morning and trudge out twelve hours later, bedaubed with black grease. Jeans and T-shirts replaced suits and ties, sweat replaced aftershave. Electricians came and went, day and night. Finally the loopers seemed to work.

To Jacek Gajda fell the task of delivering and starting them up at the Fruehauf plant in Milan, Michigan, a small town southwest of Detroit. Gajda is a thin, affable young man with a Pole's charm and a Pole's fondness for having always in hand a lit cigarette. He had come to the U.S. in 1974. By 1977, when the spiral loopers were to be shipped to Fruehauf, Gajda was the man on most intimate terms with those four demanding, recalcitrant mistresses. He took them to Michigan.

The testing in the shop had been superficial—just enough for working in theory, not enough for working in reality, in normal industrial conditions. Installed then in reality, everything that could go wrong did. "I thought Fruehauf would throw me out in two or three weeks," Gajda says, "I can't even begin to describe what hell we went through: mechanics, electrics, this thing breaking down, that thing breaking down. It was a mess. It was a lot of money sitting there not producing anything. At first it wouldn't work at all. Then it would work for five seconds, and we'd end up with tons of steel all over the floor. I almost had tears in my eyes. But one engineer said to me, 'Jacek, if something works for five seconds, there is no reason why it couldn't work for fifteen seconds.' Progressively, you will come to twenty-four hours."

The Fruehauf managers had told Gajda he had three or four months, and if it was still not working they would yank it out. But, Gajda says, "I became very friendly with them. We were working ten hours a day. [They could see how much] effort I put into it. So, when they'd have a management meeting [and decide to shut it down], someone at the end of the meeting would say, 'OK, who's going to tell Jacek?' 'Well, how about if we give him two more weeks?' And it would go on like that."

At one point Mr. Yoder, the company president, was so angry that he refused to speak to Tad directly. "He sent a telex to Sencor," Gajda recalls, "saying that he was going to rip the loopers off the floor and charge Sencor something like a thousand dollars a day penalty charges. And Tad wouldn't speak to him, of course, because he felt insulted."

Finally all four loopers were made to work. But Tad continued to hold a grudge against Yoder and the Milan plant. He sent Gajda out there to show the working loopers to other interested customers; he wouldn't go himself. In the summer of 1978, however, Gajda's father came to the States for a visit, and Tad had the idea to pack everyone into the RV and drive out to Milan to see the loopers. And there at last they were, spinning and dancing just as he'd envisioned—a thrill to see, his children obediently at work. The managers and men operating the loopers came up and introduced themselves to him with all due respect. No hard feelings.

Alas, while the loopers triumphed, Fruehauf did not. After a few years of financial trouble the Milan plant shut down the I-beam and tube lines. One looper was sold to a plant in Missouri, where it is running strip with ease. The three others wound up in the hands of a used machinery dealer, and while their fate is unknown, Gajda suspects they were viewed and sold off not as their sum but as their parts.

*   *   *

Tad wrote in a letter to me in August 1979, "Our loopers work OK at Fruehauf, but Jacek didn't sell any [more] yet. We were counting on those sales to put Sencor in the black and I am disappointed. I almost feel like Diogenes with a lamp on the agora at noon."

Diogenes worked a bit harder at his search. The spiral looper suffered in its quest for recognition. It suffered not from its technical quirks but from its inventor's extreme distaste for spending money on promotion. He thought the loopers should sell themselves. Wes Wozniak, a tall, sometimes clownish, meat-and-potatoes Pole who became Sencor's chief engineer, winces as he recounts the stymied sales efforts: "Our competitors are tremendous companies, hundreds of people working in sales. They have reps at every show, with a video. *Once* Mr. Sendzimir allowed me to go to Philadelphia to a convention. We did many proposals, but *people were afraid.* They could not visualize how it could work—high speed, thin strip riding on the edge. They'd say, 'No way!'"

Sencor sold a small (six feet in diameter) spiral looper in 1981 to a firm in Sweden making aluminum tubing for the radiators of Volvo trucks. That looper generated no complaints. At the same time, Gajda heard (through Yoder!) of a possible sale to NKK Steel in Japan. Tad asked Michael, on an impending trip to Japan, to pursue it. Through Michael's and Nissho-Iwai's efforts, NKK bought a spiral looper in 1982. The looper was installed in one building of NKK's Keihin works, a huge, fully-integrated steel plant on a rectangular, 424-acre man-made island in Tokyo bay.

The conception, gestation and birth of the NKK spiral loopers (they bought a second one in 1988) were enacted with the same drill team efficiency the Japanese had displayed building the planetary mill. An engineer from Hitachi and one from Nissho-Iwai came to the States to study the loopers at Sencor and at Fruehauf. They then took Tad and Gajda's designs and engineered their own version. Gajda made several trips to Tokyo during the design, building and start-up stages. NKK had some minor difficulties at first, and since then there's been barely a whimper. That first looper was a giant, fifty feet across, carrying steel strip a yard wide for heavy pipe. The second looper started also without problem. But the smooth rolling of the NKK spiral loopers seems insignificant in the vastness of the plant they serve—like a couple of gaskets deep in the humming engine of a Lexus sedan.

One more large spiral looper was sold in Japan, to Nippon Steel. Sales ended there. Sadly, when British Steel in 1988 asked Sencor for a quote on a tremendous Looper, Sencor had to turn them down.

The job was too big, too experimental; Tad couldn't find a builder. The matter was dropped.

But of course the matter was never dropped from Tad's internal Rolodex of ideas. The spiral looper became for Tad the missing link in what he called "closed loop rolling." Instead of having the strip move back and forth through a reversing mill, the strip would be rolled in one direction only (like his first mill in Poland), out and around and back—through a spiral looper. A brochure was printed up, with a drawing showing how it was done—as if Sencor had installed them by the dozen.

Only, they hadn't. It never *had* been done, and anyone familiar with the cold rolling of steel and with the spiral looper will tell you that it *can't* be done. The spirals of the spiral looper function well enough on heavy gauge material for beams and pipe. But on very thin gauge, cold-rolled steel, the strip couldn't rest on its delicate edge through this roller coaster of a machine the way heavy pipe steel can. At the high speeds of cold rolling, the smooth and slender strip would tear itself up.

The idea boggled Jacek Gajda. "Some Z mills go at three thousand feet a minute. Can you imagine this giant coil, tons of it, running at that speed? One [closed loop system] was built at Sencor, but it's just a toy. It's working, but at ten to fifteen feet a minute. For Mr. Sendzimir, something that works at ten feet a minute should be able to work at a thousand feet a minute. But not when it comes to tons and tons of very thin material."

But Tad was not to be swayed. He never responded to memos Michael sent him explaining these problems. It was one more beautiful idea that someday he'd figure out how to make work. He received two patents in 1985 for an Intermediate Accumulating System, which went beyond simply adding more loopers to a closed loop rolling system. He made notes for another patent application for closed loop rolling, to be found in his notebook dated June 14, 1989. He died ten weeks later.

*   *   *

The view across Tad's desktop in Jupiter, Florida, in one corner of the large living room overlooking the ocean, was screened beneath an accumulation of clutter that would provide honest employment to an archeologist. Books, parts catalogs, magazines and dictionaries (in six languages) rose in foot-high barricades around the edges. On a narrow table along the wall lay a five-foot-long row of standing, jumbled file folders, stretched out like a mummy. (He once said to Jacek Gajda, "Jacek, when I die and I go to heaven, or wherever I go, God will make me file things.") Three or four typewriters, covered against the dust with white paper napkins, sat on the floor nearby, each with its particular complaint. (These were among the dozen or so he amassed over the years; like puppies in the pound, a new one would catch his eye in a catalog or discount store and he'd eagerly give it a home.) Scattered across his desk were his various projects: blueprints, sketches, business correspondence, letters from his sisters, a stack of *Nowy Dziennik*, reports from the Kosciuszko Foundation, patents to study. On every available inch in between (the glass desk top was not visible to the eye at any point) lay paper clips, pens, bottles of Liquid Paper, bottles of mineral water, rubber bands, magnifying glasses, empty film canisters, batteries. On the wall were three carved wooden masks from Bali, a picture of a Z mill, and half a dozen fading family snapshots in rusty metal frames. Behind the desk, in the far corner, a three-foot-high mound of used manila envelopes was growing like pizza dough. Within these large manila envelopes, taped up like wounded veterans, the business of Sencor— via airmail between Connecticut and Florida—transpired for fifteen years.

When he started Sencor in 1974, Tad wrote in his notebook that he hoped for sales of $750,000 in the first year, $1.5 million in the following. Sencor's income never reached a million; it ranged between $100-200,000 for most of the firm's existence. This money came from the loopers, from the sale of a few small pieces of machinery, and from research tests done on the experimental mills, commissioned by outside firms. Tad's gifts to the industrial world sat fretfully, fruitlessly in Sencor's parlor, awaiting the proper suitor's knock upon the door.

Tad's longstanding annoyance at the lack of daring and vision on the part of American steelmakers was by 1980 somewhat misplaced. The economy was to say the least unpropitious. No one was investing in untried machines. And certainly no one was investing in machines whose performances were based merely on the testimony of their octogenarian inventor. In such climate, even the most far-sighted, innovation-loving of Tad's potential customers had to count his change, press his nose against the glass display case, return those coins to his pocket with a sigh and walk away.

Tad in his eighties looked like a man in his sixties, and thought like a man in his forties. Unfortunately, he also thought like a man in *the* Forties, or even the Twenties, or earlier still: the era of big money and big innovations when new ideas were pounced upon by hungry capitalists; the era when the eccentric, gentleman inventor was regarded with awe and respect, not bemusement and suspicion; the era of the hand-shake, not the legal contract with its iron-clad performance guarantees. The era of inventions by Bell and Edison, not invention by committee. In the 1970s and 80s, the rare company that was investing in heavy industry didn't have time for the old timers.

Tad had also, in that earlier era, a monopoly with his Z mill, and a monopoly in a booming economy. Customers had beaten a path to his door. Now where were they? He assumed that the industry shared a pervasive faith in anything bearing the Sendzimir label, as if investments in industrial equipment were made with the same criteria as the purchase of designer jeans. What there was of that faith had faded over the 1960s, due in part to the difficulties with the planetary mill. Sendzimir was a visionary, yes, but he was making mistakes...or, at least, he was wasting precious time to correct them.

Dick Martin admired Tad's skills as a businessman, but he says that by Sencor's time, those skills weren't enough. "People were in awe of him. They had a tendency to believe him. That was the key to his success: he could get people to finance his ventures. Then, in the 1970s, people started not believing him. Because of the planetary, because of the rocker mill, the reducing press. He lost his aura of infallibility. Sendzimir products didn't work." And over time, Martin goes on, the faces change. "The people who knew TS back when it was starting had gone. A new breed was coming in. It was difficult to convince new people, who'd say, 'Prove to me. Don't tell me. Prove to me.'" No one could afford to be the guinea pig.

Tad persisted in his belief that all he had to do was show you, the customer, a gimcrack model, and the scales would fall from your eyes. Hadn't he sold his galvanizing concept that way in 1931? You'd buy it and with his help get it to run—because you had faith, patience, and money in abundance. When no one showed up with these three qualities, Tad did not wake up, choose one among his assorted ideas, and say, "Alright, I'll build it myself. I'll prove to the world that it works." He muddled along, juggling half a dozen half-built inventions, assuming his 1920s Shanghai-bred knack for talking fast and jury-rigging machines would suffice in the U.S.A. in the 1980s, where standards were higher and money was not lying in the streets.

What hurt and disappointed Tad most was when he couldn't even interest the Japanese. When Tad went to Japan he would talk about his developments at Sencor, the Japanese would listen respectfully, and the next day ask Michael the hard questions. Michael was only too glad to fill them in, and you can be sure he hadn't much nice to say. He says that "Any response to Father would be extremely polite. It usually was checked through me, how not to offend him. Any new development, they would ask: 'How far is it advanced? Is there an operating unit? Is it successful? Are we supposed to do the development work? Why is this better than the other project?' Very scientific, step-by-step study. I was giving objective answers. They would accept only his *proven* inventions."

Tetsuji Taniguchi is a managing director at Sejal who reminds one of a Japanese edition of a young Gregory Peck. Tad respected his opinions and wrote to him more than once asking for his thoughts— on the oscillating press, the future of the spiral looper, linking the planetary with a continuous caster, closed loop rolling, the Nylatron mill. Taniguchi responded that these ideas were either too unrefined, like the Nylatron mill, or too limited in application, like closed loop rolling. Taniguchi visited Tad in Florida in 1988. Tad took him to his favorite seafood restaurant. They sat on the deck overlooking the

Jupiter inlet and lighthouse, watching the brown pelicans and talking about rolling mills. Tad, Taniguchi says, "told me repeatedly how so often before the Japanese customer tried passionately the new ideas of his. He complained that lately the Japanese customers are not so eager to try.

"But the attitude of Japanese customers has not changed. They are eager to develop, if the idea is very good. Some of Mr. Sendzimir's ideas had fundamental problems."

* * *

In January 1978, Dick Martin flew down to Florida for the annual meeting to discuss with Tad the goals for the upcoming year. The spiral loopers at Fruehauf were in operation at last; the ones for Japan and Sweden hadn't yet been ordered. Martin was supposed to stay in Jupiter three days. At the end of dinner on the first evening, as Martin remembers, Tad turned to him and said, "Well, what do you foresee?"

"Mr. Sendzimir," Martin replied, "to be perfectly honest, I would put all your talent, all of your money that you are putting into Sencor, and direct it towards the looper. Because I think that's the only salable product we have."

Tad eyes widened. It took him a moment to speak. Finally he said in a flat, harsh voice, "That is *not the attitude* I want in a general manager!"

"Well Mr. Sendzimir, that's the way I see it. Let's lie low on the other mills. Let's push the loopers."

"No."

"Fine. You're the boss. But that's my opinion."

Martin left not three days later but the next morning. "TS had nothing more to say," Martin recalls, "and he didn't want to hear what I had to say. I thought that was my epitaph."

Dick Martin was not an engineer—*that* perhaps was his epitaph. He was a competent and friendly manager and businessman, but he hadn't the engineering training (or the initiative) required to successfully ride herd on Tad's projects. Tad needed a business manager, but he also needed a chief engineer.

So Tad just did as he pleased, and what pleased him was to flit from one project to the next like a honeybee in July. Tad wanted a general manager who would acquiesce to this helter-skelter course, *and* make a profit out of it—so long as making a profit didn't get in the way. "Routine wasn't his forte," Martin says. "There always had to be a new challenge. When he lost interest in something, he dropped it. He did care about sales, but he always wanted to do something *else*."

My brother Jan worked at Sencor between 1978 and 1980. "There was no logical progression—try this, try that, four, five, eight projects. In the midst of all this Papa would say, 'By the way, where are the sales?' It was crisis to crisis. Lots of things were sixty percent done, eighty percent done. There was an atmosphere of 'fantasyland' even then. I know that engineering firms have to keep a lot of projects on the burners. But Papa didn't follow through. There was no focus, no plan."

Perhaps what most crippled his efforts was that he never tried to find good engineers to work for him. When he needed help, he looked for recent graduates of the local technical school—young greenish men, little more than mechanics, who came cheap. As did the steady trickle of Polish immigrants. Consciously or not, for reasons of cost or not, he avoided hiring a competent engineer. Such an engineer might have challenged him—but he also might have taken Tad's ideas and really made something of them, as John Eckert had in the 1940s. Such an engineer might have been able to develop the machines Tad was so desperately, as he got older, trying to teach to walk and talk—before they became orphans.

He put up the appearances of a serious businessman, in his eighties and nineties, albeit one who spent six months of every year in Florida. He stocked the bookcases in the office with the latest technical journals, reference manuals, and the most recent patents from around the world. But these he seemed to read just for the intellectual pleasure and stimulation, like detective novels. Their contents did not make the smallest dent in his belief in the superiority of his own inventions.[Appendix, 12]

His lengthy stays in Florida were his reprieve; the house in Jupiter, and the cottage on Cape Cod, his refuge from the petty arguments, business details and mechanical problems that in Waterbury lay in his path like waist-high brambles. "He was happiest," Berthe says, "he was truly himself, when he was away from the office—at Cape Cod working at his little desk, or on our trips to Colorado walking in the mountains. When we were driving back to Waterbury from the Cape it was like driving back to jail—you could see it in his attitude." On his walks on the beach he could dwell on the theoretical, beautiful ideas. In Waterbury, others had to marry those ideas to cold metal reality.

Relations between Sencor and T. Sendzimir, Inc., were cool. While the Sencor engineers saw themselves as an elite crew working for a respected, if difficult, inventor, some of the employees up the hill referred to Sencor as "Fantasy Island," or, alternately, "The Museum." Michael had the ability and opportunity to help Sencor, by mentioning Sencor's products to his customers. It cannot be said that Michael outright sabotaged Sencor. But while Tad did not see T. Sendzimir, Inc., and Sencor as competitors, Michael saw them as nothing but. When customers would ask him about the merit of Tad's latest inventions, Michael was not unhappy to report to them the truth: these inventions had problems. Michael's statements and actions reveal scant respect for his father's genius, and for the potential of his later ideas. He didn't believe in them. All that development was too much trouble, for one so conservative in nature. From his spot on top at T. Sendzimir, Inc., Michael could look on with concealed satisfaction as his company floated along while his famous father's was taking on water.

Dick Martin was fired in 1980, and Jacek Gajda took over as General Manager. Gajda had a slightly better time of it, because he was an engineer and he was a Pole and Tad was fond of him. "I didn't want to build a huge design office," Gajda says. "We could handle the spiral looper for Sweden, a small piece of equipment. We couldn't handle the one for Japan. But Mr. Sendzimir could never accept that, that a giant piece of equipment could not be designed by two or three people. He was completely unrealistic. The company would only make sense if it was commercially viable. At some point

I realized that that's not exactly what he wanted, although that's what he would say every day."

What exactly he wanted was to invent. And after all, at the age of eighty, after a long and successful life, why shouldn't he just invent? Why shouldn't he just tinker to his heart's content, as long as he could still pay the salaries and keep the roof up? He did want to see his inventions succeed in the outside world. But to put aside any of his ideas, his lovely children, in order to concentrate on just one...he couldn't do it. The others would perish.

"Sencor was like a toy shop, spending Papa's money," Jan Peter says, and that alas is the demeaning but widely held view of the firm. Sencor as Tad's hobby shop. Michael believes his father was content through this period. "He was living in a fantasy world. He visualized his inventions, and he was thinking on beyond. That gave him happiness. The fact that he didn't have sales never bothered him. Never." Jan agrees: "Papa had a longer view. He wasn't desperate. He was self-absorbed. He blotted the failures out. He dipped in and out of his fantasies, the beauty of this or that machine. Certainly he was disappointed, but overall he was optimistic.

"Also maybe there was frustration," Jan continues. "He was working and working until the day he died, and there was no one to hand the baton to." Michael's son, Thaddeus, became an engineer and joined his father at T. Sendzimir, Inc. When Tad once offered Thaddeus a job at Sencor, Thaddeus said he felt his future was more secure at T. Sendzimir, Inc., under his father. None of the Sencor engineers had that special combination of patience, to put up with Tad, and promise, to carry on alone. Lest pity engulf us, remember that Tad was lying in the very bed he'd spent several decades making for himself. He wouldn't hire skilled engineers. He snatched away design work from his own men. He wouldn't delegate to them or train them. He could never trust anyone to do a job as well as he, and so no one ever could. He was left on his own.

Such arrogance, stinginess, and stubbornness rang down the curtain on most of the projects of Tad's last twenty years of life. This is not to say that those projects were no good. He simply got in the way of their execution. His refusal to give his engineers leeway in working on his machines, the absence of a strong chief engineer to steer the development, the crisis in the steel industry that caused investors to stay home in bed—all contributed to the apparent failure of his later work. But in that work still lay some nuggets of gold.

In November 1984, a business opportunity presented itself from an unlikely source—the People's Republic of China. Tad jumped at it, and in the ensuing months there materialized, also from an unlikely source, the person who would carry on Tad's work. She'd been married to him since 1945.

CHAPTER EIGHTEEN

RETURN TO CHINA

1984 - 1985

When Richard Nixon made his historic visit to China in 1972, Tad was watching it on TV. When Deng Xiaoping regained power in 1979 and began to open the shuttered gates of the Middle Kingdom to Western business interests, Tad was reading about it in *The Wall Street Journal*. He followed the gradual developments not with the zeal of the modern capitalist, but with the nostalgia of the old colonialist. What had been entombed for so many years came seeping back—the distant, vivid images, the rich smells and sounds of old Shanghai. Westerners once more could go to China. Tad was a Westerner. Therefore...

But Tad was not just any Westerner. He was an esteemed inventor. He had lived in Shanghai for eleven years and built the country's first automated nail and bolt factory. He was somebody—somebody who wasn't going to just show up, like a tourist. "Tad had said many times that he would like to go to China again," Berthe says. "But he would not go unless he was invited."

In the spring of 1984, T. Sendzimir, Inc., received an inquiry about a planetary mill from a steel plant in Lanzhou, an industrial city on the Yellow River, in China's western province of Gansu. Michael suggested to the Lanzhou Steel Plant (LSP) that they look into purchasing the then-idle Ductile mill, as they hadn't the means to buy a new one. Correspondence to that effect passed back and

313

forth through the summer. In September, Zhang Wu Le, the president of LSP, invited Tad, Michael, and Gina McWeeney (Michael's secretary who had become T. Sendzimir Inc.'s Executive Vice President) to come to China for a visit in November.

Michael had a business trip planned. He said he wasn't interested (a return to his birthplace apparently did not hold appeal), and he felt the trip was unnecessary—the Chinese should go themselves to Ductile instead. But Michael told his father about this invitation, and asked him if he'd like to go.

"Tad called me from the office," Berthe says. "We were supposed to leave for a vacation in Colorado a few days later. He said, 'Instead of going to Colorado, how would you like to go to China?' And I said, 'Yes, when are we leaving?' We left a week later."

It was cold in Beijing when this ninety-year-old inventor and his wife stepped off the plane in the land he had set sail from exactly fifty-five years before. They arrived at eleven in the evening and were brought by car to a college dormitory. "We didn't know what it was," Berthe says. "They gave us a suite of rooms—bedroom, sitting room, bath and entrance. It was quite nice. We couldn't understand. 'That's not a hotel,' we said. 'No, that's the University of Beijing. Your hosts insisted that you come here directly.' The next morning, after breakfast, we were taken to a classroom, where about twenty or thirty students were seated, and the head of the department showed us a Sendzimir cold mill that they had made from drawings [from technical journals], to teach the students about cold rolling."

Tad and Berthe were soon to discover that both at the University, and at a technical institute in the city of Xian, several cold mills and planetary mills had been built, all from drawings. They were used for teaching and research, and, some, for commercial production. This was China's self-help strategy—appropriating expensive or embargoed Western technology by just looking it up in books and putting together the pieces—and it contributed, as a consequence, to the immense esteem in which Tad was held. No one could blame him if the mills didn't work: he'd had nothing to do with it.

After two days at the University, they flew west to Lanzhou and arrived in terrain similar to what they could have been seeing, in

Colorado, had they not come to China. Gansu province is sort of China's Wild West, a dry, high, dusty countryside, sparsely populated compared to the thickly-settled floodplains of eastern China. Between the brown hills, in a narrow, green belt where melons grow fat by the Yellow River, lies Lanzhou, the elongated provincial capital, Gansu's Denver. The old Silk Road crossed the Yellow River here, and to the north stand the crumbling western reaches of the Great Wall. Marco Polo came through seven centuries before; not many Westerners have been by since.

Zhang Wu Le, a warm, stocky, energetic man in his mid-fifties, welcomed Tad and Berthe to the Lanzhou Steel Plant. LSP is a collection of dusty, tan brick buildings set against the backdrop of a mountain horizontally striped with terraces, like a scrim of brown corduroy. Zhang gave them the grand tour. Tad asked specifically to see the maintenance department—if that was inadequate they couldn't possibly cope with the planetary's hypochondriacal bearings and rolls. Berthe was shown the nursery for pre-school-age children. She was instantly smitten—as she was also, while being driven around the city, by the population of pigs who resembled stray dogs as they meandered unconcerned in the gullies and lanes, unaware of their future.

Tad and Zhang Wu Le took to one another from the start. They could converse directly only in threadbare Russian, a language Zhang had studied along with millions of his countrymen in the days before China and the Soviet Union were shooting at each other across their borders. Zhang was overjoyed that he had succeeded in bringing to his city and his factory the real-life inventor of the mill he had studied and longed for. Such enthusiasm and respect were music to Tad, a music he'd not heard enough of lately. He returned their good will in kind. He felt the Chinese could do well with his planetary, remembering that resource he'd found in Shanghai six decades before: the dogged industriousness of the Chinese worker.

Tad signed a joint venture agreement with Lanzhou Steel. He would find and give them a used planetary mill (with a $100,000 loan from LSP) and the drawings and know-how to make it work; once working, Sencor would receive one and a half percent of net sales of the steel tube LSP would be making on that planetary, up to a maximum of $200,000 per year. The used planetary Tad pushed on them was not the Ductile mill, as Michael had suggested. It was the old Benteler mill, or rather what was left of it. (LSP engineers would later travel to Germany, crate up the mill, and ship it across two oceans and up the Yellow River to Lanzhou.)

Then Tad and Berthe flew to Shanghai, just for a visit. They stayed in a hotel on the outskirts. Tad hired a taxi to take them to the area north of the city center where he hoped to see his old factory. The neighborhood was now a confusing warren of low buildings and small workshops. They couldn't find the factory, for it no longer stood in an open field, as when he'd built it. They drove back downtown, to the Bund, the wide avenue along the Huangpu River. The snarl of boats and sampans in the Huangpu was in the 1980s exceeded in intensity by the snarl of cars and bicycles along the Bund itself. Tad and Berthe drove through the crowded streets over to the area where Tad had lived, then known as the French Concession. In contrast to the tightly knit, rickety wooden buildings in the other sections, here were the stately, formidable homes built by the Europeans in the beginning decades of this century, situated behind tall brick European walls, shaded by European trees. They got out and walked a bit. Tad described to Berthe the way people had lived then, the French Club where he had used the swimming pool, the Russo-Asiatic Bank (this building they did find) where Jastrzembski and Jezierski had given him his start. He said not much really had changed in the city since his time there in the 1920s; he failed to note that the overflowing population of beggars had, since 1949, disappeared.

Through a contact at a Shanghai trading company, they met a group of executives from factories in the area. One of these, a tall, elderly gentleman named Karl Tong, rang them up at their hotel later and asked in excellent English if he could stop by after dinner. He arrived around eight with his even taller twenty-two-year-old son, Harold. Karl Tong explained that he was fascinated by the fact that Tad had run a factory here in Shanghai in the 1920s. He wanted to try and find it for them. Tad pulled out of his suitcase a small, square catalog, its paper yellowed and brittle. It said on the front "General Forge Products, Ltd." Karl Tong carefully leafed through it, and said to Tad, "You know, these are things that are precious to us, because we don't have such documents. That's why I wanted to talk to you."

The next day, Karl Tong called up the Shanghai Heavy Machinery company and brought Tad and Berthe there to meet them. They toured part of the tremendous plant, then were shown into a conference room for the obligatory cup of jasmine tea with the company president and a score of engineers. One man, sitting at the side, was looking at Tad with intense, un-businesslike interest. After a while he spoke up: 'Mr. Sendzimir, I want to introduce myself. My father was your foreman. All my youth, I remember how he was talking about you. How he was happy to work for you, and how you were a good employer. Now I am Chief Engineer at Shanghai Heavy Machinery—I went into the same business." He rose from his seat, came over and shook Tad's hand. "Tad was really pleased," Berthe remembers, "and touched."

After three days in Shanghai, Tad and Berthe flew to Tokyo and on to Honolulu. They got a room for a week on Waikiki Beach. That was their decompression chamber. During that week of calm, Tad, inspired and energized by the prospects of reviving at last a planetary mill, filled with drawings dozens of pages of a large black notebook. He wrote notes on the LSP factory, on the planetary, and even—why be timid?—on how the planetary could be hooked up directly to a galvanizing operation (his, of course), giving Lanzhou what he thought was the world's first continuous rolling-galvanizing line. As Berthe fed croissant crumbs to the sparrows at the beach-side breakfast table, Tad would gaze at the blue Pacific and see gear boxes and strip winders.

Tad wasn't the only one dreaming. Berthe too was in a reverie. First, over meeting all these men who shared with her the opinion that her husband was a genius; second, with the prospect for meaningful, possibly remunerative work for Sencor. But mostly she was entranced with the Chinese people themselves. "They are so warm, so friendly, so open," she told me repeatedly after her visit.

"And those kids! I would have taken one home if I could." Since the 1950s she had been a student and lover of the art and culture of China's neighbor, Japan. In China she found a similar but richer and more ancient culture—and a people less distant, less insular. She found a people and a land she could embrace, and a well of need beckoning her underutilized intelligence and compassion. Overnight she became, I joked to her, a Born-again Chinese.

To her it was transparent that Tad needed her help with this joint venture. He was ninety; she merely seventy-one. His hands were full with his projects at Sencor, even as his mind wandered off on other errands. The joint venture would drown under the paperwork alone. This time she wouldn't be put off; she seized with no small joy the job of administrator of the LSP work. Tad couldn't argue. Four months later, in March 1985, Berthe was at the Sencor office talking to Tad's secretary, who said to her, "Mrs. Sendzimir, you look twenty years younger now."

Tad shared her enthusiasm, but his boiling point was some degrees higher. He was less the missionary, more the doting paterfamilias with a house-full of unbetrothed inventions. The object of his hopes was not so much to help China. It was to turn his newest ideas into reality—which, to his mind, would vastly help China. In May of 1985, he outlined in a letter to LSP his vision of Lanzhou Steel's future operations: making aluminized tubes from the planetary, spray casting with his technique, hooking up a continuous caster to the planetary, installing some spiral loopers, purchasing a Z-Hi mill from T. Sendzimir, Inc., for cold rolling, and eventually of course buying a second planetary to make, say, roofing sheets.

By the time this letter was sent, plans had already been made for a return trip to Lanzhou in July. LSP insisted that Tad and Berthe come for a symposium and trade show for Western businessmen. I was invited to come along.

We spent ten days in the dry heat of Lanzhou. Between elaborate, high-spirited banquets, Tad met with the LSP engineers and explained the workings of his planetary mill, blueprints spread out between cups of tea on the tables and couches of a small lounge. (In an adjoining room was a bed where Tad could stretch out and nap between meetings.) He gave lectures to engineering students, some of whom later came up to our rooms to visit bearing armloads of melons. LSP took us around town in a polished black Toyota sedan with fringed curtains on the windows, the driver leaning on the horn as if we were members of the Central Committee. They drove us out into the countryside one day to show off a large dam and hydroelectric plant (the entrance to which was guarded by a no-nonsense young man clutching his rifle with fixed bayonet—and on his feet, cloth shoes).

They took us on a brief tour of the Lanzhou Steel Plant. Berthe remarked to me with dismay that their steel-making methods were exactly those she remembered Armco was using—fifty years before. Only in Lanzhou, the workers' hard hats were made of woven bamboo.

LSP had first put us up in a suite of rooms in their "guest house," a sort of dormitory/office building near the plant. The setting was relaxed and friendly, the plumbing atrocious. The toilets worked intermittently. Water was shut off at 7 a.m., but still the bathroom floor remained at all times covered with a half-inch-deep pool. (Considerately enough, they supplied us with wooden clogs for wading into the bathroom.) We asked to be moved the next day to a hotel. That was still not soon enough to dispel from Tad's heart the first note of misgiving: "How can I trust them to operate something as complicated as a planetary mill," he wondered aloud, "when they can't so much as fix a toilet?"

The five days in Lanzhou left Tad exhausted. We flew next to Beijing, and during our three-day stay Tad ventured out only for a quick look at the Imperial Palace. He regained his strength and spirit by the time we flew to Shanghai.

Karl Tong greeted us at the Shanghai airport. He'd met up with us already the week before in Lanzhou, for the symposium. A courtly and cosmopolitan man, he would sit next to me at the banquets and continuously and insistently load onto my plate one strange, savory item after another. Tall, white-haired and broad-shouldered, imposing in his pressed gray suit, he kept his hand-held fan waving at all times. You knew when he'd dozed off, in a lecture hall, when that fan fell still in his lap.

Karl Tong was as good as his word. He had found Tad's old factory and we were brought there the day we arrived in Shanghai. When Tad had left in 1929, his factory was one building squatting amidst acres of vegetables. Now it was packed into a crowded neighborhood, at the end of an alley among two- and three-story buildings—one semi-colon in a novel of twelve million characters. Next to the factory building, a tiny, walled-in park with statues and benches had been erected as a place the workers could sit for lunch. We entered and walked around the low-ceilinged, darkened plant. (It was deserted that day, a holiday.) A layer of metallic dust covered every surface. Now they are only drawing wire; they had abandoned Tad's bolt- and nail-making operations. But Tad noticed a couple of familiar machines in a corner. He went closer to investigate, and said in amazement that these were the wire drawing machines he had cobbled together back in the 1920s. They were still in use.

Our hosts had found a veteran from that time. We drove into town to visit a man who had worked for Tad in the 1920s. He was now eighty-four and in poor health. We stopped on a busy street in a downtown neighborhood. Our guide ran up to the man's apartment to bring him down. The guide returned, walking slowly with a white-haired man in a T-shirt leaning on his arm. He and Tad met on the sidewalk and shook hands vigorously. Tad tried to say a few words he remembered in the Shanghai dialect. The man was pale and weak, and nervous among these well-dressed foreigners. But his cloudy dark eyes shone, and he said through the interpreter, "You were the best boss I ever had. Thank you for coming to see such a sick, old man!"

We stayed in Shanghai four days. Tad and Berthe met with city officials and with representatives from the Number Five Steel Plant and Shanghai Heavy Machinery. Tad, inching by car through traffic from one place to the next, became enamored of the idea of helping his old home town surmount its problem of moving seven million people back and forth each day. It seemed implausible to put a subway into the muck on which Shanghai was built. What they obviously needed was his Cableway. He had dreamed this up a couple of decades before, and had a model built of it in the T. Sendzimir Inc. building, running overhead down the hallway. It was a tram system in which the motorless cars, suspended from thick cable, would be propelled simply by gravity—the poles supporting the cables would drop away in front of the oncoming car, and raise the cable again after the car had passed; the car rolls forward as it moves down the slope created by the cable rising up behind it and dropping in front of it. Shanghai city officials expressed polite interest; letters and diagrams were exchanged over the next four years. The city fathers in the end pursued methods, submitted in bids from European and Australian companies, that were more proven and practical.

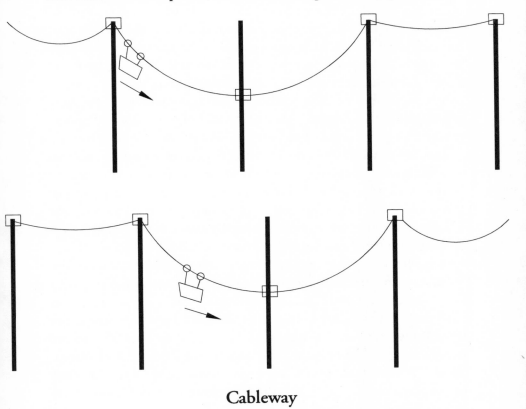

Cableway

Karl Tong asked for a favor in return for helping Tad meet business contacts in Shanghai: could Tad help his son Harold get to the U.S.? Karl Tong had himself been educated in the States in the 1940s. He loved China; he was circumspect about his own experiences during the Cultural Revolution, when thousands of English-speaking "intellectuals" were tortured and killed. But he wanted his youngest son to get a good education and make something of himself. "In China, Harold has no future," Karl told Tad. "Ten years of the Cultural Revolution destroyed our education system. It made our science and technology about twenty years behind the West." Harold, six-foot-one and muscular from volleyball, was nonetheless the baby. Karl and Harold lived together, Harold cooking for and taking care of his aging dad. When you saw them together—the seventy-two-year-old man and his twenty-three-year-old son—the respect and fondness they had for each other you could almost touch with your fingers. Tad and Berthe promised to do what they could from the States. (Harold came to the U.S. in 1986, and became a newly adopted member of the Sendzimir family. He is adored by every granddaughter. He moved eventually to Miami to work as a computer programmer. His father died in 1988. Harold was far away.)

Tad and Berthe returned to Connecticut after the July 1985 trip to China, and there they waited. Engineers from LSP went to Germany to pack up the Benteler mill and ship it to Lanzhou. Wes Wozniak—who had never seen a planetary mill in operation, but who as Sencor's chief and only engineer was the only man available—took a trip in the spring of 1986 to Lanzhou to see how things were going. Things were going nowhere. First LSP couldn't pour the foundation for the mill because the ground was frozen. Then they lost another six months because everything had to be ratified by at least three different government bodies, and for some reason the third body was inert. Without ratification, they couldn't get the necessary funds from the bank to build. So they waited. And waited. Zhang Wu Le, meanwhile, had been promoted to Vice-Governor of Gansu province, and LSP was put in the hands of a man who lacked Zhang's influence and force of will.

"I think that was one of the reasons they lost so much time, almost a year, after the signing in 1985," Berthe says. "Tad got rather discouraged. Everything else otherwise [in preparation] was done, but then nothing happened.

"I wish at that time, when they were having these problems [the bureaucratic snafus], that Tad had taken it more seriously," Berthe continues. "We always thought, well next week they'll figure it out. I wish we'd written to them that the agreement calls for them to do it within a certain period of time, and if it's not done we want to get out. I never myself wanted to get out of it, because Tad was so enthusiastic. And the planetary was there by then. You realize that this planetary had been in storage for twenty years or something."

By the spring of 1987, two and a half years after the initial agreement, still nothing had happened. Tad wrote an angry memo on April 23rd to Wozniak and Berthe, summarizing the history and his regrets:

> I presented that plan to LSP in writing but, unfortunately, I have not ascertained if they understood it and if they agreed with my reasoning. [Wozniak] has visited them last winter and found that the planetary mill was not installed and nothing done to complete the facility. LSP excused themselves claiming that no funds were available. They used the funds for other projects...This causes us heavy losses: no return on a nearly $1,000,000 investment plus deterioration of our planetary mill.
>
> In sum this is a pitiful example of how a Joint Venture actually works....I criticize ourselves for having been overly enthused and expected that the Chinese side will do their part. I must stress here that we were bringing to China most modern methods doing tremendous service to their steelmaking industry. I am inclined to believe that, with this experience, the wisest thing to do would be to withdraw entirely from the China operations.

(Tad's monetary investment was nowhere near $1,000,000. The "most modern methods" Tad was contributing to China's steel industry were in actuality a broken down twenty-year old mill, and the drawings for a process that existed only in Tad's imagination—continuous rolling directly into galvanizing.)

Berthe responded to Tad's memo that very afternoon with one of her own:

I quite understand your concern, it has been mine for months, but I cannot imagine reneging on our word and signature...I understand that you are tired and wonder why you should keep on going and fighting at your age. You have passed the normal age for the kind of work you are doing, and yet I cannot conceive you sitting outside doing nothing, or going on cruises to look at beautiful things, lovely landscapes that are not connected with your inventions.

Noblesse Oblige: you have been given a mind and a body that few have come near getting. You cannot suddenly become a common man. Their way of relaxation could not be yours! Because I love you, and because I love China, I am asking you to let me continue your work, while you are still with us, in the background, with your advice and love helping me.

Tad retreated from his attack. Over the next couple of years, the LSP venture proceeded at its glacial pace, letters crossed the Pacific with little visible effect, and Berthe would sit at her small desk in the kitchen typing memos, filing reports, and urging Tad to answer this request and that from China (usually for drawings or answers to technical questions). Berthe remembers that Tad would sit down to supper and lament: "Why can't we go back to the way it was before all this? We were so happy here in Jupiter! You used to have time to go on the beach. You weren't always talking business and worrying." She was in his hair and he didn't like it. "Tad," she'd respond, "I cannot go back to being a housewife. This joint venture with China will be the future of Sencor. We can't give up. If I don't participate in this operation, it will fail." He would turn back to his soup, feeling very sorry for himself.

But still she felt guilty. She said to me more than once, "Why am I pushing him? He's over ninety years old. Why can't I just let him sit there at his desk playing with his patents and reading Polish poetry? That's when he is happiest." I had to remind her that it was his planetary mill there in China, that it was his good name on the line, and that he was as eager as she to see it succeed. And I said that as much as he might scowl and bark (though in truth this was done at a fraction of the intensity of his younger years), he depended on her for every single stitch binding his life—business and personal—together. She had been his behind-the-scenes (and utterly unacknowledged) executive secretary and chief adviser for many years before the China deal. Tad himself often told me that he worried that she would take sick and become incapacitated—and then *he* would have to take care of *her*. That was his greatest nightmare.

But Tad had never been a pessimist. His gloomy moments were just that, moments; the sun broke through again quickly. The business with China opened up such a vast and promising arena for the inventions he was then unable to sell anywhere else in the world. As difficult as relations with the Chinese were, still there were relations. Still there was hope. In the spring of 1989, as LSP seemed no closer to starting their planetary mill four and a half years after signing the first agreement, Tad was writing memos suggesting that Sencor contact Shanghai Heavy Machinery to start...*another* joint venture, this time to produce roofing sheets.

Three years after Tad died in 1989, Lanzhou Steel invited Berthe and me to come to China to watch the inauguration of their planetary mill. We made the trip in September 1992. They'd commissioned a magnificent bronze bust of Tad to celebrate the planetary start-up. Three days after our arrival in Lanzhou, LSP held a ceremony to unveil the bust and make speeches about the great man and his vision. In a building a hundred yards behind the bust, ten minutes before, the planetary mill had been briefly switched on so we could see that the wheels do turn. They turned in limbo. A half dozen pieces of auxiliary equipment were in place. Not a single one was hooked up to another.

CHAPTER NINETEEN

THE OLD MAN

1985 - 1989

He stepped out of his bedroom into the patio at about seven in the morning, naked but for loose maroon bathing trunks. On his thin legs the skin is tight and brittle, tanned. On his calves are small gnarled blue fists of varicose veins. A few plastic bandages cling to a leg or a hand—his skin breaks easily and heals slowly. His longish, light gray hair is slept-in, pushed out of the way by a palm, back from his sloping forehead. His chest is narrow, flat, his shoulders and back rounded; he no longer reaches five foot ten. His gray eyes have faded to the paleness of the Atlantic reflecting the dawn sky, just then when the sun is breaching the horizon.

He walks now with eyes cast down, not ahead; he has a great fear of falling on the concrete. He steps carefully around the puddles left from the leaking roof, over to the side of the pool. He enters the pool without hesitating at the coolness of the water. Standing for a moment waist deep, facing the far end, he takes a breath and begins a very slow, noisy crawl stroke to the other end. Back and forth he'll go for ten laps, stopping once or twice to breathe for a moment, then plunging in again.

Berthe has already been in for her quick swim, a half hour before, while Tad was waking up and moving his limbs and rubbing his eyes in his slow, self-prescribed exercises on top of the bed. She has their breakfast on the table by the time he comes from his shower. He has combed back his hair, but has left to go their own way, like Spanish moss, the wild gray tendrils of his eyebrows. He is dressed as usual in long trousers and old Birkenstock sandals, and a loose brown corduroy shirt from J.C. Penney, his favored clothier. In his pockets are his reading glasses, pens in assorted colors, his notebook and a handkerchief. The skin on his large hands is speckled brown from liver spots, translucent; the heavy solid-gold ring stamped with the ancient family coat of arms, "Ostoya," dangles on his finger. He and Berthe exchange good morning kisses on both cheeks, and sit down to the chatter of the morning TV news. Before them is an array of boxes and jars containing the bird feed they ladle into their small bowls of yogurt: wheat germ, lecithin, bran, sunflower seeds, bee pollen, pumpkin seeds, brazil nuts, jam.

Once this battery of roughage has had its effect, Tad returns to sit at his desk, in one corner of the large living and dining room. He likes having his "office" right in the middle of the only family room in the house; he put it there so as not to feel isolated. He has had then to cope with marauding granddaughters, who know in which drawers to find the most interesting supplies: the Slinky, the titanium balls, the magnets, the multi-colored felt markers. Then comes surreptitious theft, and scolding that is quickly forgotten. (We of the family sometimes resented having to keep the television turned low while Tad was working, or having to hear his every phone conversation while we were trying to read, but now we have these calming memories of him working at his desk, part of the group—so different from how separated and mysterious he and his work were when we were young.)

Tad spends the morning reviewing patents and calling the Sencor office to talk to Wieslaw Wozniak about his activities. He quits his desk around twelve. He puts on a pair of rubber thongs encrusted with beach tar, covers his head with a canvas hat, takes up his cane and proceeds down the wooden stairs to the beach for an hour's walk. When he returns, he lies down to rest for half an hour. If an errand is to be done in town, Tad and Berthe go off for lunch to the Red Lobster, a chain of economy seafood restaurants Tad enjoys, where he'll order a fillet of whatever is fresh, followed by chocolate mousse. (In his last decade, he indulged his previously repressed fondness for chocolate desserts. This did not however prompt him to revise one granule of his sermon on the evils of sugar.)

He takes another short nap when he gets home, and returns to his desk for a couple of hours before another quick walk prior to supper. Those hours at the desk, once the calls to Waterbury are complete, are most likely spent typing witty, philosophical letters to his children, or reading Polish poetry from an old volume someone sent him. He allowed these enjoyable tasks to fill up more and more of his time as the 1980s progressed.

Supper is prefaced by a shot of vodka, then a few cloves of raw garlic, soup, television news, and feeding at the end the scraps to looper, the blind and wary dachshund (who was born and christened in the heat of the struggle over the spiral loopers.) Tad and Berthe will linger in front of the TV if there is a nature show on, or an opera, Tad sitting very close with one hand cupped behind his ear, hearing aid turned up. If not, he goes once more back to his desk until they retire to bed around ten.

*   *   *

Up in Waterbury, Wozniak proceeded each day as Tad directed, by phone or by mail or by antiquated telecopier. Tad was spending eight and more months of the year in Florida. He had to rely on Wozniak, by force of circumstance giving him the leeway his previous general managers had only dreamed of.

Much time was taken up with the ZB mill, that supposedly "revolutionary" innovation on a plate mill at half the cost of the real thing.[Appendix, 13] It was another fanciful idea from someone who favored the broad jump over the methodical relay race of improving existing inventions. None of the ZB mill ideas by themselves could have been patented—none of them were new. What was new was bundling them up into one mill. As usual, the prototype was patched together with parts from Tad's regular suppliers: Sears and the junkyard. The design was weak; the model was weaker. Tad "didn't believe in calculations, like for torque, or speed," Wozniak says. "There was no time. He just guessed." The mill's versatility was a selling point only for companies doing research—rolling different kinds of metals to see the outcome, before going into full production (on a more dependable mill). The ZB mill ended up at Texas Instruments. They were test rolling titanium aluminide for the epidermis of jets and spaceships.

Sencor was earning some income from this kind of research, for firms that couldn't interrupt their own mills to test new products. Sencor had an assortment of devices—the ZB, the Double-Three-High, the Wobbler—to try things out. United Technologies asked Sencor to roll some material for the power cell on the space shuttle, and they paid well for it. Shell Oil had them rolling plastic.

The most fanciful mill in Tad's head just then was what he called the "Nylatron mill." He had become infatuated with the new tough plastics. He thought he could use such material to coat the bearings on a Z mill—making them, he liked to think, eternal. Tad would plug this idea in every outgoing piece of mail, and ignore the detailed reports Taniguchi and others sent him explaining the fatal drawbacks of the idea. He continued also his work on closed loop rolling. He applied for a Department of Energy grant for spray casting molten steel in 1984, but was turned down. He got a patent for spray casting a year later. (Tad had for many years been carrying on a friendly correspondence about spray casting with a British inventor, A.R.E. Singer, who was developing a similar process.) And he kept trying to improve the planetary, and trying to interest someone in adding one to their continuous casting operation—if they would foot the bill.

He might have had such a chance in 1986, but his parsimony again snuffed it out. Our family had gathered in Linz, Austria, for Stanley's wedding. The day before the event we were invited to tour Voest-Alpine's tremendous steel plant. Voest is the company that perfected continuous casting. They were interested in the planetary, Berthe says, but they wouldn't simply buy it and get it going on their own. "*That's* the place for it," she insists. "*That's* the place he should have said, 'All right, we do it together. I want to prove the planetary works, right after your continuous caster. Let me put it there and I will pay for the expense. Even if I am penniless after.' But he wouldn't."

In 1985, Tad wrote in a letter to an old family friend: "Luckily, my inventive mind has opened new fields for me in NASA (outer space) and I have interesting patents of structures that can be erected in orbit, hundreds of miles above earth surface. My dream is to be taken as passenger on one of those shuttle planes to transport such structure and leave it permanently in orbit to house a colony of people who live in space."

Tad let his mind out to play, in his later years, in the open fields beyond the steel mills. One result was this suggestion to the National Aeronautics and Space Administration for his material for constructing space stations [see Chapter 10]. Another was his idea, similarly Florida-inspired, of running specially-equipped jeeps between rows of orange trees, covering the rows with immense, long sheets of plastic to protect the fruit from frost. He sent a letter to *Nowy Dziennik* suggesting that to reduce New York's air pollution, electric motors be installed in all the taxicabs, to be recharged each hour at taxi stands. He proposed in an address to the International Steel Congress a method for laying oil pipeline by putting an entire pipe factory on railroad cars, producing city-block-long lengths of pipe *in* (moving) *situ*. And in a memo and sketch from 1986 that even he had to entitle "science fiction," he explains his idea for hexagonal floating islands of "prestressed sprayed concrete over a structural steel and expanded metal frame. Or better still an archipelago of seven such islands elastically tied together. About 300 feet across...joined by short bridges for circulation..." The islands would be fishing and fish packing communities, with some vegetable gardens, able to move to the richest fishing grounds. "Compared to San Francisco, life could be a little monotonous but not much more so than in Honolulu. And Honolulu couldn't move next to Tahiti, but our island could!"

* * *

There is a tiny village in the hills of southern Poland, south of Krakow, named Lukawice [pronounced Woo-ka-vitz-a]. In that town is a wooden church with a steep tin roof, three small imperial domes, and dark brown, board and batten siding. In the entry, on the wall in a glass case, an inscribed poster tells the story of the founding of this church, in 1703, by a person whose name was Sendzimir.

On a rainy day in September 1983, Tad hired two taxis in Krakow to take us — the whole family — to Lukawice. It was a Sunday morning; along the muddy roads villagers walked with their families single file into town for Mass. We at last pulled into Lukawice just as one church service was ending. Tad and the driver went around back to find the priest.

The young pastor invited us in for coffee. He brought out and set down on the table an old ledger, the chronicle of the parish. He turned to a page, written as all the others in Latin, that described the founding and building of the church, with funds donated by this Sendzimir, an obviously respectable representative of the branch of the family who made their home here in town. Tad, smiling with pride, read over the page slowly in Latin, translating for us as he went. The taxi drivers were impressed.

The pastor chatted with Tad in Polish. He explained to Tad that the church (it was not the original structure from 1703) needed to be rebuilt; his flock was growing and at every service people had to stand outside the door. When Tad returned to the States, he sent the pastor a generous check.

We were there in Poland in 1983 to mark the fiftieth anniversary of the birth of Tad's first inventions, the galvanizing line and the rolling mill. The Mining and Metallurgical Academy (Akademia Gornicza-Hutnicza, AGH) in Krakow held a celebration in his honor. (They had given Tad an honorary doctorate in 1973.) Family and friends attended the formal symposium, along with professors of the Academy, officials from the Polish steel industry, and a few old men who had worked with Tad in Katowice in the early thirties. They spoke, with pride and humor, of their acquaintance with Poland's most renowned inventor. For three days we were taken around town from one formal dinner to the next; even the Communist mayor of Krakow held a reception for Tad. In between we had a few moments to visit with and be spoiled by the large collection of new and old Sendzimirs in Krakow.

Tad's relations with Poland had remained strong through the 1970s. He'd been back several times; T. Sendzimir, Inc., had sold a few mills. In 1980, Tad was negotiating a plan to send over both his Wobbler mill and the reducing press, and to set up licensing agreements so that his mills could be built in Poland. This plan was abandoned without a word when martial law was imposed in December 1981.

By the time of the celebration at the AGH in 1983, martial law had begun to thaw. Even so Tad was not of the mind to renew serious business talks. He continued writing to professors at the various technical schools, rhapsodizing about the nylatron mill and spray casting and strip for space stations. And he kept up a detailed correspondence with his relatives, especially with his sisters Aniela and Terenia. Every year he sent a large check (by the standards of what U.S. dollars could buy in Poland at the time) to Terenia, who followed his instructions for dividing it among the cousins and nieces and nephews. Along with his letters urging his sisters to take daily walks and eat fresh vegetables, he would send bottles of vitamins.

While Tad's commercial ties with Poland were wilting, Tad's emotional ties were coming into autumnal bloom. The Peripatetic Businessman was slowing down and the Son of Poland was stepping into his place. Tad spent more and more of his time over the last decade of his life reminiscing, reliving and reciting from the deep well of Polish culture, history and experience. A safe bet for a birthday or Christmas present for him was always an aged, leather-bound volume of Polish poetry, if we could track one down in an antique bookstore. He would sit at his desk hunched over such books, magnifying glass in hand, gently and slowly tapping the desk with the middle finger of his free hand to the rhythm of the stanzas. He'd recite verse after verse from memory to any guest who spoke the language.

In a brief letter to Jan in 1986 he reveals his wistful disappointment in his illiterate children:

> Dear Jan, I remember some years ago you seemed to be

sensitive to poetry; you even produced some, always mysterious like a jungle. I never told you how much poetry meant to me. But unfortunately no one of my family except Michael speaks Polish, and Michael is too busy to think about art. I see no way of introducing my wife and my children to this fabulous enchanted kingdom which is Polish poetry.

As he moved through his ninth decade, he took great pleasure in placing himself in Polish history. He was the scion of an ancient line of distinguished Sendzimirs, he repeated over and over in letters to us, in rambling memos, and in the cursory memoirs he began to write in 1984 (and abandoned in 1985 when he got too busy with China.) The story would begin around the year 1130 with an army commander under King Boleslaw III, and continue through to 1809 with Tad's great-grandfather defending the city of Plock. Tad took pride and also comfort in these stories. He had fulfilled, in his lifetime of achievement, the mission of upholding the honor of the family name; maybe now he could rest in peace. In the last few years of his life he was putting even greater emphasis on the achievements of his ancestors than on his own. He became a mere footnote. He became almost humble. He talked much about his family's place in the history of Poland, little about his own place in the history of technology. (But still, in his business letters, he never failed to claim that in his nineties he was still working on the cutting edge.)

The stories in the letters to us served an additional purpose. "I've done my part," he was saying. "This is your legacy. These are your genes. Now come on, do something with them." Tad was both the supreme individualist—insisting that all his accomplishments were thanks to his own personal brilliance and will power—and the fatalist who was merely fulfilling heredity's orders.

*   *   *

Tad grew philosophical. This was not inspired by gloom over his mortality. Quite the opposite: he became playful, relieved at ninety of the duty to be serious. As a young man he had studied philosophy to refine his skills in logic. Now he returned to it, to muse on life and man and God, as he sat before one of his colicky typewriters, staring out the window, ignoring the entreaties piling up on the desk from his engineers and accountants. He typed memos to himself (and then made copies and sent them to us). One from 1986, entitled "GOD," went like this:

> God has created man. And man has created God. Man was to resemble God, be his image. But man is created to walk on the land. So obviously God must be walking among us some-where....Men were fewer at biblical times, so it must have been easy to spot God and maybe even talk to him....I cannot imagine the purpose of locating [God] somewhere up in the air, floating and looking upon mankind from that elevated position. To police observance of the ten commandments, it would definitely be better to stay among men on the surface of the earth. But I still do not understand what was the purpose of creating man, now that man has spread all over and that we are threatened by a population explosion. Has THAT been originally planned?

Tad's mind dwelt on less lofty entertainments as well. One favorite pastime was wordplay. He filled a thick file folder with scraps of paper containing such lists as: "chaotic, glue stick, drum stick, chopstick, plastic, gymnastic, chauvinistic, altruistic, al coholic, realistic." Or, "Investigator, Alligator, Perpetrator, Fumigator." Some of his lists were in Polish, others had additions in French and German. These were gymnastics for the brain, a muscle he believed needed its exercise like all the others. The exercises also served to prime the pump for his puns and witticisms. While we were watching a television show on conserving wetlands, Tad went over to his desk and scribbled a note: "This is a concentration of conversation on conservation." He asked one employee, after giving him for Christmas a compass, "Will it enable you to be compassionate?" One much repeated, and probably stolen, was: "When Richard the Lion-Hearted got sick, did he see a doctor or a veterinarian?"

He philosophised, exercised (and procrastinated) also in his letters to the three of us, myself and my brothers. The letters became less formal, more amusing and good-natured, even though, in Stanley's case, his worry remained. The letters were his opportunity to continue his sermons, replay his anecdotes, expound on art, life and health, and show his love. Just as he never left aside any of his inventions, always trying to improve them, just so he was always trying, gently, to improve us. Letters between Tad and Jan were the most frequently exchanged, but still Tad would playfully worry that his epistles had hit their target: "I hope this letter won't take too long to reach you though it depends if you shall not be on the move like a hydrogen atom in closed bottle at elevated temperature."

The true flavor of these letters from Tad cannot be conveyed adequately on this neat, typeset page. Tad would buy his increasingly sophisticated typewriters and never get further than the On-Off switch. Every third word in his letters was misspelled, sometimes quite amusingly. Lines were xxx'd out and written over. Punctuation marks were sprinkled into the words. The letters often had no margins—the last word of each line fell off the paper. The "self-correcting" function of these machines still requires human intervention; Tad was too busy to bother.

Despite his longings for a poet in the family, Tad supported my efforts at prose. It had been his idea that I write his biography, and he made only a few corrections on the chapters he read. Most of all he was pleased—"thrilled" wouldn't be too strong a word—to have me coming down to Jupiter and asking him to explain his inventions. "Finally," he'd say, "there will be one among you children who understands my achievements."

I know that on that level—achievement—my brothers and I were a disappointment to our father. We were intelligent, but we had not, in our thirties and early forties, made our mark on anything, much less come close to his standard. But here was the silver lining to his lifelong preoccupation with his inventions: *their* success was what mattered. Tad's ego was not so dependent on what his flesh-and-blood offspring made of themselves, as it is for many fathers who make enormous demands on their children. Tad was not in despair when we didn't turn out the way he'd have liked. His other, mechanical, children had brought home the awards. He said to Berthe more than once that he felt quite proud of us: "They are all warm, kind human beings."

*   *   *

In his philosophical musings, Tad made as many references to the devil as to the devil's counterpart. But in Jupiter Tad practiced only one religion, and he did so with a convert's zeal. That was the religion of Health. His long walks were his prayers. His swimming and garlic-eating were his sacraments. His books—the dozens weighing down his bookshelves and sitting in stacks on his desk, books on such themes as "Throw Away Your Glasses," "How to Increase Your Brain Power," "Reverse the Aging Process," "Long Life Through Fasting," "The Wonders of Garlic"—were his scripture. Florida was his church; the Jupiter beach was its altar.

The universal theme in his sermons was "use it or lose it." "The moment I decide to sit comfortably in my armchair, my career, at least in this incarnation, will come to an end," he wrote in a letter to me in 1988. "Mandatory retirement is a death trap. [If] I relax or slow down, I shall get rusty and be soon ready to face the encounter with eternity." In 1987 he came upon an article in the magazine of the American Association of Retired Persons, entitled "How We Age." He sent a copy to every English-speaker he knew. (The article expounded on his own anthem, Use It or Lose It, and explained how, with advances in medicine, today's elderly are healthier and more active than the elderly of a generation before.) "While I may hope to reach the age of 100," he wrote in a letter sent with the article, "my children might reach 110. Not only that: my 'savvy box' is more efficient, has more storage capacity than my father's. That leads to better models of human beings in the future."

Alas Tad's fanaticism led him to be not so much the better model of a human being in the present. Berthe's burden (besides sharing a bedroom for forty-five years with a man who ate raw garlic every night) was that Tad's preoccupation with keeping himself healthy ran to excess: he was a hypochondriac. He swore by his methods and cures, but not to the extent that he would look the sudden chill or the cold rain in the eye and laugh. At the slightest cough he'd take to his bed. By mid-morning, he might get up and plod over to his desk, bundle blankets around his shoulders and legs, make a few phone calls to let everyone know that he was still working despite being close to death, and return to bed. Slowly, miraculously, in a few days he'd bring himself to admit that maybe, maybe he was feeling a little better.

In 1987 Tad (then ninety-three) was leaning on the edge of the round dining room table, supervising the TV repairman. The table tipped and dumped Tad on the floor. He broke a hip. Two days later the surgeons put a pin in it. Four weeks after that, Tad was back on the beach. Of course, the first week had been pure gloom: he thought this was the beginning of the end. He could feel the rust forming. With the help of exercises and a physical therapist—and a more positive attitude—he made a quick recovery. Otherwise, his program of diet and exercise did its remarkable job keeping his body and mind vigorous. His one serious physical ailment came from the very Florida climate that had been keeping him alive: skin cancer. Over the last five years of his life, one tiny growth after another had to be removed. It is possible that one of these, in a roundabout way, was the precursor to his passing away.

(I was less concerned about Tad's health than I was about the health of everyone else in Palm Beach County—when Tad was driving. It is nothing short of a miracle that this man never had a serious accident during his long and perilous life behind the wheel. It is nothing short of criminal negligence that he was allowed to keep his driver's license into his nineties, no questions asked, no tests demanded. His erratic, blustering driving style went from frightening to homicidal as his eyesight and reflexes deteriorated. But he prided himself on his excellent driving. What truly terrified him was the prospect of losing his license. He'd been driving cars for seventy-five years—he'd been driving cars almost as long as the human race had been driving cars. He wasn't going to stop now.)

*   *   *

In Colorado, south of Leadville, there is a hillside where Tad and Berthe liked to walk. It overlooks a broad valley framed on its opposite bank by mountains named after Ivy League colleges. Tad bought 160 acres of land on this slope outside the town of Buena Vista in 1973. They came here every couple of years for the view and the peace and the air. Berthe looked for arrowheads. Their habit was to fly into Denver, rent a car, and after a few days in Buena Vista travel south to Taos and Santa Fe. They took great pleasure in the mountains, rocks, art and history of the Southwest. Most of Berthe's jewelry is Zuni. Tad more often than not passed up the silk cravat in favor of a simple bola tie.

Tad in his sixties went abroad a dozen times a year; Tad in his nineties was not quite earth-bound, but he'd slowed up a bit. Most of the year was spent in Florida. During the summer months, he and Berthe would return to Connecticut, visit Cape Cod, and try to fit in a trip to Colorado or to Europe. In 1983 they went to the Soviet Union. Later that year they were in Poland for the 50th anniversary ceremonies. In 1984 they went to China. In 1985 they made the trip to Austria for Stanley's wedding, and a month later were back in China. Tad did not return to China after 1985, but he never stopped talking about the trip he was planning: he would take us to Beijing—via Europe; in Moscow we'd board the Trans-Siberian Railway and repeat his 1918 journey across the U.S.S.R. (this time inside the railroad car, not on top).

Foremost on his mind in the mid-eighties was a return to his hometown of Lwow. Travel was becoming easier in the Soviet Union. Smaller cities like Lwow could be reached. He wanted to show Lwow to his children, and to find his home on Saint Teresa Street, to see if the pictures his mother had painted were still there above the door frames.

In August 1987, after several false starts, we arrived at last in the Soviet Union: Tad, Berthe, myself and my brother Jan. We took off from one of Moscow's domestic airports, and two hours later landed on a wide plateau of farm country. The plane pulled up to a structure the texture, shape and color of a sand castle, "Lwow" prominent in block letters in Russian and Ukrainian on its cornice. A 50-year-old woman in tan babushka and blue coveralls was sweeping between the standing aircraft with a straw broom. Inside, the airport had the casual, buzzing atmosphere of a Nebraska county seat, surrounded by farmland but with a backlot full of old war planes and helicopters.

In the twenty-minute taxi ride we descended from the plateau into a green urban basin, rimmed with parks, studded with small hills and baroque church spires. Berthe, Jan and I watched Tad anxiously for signs of recognition as we passed from the modern apartment blocks on the outskirts to the tree-lined cobblestone streets and stuccoed houses of the center city. He couldn't place where we were until we pulled up to our hotel, the Intourist, in the center of town. Looking up at the four-story structure, he remembered that it was built when he was about six or seven. He turned, surveyed the surrounding buildings, the Roman Catholic cathedral two blocks away, the statue of Adam Mickiewicz (Poland's poet laureate) in the middle of a traffic circle, and remarked that indeed, nothing had changed since then.

Nothing seemed to have changed (or, let's say, been repaired) inside the once grand hotel since then either. The elevator was permanently out of order. Loose, frayed oriental carpeting covered the marble stairs up to the third floor landing, where a huge reproduction of "Lenin Reading" was the only reminder that Emperor Franz Joseph had been replaced. An old-fashioned pull-toilet gurgled from our bathroom; the hot water came intermittently. "What difference if we were in tents in the park?" Tad commented the next day to Berthe, with the sarcasm he'd succumb to when tired or frustrated.

We spent four days in Lwow. In between the prolonged meals and Tad's frequent naps, he showed us his city. Hailing a taxi from the sporadically served taxi line in front of the hotel, Tad would get in the front seat and give the driver directions. He took us to the main building of Lwow University, the ornate structure that had been used by the Austrian parliament and bureaucracy at the turn of the century. He pointed up to a window on the second floor and said, "That's where my father's office was." We went next to the central square, the Rynek, and Tad explained as we walked what businesses and shops had occupied the narrow-front houses, built by sixteenth-century nobles, when he was a boy. The following day we climbed to the top of Wysoki Zamek, a man-made hill dominating the center of Lwow, raised up by patriotic Poles in the middle of the nineteenth century to celebrate the union of Poland and Lithuania in 1569. At every intersection, the large yellow tanks of *kvas* vendors dispensed their lightly fermented drink. Stout gray veterans, bearing chestfuls of WWII ribbons, filled up the park benches where sat, one hundred years before, the similarly august heroes of Poland's 1863 insurrection against the czar.

Tad brought us to the Lwow Polytechnic, where he had studied mechanical engineering. The large Italianate main building glowed under a fresh coat of Pompeiian pink, as it had eighty years before. An enthusiastic history teacher showed us around. He'd never heard of Tad's rolling mills or the names Tad mentioned. A 93-year-old cannot expect to run into some of his old professors.

So little of the Lwow Tad showed us had changed. He was back in his nineteenth-century hometown, walking carefully along the cobblestones laid before his birth, remembering the concerts at the Opera House he had attended as a child. He commented more than once that the city was fifty years behind times. The crumbling plaster on the rococo facades, the dusty, old-fashioned items in the small shop windows, and the rare sight of a woman not in skirts reinforced that impression. The Lwow we saw was like a museum, everything in the past tense. Yet through the gray haze from the top of Wysoki Zamek we could see white squadrons of modern apartment blocks and factories stretching beyond Lwow's rim. Buses, motorbikes, cathode ray tubes and TV sets were rolling from the assembly lines of Lwow, I found out later. The Soviets had not left this area to stagnate.

Throughout our stay, Tad was calm and unemotional. He was glad that so much was still standing. Yet his descriptions of the past were spoken deadpan. His gray eyes seldom brightened. Two factors, I believe, dampened what might have been higher spirits. The first was weariness and the strain of traveling—he was after all ninety-three. The second was the fact that, while the Soviet government hadn't removed all the Polish statues and buildings, they had removed all the Poles. This Lwow was not the Polish city he had grown up in—it was a city invaded, annexed and transformed by the enemy. All the street and shop signs were in Russian or Ukrainian; the people in the restaurants and the hotel were not speaking Polish. Imagine, on a larger scale, Berthe returning to Paris, if Hitler had won; the magnificent buildings and boulevards unchanged, the neon signs on the Champs Elysee bearing advertisements in German. Still this image should not be overplayed. Tad was not a bitter man, nor one much given to political rumination. He seemed content just to have set eyes once again on his old city. He could easily steep in the glories of the past and blink out the realities of the present.

Tad's emotions did rise to the surface, briefly, when we set out at last on our main objective: to find the house where he grew up. No Sendzimir had lived in that apartment since 1940, when the Soviet army evacuated the Poles (including Tad's mother, his sister Terenia and her two children) to camps in Kazakstan for the duration of the war. We had no idea if the building was even still standing.

The cab driver told us there was no Saint Teresa Street, so Tad directed him to the neighborhood, past the Greek Catholic cathedral towering at the foot of his street, past the park he had cut through on his way to grammar school. Still Tad didn't recognize the street names. We trolled around several blocks of neat, three-story apartment buildings, flush up against the sidewalk, of identical beige squareness and identical chipped plaster ornaments. Finally, one corner caught Tad's eye, and he asked the driver to pull over so he could go by foot. Jan, Berthe and I followed twenty steps behind as he inspected each doorway. At the last house before a small park, a house like each of its neighbors, he stopped and said, "This is it."

Tad climbed the two steps up to the left side door and knocked. A young woman with blond hair tied in a bun answered. With a polite smile she let us in. She led us through a narrow, cluttered hallway smelling of onions and small children and into a tiny, comfortably furnished sitting room. There, above two doors, were my grandmother's paintings, faded, but still showing an innocent, amateur charm; one was of a peasant girl in a field of wheat, the other a blue-black lake in moonlight. Only then did we know we had indeed found the right place. Tad's eyes moistened as he stood gazing at them. He had always said, "When we visit Lwow, I will show them to you."

In a few minutes, the lady of the house, a friendly, attractive woman of about sixty, came in. She led us into the living room and showed two more of my grandmother's paintings. She and Tad chatted in Russian for ten minutes. We thanked her, exchanged addresses, and walked back to our waiting cab.

On the evening of the following day we boarded an overnight train to Kiev. We spent three days walking around that vividly green city—of which much had changed since Tad's stay there during World War I—and flew from there to Warsaw. Tad and Berthe returned to Florida after this tiring trip, and Tad never set foot out of the state again.

* * *

In March of 1989, Tad received a call from a man in New York, a Polish film director, who was embarking on a project for New York's Polish television station: a series of films on famous Poles in America. Tad was to be the first. The director, Antoni Dzieduszycki, had already set up interviews in Waterbury. Could he and his crew come down to Jupiter to film Tad and Berthe in their home? Tad shrugged. Why not?

They arrived by car a couple of weeks later. Dzieduszycki, a lean man in his forties with a moustache and a quick smile, turned out to be an enthusiastic, sympathetic listener. He was pleased to find that his first subject was a man of such warmth and erudition. He'd sit with Tad on the patio overlooking the ocean and let him recite verses from Slowacki as the camera rolled. They filmed him walking up and down the beach, swimming in the pool, working at his desk, eating his garlic. Tad quickly ascertained (or decided?) that Dzieduszycki had noble forebears. Nothing could have better served to warm Tad up to his interviewer.

This week in the spring of 1989 was a distracting but pleasant break for Tad, a felicitous interlude before the difficult months to come. With the film crew he found an appreciative, uncritical audience. He could ignore the glaring floodlights and ramble on in Polish about his ancestors, the history of Poland, poetry and philosophy, his inventions, his latest projects to advance the human race. They wanted to hear everything; they recorded everything. And they produced from all this, on their shoestring budget, an hour's worth of film that arrived in video cassette, by special delivery, on the morning of Tad's birthday in July. He couldn't have been more pleased. The film was broadcast from New York's Polish TV station a week later. Everyone who has seen it has commented on how vividly and gently Tad is portrayed, strains of Mozart in the background as he walks on the beach, stanzas of poetry flowing from him as the wind tousles his hair.

*   *   *

No individual, actual or imaginary, can pass his 95th birthday more than once. I hope to pass that day the next 15th of July. You are invited to help my family and myself to celebrate and offer congratulations or sympathy, depending upon how you feel about it.

Tadeusz

This was the draft of the invitation to the ninety-fifth birthday party that our family was slowly trying to plan in the spring of 1989. The troubling question was: where? Tad and Berthe were in Jupiter. Most of the friends, relatives, and employees present and past—all of whom needed to be invited to this event, the like of which was not soon to be repeated—were in New England. Would Tad feel up to returning to Connecticut, and when?

In early June, hopes for this return disintegrated when Tad went to his dermatologist for a check-up. The doctor, as always, found more potentially cancerous growths to remove. But he found one on Tad's calf that he felt was too large to safely cut out in his office. He told Tad that his skin in that spot was too thin and brittle. Tad would have to go into the hospital, have the growth taken off by a surgeon and replaced with a skin graft. He'd be in the hospital at least two weeks. And then he'd have to stay off his feet for a month.

Tad was silent as Berthe drove him back to Jupiter. He stared bleakly out the windshield at the traffic on Route One. Finally he said in a voice thin as a dagger, "What if I just don't have it done? I've lived long enough."

To let such a growth remain was a death sentence, he well knew. But to him, so was an operation. So was enforced immobility.

Stanley had come from Europe with his wife and daughter for a month or two. He went along with Tad and Berthe to meet the surgeon. "This guy is a schmuck!" Stanley declaimed when they were leaving the office. The surgeon had talked to and about Tad as if to and about a stick of wood. Stanley called the dermatologist and got the name of someone else. When this second doctor saw Tad, he pooh-poohed his colleague's prescription. A week later Doctor Number Two removed the growth from Tad's calf in an out-patient clinic. He stitched up the wound without using a skin graft. Tad had to keep his leg up for only a week or two, and he couldn't swim.

This time however, recovery was slow and painful. In 1987 when he'd broken his hip, after a week of despondency and self-pity he bounced back. His 1989 despondency would not lift. It's as if, in that first car ride back from the dermatologist's office, the idea that he'd lived long enough caught hold like a bur and wouldn't come free—no matter that its source, the threatened skin graft and hospital stay, had been quashed. I believe that Tad in that moment decided to die. Why? I don't know. I suspect that he was simply tired, and that he saw that none of his projects were so near fruition he had to hang on to see them through. For almost ninety-five years he had used his will power to grasp and steer his life. In the summer of 1989, he used that will power just as assiduously to let it go.

But first he had to say his good-byes. And though he realized (or decided?) he wasn't going to make it after all to a hundred, he was certainly going to make it to ninety-five.

I flew to Florida for the week of his birthday in the middle of July. Stanley and family were there, as was Harold Tong. Jan was absent—he was in Europe for the summer with his family, developing some projects related to his ecological work.

The man we found at home in Jupiter was not the man we'd always known, so lively and active. By July he was on his feet, but with the help of two canes. He was thinner than we'd ever seen him; his walk was slow; the light in his eyes intermittent. He'd get up for an hour, then shuffle back to his bedroom to lie down for two. He did walk on the beach, but he'd go for only a hundred feet in one direction, using both canes to steady himself, then turn around and come back. He couldn't swim because of the still-bandaged wound.

I took a lot of pictures of him on his birthday. He sat on the couch in the living room and merrily opened presents. We watched the film about Tad from the Polish film-makers, which had arrived just that morning. He had the energy to sit and chat with all of us there, and that indeed was the present he most appreciated, having his family around him. Later on, Jan called from Europe. Tad asked him once more, "When are you coming back? Next week?" Jan reminded him no, not till the end of August. Tad was disappointed, and anxious.

Tad had a fainting spell on the beach that very morning. This gave everyone a fright. (Only later did we guess that it might have been mild heart failure.) We arranged it so that Harold, on his summer break from college, could stay in Jupiter and go out with Tad on his walks, in case he needed help.

I could not stay. When Tad and Berthe drove me to the airport and said good-bye on the curb, Tad embraced me more strongly than usual. The look in his eyes was unmistakable: I will not see you again. It was not a look I had ever seen before. Before it had always been, "Till next time. Please come back soon." I dismissed this look at the time. He'd recovered before, I figured, and he would again, since apart from his great age he had no diagnosed health problems. Over the next month I'd call them in Jupiter several times a week, as usual, but I seldom spoke to Tad. His hearing was poor on the telephone. I'd find out from Berthe how he was doing, and ask her to give him a kiss for me.

She herself saw nothing coming. She'd lived with this dynamo for forty-five years, and even in the face of his faltering it was impossible to think he wouldn't last forever. She'd heard his gripes and aches and pains often enough before—he'd always, eventually, recovered. She did her best to get him to take it easy. Stanley asked Tad one day at lunch whether, given how he was feeling, he might think of slowing down...retiring. "Oh no!" Tad replied. "I want to stay in full control till the very end."

Michael flew down to Florida for a visit at the beginning of August. When he and Tad parted, the impression he got, he remembers, was the same as mine: our father was bidding us good-bye.

Katherine and Tatjana, Stanley's wife and daughter, flew back to Paris at the beginning of August. Stanley remained. He was deeply troubled over the state Tad was in. He spent much of his time getting him comfortable, urging him to see other doctors, and trying to instill into him some fight. Tad was touched by his son's solicitousness, but it hadn't much effect on his resigned attitude. By the middle of August Tad's condition seemed stable and Stanley felt that he could go. When Tad said good-bye at the airport, Stanley, in hindsight, admits that it was more emotional than ever before. "But I was in a state of denial then. I would never have left if I had the slightest idea that he'd die soon. I saw my role as cheering him up, trying to make him feel all right. So if he was trying to say a final good-bye then, I was totally blocking it out."

That left only Jan. In the last week of August, Jan returned with his family from Germany. They arrived in Miami, came up to Jupiter, and spent two days with Tad and Berthe. As usual, serious talk was put off till the last minute. Jan told his father about his trip to Eastern Europe, and they talked about the real estate projects in Florida Jan was taking care of for him. When they were almost through, Jan says Tad "turned and said, out of the blue, 'I want you to know you're my spiritual heir.' I think it was his way of telling me that he was proud of me and of the work I was doing. That I was a scientist like he was, that I was interested in Poland."

Tad now was free.

"I did not realize the end was near," Berthe says. "He was so alive. The day before he died was a Friday. He would always call the office late Friday afternoon just to say goodbye before the weekend. He called them that afternoon and talked to everyone. He seemed fine."

The next day, one week after Jan left, was September 1. Tad took a long time getting out of bed. He told Berthe that he felt a bit tired that morning—maybe he shouldn't go out. But he got up anyway and slowly put on his robe. He met Harold at the door to the beach. They went out onto the patio, and carefully walked down the wooden stairs to the sand. The sky was clear, the ocean still, the sun just above the horizon, the air becoming white with its late summer heat. Harold had Tad's arm in his. They took a few steps, maybe ten, toward the shore. Tad said, "Harold, I'm weak. Let's go back. I'm sorry to be such a bother." He mumbled a few words in Polish. And then he collapsed.

Harold ran to get Berthe. They called an ambulance, then carried Tad, breathing but unconscious, back up to the house. The paramedics arrived and couldn't revive him. They drove him to the Jupiter Hospital. Doctors in the emergency room tried again, unsuccessfully. He died less than an hour later. His last conscious image had been that beach at dawn, for twenty-five years his source of strength and inspiration, his most cherished spot on the face of the earth.

EPILOGUE

Two hundred people filled and flowed out of the tiny chapel in Bethlehem, Connecticut, for Tad's funeral Mass. It was a cold, gray morning in mid-September 1989. A string quartet, squeezed knee to knee in a corner up front, played sixteenth-century Polish hymns, Chopin and the Polish national anthem. Michael gave the eulogy. The casket we'd ordered was, of course, stainless steel. At home, condolence notes and telegrams from around the world were rising in stacks.

In February of 1990, a letter came from the Solidarity-led Workers Council at the Huta Lenina steel plant in Krakow. Could they, they asked, be allowed to use the name of Tadeusz Sendzimir in renaming their steel mill? Jubilant Eastern Europeans had been obliterating Lenin's name and tearing down his visage since the fall of the Berlin Wall a few months before. The workers at the plant outside of Krakow were about to do the same. Sendzimir—Poland's most famous name in steel—seemed an honorable replacement. Of course we agreed (despite our reservations about giving our name to a plant whose toxic fumes were eating the faces off the monuments of Krakow).

On May 2, 1990, our family arrived in Krakow for the ceremony to re-christen Huta Lenina, scheduled to coincide with St. Florian's Day, the patron saint of firemen and steel workers. The trees wore spring's soft, freshly-minted leaves. The air too was soft and clear, briefly, and warm. The city had never to us looked so beautiful, so like Tad would have remembered from his childhood visits, when Krakow was a town of learning and culture, not smoke and industry.

On the morning of May 4, we were picked up at our hotel and brought out to the plant for the ceremonies. Driving up the long avenue leading to the plant entrance, we could see the tremendous stainless steel sign, thirty feet above the ground, heralding in silver letters as tall and proud as stallions: HUTA im. T. SENDZIMIRA.

As we waited for the ceremony to begin, one of my Polish cousins whispered to me, "I wonder who is more surprised, Lenin or Tad?" Surprise was my own emotion too. Just two and a half years before, I'd stood in this exact spot, under Lenin's sign, under (I couldn't help imagining) surveillance, intimidated and nervous, waiting to interview some of these bureaucrats, waiting to see for the first time Tad's galvanizing line. Now Solidarity plaques had replaced the hammers and sickles on the walls of the administration buildings. Now a small brass band was playing and red and white ribbons flew from the giant sign. Now I was being treated like a celebrity, not like a busy-body American. I kept looking up at the sign and, so to speak, rubbing my eyes.

First came speeches in a large hall inside, and the flourished signing of over-sized, official documents. Then, outside again, Michael and Berthe cut the ribbons. The local cardinal, Macharski, said a few prayers and blessed the crowd. Two buses pulled up to take the whole family, sporting our white plastic hard hats, for a quick tour of the plant. (One elderly aunt kept chuckling, repeating in a mirthful, amazed, ironic voice: "*Our* Huta!") They brought us back for an elaborate lunch and more speeches. Later in the afternoon, we went to a crowded wooden church in Nowa Huta, the barracks-like (in form and function) suburb near the plant, for a commemorative Mass sponsored by Solidarity. In the evening, Michael hosted a cocktail party in the best restaurant in town.

The evening before, we had gone to a relative's apartment for the family gathering, the traditional event organized each time Tad had returned to Krakow. Again the tables groaned under the weight of cakes and canapes. Again the rooms were squeezed with Sendzimirs. It all seemed the same, but it was not the same. Tad's absence was pronounced. There was no nucleus at this event, as he had been. (Michael had become the patriarch, it seemed, but it was amusing to see him acting as such in the presence of women who had baby-sat him when he was in short pants.)

I recognized only later that Tad was still the core and focus, in absentia. He was why we were all there. He'd made it possible, through his continuing love for Poland, through the fame that had that May brought us all to this spot, and through the support that had seen his Polish family through fifty years of turmoil. He could be honored, he could be imitated, but he could not be replaced.

APPENDIX

Chapter Notes

1. [Chapter 7] Armco increased the speed of the line by adding exit rolls—two rolls placed on either side of the strip as it leaves the zinc bath, which lightly squeeze off the excess zinc. They investigated solutions to a problem with stiffness of the strip, which had already been noticed in Poland, and they successfully coated strip with aluminum, tin and other metals.

2. [Chapter 7] Armco's granting of licenses came only after bitter experience. U.S. Steel approached Armco for a license in the early 1940s and was refused. Weber Sebald, Armco's short-sighted president, wanted to keep Armco's monopoly on the product. U.S. Steel proceeded to successfully duplicate the process on their own, with just a slight modification: wet cleaning of the strip instead of Tad's (now suspect) initial oxidation. The reducing atmosphere was the same as Armco's, as was the final product. Armco sued. U.S. Steel claimed, with some justification, that the steel didn't need that initial layer of oxide. Armco claimed U.S. Steel *was* producing that oxide layer, even though it was invisible, and so was violating their patent. Armco eventually lost. The court agreed with US Steel, both on the oxide layer and on how prior patents (those patents he had seen and tried to work around) were shown to invalidate Tad's claims. By the conclusion of the case, however, even Tad's patents had expired.

3. [Chapter 10] The most significant improvement in the 1950s came with what they called "power crown adjustment," the ability to decrease or increase pressure at specific points across the entire width of the strip, much the way an offset printer can turn one of many screws along his ink tray to put more or less ink on the corresponding section of the printed sheet. The power crown adjustment boosted the Z mill's reputation for precisely uniform strip shape.

The advantages of the Z mill were summarized thus in a 1961 Innocenti (the Z mill builder in Italy) brochure: "Extreme accuracy of gauge; Highest standard of surface finish; Shape instantly adjustable; No limitations in strip width; Minimum number of passes; Freedom from camber and edge cracking; Elimination of intermediate annealing; Quick and easy roll changes; Low original costs; Low tooling costs; Economy in maintenance; Low foundation costs; Lighter building and cranes; Lighter roll grinding facilities."

4. [Chapter 14] Frank Hall, with Charles Batten, had actually come upon the planetary before coming upon Tad. Ductile had bought up a tube-making firm, and a director in that firm, Edward Picken, had already been granted a patent on a mill very similar to the planetary. But the model was mechanically hopeless. When Hall found out about Tad's planetary and saw the pilot mill in operation, he began negotiations with Tad. Tad bought the Picken's patent from Ductile to settle the matter of patent infringement.

5. [Chapter 14] The strip from the planetary varied only plus or minus two-thousandths of an inch in thickness along the length of the coil; the strip from a conventional mill could vary six to eight-thousandths of an inch. (Apart from wasting metal, such uneven thickness brought grief further down the line, when the strip had to be stamped into its final shapes.)

6. [Chapter 14] Rolls overheating; work rolls out of synchronization; high costs running the furnace; heavier gauge on the edges of the strip, producing what's called a "dogbone" shape; scale on the slab and scalloped edges on the strip; problems with the hydraulic cylinders on the feed rolls of the big mills; delicate work roll mountings and disagreeable gear boxes, and all those bearings.

7. [Chapter 14] "Low original investment; small operating crew; modest space requirements; close gauge accuracy both along and across the strip; no heavy ends—uniformity of product; flexibility in rolling program; precise control of rolling temperature; short heating cycle."

8. [Chapter 14] The reversing Steckel mill was one alternative to the conventional hot strip mill that some steel plants chose over the planetary. The Steckel consists of one or two stands of four-high mills. The slab passes back and forth through the mill,

instead of moving in one direction through eight or ten stands, as on a conventional mill. The Steckel has its own problems, but in general it was felt to be more reliable than a planetary, and it's far less complicated. The strip produced is not as good in quality, but is certainly acceptable. Reports differ on whether the Steckel is more or less expensive than the planetary. For many smaller plants, the Steckel was a dependable choice.

9. [Chapter 14] The rocker mill, the double-three-high mill, basket cages, the reducing press, the synchro-feeder, the eccentric press, the beam-backed mill.

10. [Chapter 17] The roller anvil planetary, a mill with one assembly of rolls instead of two, rolling against something like an anvil; the rocker mill, a planetary for non-ferrous metals which could roll metal cold; the double-three-high mill, more or less a competitor of the rocker mill, but simpler; the beam-backed planetary, developed to tackle the scallop problem, and to counter the weakness of the double-three-high; the wobbler mill, a predecessor of the rocker mill; the universal planetary mill, for reducing strip vertically and horizontally, to produce bars and rods; and finally the "Christmas tree mill," just done up in drawings and a wooden model, a planetary mill with only partial housing. There was the reducing press, a machine developed for Ductile to make the slabs smaller before they hit the planetary; the synchro-feeder, another device to improve the planetary by feeding the slabs at the moment of least resistance; and the oscillating press, similar to the reducing press. And there were experiments being done with the planetary on making clad metals.

11. [Chapter 17] The high-speed oscillating mill, a cold mill; the cross tensiometer, to detect imperfections in a strip during rolling; a bearing tester; the hydraulic descaler (for the planetary); and the three pass S mill, a cold mill where the strip went through one set of rolls and snaked down to a lower set.

12. [Chapter 17] This hell-bent naivete about his own ideas got him into trouble on one occasion, when he seized the chance to sell a galvanizing line to Argentina. The Argentines only wanted a simple line, and Tad gave them one—his, circa 1932. Since no one at Sencor or at T. Sendzimir, Inc., knew anything about galvanizing, Tad called in Ted Bostroem, who worked on it for a

couple of days and then said to Tad, "Incidentally, Tadeusz, we didn't discuss my compensation. How much are you going to pay me?" "Seven dollars an hour, the same as everyone else here gets." Bostroem: "I think you're joking." Tad: "No, I'm not." Bostroem got up, shook hands all around, and left. Tad then hired an engineer who had just been laid off from T. Sendzimir, Inc., and who barely knew the difference between a machine applying a coating of zinc to steel and one applying a coating of chocolate to candy bars. Finally, the sketches—they couldn't even be described as drawings—were sent to Argentina. The Argentines built it, spent a lot of money, and it never worked. They would call Sencor asking for help, but no one there knew anything about it. Tad simply ignored them.

13. [Chapter 19] The design of the ZB mill was unique in that Tad built the housing from plates and columns, not heavy cast iron, at maybe one-tenth the cost. Sort of like making a boulder out of strategically placed shards and stones. The result was versatility: the flexible housing made it easy to change the diameter of the workrolls, to roll many different jobs. Tad also put all the drives on top of the mill, instead of off to the side, which made the mill more compact, more conserving of space and energy.

BIOGRAPHICAL AND PROFESSIONAL DATA

Honors Received by Tad Sendzimir

1938   Golden Cross of Merit, Poland, presented by Dr. Ignacy Moscicki, President of Poland.

1949   Bronze plaque for Fundamental Achievement in Galvanizing, American Zinc Institute.

1964   Bablik Gold Medal, International Zinc Institute, Paris.

1965   Bessemer Gold Medal, Iron and Steel Institute, London.

1967   Doctor, h.c. (Science), Alliance College, Cambridge Springs, PA.

1972   Golden Cross of Merit, Officers Grade, Poland.

1973   Doctor, h.c., Academy of Mining and Metallurgy, Krakow, Poland.

1974   Brinell Gold Medal, Royal Academy of Technical Sciences, Stockholm, Sweden, presented by King Gustav.

1976   20th Century Pilgrims Award, presented by Mrs. Ella Grasso, Governor of Connecticut.

1977   Award from the Polish Heritage Society.

1980   Doctor, h.c., Mining Academy, Leoben, Austria.

1982   Fellowship, American Society of Metals, St. Louis Convention.

1983   Commandery of the Cross of Merit, Republic of Poland.

1984   Distinguished Friend of Alliance College and Trustee Emeritus.

1986   Award for Dedicated Service to the Citizens of Connecticut, from Governor Wm. A. O'Neill of the State of Connecticut.

1986   New York City's Liberty Award, presented by New York Mayor Ed Koch.

1987   President's Award, Association of Iron and Steel Engineers, Pittsburgh, PA.

1990   Poland's largest steelworks, Huta im. Lenina, renamed Huta im. Sedzimira, Krakow.

Milestones in the History of Tad Sendzimir

1894 TS is born, Lwow, Poland.

1915 TS evacuates to Kiev, Russia.

1918 TS evacuates to Shanghai, China. Founds China's first mechanized nail and screw factory.

1924 TS marries Barbara Alferieff.

1929 TS leaves China for United States.

1930 TS returns to Poland. Begins intensive work on galvanizing and cold rolling mill inventions.

1931 First Continuous Galvanizing Line put into operation for rolling low carbon strip at Nowy Bytom, Poland.

1935 TS signs agreement with Armco Steel, Middletown, Ohio. Founds Armzen. TS moves to Paris, France.

1936 First Galvanizing Line started in U.S.A. at Armco's works in Butler, PA.

1939 First Z-mill in U.S.A. TS settles in Middleton, Ohio.

1942 First Z-mill rolling silicon steel—for air-borne radar. TS divorces Barbara Alferieff.

1945 First Planetary Mill in Chicago. TS marries Berthe Bernoda. Moves to Waterbury, Connecticut.

1946 First stainless production on a Z-mill in U.S.A. (Today, over 90 per cent of stainless steel rolled in the world is rolled on Sendzimir mills.) TS becomes U.S. citizen.

1953 First production Planetary Mill in U.K.

1956 First Z-mill in Japan. TS dissolves Armzen, founds T. Sendzimir, Inc.

1966 First wide stainless production Planetary Mills in Japan and Canada.

1974 TS founds Sendzimir Engineering Corp. (Sencor).

1977 First Spiral Looper in U.S.A.

1982 First Spiral Looper in Japan.

1989 TS dies, Jupiter, Florida.

Patents in the Name of Tad Sendzimir

In the United States, there are 73 patents in the name of Tad Sendzimir, with foreign equivalents in Australia, Austria, Belgium, Canada, England, France, Germany, India, Italy, Japan, Mexico, New Zealand, Poland, South Africa, Spain, Sweden and Switzerland.

INDEX